MW01343793

We Come Bearing Curses

by
Zachariah Chamberlin

To request permissions, contact the author at zchamber76@gmail.com.

Paperback: 9798852307064
eBook: B0CL4BL91K

Library of Congress Number: TXu002382948

First paperback edition 10/20/2023.

Edited by
Alyson McNitt
Joseph Nassie

Copy Edited by
Brian Hershey

Cover art by
Zachariah Chamberlin

Printed by Kindle Direct Publishing in the USA.

To my children- Z and I
The reason I smile every day.

To my mom
Thanks for the Friday Fright Nights

"Trigger Warnings-

This is a story about childhood trauma & survival.
There is pain and healing within these pages.
Take care of your mental health as you read this."

-PROLOGUE-
JACKIE'S BAD DAY

Are you fucking kidding me?" Jackie Davids said as she finished packing the last bag of groceries into the trunk of her snow-white SUV. "Fuck, fuck, fuckity-fuck-fuck!" she growled as she looked at her cell phone, trying to will the impassive clock to be wrong. The searing light of the clock burned its response into Jackie's eyes. She had been stuck at the store for over an hour and was late for making dinner.

She drove an hour daily to her realty office outside of Haven Shire and often spent the whole day with clients. Her buyers today were a pain in her ass. She showed them six properties in the surrounding countryside and within the local hamlets surrounding *The Shire*.

She was tired and frustrated and wanted a little time to herself before James and Dustin got home. That was not going to happen now. If only her clients would just pick a fucking house already.

The newlywed couple was trying to make sure their first home was perfect. There weren't many houses available for someone in the market for the recently renovated, cozy yet spacious, historical, yet modern home. Oh, and it needed to be near town but not too close.

Jackie finally freed herself from the quarreling couple and sped home for a much-needed glass of wine. James was closing a big construction deal and Dustin would be hungry and wired from his Boy Scout meeting. She just wanted to get home and decompress before all the noise.

It was when she had nearly got home that Jackie realized that she had forgotten to stop by the grocery store and pick up items for Dustin's scout troop bake sale. God forbid she buy "store-bought" cookies instead of taking the time to bake the confections. Jackie considered the withering judgment of the other den mothers and how they would gossip.

Rather than face that fate, she quickly stopped at Corner's Grocery store and picked up the ingredients along with a few other things they had run low on in the pantry. The errand had intended to only last ten minutes, but Jackie had somehow dragged it out to over an hour.

"Shit, shit, shit, fuuuuck!" she exclaimed again as she slammed the SUV's back gate and rushed over to the driver's side door.

As Jackie made her way to the driver's side door she noticed the throng of people outside the church. They were all lined up awaiting entry into the homeless shelter's soup kitchen. After five years of campaigning, Father Curry had scraped enough money and support to build the add-on to the ancient church. It was a prudent addition since it kept the homeless off the streets and provided services that kept the transients busy and out of the public eye. It seemed their numbers had swelled as of late, which made Jackie uneasy.

It wasn't as if Haven Shire was easy to find, or even easy to get to by any other means than the single road that led into town. Despite this, over the last few years, the number of transient strangers had increased. For the most part, they kept to themselves, which made them more creepy to Jackie.

On more than one occasion, she noticed a man or woman shuffling out of an alley, or simply staring aimlessly toward the sky or hills, or even peering from behind a bush or corner. They all seemed to be watching and waiting it seemed. This creeped Jackie out.

As if spoken into being, Jackie felt eyes on her. She snapped free from her thoughts to find that everyone awaiting entry into the church was staring at her now. Emotionless gazes were all fixed upon her.

"What the fuck are you looking at?" Jackie muttered to herself.

The side door of the church opened, and Father Matthew Curry stood calling to the herd of homeless to enter the shelter of the church. Two men exited the church from behind Father Curry. Jackie recognized them immediately as the last transplants Haven Shire had welcomed in decades, Jerry and Mike Allgood. They were the sweetest couple, but Jackie knew that this town would never fully accept the colorful gay couple into their community.

Jackie watched as the men walked into the crowd and began herding the homeless into the cafeteria. Despite their warmest attempts to urge the wanders toward a hot meal and bed, their glares still clung to Jackie.

She was about to throw the door open when something tapped her shoulder. She turned and nearly shouted as she faced a grizzly visage before her. A homeless man of undiscernible age stood just inches away from her now.

The derelict seemed somewhat shaken by her startled response and looked at her with wide jaundiced eyes and zit-peppered skin. His teeth were yellowed, sparse, and carried a foul stench of tobacco rot on his breath. irises that were milky pale.

Collecting himself, the homeless man averted his gaze with his milky white irises and adopted a pitiable expression. Jackie stifled any further response as best as she could, and was honestly concerned for the man, but his smell was overpowering.

"Pardon me, ma'am, do you think you could help me out?" the man said. His voice sounded wet and gravelly, like a bag of pebbles was rolling around his tongue as he spoke. The saliva was heavy in his mouth, and he smacked his lips as he spoke. His breath billowed like the black exhaust from an old truck, impeded only by a few slimy teeth.

Jackie was distantly aware of the man's plight, but she couldn't hear what he said, as she was focused entirely on the shiny white pustules that dotted his face. Her nose absorbed his odor and shared its findings with her taste buds.

One abscess notably held her attention. It resided just above his left nostril and took much of the real estate on his nose. It had a brown dot in its center, surrounded by streaks of red that seemed to swirl within the contents of its mass.

As the man spoke, the pimple seemed to quiver, ready to erupt any moment, spraying the infection all over Jackie and her pristine white cardigan. Jackie stood against her car, transfixed in horror at the man's face; her arms curled across her chest clutching her purse. Jackie's mask of patience and concern melted into disgust.

Suddenly, she realized the man was no longer speaking. His face screwed up in confusion. Jackie was shaking, her body tense, and she felt her face tight with fear and repulsion. The beggar appeared perplexed, even concerned at first, until the realization hit that Jackie was thoroughly horrified by his condition.

"Jesus Christ, I was just asking for change lady. I don't want to hurt ya," he said in his wet, gravelly voice.

The man's gaze narrowed, his gaze longer pleading with this woman, and instead looked disgusted. Jackie's cheek flushed as she realized she had tears streaming down her face. The beggar took a slow step back and raised his hands in resignation, shaking his head in surrender at the pitiful, trembling creature before him.

Jackie, embarrassed by her reaction, began to speak, but the man's stench filled her nose again, and she had to avert her face and wave away the smell before she vomited. The cloud of old sweat and piss covered the man like a cloak. An odor so intense that Jackie's skin felt greased by it.

The old vagrant's look of pity turned to hurt, and his face reddened. "Oh, am I that disgusting to you? Huh?!" he asked. "Are you new here or something? Because take a look around ya. We are everywhere in these parts."

"Just get away, please," Jackie said, pulling out a couple of Kleenexes as she did so. Futilely trying to block the smell, she raised the thin paper cloths to her nose. "Just go away and leave me alone."

The homeless man's body shook with rage. "You know what bitch? Never mind. Go fuck yourself and have a nice day." With that, he snorted up mucus and spat the massive glob of spit, blood, snot, and whatever else lived between his teeth at Jackie's feet.

At the sight of the expectoration, Jackie screamed and shivered so hard that a witness may have thought she was having a seizure. She began to retch behind her tissues. Desperate to leave, Jackie renewed her attack on the door handle, trying to pry open her door.

The homeless man wiped his face with his left hand, across his nose, grazing the quivering pustule with his sleeve as he did so. White and yellow fluid exploded from behind the man's forearm, quickly oozing down the man's cheek. Jackie began to hack and retch as violently as a cat trying to rid itself of a hairball.

Jackie clumsily grabbed the door handle and pulled at it so hard that the corner of the door clipped her jaw. She screamed, jerked, and gagged as she fell into the driver's seat and began fumbling for the power button on the console.

She now understood why all those women in the slasher films died as they fumbled for their house or car keys. It was easy at the time to scoff at the cleavage-toting, scantily clad, witless bimbo fleeing from whatever knife-bearing killer was featured in the Friday night horror flick. Jackie could almost hear the nerve-racking musical score playing as the victim played out her last moment on the screen.

Jackie grabbed the door handle and pulled, trying to close it, but then she felt something resist her, wedging the door open. The vagrant held the door open and stared hard at her. His face was now bloody and contorted with disgust and hate. Jackie imagined could feel his hot, rancid breath caress her skin, eyes, and lips as he panted with fury.

"Hey lady, you've been a real fucking peach!" he shouted. "I hope you have a great day, and God fucking bless!"

With that last sentence, and with a mouth sputtering froth and foam, he slammed the door. His hand and forearm, covered in blood and pus, wiped across the window, leaving a trail behind it.

"Fuck you!" Jackie screamed from behind the haze of ichor. She didn't know when, but she found the start button and smashed it so hard with her finger that she feared she may have broken the digit.

Tires screamed at the abrupt takeoff and the ordinarily quiet engine roared. Smoke began to fill the air as Jackie peeled away. Her car swerved serpentinely until she held the wheel and got the mass of plastic, metal, and rubber under control.

Jackie scanned the exit of the store parking lot, barely taking time to look for oncoming traffic, and pulled furiously onto the street. Her breathing came rapidly, and her head swam from the combination of adrenaline and hyperventilation.

As she sped down the street, Jackie noticed more derelicts coming out of alleys and standing on street corners. All of them fixed her with an eerie gaze and appeared to all move in unison as she drove past them. "*Or maybe you're just freaking out,*" Jackie thought.

"Calm down, girl," she said soothingly to the car and herself. "What the actual fuck is going on with this place?"

This statement was an evaluation of the world in general. Haven Shire, where she'd grown up, was no exception to this criticism. People these days don't smile or wave as they walk down the sidewalk. Social functions have also lessened in recent days.

Her neighbors seemed apathetic with an oppressive feeling of despair that clouded the small community.

Outside interests bought them out and shut down the factories, causing unemployment for many who lived in this rural hamlet. Opioids and alcohol became a coping strategy. Attempts to renew hope with local businesses were met with the pandemic, forcing many to shutter their stores for good.

As desperation increased, so did desperate acts. It seemed the town had become a beacon to those who wished to never be found or had nowhere else to go. The once scenic parks and bridges of the county become camps for the destitute.

Fear reduced the citizens to hiding in their homes and isolating themselves from each other. Instead of participating in the usual small-town craft fairs or harvest festivals, the streets were empty and cold. Her cousin Robert would share details of his exploits with the city police department.

Teens beat an elderly man to death last week, some racist painted slurs on the church! Why would anyone do that? Jackie thought. *My cousin, Robert, grumbles a lot but for good reason.*

Jackie didn't have the answers. She still regularly attended the PTA and scout meetings and volunteered at church, but Jackie found herself becoming as fearful as the other townsfolk. She often cried at night, when everyone had gone to bed, thinking about the state of her once-picturesque hometown.

The expression on the vagrant's face, the way he yelled at her, assaulted Jackie again. She shook the memory away as she sped down the street. The anger helped her focus and collect herself. She was now free from the fog of fear and confusion. Now she was just pissed.

"That freak! What the fuck was his problem?" she complained to herself. "I'm calling the police as soon as I get home. I hope they use the taser on him. Shock the literal shit out of him."

She slowed down as she traveled down the unkempt remains of the downtown streets. She longed to be home, sitting with her family and sipping on wine. She couldn't wait to wrap herself in the comfort of routine.

Visions of the homeless man pushed their way into her mind again, causing Jackie to cringe. She was truly disgusted. What if that man had assaulted her? What if she had her child with her?

Fumbling for her purse in the seat beside her, Jackie snatched up her cell phone. She knew the dangers of cell phone use while driving, but this was important, God dammit! It's not like the streets were busy in Haven Shire anyway, right?

Unlocking her screen with a series of thumb swipes, Jackie was stunned to find she had received an email from her buyers. They finally chose a house! Jackie squealed with joy. This would require a call for celebration but first, the buyers needed to be contacted for further instruction.

Jackie's rage began to melt away in the light of this new fortune. James was the first person to appear in her mind when Jackie considered who to share the good news with. He had been patiently listening to her vent about these clients for several days now. She wanted to call straight away. As Jackie pulled up James's profile for speed dial, she accidentally tapped the video call icon instead.

Her camera app activated, bringing up her face on the screen. Jackie glanced at her reflection and noticed a yellow and green blob of mucus clinging to her left cheek. Her face was so wet from the sweat she hadn't noticed it.

The realization that the vagrant had splashed his filth on her hit Jackie like a slap. The cab of the SUV exploded with her horrified screams as she dropped the phone and searched frantically for tissues. She heard the phone falling to the floor distantly as she discovered a travel pack of Kleenex in the overhead compartment.

Jackie tore open the package and gutted the plastic wrapping filled with its cottony salvation. Clutching a handful of tissues frantically she wiped away the stinking, slimy filth that was the parting gift of the homeless man. The interior of her car suddenly exploded into chaos as airbags deployed as Jackie wiped away the remaining smear of mucus from her face.

Jackie didn't see what she hit. She only felt the impact on the front of the SUV and the explosive shattering and thunder-like crash of her windshield. Jackie slammed on the brakes, and the vehicle began to fishtail until it stopped. Her knuckles were white as she gripped the steering wheel. Whatever she had struck had rolled off the hood and onto the pavement.

Jackie coughed, her throat irritated by the dusty remnants of the airbags. She tried to sit up straighter and look through her windshield, but the seatbelt had pinned her to the seat. The contents of the shopping bags rolled around the trunk and the sound of carbonated liquids hissed angrily.

Jackie slowly opened the door and stepped out of her car. She looked around at the crumbling ruins of the neighborhood street, looking for witnesses. A mix of fear and relief flooded her. There wasn't a soul around if she needed help or anyone to witness this lapse in judgment. She could hear James's voice now chiding her for her phone usage while driving.

That's when she heard a low and pitiful whine in front of her vehicle. Jackie slowly walked around to the front of the car. A deer was lying on the street, lazily bobbing its head up and down—a buck. Massive antlers topped his head. The deer's injuries blanketed its hide in blood, and Jackie could see exposed muscle tissue. The impact left the animal's legs twisted and broken. Jackie could also see the deer's neck bulging, and his head lolled clumsily.

Fresh tears filled her eyes, this time out of pity. She hurt an innocent creature just to make contact with her client. Jackie wanted to throw up, scream, or be anywhere but there.

The deer suddenly began to bleat and howl, this time with something wet and thick filling his throat. Panic rose again, filling Jackie's stomach and crawling across her skin. She raised her hands to the sides of her shaking head, trying to deny this reality.

"Oh God," Jackie whispered. "He's suffering." Jackie began to tremble as she considered her next course of action. "I can't just leave him like this. I have to call for help…" she began. Then she paused. "…and tell them what, I was dicking around on my phone when I hit this deer?"

Would the police arrest her? How would she tell her husband? Her son? She hurried back to the car, brushed away the deflated airbags, and grabbed her phone. *Call James…he'll know what to do.* Finding his number was easy, and she tapped James's portrait, initiating the call.

The gurgling pleas from the deer grew louder and more desperate. She felt something in her throat pinch and Jackie's hands shook so fiercely that she feared she'd lose the device. The guilt of having harmed this poor animal was conflicted by her prayers that it would quickly die.

Ring. Ring. Ring.

James's voice shouted cheerfully through the speakers, and immediately, Jackie began to tell him how glad she was to hear his voice. "Oh, thank God, James, I need you. There's been an acci…." Her story was interrupted by James's voicemail message. *"…so be a pal and leave me a message, and I'll call you right back,"* James's voice concluded.

"Shit! Fuck! Come on, James! Answer your goddamn phone!" yelled Jackie. She hung up and redialed the number. Same number of rings, same voicemail. She tried again and again, the same outcome. "Fuck!"

Just as she began to collect herself, fat droplets of rain began to pour down. The rain was slow and gentle at first but picked up the tempo with every passing second. She realized the deer was no longer calling out in pain.

Jackie looked around the car's front end and found the deer lying still, no longer rolling his head around and no longer breathing. Her sobbing began anew as the rain pelted her without mercy. Her head and shoulders sank, and she walked back to the open door of her car. She climbed into the driver's side, brushed dust from the airbags away, and buried her head into her forearms across the steering wheel. After a few seconds, she felt a vibration from her phone.

Jackie excitedly looked at the face of the cell. Maybe he just texted her? James might be busy, and she didn't leave a message. Jackie just needed him to tell her what to do and reassure her it would be ok. With trembling hands, she snatched up the phone.

Her heart sank, and Jackie exhaled a pitiful moan as she discovered that her phone's battery had run out, and the vibration warned it was shutting off. Jackie dropped her phone on the seat next to her in complete resignation. A sad chuckle escaped her throat.

"Why the fuck not…" she began. "Just par for the course, the perfect way to end a shitty day." She looked around and got her bearings at this point. She wasn't far from home. Five, maybe six blocks at best. Jackie took a long-resigned breath. "May as well get to it."

Jackie buttoned her cardigan and checked once more in the mirror. Her eyes were red and puffy, and the evening's events had severely smudged her mascara. She looked for remains of the filth and slime left over from the homeless man's assault. When she was somewhat satisfied that no more of his foul pustulant discharge was on her, she closed the overhead mirror and took a deep breath. She looked out at the darkening street, now being punished by rain.

Luckily, Jackie always packed an umbrella for a moment like this. Pulling it from the door compartment, she unfolded it to shield her from the rain. The water was pleasantly cool. It was nearing the beginning of fall, and the summer heat wasn't giving up without protest. The rain was a welcome reprieve.

So, she walked, carefully avoiding deep puddles of water. "First thing I'm going to do when I get home is shower. The boys can feed themselves for a change," she said to herself.

Despite her anger at feeling abandoned by James at that moment, she smiled to herself. She was heading home, and there was some comfort in that. No matter how perverse this town, or the world, had become, Jackie at least had someplace to go.

She trekked cautiously on the sidewalk. There hadn't been any repairs to the path and street in over a decade. The city council blamed a lack of tax revenue, but Jackie wondered if anyone cared. The streets were a series of cracks and potholes, the splits in the asphalt now home to weeds and grass.

To occupy her mind, she pondered the mysteries of Haven Shire. Why aren't there more children? People used to announce a new addition regularly. What else was there to do in this town besides working, drinking, and making babies? She couldn't remember the last time she went to a baby shower for a neighbor.

Maybe this town needs new blood, Jackie thought. There are plenty of available homes and empty lots, but most had been bought by the Marcus family. There had been only one couple who had recently joined her community. They were beautiful, friendly, and gay. Jackie enjoyed their company, even if she disagreed with their lifestyle choice.

Jackie continued walking and suddenly realized she had nearly walked past her street. She was so deep in thought that she hadn't even noticed that it had gotten considerably darker. Despite her umbrella's best efforts to ward off the rain, the ceaseless downpour had soaked Jackie's clothes throughout.

She turned and began moving toward the walkway that led to the front door of her home. She noticed that none of the streetlights that usually brightened the sidewalks at night were working. The darkness around her seemed particularly thick, like a black sheet drawn over her neighborhood.

Jackie was confident her small neighborhood was safe, and anyone home would aid her if she needed it. She trained in judo in college and felt sure she could protect herself. That and the arsenal of self-protective measures in her purse also boosted her confidence. Jackie envisioned the tactics she would employ if someone tried to attack her.

"Where was that bravado with that asshole in the parking lot?" she quietly berated. If he had been just a thug or punk, it would have been different. It was his stench, and she couldn't deal with the sores, pus, and spit. Jackie let loose a shudder when she thought about the phlegm on her face again.

She carefully stepped to avoid walking on the grass or tripping over cracks and potholes on the sidewalk. The last thing her day needed was for her to break a heel or ankle trying to get into her own home. Jackie noticed the dining room light was on through the window. It appeared as though someone was sitting at the table.

"Oh, James, you just wait," Jackie said. Suddenly, she realized she had forgotten her house keys with her car. She tested the door and found it unlocked. She forgave him a little just then but would give him shit about not securing the home.

"James, I'm home!" she announced, not even trying to hide her irritation. "It would be nice if you answered your phone. You wouldn't believe the night I had… I really could've used your help!"

No answer.

She walked to the kitchen, glancing in the dining room along the way. The bulbs bathed the space in the florescence she hated. There sat James, hands on the table, sitting straight up. Just sitting there, so still, stiff even.

"Babe, what's up?" she asked as she continued to the cabinet holding the tumblers and wine glasses. She pulled out her favorite tumbler, which was intricately cut in such a way that it refracted the light perfectly. Jackie pulled a couple of ice cubes from the freezer and walked toward the dining room.

"James, what's up? Didn't you hear me?" Jackie walked up behind him. She noticed the table then. The candles gently bathed the room with warm light, plates with proper cutlery and napkins sat neatly arranged, and wine glasses stood guard over the place settings.

"Oh, sweetie," she cooed.

James was a kind and considerate husband, but he rarely would surprise her with homemade dinner or other thoughtful gestures. Not that she resented this; Jackie was pragmatic and not exactly sentimental. After this day though, the motion wiped away all the anger of being stranded and forced to walk a few blocks. Jackie dipped to give James a hug.

Jackie felt something wet on her face and suddenly felt how cold James was. The skin on his hands was pale, too pale, and his neck and shoulders were stiff. She pulled away immediately when she looked down at the plate in front of him. The white porcelain framed what Jackie's brain first processed as some cut and bloody meat sitting in its juices. She stared; her mind could not understand what she was seeing.

It had hair—eyebrows and lashes—and holes. The teeth sat locked in a tight grimace, and above it were flared nostrils and empty holes for eyes. Oh God, it had eyes. Jackie wiped the side of her face, her palm sticky with a thick, dark red liquid.

"J.. J…Ja...James, baby, what is this…?" Her eyes filled with shock and horror as she peered down at James. He wore the same clothes she had set out this morning, his light blue button-up shirt, navy blue tie, and blue jeans. A heavy, sturdy metal watch shone on his right wrist in the candlelight. She tried to repeat his name, but the words came out as a mixture of moans and random sounds.

"Wha..wha..guh…guh…ffff…. ffff," was all she could manage as she examined his head. His face wasn't just the only thing missing. So was the front of his skull, back to the curve of his jawline. Blood had flowed down his neck and shirt. The perfectly pressed blue shirt stuck to his chest and soaked the red into its fabric. Blood pooled in his lap and his crotch was soaked.

His skull's details displayed a perfect cross-section, complete with the structures, muscles, and organs—all except the brain, eyes, and tongue. The brain was gone, leaving a surreal cave for something to live in. His eyes were just sockets staring out into the void. His tongue lolled out of his "face" lazily and hung there.

Jackie moaned louder and louder and in increasingly higher pitch until it became a scream as she backed out of the room. Her eyes were wild with grief, horror, and disbelief. She dropped her glass tumbler and began retreating to the hall that would take her to her bedroom. She had to call the police, call for help.

Wait, Dustin...where was Dustin?

She screamed for him as she turned away from the gruesome scene, nearly tripping over her feet as she did so. Again, the image of desperate bimbos running from their killer popped into her head. She had to get Dustin out of this house. Just as she was about to reach the stairwell, she saw someone walk out of the darkened living room and block her path.

Jackie began screaming in protest and for help, calling for Dustin to run only to realize it was him in front of her. She sobbed at the sight of her son and breathed a sigh of relief. Jackie fell onto the boy, embracing him in a tight hug.

Without warning, a sharp pain tore into Jackie's leg. She yelped in surprise and from the burning sensation that crept up and down her thigh. She looked down and spotted a large syringe sticking out of the meatiest part of her left leg. Whatever the contents were in the needle now coursed throughout her.

Jackie grabbed the syringe and pulled it out of her leg, which was now numb. She looked at the giant needle and back toward Dustin. Dustin looked so much like his father, with his dark hair, pale skin, freckles, and that dimple on his left cheek when he smiled.

His smile. Why was he smiling? What was wrong with his eyes? Instead of the sweetest chocolate brown hue with flecks of green around the irises, she was looking into pools of endless black. Empty and cold, they looked slick, like ink poured into the sockets of his sweet boyish face. Jackie tried to turn and run but fell hard onto the hardwood floor leading into the kitchen.

She reached out to Dustin and tried to plead for help. Instead, Jackie couldn't formulate the words and just gave a pathetic moan. Jackie suddenly felt so tired and confused, and she moved slowly. She tried to crawl away, but it felt like she was swimming; her arms were heavy. She couldn't even lift her head to turn and look anymore.

Darkness started to creep into her field of vision. Jackie was vaguely aware that others entered the room. She felt pinned by her own gravity as she laid her cheek on the cool tile of the kitchen floor. As she began to drift away, Dustin's Converse shoes came into view before her. Black leather shoes joined his in front of Jackie.

"Good job, kid," said the other presence. His voice sounded warm and light. It was so comforting that Jackie felt lulled by it. She wanted to fight, but her mind and body demanded sleep. Sleep. Then she would find a way to get out of here. She just needed to close her eyes for a moment.

Jackie awoke with a start, but her mouth seemed unable to form a scream. She began taking deep breaths. She could feel the air moving as she inhaled and filled her lungs. She couldn't turn her head, stand, or flail her arms for some reason. She was trapped inside her body.

Jackie tried to speak, but she could only manage a muffled moan. Her gaze scanned the room, trying to orient herself. She was sitting at the dinner table now. Thick rope coiled around her chest, arms, and abdomen, tying her to one of the chairs.

Immediately, she began to lose control of her breathing, going from slow, controlled breaths to panting as she wrestled with the scene before her. Sitting at the head of the table, sat the corpse of James. Jackie's mind tried to call for a retreat, but the truth of James's corpse anchored her to reality.

Upon viewing his twisted corpse, she began to moan loudly, her scream of terror muffled by frozen lips and jaw. The lights were now on, and she could see every detail of James's mutilated body. She trembled violently as her body refused to respond to her mental screaming and the need to run as far and as fast as her legs could carry her.

She caught movement from the corner of her eye. Her eyes tried to find the source, finally landing on a figure casually walking into the room naked. The man moved robotically and sat across from her.

Under the warm glow of the small light fixture sat James. Jackie's brain couldn't process what was happening. She struggled to understand the man sitting across from her and the corpse of James sitting to her left. The man across from her looked precisely like James had looked like before his death.

Both shared the same dark hair, mustache, muscular body, and even the strange mole perched above his right nipple. He was every bit the same man, except for the eyes. The eyes were vacant, devoid of emotion, as though James's face was a mask. They barely blinked as he sat there emotionless.

The James-thing in front of her suddenly began twitching at the corners of his mouth. To Jackie, it appeared as if he was trying to convey something to her, trying on this new face and using its muscles for the first time. Each corner of his mouth curled and shook as his lips parted and the James-thing bared his teeth. Suddenly it hit her. This fucking thing was trying to smile at her!

Jackie tried to scream at this abomination. Her moan was so loud and guttural that her body vibrated with rage. Tears and a line of drool ran from her lips and lazily fell onto her lap.

"Now, now, shush," came a voice in the kitchen. "That's quite enough out of you. I would hate for you to have an aneurism with all this fuss."

Jackie listened for some clue as to who the man was. He sounded familiar, but Jackie couldn't think straight with the madness before her. She heard clinking and shuffling about.

Is he in my fridge? Jackie thought.

"I hope you don't mind," the man said as if reading her thoughts. "The boy and I are famished. Aren't we, Dustin?"

Jackie heard the soft click of the refrigerator door closing and someone walking around in the kitchen. As if he had all the time in the world, the man slowly walked into her line of sight and stood directly behind the James-thing. The man was young, slender, and well-kempt. He had an air of confidence about him, and shock quickly gave way to recognition. It was Thaddeus Marcus, son of Judge and Maria Marcus.

Thaddeus looked at Jackie with such disinterest that it made her feel as though he didn't even register her presence. He seemed, in fact, more interested in the half sandwich he had made for himself. After taking a few bites and swallowing them, Thaddeus raised a glass of whiskey to his lips and took a deep gulp. He wrinkled his nose and looked disapprovingly at the golden-brown liquid.

"This did not pair well at all," Thaddeus stated flatly. Seemingly disgusted with his meal, he handed the remains of the sandwich to the James-thing. It looked up, somewhat confused by the gesture, and slowly took the sandwich remains from Thaddeus. The copy sat there momentarily to ponder the gift given to it and then opened its mouth wide and shoved in the whole thing.

The James mimic appeared as though he would even bite off the ends of his fingers as he tried to jam the bread, meat, cheese, and other contents deep into his mouth. Then he gently pulled his hand out from within his gaping maw. He sat there momentarily, mouth agape, and seemed unsure what to do next. He slowly began to chew his mouthful of food. Cautiously, he moved the contents around in his mouth. Then his gaze returned to Jackie as he slowly mashed the sandwich between his teeth.

Thaddeus looked down at the James-thing as a parent would while watching their child eat their first solid meal. His face was a mix of pride, warmth, and caution. "That's right, chew, chew, chew. Wouldn't want you to choke," Thaddeus instructed.

After Thaddeus felt confident the James-thing wouldn't be undone by his snack, he gulped down the remaining liquid in the glass and gently set it on the table. His gaze rose to meet Jackie's; he crossed his hands and breathed deeply. At first, he appeared to be at a loss for words as he stood there for several moments as though considering what to say.

"I have no words to help you understand nor the ability to ask consent for what I'm about to do to you," he began. "I'm just following orders, you see. Judge needs bodies and souls. Your number just came up."

Jackie began to whimper and cry.

"Tut, tut, tut," Thaddeus said, as he feigned concern and wagged his finger. "I need you to stop doing that. I need your face to not be too puffy from all those tears."

Thaddeus simulated taking a deep relaxing breath and tried to prompt Jackie to do the same. She didn't.

"Well, if it's any consolation, you will be playing a part in changing this sick and weak planet. Judge has a vision, you see. I don't share it, but doing as he asks keeps him off my back, and I get to do what I want," Thaddeus stated coolly. "He thinks he's going to be an architect, providing materials and resources, and his gods will be using these resources to build a whole new reality." He punctuated this last statement with his arms raised and gesturing to the space around him.

"Now you, a mother, know that when we give birth to something new, there is pain. Pain, blood, and some trauma. I'm afraid this period of growth, rebirth, and change won't be pleasant," Thaddeus continued. "I wish there were a way to make it all painless."

It was a blatant lie, and he didn't hide it. "Sadly, they need your pain. They need you to sing their hymns with your pleas and tear-filled screams." He said this nodding his chin at the shadows, accented with something that imitated pity.

"I will not draw this out any further since I just can't stomach to watch you blubbering and suffering so…" he said with a wave of his hand as he began to move to the corner of the room. Beyond the dining room, Jackie saw forms standing in the inky dark of her living room. Each form, a silhouette, backlit by the storm outside.

Jackie was trying to blink her tears away to get a better look. They all seemed to be wearing robes, pointed hoods, and holding empty gold plates. They whispered something in hushed tones and swayed slowly from side to side.

"Oh, I almost forgot. I want to assure you that your son will be fine. I promise to keep him safe and healthy. I believe Dustin and I will be fast friends. We both like sandwiches and drawing."

Jackie began growling and trying to scream again. Then she stopped and froze as Dustin came into view with a gold plate. He carefully laid the plate on the dining table in front of Jackie. In a robotic fashion, Dustin walked around the table to the chair opposite her. He climbed onto the chair and then on top of the table.

Slowly, Dustin sat himself down, cross-legged, in front of Jackie. He moved as though he was sleepwalking. Jackie's eyes drifted to the plate before her and saw a strange mask peering up at her. Jackie had taken an Asian culture course in college and recognized it as a Japanese Noh mask. Its surface was porcelain white with deep black holes for eyes and one to match a mouth.

There were no other features, no nose or cheekbones. There was nothing to distinguish the gender of the mask or its emotional state.

Dustin slowly raised the mask before her, eyes facing her, peering at her with their endless black stare. Even though the visage faced her, Jackie couldn't see through the eyes and mouth. She felt drawn into those pools of nothingness, unable to look away.

Jackie distantly noticed the whispering in the next room began to pick up in pitch and tempo while the figures swayed back and forth in rhythm. She couldn't distinguish the words and knew their language was not any tongue she could recognize. Their intonations reminded Jackie of responses she made during service.

She looked back to Dustin, her eyes pleading; she was trying to moan his name. Suddenly she realized she could move her head slightly from side to side. Her fingers were starting to heed her commands.

She thought she might be able to slow him long enough to grab Dustin and escape. She just needed to reach him, break whatever spell had hold of him. Dustin sat before her, whispering the same prayer as he turned the mask upside down. Jackie could feel her lips start to part. Her teeth chattered.

Dustin's eyes met hers, and all Jackie could see were the pools of inky blackness. There was no look of recognition on his face, no love, no pity. Dustin turned the mask around to face him, and Jackie understood why she couldn't see through the sockets. There were fleshy knots with small spikes protruding in various places filling the mask. Each spikey tube was a pale flesh tone, segmented and pulsating. Jackie kept trying to jerk away. She felt her torso begin to move. She just needed a little more time!

The knotted mass of fleshy tubulars on the back of the mask began to writhe and unfold as if its succulent rolls were unclenching. Jackie fought and shook and felt her feet and toes started to loosen. She stared in horror at the rolling and spiky mass. She thought back to a caterpillar she saw as a child. Not the cute furry ones, but ones with chubby rolls and tiny fleshy spines all down their backs.

The folds rolled out in a flash and reached for Jackie's head. The meaty appendages passed her face and grabbed the back of her head. Jackie felt the spikey protrusions bite into the back and sides of her scalp. They held her head like a set of fingers gripping a baseball and began to draw her head toward the center of the mask. Jackie looked into the center of the mass and finally found her lips and mouth working as she screamed.

The center of the mask was now exposed, and Jackie could see an orifice, drooling, and stinking like rot. Slowly, the circular mouth opened up to display rows upon rows of needle-like teeth. Jackie's eyes watered from the stench as the mouth widened, and the mask was filled with pink slimy flesh and circles of teeth. Each tooth moved independently, seeking purchase into flesh. The teeth on the outer row of the mask became more agitated, vibrating, and now clacking.

Jackie tried to recoil from the thing that grasped her and felt spikes from the arms of the beast dig deeper into her skin. Beyond, Dustin held on to the mask as he drew in Jackie's face in a controlled manner. Jackie's scream became shrill as the mask closed in on her.

The chittering stopped suddenly as the tiny needle-like teeth dug into the sides of Jackie's face. Her muffled protests increased in desperation as each fang hooked into her flesh suddenly began vibrating. Like a dentist's drill, the bony click was replaced with a high-pitched squeal. The fangs chiseled and burrowed into her temples, cheekbones, jaw, scalp, and neck.

Blood oozed out from the sides of the mask and ran down the length of Jackie's face and neck. The teeth buzzed and vibrated until there was an audible crack. Dustin released his grip on the mask and watched Jackie futilely attempt to shake the living artifact off her face.

The paralytic used to incapacitate her had begun to wear off, and her face shook violently. Her body was still too drugged for Jackie to move her arms and instead they trembled helplessly. The living mask was getting more aroused, and the clicks and rattles of the beast picked up in tempo. Beneath the veneer, Jackie was blind and on fire with pain as the needle-like teeth drilled their way into her bones from different angles.

More teeth poked and prodded around her mouth, nose, and forehead. They traced her face, picking up on every nuance and wrinkle. Jackie felt the points probing her lips, nose, and eyes, filling her flesh with searing pain.

The teeth stopped their work and retracted from their drill sites. The onlookers could still make out moans and whimpers from behind that awful mask on Jackie's face. Her muffled pleas failed to reach Thaddeus Marcus, who stood disinterested in the corner, seemingly bored with it all. She pleaded with the dark witnesses in her living room and with Dustin, who sat cross-legged, staring curiously as the mask returned to its brutal work.

The mask shifted, scuttling counterclockwise, the tentacles readjusted their grip, and the teeth that bit into Jackie's flesh and bone began to drill again. This torture started Jackie's shrill screaming and writhing anew.

This process continued until the face of the mask was no longer upside down and the eyes and mouth were in their proper anatomical position. Jackie's screaming had ceased. She twitched intermittently, and her head lolled forward. Her shirt and lap were covered in blood, just as James's corpse was when Jackie had found him. The mask's limbs relaxed as the creature seemed to calm.

Thaddeus looked up as if he had nearly fallen asleep during Jackie's torturous and gruesome end. He quickly moved around the table and placed a hand under the creature, cradling it in his palm. Dustin put the plate before Jackie, moved away from the table, and stood in the corner.

Thaddeus tipped Jackie's head back, looked at her limp head and exposed neck, and then asked someone within the congregation to come forth. The group parted and one of the attendees solemnly moved forward. The cloaked and hooded figure walked like a mourner toward a casket. Its head bowed in reverence and supplication beneath a hood and hands tucked inside the robe's sleeves. The form beneath was indiscernible as the robe's folds entirely obscured its shape.

"Come on, come on! I don't want to stand here all night, for fuck's sake!" Thaddeus snapped. The attendee seemed unfazed by his impatience and moved to stand beside Jackie's body. Thaddeus whispered a chant in a language only a handful of human beings could speak and fewer understood. The words seemed to roll from his tongue and lips like smoke. Upon hearing them, the creature covering Jackie's face released its many arms from her scalp.

The tiny protruding barbs were wet with blood, and some had clumps of hair and scalp still attached as the beast began to pull away. Thaddeus carefully inserted his fingers and thumb into the orbits that made the eyes and mouth of the mask. He gently pulled on the creature's center. A wet, sickening suction sound came from beneath the creature's body, and finally, there was a soft pop as the mask pulled away from Jackie's head.

Thaddeus chuckled like a child as he placed the creature on the plate before Jackie. He whispered a few more twisted and melodic words to the beast, and it released its prize from its teeth. The contents fell to the plate with a tap. Thaddeus continued his grin until he realized "eyes" were on him.

Thaddeus knew his father was watching the ritual. Judge remained a true believer through all the years. Thaddeus knew Judge had presided over such ceremonies, but his father had other concerns tonight. He felt his father's gaze through the eyes of those in attendance and any slip or error would result in physical and mental punishment.

"Oh, my apologies, the 'pop' always gets me," Thaddeus admitted and returned to finish the ritual. He turned to Jackie's body while the attendee cradled Jackie's skull as gently as a mother holding a baby. Her skull, no different than her late husband, sliced cleanly, exposing the sinus cavity and the back half of her mouth. The eyes were still intact; they stared at the ceiling, and her tongue lay limply in the back of her throat. The brain was visible and intact. The congregant began to lean forward when a wet, bloody gurgle suddenly rattled in Jackie's throat. Thaddeus jumped back, startled, and, after a beat, roared with a laugh.

"Jesus, bloody…! That always gets me!" Thaddeus said with a laugh. The attendee stopped and stared out from its hood. Thaddeus looked around the room, fell silent, and gestured for the rite to finish. The attendant pulled back the hood of its cloak to reveal a smooth, stone-grey scalp.

It had no discernable ears, and the figure was gaunt. The fingers ended with pale nails that were pointed and sharp at the tips. Its face was void of eyes or nose, only a small hole in the center of its skull where a human nose could have been.

Slowly that hole rotated and opened into a cavernous maw filled with rows of short, needle-like teeth. The teeth resembled the creature that previously held onto Jackie's face. Each tooth was a jaundiced yellow, and the mouth salivated as it leaned into the open face of Jackie's body and began to devour the exposed brain and eyes hungrily. Thaddeus winced at the sloppy nature in which the congregant ate. He didn't want a mess to clean up, but what could he do?

The creature finally finished, shuddered as if reacting to some form of ecstasy. The gaping hole in its face twitched as it finished chewing and slurping the last of Jackie's brain. It took a step back, almost a stumble, and straightened. The congregant walked up to the plate, removed the mask-with-teeth, and seemed to stare at Jackie's visage.

The creature gently took the mask off the plate and placed it on its face. In almost a reverse of what had happened just minutes ago to Jackie, the congregant let loose a shrill cry as the mask clamped down onto its skin and began to sew itself onto its skull. The congregant threw its hands out wide and began to shake its head back and forth as if trying to resist the merging of the mask. It reached up and clutched its head and howled in pain.

Thaddeus Marcus had witnessed this process a few times, often forced to watch by his father, but it never ceased to fascinate him. He knew what the congregation looked like beneath their robes. They were named the *Formoria* because legends suggested they were the first creatures on this plane. They also had no agreed form. Some walked on two legs, others on giant tentacles, some on long spidery legs. No two were alike. Being forced to take on a shape, a single design, was an insult and sacrilegious to these otherworldly beings.

The First Tribes came with their rituals, religion, and their order. They hunted or imprisoned Formoria. They murdered them with iron, fire, and magic. Those that lived were forced to take a name and a shape, thus losing their power and identity. Others fled beyond the Veil to serve their gods in our nightmares and insanity. That was the only way they could influence our existence now.

Thaddeus hated them all, but not half as much as he hated all of humanity. Thaddeus knew that if his father were to change this world, he would need these creatures to create chaos. He required their Old Gods to grant him more power and strength. Thaddeus didn't care about the machinations of the Old Gods or his father. He only wanted to be free to feed his appetite every day until he died.

The congregant threw off its robe, exposing its stony-grey skin, which clung desperately to its bony frame. The Formorian fell to the floor, writhed, and then the creature's body transformed. Skin tore away, exposing new, pink flesh and hair beneath. The maw closed, muffling the howls and screams behind a wall of flesh. The head twisted, and bones snapped and knitted repeatedly as it began to build features and contours.

Grey skin filled with blood and turned red, then rosy-pink, and finally light peachy in tone. The slits where the eyes, mouth, and nose should be, formed and widened. Curves and folds across it's body filled in the details of the thighs, hips, buttocks, and breasts. The creature's breathing began to slow and it ceased its howling. It stood slowly, trembling from its rebirth.

The congregant raised its hands to its face, feeling the new form and visage the ritual had bestowed upon it. The Formoria probed its new mouth and teeth. Even as it was learning to move its new limbs, it continued growing. Bright blonde curls sprouted from the top of its head, and freckles and birthmarks dotted its skin.

Thaddeus moved over to the creature that now looked like Jackie and placed the heavy robe around its shivering body. He eased the mimic to a chair. The impersonator looked up at Thaddeus pleadingly, tears streaming down its face.

"Soon, my dear, never fear. Soon you can tear off this disgusting costume and return to your true form."

Thaddeus looked to the congregation and spread out his arms. "Let us welcome our new brother and sister—James and Jackie Davids." The others stood straight and removed their hoods, each showing their face. The faces of other community members intermingled with the twisted, mangled, and toothy abominations. The group stared at the Jackie look-alike with reverence and a touch of anticipation, eagerly waiting for the final communion that would punctuate this macabre ceremony.

"Oh yes, how could I forget," Thaddeus said with amusement. He strolled over to Dustin, still in his trance-like state. His eyes were still reflective pools of pitch, his face emotionless. Dustin stood in the corner staring at the scene before him. The congregation filed in and filled the room, each watching Dustin. Even "Jackie" and "James" took their places, standing behind the now cooling corpses of their counterparts.

Thaddeus walked up to Dustin and placed his middle finger on his forehead. He murmured the same spidery language he had spoken earlier. Before removing his finger, he said, "Time to wake up, my boy. Wake up and see all the terrible things you've done."

The crowd in the room shivered. Some chuckled, but each attendant held their breath as Dustin first closed his eyes and then opened them slowly and blinked several times as if he had just awakened from a long night's sleep. Dustin took a sudden deep breath as if he was shocked awake. He looked around the table, puzzled as he tried to understand what he saw.

The look of confusion began to twist, his eyes filled with tears, and Dustin began recognizing the corpses at dinner. He looked up at the copies of his parents, and confusion struck hard once more. They looked like his mom and dad, but something deep within him knew the truth. His mind and body rejected these forms.

Dustin felt his crotch get wet, his stomach twist, and his bowels loosen. He saw the rest of the congregation. Tears streamed down his face, his mouth opened into a moan, and saliva drooled from his tongue and lips. The sight excited the attendees, and those who played at being human began to smile unnaturally.

Those without human lips, gums, or anything resembling a human grimace, began to click and growl and hiss their pleasure. They then leaped upon the boy, teeth and claws tearing into his young flesh. They took their communion, which signaled the end of the ritual.

The neighborhood began to stir from outside the home, the sun climbing slowly into the skyline. The residents of this sleeping town would not hear the shrill screams of the boy who helped feed his parents to abominations. The house sat eerily quiet and still, with no one the wiser.

# # # #

Beyond the quiet neighborhoods of Haven Shire lay the hills upon which the Forgotten Church was built. Those living in the hamlet had forgotten the ancient power slumbered there. Not Judge Marcus. The tall, muscular man stood at his laboratory window, looking at the ignorant community below. He pictured every citizen below screaming in terror and agony, a nice distraction from his impatience. They were coming. He felt them clawing at the Veil. He heard their calls, and his soul ached with the same hunger.

"Just have to be patient," Judge muttered as much to himself as he did to those he sensed. He turned his attention to the new materials he had acquired now from his trafficker. Six young Asian beauties delivered for him to educate and improve. Maybe, he could spare one for now. Just one to sculpt and improve. To make fit for service.

"I deserve this," Judge said to himself. "I've worked so hard. Don't I deserve to enjoy myself from time to time?"

From the other side of the lab, Maria scoffed. Judge was surprised to find her there and wondered how she got past his magical wards. No matter. Maria may be his wife, but she no longer satisfied him. He needed more. More pain, more screaming, more blood. As Maria left the room, no longer interested in Judge's antics, Judge ran two fingers across the naked and trembling flesh of the Asian girl on his table.

"I wonder how long you can entertain me. Feed me," Judge whispered as he traced the lines of her ribcage. "How much can we teach each other?"

The girls all screamed in horror as Judge picked up a scalpel and got to work.

-CHAPTER 1-
THE FOG OF HAVEN SHIRE

Officer Holts was surprised by how little blood there was on the scene. There was copious amounts for sure, but he had expected so much more. He scanned the room and tried to imagine the scene before the gun had gone off.

He looked up to the ceiling, examining the spatter of blood, tissue, and bone. The force of the shotgun blast had sent the tissue up into the popcorn coating and impaled some of the pieces into the drywall. What had not coagulated yet still dripped slowly to the floor.

"Fucking hell, what gauge did you say the shotgun was again?" Holts asked the detective in the next room.

"Twelve-gauge…I think," Detective Andes yelled back. Holts heard Andes flipping through his notepad and muttering a confirmation, "Yep! A twelve-gauge, pump-action Mossberg!"

Officer Holts scanned the floor beneath the dripping ichor with his flashlight. He found the shell casing under the foot of the desk where the victim was sitting. On top of the desk sat a worn copy of a textbook. He recognized it from the copies that sat in piles around the office. Some of them had the cover torn off, whereas others were neatly piled on chairs. On the wall opposite the desk, several boxes were stacked. Holts walked over to one of the boxes and peered inside to find it was filled with similar copies of the book.

"Do you think this has to do with the fact that his books didn't sell?" Holts yelled to the detective in the next room.

"How the fuck do I know, Holts?" the man snapped back irritably. "He wrote that garbage like, twenty years ago or something. Did you find a note yet?!"

"Still looking," Holts replied with a sigh as he made his way back to the desk. As his flashlight came back to the simple piece of furniture he saw something flash under his light. Something yellow. The corner of an envelope poked out from within the book. Half of the envelope was wedged between the pages. The other half was covered in blood spatter and tissue.

Holts carefully opened the book and found that the envelope had been used as a bookmark for a chapter that had several highlights throughout. Stealing a glance around to make sure the detective wasn't watching, he began to read the brightly highlighted sentences.

All across the globe are spaces that refuse to bend to any law. That's not to say they are lawless, just that they don't follow the rules of nature, science, or society. People find these places, most of which are harmless, and they are fascinated or charmed by the strange beauty of that parcel of the world. Then there are those lesser-known places that go untouched by tourists, environments with their own laws.

The Tribes of the First People, called by many the Children of Adam, or Tuatha De' Danann by early druids, claimed Earth as their own. They worshipped the Earth and gave thanks to her bounties. They cultivated beauty and had access to magic. They sought to tame the world and shape it to their needs.

The Formoria was born in the dark, chaotic void of space. They originally had no form, no purpose that any human would understand, and they warred constantly. They worshipped the greatest and oldest of their kind. The Great Old Ones, The Outer Gods, and their progeny populated the void and several planets and solar systems.

They all had existed for so long that no one could determine their origins. Town elders and scholars of the occult postulated that they traveled the multitude of realities for no reason other than to consume and create chaos. Other intellectuals, and some fanatics, believed these beings were the physical manifestations of chaos birthed to oppose those who rule by law and order.

Regardless of their origins and intentions, their rule of this universe ended with the birth of sentient life on our plane of existence. Nothing could be more opposed to the chaos, warring, and nebulous nature of the Formoria and their deities. At birth, The First Tribes empowered humans with compassion, love, hate, grief, and shared purpose. Initially, they were a species working together toward bettering themselves and working in harmony with their environment. All these worked in direct opposition to the Formoria and were therefore challenged the Formori's existence.

The First Tribes gifted their children with the ability to create form and structure from imagination. They inspired those who worshipped them with dreams and ambition. They imprisoned those chaotic creatures in bodies with anatomy, emotion, and means to die by mortal hands. The human tribes hunted down the Formoria with fire, alchemy, and weapons of iron and wood. The universe produced light that burned the flesh of Formoria and blinded those beings so accustomed to the darkness. The only thing the Formoria could do was flee before this power.

The First Tribes used their final curses and rituals to create a realm the Formoria were accustomed to, a dark patch of reality filled with the waters and fruits the Formoria so loved. They took with them their deities because where worshippers go, their gods must attend to them. Once lured into this dimension, The First Tribes shut the door behind them and placed The Veil around our plane of existence.

This Veil hid our reality and prevented entrance from these monsters. They quickly discovered they were trapped and have since raged against the deception. Their gods still have the power to reach beyond the Veil through our nightmares, and they promise servants portions of their power and glory if they are given purchase into our world. It is only a matter of time before those beyond the Veil return.

-Robert P. Holcombe Ph.D.

"The Complete History of Old Gods and Monsters"

"What a weirdo," Holts muttered to himself.

"What'cha got Rook?" a stern voice barked from behind Holts, causing him to jump in place. The envelope in his hand opened just enough for a handwritten letter to fall out onto the floor. Holts picked up the letter quickly and began reading it aloud.

Haven Shire is a curiosity. Travelers have discovered this valley many times over the centuries. Each settler fell under the magical charms of the glen and was inspired to remain in this slice of paradise.

According to the oral history passed down by elders and chieftains of the valley, the first tribes of man cultivated the land. The rich soil, clean waters, and abundant wildlife kept them in the valley, and those who dwelt there gave thanks to their gods for the gifts given to them. They were healthy, productive, and the connection to the land was intimate.

Over the centuries, those who dwelled in the valley were discovered, often by accident, by other tribes and settlers. Instead of warring over this hidden treasure, as often was the case with human beings, the land inspired peace and community.

When my family first arrived in the secluded little village, they were pilgrims in search of fertile lands and freedom. They ministered to the population, raised crops and livestock, and for a time, they were happy. Everyone in the community seemed to co-exist blissfully ignorant of the machinations of politicians and capitalists.

The town needed to modernize to accommodate the growing population. Engineers introduced electricity, radio towers, and methods to bring the world to this Eden. Despite being dragged to the modern era, Haven Shire's people fought to remain unsullied by greed and lust.

Looking back at the town my fore-parents grew up in, it seemed the village was the backdrop for "Leave It to Beaver" or some other seemingly peaceful TV utopia. The neighbors were friendly, people broke bread without prejudice, and justice was dispersed fairly.

The valley's defense against modernization and progress waned, however. A new god, new technologies, and hunger began to weaken the magic. The instructions of the first tribes eroded, and the connection to the land faded over time.

The land was not defenseless, as it was a gift from the First Tribe to the tribes of man. A constant mist that rolled down from the hills, blanketing the valley. Only those invited were permitted to see the land, and if they decided to leave by chance, they soon lost all memory of the place and its location. Also, the lands would "take" a local citizen or passerby to prevent overpopulation and further corruption.

Just like any fruit, the magic began to spoil over time. The modern advances in human technology grew too powerful for the magic of the land to keep pace. New pilgrims arrived but no longer thought to thank the land and their gods.

The increasing community took too much and cared too little for their home. As more people came to live within the misty hills of the Shire, so did the need for modern conveniences. This hunger for comfort further disconnected the tribes from the land.

Monotheistic teachings and prejudice took root, dismissing and condemning the original legends as heretical. This lack of love created rot, rot invited disease, and soon the whole fruit began to spoil. This spoilage over time invited further corruption.

Haven Shire today has seemingly lost all its magic. There remains the curious mist that covers this outwardly scenic village. Those who commute in and out do so as they please. Those who lived within the valley no longer enjoy life removed from the business of the world.

There is still the occasional disappearance of community members and travelers. People assumed that the slow-paced life of the Shire was too much for some and they left. It is unknown to the residents what feeds the mystical nature of these woods and hills, and many found a reason for the pervasive fog. Explanations ranged from the magical to the ludicrously mundane- topography, nearby hot springs, or an errant wind current.

The people who live here now spread selfishness, greed, wrath, and sloth. They lust, devour, and envy as all humans do. This cancerous evil begets itself. It has metastasized in our hearts and spreads a creeping sense of despair, xenophobia, and paranoia to every corner of the Shire.

Strange figures in the shadows, rumored monsters in the woods, or loved ones stolen at night erode the community's peace. No one seemed to wish to voice this truth as it might cause a stir in the otherwise quiet town. Or if one, such as I, makes light of the growing threat to our lives, they may be condemned as insane or a fool.

I hope someone discovers the cause of the disease and cuts it from the body. Sadly, I will not see this in my lifetime. I have recently been diagnosed with stage four pancreatic cancer. My corruption and illness mirrored what had occurred to my beloved community. My life here is no longer tenable as I cannot live alone without support, and I would not want to invite others to become besmirched as the town has.

I choose to leave this place I love so dearly on my terms. I have been assured that the shotgun blast will end my life quickly and with minimal pain. To those whom I leave behind, I pray for you all and hope to see you again soon.

Farewell,

Robert P Holcombe, Ph. D.

"Well I would say you just found a clue there rook," the detective sneered. "Who's it written to? I'll make the call."

"George Thatch," Holts said, then his eyes shot open wide. "Sergeant Thatch, sir?"

"Shit boy, you may make detective one day yet," the detective laughed. He took the note and envelope from Holts and examined it briefly. After a few moments, he shoved the articles back at the Holts, who fumbled for the papers in an attempt to not drop them on the floor. He looked around the room and then back at the rookie cop. "You be a peach and run that up to the Sergeant, would ya? I got enough weird shit here to deal with."

"Yessir," Holts agreed. He wasn't the detective's favorite, and the feeling was mutual. He liked Sergeant Thatch and maybe this would help get in his good graces if it turned out to be something important. Officer Holts turned the letter over and found a few lines left.

P.S., George Thatch, you will undoubtedly find this letter first. I am sorry to put the burden of my death onto you. Please excuse the mess. I will miss our talks over coffee.

P.P.S., George, can you clear my browser history? Hate to fuel the town's gossip.

-CHAPTER 2-
HISTORY HAS A MEAN GRIP

Breathe. His body trembled, and his chest felt so tight. *Breathe, slow it down,* George Thatch thought as he sat in his patrol car. His eyes were closed, and he took another slow breath. He looked up into his rearview mirror. His grey hair and sleep-deprived eyes made him look like he was in his forties, despite being only thirty-five. Often, this effect was referred to as police miles.

George's skin and bones felt like they wanted to run in opposite directions, just fall off his body and fly far away. His chest was tight, and his guts felt like ants were crawling around inside him. He was sweating, and his hands trembled.

"Fucking PTSD! It's not real!" he scolded himself. "Breathe, goddamn it! This isn't real!"

He thought of the bloody note he held, sealed in the evidence bag. George had read the message left for him at the scene of a suicide. He knew Robert Holcombe, or as the students called him, 'Crazy Bob.' He was a history teacher, volunteered at the local library, was president of the Haven Shire Historical Society, and was an all-around quack.

George would run into 'Crazy Bob' as he got coffee and be held prisoner by far-too-long of conversations. He politely listened to conspiracy theories, legends, and lessons on how the new generation has no respect for traditions. He patiently listened because he felt a little sorry for the man.

He thought of the gore left behind by Holcombe after he took a double-barreled shotgun and blew his face off. He didn't die immediately, much to Mr. Holcombe's disappointment, and the blood trail he left indicated he nearly crawled out the front door of his house. George was aware that survivors of suicide often panic in those moments right before death, filling his brain with images of Holcombe trying to call for help in those last painful seconds.

"Fuck," George swore as he considered the contents of the message. He pulled on a pair of light blue gloves and reached over to the clear plastic bag next to him. The envelope was spattered like a Jackson Pollock canvas. If the artist used blood and brain matter as his medium.

Robert Holcombe knew a secret. He was privy to knowledge about Haven Shire that George thought only he and his brother knew. George had hoped he would never have to unlock that heavy box which contained that night in his memories. He locked them away with imaginary chains of iron and nailed shut with railroad spikes.

"Oh God, that fucking railroad," George muttered aloud. Like quick flashes of lightning, the memories blasted his vision. The icy grip around his chest, spine, guts tightened. He couldn't breathe again. No matter how deep he inhaled the air couldn't reach deep enough into his chest to help. He needed to focus. *"Breathe, motherfucker! Breathe!"*

When George felt like his world was spinning out of control, he focused on what he loved most, his girls, Ava and Rose. His "Thatchlings," Amanda called them, often *not* as a compliment. They needed him and he needed their smiles and laughter. They were safe, still untouched and poisoned by this town or the world at large.

The memory of his family sent his eyes to find the family photo, nestled in the overhead visor. Almost like a Pavlovian response- memory instigates the need to look at what he is currently missing, initiates more memories of what is falling apart back at home. His wife, Amanda, had left the night before after their last argument. She wanted him to talk more, be present, and open up with emotions. He wanted to do nothing but forget what he saw and just be a good dad.

"You're so distant ever since 'that' night, you have to talk about it with someone," Amanda said before leaving. "At least find some way to get the nightmares to stop. You scare the girls with your screaming, and you are scaring me!"

George rubbed his eyes and tried to blink away the slamming door and the sound of his girls crying. That memory was instead tossed aside to make room for the scene of Holcombe's suicide. The bloody mess of it all, and the note, still tucked neatly in an evidence bag.

George read the note that Officer Holts dropped off once but quickly folded it shut until he could be alone with its secrets.

Holcombe somehow found out something that explained this strange hamlet, and it drove him insane. Sure, the cancer didn't help, but he saw the truth of this place. If it wasn't for the girls, would have George done the same?

When the girls were born, George's love warmed him to his core. Amanda was always the stoic and sensible one, but even her gaze softened when her girls were playing together. George would catch her looking at him, playing with the children, and see her stoney façade eased.

George's love for his daughters came at a price, though. Nightmares replaying the awful things he'd seen and heard. He was also assaulted by visions of the horrors that could befall his girls. Sometimes, Ava was stolen from him, hit by a car, or gunned down. Or dreams of Rosie being diagnosed with cancer, dying of SIDS, or being attacked by an animal. His dreams knew what made him vulnerable and twisted its knife to remind him that this town, this world, was ready to take what he loved at any moment.

"Jesus! Fucking-"George screamed into his hands, still holding onto the bloody evidence. "Why can't you just leave me the fuck alone?"

"Because you can't leave here," a voice from his past whispered, *"You can't just get up and quit like that little bitch and her queer son."*

"Yeah well, fuck you too, Dad," George said to himself. He wanted to forget it all. All the way back to that day he found his dad, drunk and dead on the sofa.

George was still haunted by his parents no matter how much he fought, or how much he drank. Edward's voice was always there, screaming at him from the top of those basement stairs. Or his mother screaming into the darkness, fending off unseen demons. Then there was that kid. Even on the good days and nights, he dreamt of the boy he murdered.

Mickey Corners. His pleading eyes. His black eyes. His mouth begging for mercy. His impossible smile. The thing that scratched the inside of George was like someone trapped alive in a coffin. Mickey-*Fucking*-Corners. George's terrible secret.

Not a nickname; that's his real name, George thought every time this memory intruded on his life. He always gave a slight chuckle at the absurdity of the moniker right before the scene of his death played out inside his mind.

-CHAPTER 3-
BLUE CANARIES

George hated running, not cardio training, just running. If challenged, George would hop on any bicycle, swim any distance, or perform burpees until he puked. If asked to jog, though, even just for light exercise? The person would receive one of two answers depending on who you were. One answer was for polite company.

"No thanks," followed by a polite excuse or canned quip. This was reserved for those George didn't know well or if they had the best intentions. If he knew you, worked with you, or didn't like you, the answer was something like, "Um, no. Go fuck yourself for asking, and would you mind eating a dick while you're at it. Thanks."

He insisted on tentative politeness on either occasion. Hand gestures were optional, depending on the circumstance or venue in which such a conversation went down.

The new owner of the factory, Judge Marcus, insisted the grounds kept clear of the "flotsam and jetsam," and he paid well. The "flotsam" he spoke about was anyone who loitered on the grounds. Marcus shut down the factory and never reopened it. This was a blow to Haven Shire since many of its residents were employed there.

George wanted a cushy gig that allowed him to listen to his Jayhawks basketball games or read his L'Amour western novels. Again. For the seventh time. Instead of doing any of that, here he was, chasing some crazy, possibly strung-out weirdo away from quite possibly the strangest scene he had ever stumbled upon. "Go fuck yourself and EAT A DICK!" he growled as he continued his pursuit.

George focused on the words of the Western novel and tried to tune out the outside world. He didn't hear the wind buffeting the side of his Explorer. George no longer noticed how degraded the parking lot had become or the weeds and grass lazily waving in the wind. Reading is how he stayed calm when he began to feel life's stressors strain his emotional defenses. The last thing he needed was to have a stroke in some cheap, hand-me-down patrol car, smelling of old dog food in the middle of a closed factory parking lot.

The hairs on George's arms and neck suddenly stiffened, and he felt a charged sensation across his face and chest. George got this "tingle" occasionally when talking to a perp and they were lying or if he was about to stumble into danger. He threw his book aside and shut off the radio. The light was getting low as the sun descended, but it felt as though the very colors of the day were draining away. The shadows lengthened and grew dark. George scanned the sky to check for storm clouds. Nothing.

He tried to recount the number of times lightning struck a victim on a sunny day. Not a one that he could remember. He listened for any sound of an intruder and found only silence. Real silence. No animals—birds, bugs, coyotes, farmstock—no distant sound of the town or wind. George got out of the car and checked his holster.

His fingers traced the corners and curves of his Glock Model 22's grip. The "tingle" began to recede, but the hairs on his neck and arms still stood. Almost as if his body and lizard brain were aware of something he wasn't. He felt like a deer with someone's sights trained on him.

George walked around to the car's passenger side, grabbed his flashlight and portable radio, and fit them into their holsters. Times like this, he wished he had brought his shotgun. Seeing his department-issued, pump action, 12-gauge Remington alone was usually enough to deter most criminals from doing anything stupid. He parked between the main factory floor building and a machine shop. He hadn't seen any cars on this road all shift, much less any sign of life on the campus.

Just as he closed the vehicle's passenger side door, all his senses suddenly began screaming. His skin buzzed as though it housed a hive of hateful wasps, his head throbbed, and goosebumps flared up his back, neck, and arms. George was suddenly bombarded by the screams and howls of every animal within a mile of the factory. He heard them almost as if they were right next to him. Wincing at the chaotic chorus, George covered his ears with his palms.

Somewhere beyond the noise, he heard the apocalyptic klaxon of a tornado siren. The tone reverberated so lowly and loudly that George could feel his bones vibrate and his bowels shift. George shut his eyes and took several slow, deep breaths, trying to command his body to calm down.

Where was this coming from? It feels like it's coming up through the ground, George thought.

He looked down at his feet and felt his soles buzzing from below. George realized then that it was his body that was vibrating, not the ground. The dirt and rocks weren't bouncing and dancing to the low hum of the horn. George was being told to move, but where? What was beneath him?

"Under?" he started. "Shit, the basement! That's got to be it!" George held one hand to the wall when he let one hand drop from his ear. The cacophony that assaulted him caused George to become dizzy. He felt nauseous as his world swam and spun. He hurried the twenty-or-so foot distance between the Ford Explorer and the side entrance to the main factory floor. Once he reached the door, he tried to pull down the door handle.

His body jerked as the door resisted his pull, and he fell off his unsteady feet onto his hands and knees and gravel. George tried to recover from the shock and coordinate his efforts quickly, but his stomach had enough of the world spinning, and he vomited.

After the retching subsided, he shakily reached into his pocket and fished out the ring of keys that gave him access to the three buildings on the factory grounds. Each skeleton key was a match for its structure and numbered to indicate which building they unlocked.

George pulled the key marked with a faded "1" written in blue marker and taped around the end. With a trembling hand, he pushed the key into the hole and turned. Without retrieving the key, he grabbed the door handle and threw the door open. He gagged once more for good measure and crawled into the building. The entire world abruptly stopped screaming when the door slammed shut behind him. George sat with his back against the wall.

The cool stone helped soothe the drumming of his heartbeat in his ears and helped to clear his head. He slowed his breathing and tried to spit the flavor of vomit and bile from his mouth. The world ceased its spinning, and howls and screams stopped. His skin still buzzed, and something within him continued to pull in the direction of the basement.

George slowly opened his eyes and looked around at his surroundings. The main assembly floor was growing dark as the day was winding down. The shadows deepened, but the heavy motes of dust that floated in the air were still visible.

When George turned on the flashlight, he wondered if the tiny particles floating around were dust or the floating remains of the product manufactured and packaged here. He pulled out a painter's mask and put it on, but after catching a whiff of his breath, he decided to take his chance with the dust.

What little sunlight remained left orange streaks across the grey conveyor belts and packaging machines. The spotlight of his torch cut through the shadows, but nothing seemed out of the ordinary. Rat shit and bird droppings peppered the various pieces of equipment. Occasionally, George would catch movement out of the corner of his eye but found nothing upon investigation.

After scanning the immediate vicinity and checking for threats, George let out a sigh pent up within him. He didn't see anything, so why did he feel like he was in danger? Cold sweat covered George, and his guts churned and growled. He even felt his groin pulling up toward his core, seeking warmth and protection.

"What the fuck is going on?" George asked. "I think I've finally lost it." His voice trembled with that last comment. His worst fear was to turn out like his parents.

# # # #

His parents, Judith and Edward, got pregnant with George in high school. At the insistence of Judith's parents, they were wed, and Edward went straight to work in the limestone mines in the hills just outside of town. Judith was beautiful with flame-kissed red hair, porcelain skin peppered with freckles, and an almost fairy-like air. Even with no wind, she always seemed to sway gently back and forth like a tree in a meadow.

Judith had a soothing way about her, but her eyes held such a wild way about them that made it hard for people to maintain eye contact. Soon after the boys were born, Judith began to see and hear things no one else could, and what she saw frightened her and those she told. Judith claimed that ghosts blanketed Haven Shire and that monsters clung to the shadows of alleyways and surrounding woods.

Judith was committed by Edward to the state mental hospital. George never knew what had happened to his mom while she stayed there. He visited her once with his father and brother, and Judith just sat in the lounge, staring at a corner of the ceiling. She was filthy, non-communicative, and drooling all over her gown. Electricity and pharmacology snuffed all the light and magical glow about her.

On one clear moonless night, Judith escaped the hospital. She was found a month later by Finn, cold and wasted away on the front porch of their home, rocking on the swing she would sit on with her boys. She whispered something to each of her boys and then gave up. Her eyes fixed on them as her soul left her withered body.

Edward Thatch was the son of the town's preacher, who tried his best to impress upon him the importance and need of a religious education. It was only a matter of meeting a catalyst, such as one found in Judith, which allowed Edward to rebel against his father's strict discipline. Judith lived outside of the community, both physically and socially. If this troubled her in any way, she didn't show it. She seemed to stroll through town merrily, unaware of the stares and whispers of her neighbors.

Upon hearing word of Judith's pregnancy, Edward's father disowned him. After all, Edward's father groomed him to be the church's next leader, attended by almost every citizen of Haven Shire. He played baseball, and many college scouts took notice. This all changed when it was discovered that Judith was pregnant.

Edward was the most popular guy in school, and everyone wanted to be his friend. Teen pregnancy terminated any chance of a scholarship or social life. Edward was no longer his father's bright boy and was treated now as a sinner and defiler of innocent girls by his father and the community.

Edward went to work, and soon his friends stopped inviting him to the games and after-parties. Girls used to look at him with lusty eyes and romantic notions. Now, they giggled behind their hands and whispered when he was around. None of this seemed to bother Edward initially, even when Judith was so pregnant that she needed help sitting or standing. He only had eyes and ears for her and did all he could to provide for her.

After George was born, Edward worked to be the best provider for his family. He worked double shifts and quickly earned a promotion as a foreman at the quarry. Soon, he had enough saved, and they bought a small home outside town.

Edward noticed Judith had begun talking to herself. He saw how her eyes flitted and attempted to catch the movement of something just outside his periphery. Edward prayed the open air and country life would soothe her nerves. The farmhouse sat on a few acres, sufficient for him to grow a few crops and for Judith to plant her herbs and raise chickens if she wanted.

Then Phineas was born, and Edward was no longer the focus of Judith's affection. He watched her as she doted on the children. When Judith's visions worsened, she became ferociously protective, even possessive of the boys.

To Judith, it was just the children and her against the monsters and specters of Haven Shire, and for some reason, Edward was shut out of that world. She would spend hours guarding the home with totems and hand-crafted crosses. She would even have the children join her in crafting these talismans.

She sometimes kept them home from school or neglected social engagements to hover over them. One day, Edward caught her speaking in tongues and dancing around the boys. He called for the doctor when she began painting strange symbols on the children's bedroom walls in what he had assumed was chicken blood.

If Edward made any inquiries about their activities, she would dismiss them and him along with them. As the years passed, Edward often would come home from work, and she barely even noticed his presence. Over time, Judith stopped being affectionate or giving him a kind word. He felt like one of the specters she so feared.

It was only a matter of time before Edward was sick of hearing her speak about what she saw or heard. He first tried to reason with Judith, but Edward began to hate her for a life taken from him. Edward hated her for all of it. He hated her lack of attention, absence of intimacy, and her mental state separating them. He hated her because she was so goddamn beautiful and inaccessible, and the thought of living without her made him weep in the dark lonely hours of the night.

So, he drank. Soon, that was all he did. He was fired from the foreman position after a terrible oversight cost one man his hand. Edward picked up any handyman or contractor job available. Few called him back for employment. After Judith died, Edward barely left the house. He was content just to stay as drunk. He wanted to forget it all. Judith. His father. His potential.

When George and Finn were old enough, they worked to keep the lights on and food on the table. Mowing, bagging groceries, and waiting tables, George quit attending high school to put food on the table. They had to hide any cash they had. Otherwise, Edward would have taken it and drank it away.

Edward never hit George or his brother. Words were his weapon of choice. He could wield phrases like a razor and throw insults with practiced ease. He shackled the boys to him and their home with guilt and shame.

"It's your fault she went insane, you hateful little shits!" he'd slur. "If it weren't for you, she'd still be alive today! I should've taken the hanger to ya before you were born!"

Edward also found creative ways to punish his boys for getting into any trouble he perceived. Any slight landed them locked in a basement for the weekend without light or food. Growing weary of the crying, he built an outhouse far from the house.

Edward also forced manual labor on the boys to keep them out of the house. Hand-pulling weeds without the benefit of gloves was his favorite. He would place a burn barrel out, and George and his brother would have to fill it by sundown. They spent the night in the outhouse if they failed. There were no pillows, no blankets, just the tattered, thin pajamas and each other to stay warm.

At the age of sixteen, George earned his GED. This was his way out. He could get a decent job, maybe rent an apartment for himself and his brother, and get the fuck away from Edward. George was coming home to share the good news with Phineas, only to find the house cold and empty. Instead of the barrage of slurs and insults that George had grown used to, he found Edward lying cold and stiff on the sofa.

Edward's jaundiced eyes were fixed on the window; drool pooled at the corner of his mouth, now laid agape in a silent howl.

George tried to move him and found Edward fused to the couch in his piss and shit. George gave up on Edward and began calling out for Finn. He frantically ran up to his room, searching for any sign of him.

The space was not just empty; he knew that. It was cold and felt abandoned to him for some reason. Finn's bed was neatly made, his drawers were empty, and toiletries were gone. On the wall above the head of the bed, a message was left in sidewalk chalk. No explanation, no reason. Just three words:

Mother was right

# # # #

"Okay, dickhead, pull yourself together," George told himself. "Let's just check this place out and get back to the game."

George had considered keying up his radio and calling for backup but reconsidered. What would he tell them? George hadn't found anything to report. The noises he heard and sensations he felt. "Might as well turn in your resignation and check into the looney bin," George said louder than he had intended. Besides, he knew two other fuckwits working this gig. They would be more likely to shoot him or themselves by accident than provide some form of support.

George felt the vibrations in the basement, buzzing around in the soles of his feet like bees. He had to know what was happening. His body tingled from his scalp to his toes. He learned to trust this instinct, but it had never been as bad as this. In the past, his intuition had kept him from walking into a building, or perhaps it warned him that someone would do him harm. It had even alerted him when someone close to him was sick.

For example, his wife's mother had cancer. He couldn't explain it, but he just "felt" like something was wrong. When he asked her, she admitted she had colon cancer but was not ready to tell others. She wondered how he knew, of course. He just shrugged and made some awkward excuse.

He walked along the wall and pulled his Glock from its holster. He removed the safety on his gun and used his flashlight to light the way to the concrete stairwell to the basement. The basement functioned as a storm shelter and storage for the factory.

He crept up to the bright yellow rails that blocked off the stairwell. The paint was peeling, and rust was visible beneath, especially in corners or where spot welding occurred.

At the top of the stairwell was a chain hanging from its perch on the handrail. Connected to the chain was a small rectangular sign that read, *No Exit. Use caution.* The warning sign had a picture of a stick figure in mid-fall. George did his walk-through in that very spot that morning, and the chain was hung across and latched to prevent anyone from falling down the stairs into the basement. Now, it hung limp, with one end of the chain coiled like a snake on the floor. He swung his flashlight toward the stairs. Nothing.

George took a breath and began a slow and deliberate descent into the basement. He suddenly remembered how cops were usually the first to die from exposure when entering a structure with an unknown emergency. There were stories of police lying face down in the entryway of a house because carbon monoxide levels were so high that those cops who entered were immediately incapacitated.

Firefighters often joke about sending in the "blue canaries" whenever someone calls 911 for a strange odor. Such banter was all in playful fun. Good times. Not this, though. This felt like shit. It felt as though every instinct told him to run away. So why was he walking down into a dark basement, with God knows what that awaited him?

Because you need to know if this shit is all in your head, he realized. If he had gotten to the basement and found nothing, he would have been crazy, just like Mom and Dad. It's hereditary, after all, right? If he had gotten down there and found a meth lab, or a sex trafficker, or the boogieman itself, he would deal with it. Better than being crazy.

As he descended the concrete steps, he listened for anything. Literally anything. It was so quiet in the building above him. The farther he descended, the deeper the dark of the shadows. When he reached the basement floor, his flashlight lit only the tiny space. It felt like the shadows coalesced around the light, giving only a small path to travel, and nothing beyond was visible.

The tunnel was claustrophobic. Not that the tunnel was cramped, but it felt as though the atmosphere was thicker. Even walking through the dark seemed to drain the strength from him, like gravity was heavier here than anywhere else. George shook the thought and focused on what little he could see.

George had seen the floor plan of the factory and had walked it often enough to know the layout. The basement was finished, and he knew if he took a left, he would find himself in a small machine and tool storage room. On his right was a cage that stored gas cans, cleaning supplies, and other chemicals and cleaning utensils.

George found the gate was open, unsurprising, since there was nothing to store. The floor was bare, except for the occasional rat droppings or candy bar wrapping left by one of his coworkers. As he scanned the room, he tried to orient himself best by locating the support pillars. Someone painted one bright white with a red ring around its base. It reminded George of a bone sticking out of grey flesh.

Just twenty feet away, George discovered a second pillar. Each post was thick and capable of bearing the great weight of the floor above him. There didn't appear to have been any traffic down here for some time. Dust motes hung in the air like tiny spiders in invisible webs.

The basement maintained the same stench of old dog food as above but with notes of mildew and stale air. There was something else, too. George couldn't quite place the odor; ozone, maybe, not strong enough to overpower the stench of whatever-the-fuck made up dog food. They say lamb, salmon, beef, etc. Who knows? It could be a horse, for all anyone knew. George hated this place, the stench of it, the feeling it created across his skin and bones.

George turned around to head back to his book and maybe the end of the basketball game. Just as he made one last pass with his flashlight, a shadow caught his eye. Nothing was remarkable in the basement, but the seams of the farthest corner of the room didn't match. The lines of the bricks didn't line up as they should, and as he moved to his left, there was a shadow that indicated a hallway. It felt like his brain couldn't accept it was there for some reason. It seemed to disappear the moment he looked away, only to return when George refocused and looked closer to find it again.

George paused, and his face screwed up with a look of confusion. A hallway or passage had been built, bricked over, and then painted. No one reported this renovation. He also knew that it wasn't on any of the floor plans. It seemed as though it was camouflaged. He walked to the passage, eyes focused and his gun drawn. His skin and bones told him he should leave. The base of his skull held pressure, and his insides felt like they wanted to fall straight out of his rectum. A cold sweat prickled his skin, and then he felt it—a breeze and, with it, the scent of ozone.

George took a slow, deep breath and pressed forward. The passage narrowed before him into darkness. It was a darkness so thick that his flashlight glare dared not tread more than a few feet ahead. George guessed the first one hundred feet of the passage was bricked and painted like the factory walls, and the floor was smooth and polished. The foundation gave way to unfinished walls. Roots from trees and grass above hung from the ceiling and lined the passage.

George was more careful with his steps than before as he felt divots of rock and clay on the soles of his feet. They teased the toes and heels of his boots, tempting him to stumble. He treaded carefully while also trying to draw a map of the tunnel in his head.

George retained a mental map, a helpful trick a firefighter colleague taught him, and George reminded himself which way was north and of the distance from the beginning of this new adventure. He calculated he had walked in a strange circular pattern, a maze of sorts, which spanned the length of the entire factory campus. He was moving toward the center of something.

The closer he got to the center of the spiraling passage, the colder it got and the more electricity he could feel in the air. He also began to smell the stench of rotting vegetation and animals. The dirt on the walls around him and beneath his feet gleamed against the light of his flashlight. He felt his heel slip on the slimy and viscous stuff that coated the walls and floor.

"What the shit is this place?" he said to himself. For a moment, George thought his eyes were finally adjusting to the dark, but the farther he walked, the slime coating took on a brighter luminescence. He shut off his flashlight and closed his eyes.

George allowed time for his vision to adjust to the dark, and when he opened them, he confirmed his theory about the glow emanating from the soil and vines. There appeared to be an orange glow coming from trails of slime that streaked up and down the walls and across the floor. They almost looked like veins filled with orange magma, and George thought to be careful not to step on the streaks flowing down the hall in case they were radioactive.

He holstered his flashlight and placed both hands on his sidearm. George felt this strange trip down this rabbit hole was near the end. This thought was confirmed when the narrow hall widened into an ample space. The room's floor dipped suddenly, and George could see he stood on the edge of a bowl-like structure.

Several large stones jutted out from the floor and around the room. The center of the room glowed a hot orange, and the stench of spoil and decay grew strong enough to force George to cover his face with his arm. The roof curved upward, forming a dome with several vines and roots snaking around him. The roots dropped and hung low in the center of the roof. Some draped down to the floor. Within their withered and ropey appendages, he made out what appeared to be rocky clods with grassroots springing forth.

Each large root glowed with veins of the same orange mucous, some dripping onto the floor. George followed the roots to see where they terminated and if they led to another way out, but instead, he found they surrounded a four-foot-high slab of stone in the center of the hot orange glow of the pool within the bowl of the room. The stone slab was rectangular and bore intricate carvings on the side.

George pulled a handkerchief from his back pocket and tied it around his nose and mouth. It did little to block the stench, but he wanted his hands free as he slid down the embankment toward the center of the room. When George reached the bottom, he realized how stupid he was acting. He lost any tactical advantage at this point.

George scolded himself for letting his curiosity get the better of him. He didn't check for any additional entrances or egress points, and the bowl-shaped floor George was now in cut off his field of vision. He didn't even know if this orange substance was poisonous and could kill him.

"Blue-*fucking*-canary," he chided. "Real fucking smart, jackass." He wondered why he was doing this instead of calling for backup, the EPA, the FBI, or some agency with more smarts than him. "All right, this is dumb, no doubt about that. I'm just going to check this out, and then I'm getting the fuck outta here."

George snuck between the jutting boulders the best he could, carefully checking and ensuring no one was watching him. He crept up to the last boulder. There was no cover for him if George got closer to the slab in the center of the bowl. He pulled out his flashlight, lit the slab's side, and tried to make out the etching and carvings.

He was only six feet away, but the sides were covered in carvings depicting a mass of creatures as far as he could tell. The carvings displayed them writhing, curling around, or embracing each other. Some were even devouring others or themselves. A perfect round globe was in the center of the mass of tentacles, teeth, eyes, and talons. The corners of the slab were carved into what appeared to be a series of totems. Gods maybe? Each figure held up another, with runes etched onto their breasts or bellies.

The totems culminated with a multi-limbed naked woman, her arms more like insect limbs that ended in hooks. Her head sported human features, long hair, thin lips, and a nose. Her eight eyes were round and spread across her forehead, and her mouth parted just enough to expose sharp, jagged teeth.

She sported the oversized version of a woman's sex at her groin, sprouting a long snake-like appendage which, at its end, bloomed something like a four-petaled flower filled with rows of thorns and a circle of teeth at its nucleus. She held up an octopus-like creature upside down with eyes peppered across its bulbous form. The tentacles all reached up at the four corners of the stone slab, the eyes of the beast hateful and hungry. At first glance, George mistook the carving for a perverse tree.

He was about to see what else he could discover from the slab when he heard others enter the room. George froze behind his hiding spot and tried to make out the direction and distance of the noise. He moved to another boulder. This one was wider and taller and would provide more cover.

George peered around the corners and tried to get the exact location of those heading his way. He heard shuffling footsteps and a low moaning noise coming from above and on the opposite side of the bowl from him. George was lucky…he thought he would've been spotted if he had stayed where he was. Now, he could better understand what was happening in this room and decide what to do.

George listened to the moaning as it got closer. He could hear whispering as well but could not make out the words. Whoever they were, they whispered in unison and reverently, like they were praying. He went to pull his phone from his pocket to text his partner. Jack took him in when he was just a rookie, and he knew that if anyone had his back, it would be him.

Of fucking course, he thought as he found his pocket empty. George remembered leaving it on the seat next to him in the SUV because he got tired of trying to pick out the right shade of pink for the girls' room. The shades of pink all looked the same, honestly, and his wife, Amanda, would change her mind tomorrow anyway.

I'm such a dumbass, he sneered. *Okay, just play it cool. Stay calm, and you stay alive.*

He looked at his position and decided that he would try and stay concealed to determine just what the fuck was happening. He was entranced by the stone slab, the shit-smelling slime, and all the bat-shit craziness of this mess. Suddenly, his alarm bells rang loudly…he could feel it in his jaw and ears.

He peered around the rock, hoping to see where the praying was originating. There were two figures; one wore the skull of a bull, and the other the skull of a big dog or a wolf. Their heads and torsos were covered in fur that matched the same animal.

The figures were lit by the luminescent slime, displaying they were both naked from the waist down, and their arms were exposed. From what he could see, they had fresh cuts covering almost every inch of their exposed skin, even their cocks. The cuts matched the etchings and grooves on the rock slab in the center of the room. Across their skin were patches of scripture, still weeping blood from the fresh carvings.

The masked men moved carefully with an improvised stretcher. It appeared as though the stretcher was cobbled together by whatever was available. One handle was made from a broomstick, and the other a thick branch. The bed of the stretcher was made from what appeared to be a filthy bed sheet. The contents spread across the top of the stretcher were wrapped in burlap and then sewn shut with a thick leather cord. George watched the procession move into the room and carefully moved down the edge of the bowl impression.

"What the fuuuuck?" he whispered. As he watched them navigate the slope of the bowled floor, he noticed a little movement from the burlap. It was barely perceivable at first, but then he saw it again. There was something or someone alive in that sack!

Well, shit, he thought. He prepared himself for action. George could take them now while they were off balance. He considered whether he should charge straight toward them or try to move to a position allowing him to flank them.

"Fuck it," he said through gritted teeth. He tensed his muscles and grabbed his flashlight before taking a steadying breath. He tried to ignore the pounding in his head and the hive of vibrations under his skin. He had to act now! He moved to a crouched position and mentally set himself to jump out and catch the masked figures. They didn't seem to be carrying weapons. Such a thought bolstered his confidence. He rolled onto the balls of his feet and froze.

He suddenly felt all the buzzing in his head and skin coalesce to his back, along his spine, and the back of his skull. His hearing became hyperacute, and time seemed to slow as he heard the whoosh of air behind him. His skin prickled like something near him invaded his boundaries with dangerous intent. Whatever it was, it was moving toward his head and fast.

George ducked and heard something heavy crash hard against the rock in the space his head used to be. Small stones and dust slipped onto his neck and down his shirt. Within a second, he sprang forward and twisted in the air, landing hard on his back with his pistol drawn and flashlight glaring at his attacker.

The figure was tall, made even more so by the stag headdress and twelve-point antlers above the head. Like the other two masked litter bearers, this figure wore a simple fur cowl extending down to the waist. It was also a woman, George could see, for she was naked, and her chest, stomach, and arms were exposed, but unlike the other two, she wore a long animal hide skirt.

The woman also sported the same carvings in her flesh as the other two; some of them were shapes of twisted, coiled creatures, and some of them were a form of script in a foreign language. She carried a pick hammer in her right hand, its long spike jutting from one end and a sledge on the other. She hefted the tool over her shoulder, preparing for another swing.

The litter bearers stopped unalarmed. They looked on as the stag woman lifted the pick-hammer with practiced ease. George noticed that the stag woman was taller and broader at the shoulder than the other two. Muscles in her forearm flexed, and the veins bulged as they pumped blood and oxygen up to her hand as she hefted the weapon above her head.

George quickly aimed and fired. The bullet struck the top of the mask and threw the woman's head back violently. She fell straight back onto the ground. George turned and began scrambling to his feet when he suddenly heard an animal growl from the litter bearers.

As George moved to steady himself, the figures tipped the poorly constructed litter, dumping its contents onto the bowl floor. The one wearing the bull mask growled and ran around one side of the stone altar. He had no grace in his movement as he clumsily charged George. George could see the bull was berserk and blind in his rage. He lifted his gun and fired three more rounds at the charging bull-servant.

One bullet struck the man's shoulder on the right side above the clavicle. The second grazed his right shoulder. The third stopped the rush, as it smashed dead center in the chest. The assailant stopped and stood straight momentarily before dropping to his knees and falling forward onto his face.

The man wearing the wolf mask seemed less aggressive than his partner and barely moved from his spot.

"Get your hands up, you sick fuck!" George commanded.

The man began to comply, his head shaking.

George kept his gun trained on him as he moved toward the downed attacker. Keeping his eyes on him, he knelt and checked the man's pulse. Dead or well on his way. George focused now. There was still the bag he had to check.

"Okay, fuckface, get your ass down on the ground!" George told the wolf-servant. The man nodded in agreement behind the bone and fur mask. He slowly moved to the slim-streaked dirt floor. The wolf-servant kept his attention on George as he moved around the slab toward the jumbled mess wrapped in burlap.

When George reached it, he nudged the burlap bag with a free hand. It moved, and he heard a sobbing moan come from within. He assessed the stitching on the side of the sack. It was sloppily hand-sewn, and he didn't expect it to hold up to any significant resistance from whatever might struggle to get out.

George set the flashlight down on the ground next to him. He didn't need it to see because he was using it to blind his attackers, which would buy him an extra second or two as he shot his pistol. George had learned that seconds were vital in such situations, and the stunning brightness also interrupted the brain's ability to complete a task or follow through with a plan.

If there was someone in this bag George could save, he needed to see them. The wolf-servant continued to lay on his belly, but he didn't quit staring at George.

"Get your face on the ground!" George yelled.

The masked man did as George told him.

George reached into the side pocket of his cargo pants. He found the clip that belonged to his folding utility knife and flipped the blade out with a loud click. George found the knot that secured the stitching and made short work of it with the blade's sharp edge. He then folded the knife and carefully slid it into his side pocket. He began to tug furiously at the thick stitching of the primitively assembled sack.

George's gun and eyes stayed trained on the man lying face-down in the slime and clay. Satisfied he had loosened it enough, he looked down to see what was inside the bag. What George saw gave him enough of a start that he yelped and stood straight to distance himself from the sight before him. He shook his head at the picture before him, questioning its existence.

The girl was young; she couldn't have been more than fourteen. She was filthy, apparently hadn't bathed, and appeared to be forced to dwell in her waste. She sobbed through lips sewn shut, and tears leaked between threads that sealed her eyelids. Snot bubbled from her nose as she tried to track the figures in the room.

"Wha..wha..." George stammered. The poor girl reminded George of a newborn infant seeking a breast. She desperately bobbed her head around when she felt light and air on her skin again. George rushed over to the girl and pulled at the sack further, trying to give her some freedom of movement. He paused when he tore it open and exposed the poor girl. She was naked and covered in bruises and minor lacerations as well. She tried to move her limbs, but the flesh on her arms was sewn with thick leather strings to her body, much like her eyes and lips.

The girl's arms held fast in a cross position, the stitching beginning with her armpit and securing her biceps and elbows to her flanks and ribcage. Her left arm was straightened, and her palm faced down to cover her genitals. Her right arm was bent, and her palm, also face-down, cupped her naked breast. Both were stitched and secured, hand and fingers tied and knitted to her genitals in a mock pose of modesty. Her inner thighs and legs were also stitched closed from her groin down to her ankles, and her feet were bound together with the ends of the stitching. She tried to struggle, but every new movement only brought the poor child more suffering.

"Oh God, oh God, what the fuck did you sick fucks do?" He turned to the wolf-servant lying face down, mask now covered in the foul orange glowing ooze. George could feel hot bile and rage filling him up. His teeth ground against each other so hard his face hurt. He could barely see until he blinked the tears of anger and pain away.

George knew he had to consider his options now. He had an accessory to the crime, a victim, and two bodies. The girl needed medical attention immediately, and part of him considered incapacitating the piece of shit in front of him somehow and taking her to the hospital.

Suddenly, George felt something heavy slam hard into his right side. The force of the strike was strong enough to pick him up off the floor and knock the wind from him. He landed hard on his left shoulder. He felt a muted, wet pop in his left shoulder, and his right ribs burst into a fiery explosion of pain.

George quickly rolled onto his back and tried to raise his gun. The stag woman stood before him with her pick hammer high above her. Now, he could see part of the woman's face as the headdress was broken in several places.

The woman's hair was wild and filthy, matted by the dirt and slime of the room's floor. Blood flowed from the top of her scalp, and he could see his bullet had grazed the front of her scalp where the hairline began. The wound split the skin open, and he saw the glint of exposed skull.

He quickly learned his left arm was useless. The moment his hand pressed to the floor, it sent roaring pain up into his shoulder, and he nearly swooned from the pain. His vision blurred, but he knew he had to move quickly.

He heard the woman scream with rage as she brought the pick hammer down. The point of the pick slammed into the clay between his legs, narrowly missing his groin. George suddenly realized that there was something off in this woman's glare.

Black? Her eyes were black. George thought as he rolled over to his right side.

He felt a sharp pain in his ribcage and the middle of his back. The muscles cramped, and intense pain reached from his ribs to the right side of his neck. He glanced down and saw that one of the woman's antlers had stabbed him between his fourth and fifth rib. Blood was pooling around the wound. The stag woman moved slowly, bringing her weapon down again for a killing strike.

I'm going to die, George thought. *I won't see what my baby girl grows up to look like.* He closed his eyes, raised his right arm, pistol in hand, and tried to aim in time. It was time he didn't have. There was a loud thump, and sharp cracks filled the room. A grunt and exhalation escaped the stag mask as the pick found its mark. A wet squelching sound as blood and tissue grabbed onto the tool's sharp edge punctuated the attack. George opened his eyes even further in horror at the sight before him.

The stag-woman brought her weapon down hard onto the unsuspecting girl at her feet. The pick hammer stabbed deep into the center of her chest. She whipped her head around momentarily, just before it fell still, and she coughed up a small fountain of blood through her stitches. She stilled, and her head rolled to the side, blood oozing from the corner of her sealed mouth.

"No!" George howled in anguish at the sight. "No!" he wailed again, tears streaming down his face. George raised his right arm, rage overcoming his pain, and began firing shot after shot into the stag-woman as she yanked the pick-hammer free for another attack. The first bullet struck her left hip, causing her to flinch, but the next three shots thudded hard into the center of her torso. This rain of bullets straightened her, and she fell to her knees.

The pools of black that served as her eyes were wide, and her face held a confused look. George growled and fired another shot. This one entered just a couple of inches below her chin. Blood and tissue exploded through her matted hair. The stag-woman jerked momentarily and then fell forward, her head landing on the bound girl's legs.

George moved to his knees, and even with explosions of pain, he scrambled to the bound girl on the floor. In the center of her chest was a large hole from the pick-hammer, filled with pooled blood. She was limp in his arms and so still. George looked at all her injuries and the indignity and pain that marked her skin. He brushed her hair away from her face.

There it was. George knew this girl. She had been missing for a month, and many believed that she had run away. Jessie-something, Jessie Corners was her name. Her parents attended the same church as Amanda and his family. Her mom was an elementary school teacher. Her dad was a truck driver and had died during the COVID-19 pandemic. Now, here she was, dead as well.

"Sorry, kid," George said, tears clinging to his cheeks. Then, from behind him, he heard a shuffling noise. George turned swiftly, gun low to his hip, every motion sending new waves of pain. The last member of the procession had picked himself up off the floor but appeared to be in shock.

"You stay right where you are, you piece of…" Suddenly, George felt dizzy and fell to his left knee. The motion sent fresh waves of pain through his torso, back, and left shoulder. He would have fallen onto his face if he hadn't caught himself with his gun hand, which reached out for support and found the stone altar next to him. The wolf-servant took advantage of George's moment of weakness and darted up the side of the bowl. He clutched and grabbed for vines and rocks and quickly scrambled to the top.

The force of the bullet knocked the servant onto his face. George's face twisted into rage and pain. The thought of these sick fucks torturing this little girl made his eyes burn, and his body feel like it was on fire. There were memories of the girl at "touch-a-truck" day and ice cream socials. This town was small, and the community used to be close. Now, something has come into his village and taken a little girl.

"No," George growled behind gritted teeth. "No fucking way you are leaving here alive." Despite his pain, blood loss, and the antler protruding from his ribs, he climbed the bowl after the last servant. The wolf-servant hadn't gotten far by the time George made it to the lip of the bowl. George saw him hobbling and limping around the corner from the hallway he and his party had entered.

George was also limping, but only because every step he took set off explosions of pain in his shoulder and rib cage. Luckily, George was moving faster than the servant. He listened as the wolf-servant whimpered and cried as he made his way forward. His suffering made George smile ever so slightly. He would ensure this guy hurt before he called for a unit to put him away.

He followed the tunnel until it turned from rocky, slimy, and root-covered terrain to a smooth concrete floor and brick walls. He needed another light source without the luminescence provided by the slimy veins of the strange roots.

With shaky hands, George fumbled momentarily, looking for his flashlight, but it was gone. He wouldn't be able to wield it and his pistol simultaneously anyway. His left arm was useless, and it would be stupid to holster his sidearm. He knelt on the floor. This slight movement caused him to growl in pain. He searched his pockets and found a glow stick.

He only took the first aid classes needed to be a cop, and aside from what he had seen on TV, there was no telling how much damage he was sustaining walking or running. George took a moment to weigh the option of pulling the antler from his ribcage. If he pulled it free, he could risk bleeding out. If he left it in, he could worsen his injury or puncture a lung. "Fuck it," George hissed and pulled the bone protruding from his ribs. He put the antler into his back pocket for now.

George learned to keep emergency items, like the glow stick, in his cargo pockets in case of emergency. Of course, chasing down homicidal cultists wasn't on his list, but he hadn't considered every potential scenario. He bit into the plastic wrapping and tore it open. He dumped out the contents of the packaging, consisting of the glow stick and a thin piece of twine tied to it so that one could wear it around the neck.

He picked up the end of the stick and used the ground for leverage. Leveraging one end of the stick against the floor, he bent the rod in the middle until it cracked and glowed dimly. He raised the glow stick and shook it gently to avoid more movement pain.

He put his head through the twine loop, stood up, and proceeded down the hallway, using the wall for support.

The stick projected a sickly green glow that didn't give off too much light, but there was enough for George to see a short distance down the hallway. He heard shuffling up ahead and hurried the best he could to catch up to the sound. He came to an opening to a small room, which was only big enough for five or six people. On the far wall, there was a large opening. He saw bricks had been removed, and the hole opened into a room beyond. George carefully approached the space. The room beyond was a finished basement, similar to the one under the factory floor.

George listened carefully but didn't hear anyone. He hoped no one on the other side was waiting to ambush him, and he peered through to learn more about the space from which the servant had escaped. George saw that the room was empty, but some light poured from a small set of concrete stairs that led outside.

George stepped through, looked back the way he came, and discovered the spot was an optical illusion. Just like the hall that led him to the strange bowl-shaped room, the entrance was concealed. From a different angle, someone would miss this portal completely.

A mystery for another time, he thought. He jumped as he heard the slam of a heavy metal door. George caught movement from a shadow leading up the stairs. Someone was trying to close the second panel of the door that led to freedom from this cellar.

"Shit, shit, shit!" George said as he tried to hurry to the exit. The wolf-servant was hurt more than George realized and that the doorway beyond the stairs was weighty. He heard the servant grunt and cry as he lifted the gate and struggled to shut it. George got to the base of the stairs and saw that he was in a storm shelter.

The moon was large and complete, lighting the stairway with its pale blue hue. The door rocked up and down as the servant tried to lift the heavy steel door from the other side. George moved quickly. He did not want to be stuck in this basement and be forced to return to that room.

When George was near the top of the stairs, the heavy metal door was at ninety degrees and about to tip over. As he emerged from the stairwell, the door tipped toward him. He caught the door with his right forearm and pushed back. The weight sent waves of sharp pain throughout his torso and back, but the culprit he was chasing was hurt and weak enough to decide that running would be better than facing him.

George growled in pain and rage and gave chase. "Freeze, motherfucker! I swear this will be much easier for you if you give up now!" George lied. Flashes of that poor girl raced through his head. This piece of shit would pay for what he did to her and him and for making him run after his sick ass.

He watched as the wolf-servant tried to hobble away from him. The man was skinny, and blood ran down the back of his leg. He ripped off the headdress, exposing his upper torso and head, and his breathing was labored.

As he ran, the wolf-servant's breath sounded haggard as he took gulps of air. George looked around quickly and realized that they had exited through a storm shelter in the nearby railway. In the dark, the moon lit the side panels of box cars, flatbed cars, and shipping containers. George watched as the man ducked behind a railcar.

"You there behind the railcar! Come out with your hands up!" George commanded. "You've got nowhere to go!" He approached the railcar carefully.

Loose pebbles and dirt covered the ground beneath his feet. Even though he tried to tread carefully and quietly, wherever he stepped, the loose rocks crunched and ground beneath his boots. He got to the corner of the railcar and took a glance. No one was there.

George turned to look to the other side of the car, but his nose and left cheek were met with something that crashed so hard that the blow slammed his head against the railcar. His eyes filled with fireworks and stars, and tears filled his eyes. He could feel warm liquid pour down his cheek and the back of his throat.

He heard the servant reset his stance as he prepared to swing again. George moved on instinct and ducked. He heard wood crash against the railcar and felt splinters splash on his head and shoulders. His vision was starting to blur, and he felt the world getting more distant.

George raged and fought against the oncoming loss of consciousness. He tried to raise his gun but felt the improvised club hit his hand and forearm hard. His hand went numb, and his ears rang as the pistol fired and fell into the gravel. His grip was too weak to hold on to his gun as the servant kicked at his hand, throwing the pistol into the shadows beneath the railcar.

George looked up at the servant. He wasn't a servant…he was just a boy. The kid was no more than sixteen or seventeen at best. He was skinny as a rail, the ribs and collarbones visible. His skin showed old and fresh cuts that matched the symbols and signs on the altar. George looked up at his attacker, and recognition slapped him suddenly.

"Mickey? Mickey Corners?" he said. Mickey was the kid of the grocery store owner in town. The Corners were a good family with good standing in the community. Mickey Sr. was a jolly man who often played Santa Claus for the kids in the town square. Mickey Jr. may not have his father's build, but he was always a good kid. "What the fuck, kid? What are you doing?"

Mickey's eyes were wide, fearful, and he seemed lost. His eyes darted around in confusion. George had to take advantage of this moment somehow. He had no weapon, and his pistol was too far away. If George went for it now, Mickey may panic and either run away or club him to death. George's ribs and back were screaming at him, and he could feel blood running down his side and into the right hip of his pants. That's it!

George turned his right shoulder away from Mickey. He reached back slowly and could feel three inches of the antler in his back pocket. This was a dangerous gamble, for sure. Try to go hand-to-hand with this kid, wrestle away the plank of wood he was holding, and pray he didn't pass out first. George gripped the antler and gave a quick pull, freeing it from his pocket. It was dark enough that Mickey didn't see him palm the improvised weapon.

"Come on, kid, drop the club, huh? You don't want this to get worse for you," George tried to reason with him. Maybe he could avoid a fight if he were lucky. "Look at me…you know me. It's Officer George from the after-school cadet program."

Mickey suddenly stiffened in recognition. "George?" Mickey finally spoke in between his gasps. "What's going on? How'd I get here?" he said, tears rolling down his face. He looked down at George, stepped forward, and wailed in pain. "Why? Why does my leg hurt? What's all this blood from, George?"

"Mickey, first I need you to drop that board, and then we'll talk," George said. "Drop it for me now."

Mickey looked at the board as if for the first time and dropped it in surprise.

"All right, now I need you to listen to me. I need you to get down on the ground."

Mickey began to comply with George's commands as tears streamed down his filthy cheeks.

"Mickey, do you know where you are? What's the last thing you remember?" George asked.

"Uh… Ummm… my mom and my brother and I were on our way to pick up my sister… and then… then the next thing I remember was sitting in this room, and everyone was wearing masks," Mickey stammered and spoke so fast that George had difficulty understanding. "Then I was here… oh, God… George, where was my mommy? Where's my brother? My… My…" Mickey began sobbing like a little boy, calling for his mother and anyone to help him.

A wave of memories, and the reality of this situation, crashed like a train into George. The stag-woman. The bull-servant. The girl. This was Mickey's family. He suddenly recognized the stag woman, her hair, her glossy black eye, the part of her face he could see.

That was Mickey's mother. The little girl, all filthy and bloody and covered in wounds and stitches, was his sister. The other must've been his brother. George's thoughts came in faster as the truth was now in front of him. George had just killed Mickey's family. People he knew! People who were his neighbors and whom he had sworn to protect.

"Oh, fuck," George said quietly. He took a deep breath. Everything hurt so much, and now there was this. Tears streamed down his face. "Mickey, what… I mean... oh God, kid…" He looked up with the words tumbling out of his mouth, unable to form a sentence. Mickey held his head in his hand, palms pressed against his eyes.

"Okay, Mickey, I need you to help me get up," George started. Then he saw a smile. Mickey wasn't sobbing any longer. From him, George could hear a low guttural chuckle coming from Mickey's throat. His lips curled back into a smile, an impossibly large one. It seemed as though the corners of his lips were about to touch his ears.

Mickey Corners moved his hands to reveal his wide-eyed stare. Like his smile, his eyes seemed almost too big for his face. They were slick, glossy, and as black as ink. Not a bit of white showed, not the slightest bit of sorrow, fear, or humanity.

"Mickey, what the hell, kid? What's going on?" George yelled out.

"You almost got away, didn't you?" Mickey said with a guttural, wet laugh. George began to stand, and Mickey just stared at him. He stared with that impossible smile, the watery laugh, and those black eyes. George was nearly on his feet when Mickey rushed forward and grabbed him by the front of his hair. He suddenly seemed impossibly strong. "Sorry, officer, but I need this boy, and I can't let a little thing like you get in our way."

George yelled out as Mickey, a boy half his weight, pulled him up to his feet by his hair. George struggled until Mickey raised his right fist and struck him squarely in his cheek and jaw. The force of the blow was enough to rip his hair out and bounce him off the tail of the railcar.

"I was really hoping to use you later, y'know? A big, strong lad like you. You've got that sense about you, too!" Mickey taunted. "Too bad that can't help you now." Mickey grabbed George by the shoulder. George howled with pain as Mickey pulled on him and moved him to a kneeling position. "I just want you to know that I'm going to take my time with you, George," Mickey said with a grin.

"Mickey…stop!" George uttered.

He got closer, close enough that George could smell his breath. "When I'm done here, we will fuck this town. Fuck it and fill it up until it pops," Mickey chuckled with a gurgle. He flung George and sent him to land hard on the ground between two railcars.

George felt like the world was growing dimmer and more distant. *Get up! Get up!* he heard someone say. *Get the fuck up!* Was that his own voice so far away? George wanted to be done with this. All of it. The pain here, the pain of his memories, and knowing that he will hurt forever as long as he lived.

"Mickey tells me you have a wife. She's quite a catch, too. You know, he used to watch her at the games? The city pool. Church." A boy who looked like Mickey said with a knowing grin and a watery, deep voice. "Man, this kid went through tissue like you wouldn't believe! All on account of your wife!" Mickey roared with laughter at this. "I hear she's pregnant, too! Good for you."

Mickey was closing in; George could feel him walking toward him. He could feel how close he was, yet he was far away. "You know, maybe I'll make her my first visit. Do her while poor Mickey watches."

George felt Mickey's weight on top of him as his fingers snaked through his hair and pull his head up off the gravel.

"We'll show him what we like to do for fun," Mickey said, breathing heavily into George's ear. He pulled George up to his knees. He stayed close to his ear, and George could feel the heat of his breath, spittle landing on his cheek. "Maybe I'll keep the baby for myself."

Suddenly, there was a roar in the distance— a freight train. Mickey looked up and then he heard another cry. This one was more animalistic, filled with rage. George felt that roar in his chest and his guts. It all seemed distant, but that scream told him he was still alive. George burst into rage.

He felt the antler in his hand. George turned around so fast that his hair was pulled free from his scalp. He turned and punched out with his right hand. The pain, rage, and sorrow focused on his hand and into the tip of the antler, which now punched into Mickey's throat.

"Fuck you!" George coughed and pulled himself forward along the gravel. Where was his gun again? George blinked, trying to clear his sight.

Mickey stumbled back a step. The smile was still on his face as blood spurted from the wound in his neck. The piece of antler jutted out, and blood poured around it. He still smiled that impossible smile, but now blood filled his mouth and poured down his chin. His black, tarry eyes were so wide and full of surprise at this sudden show of willpower. His left hand gently touched the implement protruding from his neck. He giggled and then sputtered lines of blood from his lips.

George slumped against the flatbed railcar, his right arm desperately holding him upright. He watched as Mickey's smile faded and his wide eyes filled with tears. He looked at George, and the darkness of his eyes retreated as if draining into his skull. His face twisted in pain and confusion.

"George, what… what hap…" He tried to speak and swallowed hard to clear the obstruction in his throat. His hand still touched the protrusion lodged in his neck. George watched as the color drained from his face, his eyes filled with horror. He stumbled backward, then turned to run.

"Mickey? Mick-aaargh!" George screamed as pain charged through him, "Mickey, stop!"

George heard him coughing, sputtering, and stumbling through the gravel. Then he heard the train again. George could see the lights of the charging engine. He yelled again and stumbled after Mickey but fell onto his knees instead.

George's hands braced his fall, and he screamed out in pain. He felt his right-hand land on something. His gun. The train was so close, and he could feel it shake the ground beneath him. He got up to his feet and began to stumble as quickly as his legs would take him.

Just as George rounded the corner of the railcar, he found Mickey. Bright red streams of blood squirting in unison with the young man's heartbeats. It sprayed between his fingers and spit from his mouth as he cried. George looked down and found the antler. Two and a half inches of the point had bitten into the boy's neck.

"Mama," Mickey gurgled as tears streamed down his face and snot oozed passed his lips and mingled with the blood there. The slimy mixture hung from his chin and spilled to the ground. "Mama! Oh, God help me!"

"Mickey, stop!" George called after him. His heart broke to see this child hurting like this despite what he had done. His mind couldn't yet reconcile the boy he knew with the person who would help kill his own sister. "None of this makes sense, Mickey! Let's get help!"

Mickey turned and faced him, fat tears rolling down his face. The front of his shirt was completely red, lines of saliva and blood oozing from his lips. Then he was gone. The train roared past, horn blaring, brakes screaming. No way with all that weight, all those railcars. No way to stop and avoid fate. Reality's inertia ran through George as it had Mickey.

The protesting of the brakes continued until the train came to a complete stop. George tried to cover his ears to block out the trauma and the sharp decibels tearing his eardrums, but he might as well have been attempting to stop the moon from casting its glow. George stumbled over to where Mickey was.

Once George crossed the railway, he scanned its length. The rising moon was so bright, almost as if to say, *"There you go, see what you've done now?"* It was all too easy to find Mickey. His legs were twisted and torn, and his left arm was completely ripped from his shoulder. He looked up at George. His eyes were wide, and his breathing was fast and shallow. He was in shock; George could see.

"It hur… ts... Geor… Ge… Hel…" He tried to speak through short, quick gasps of air. "It… t… t... hurts… George… pl… pl...." He wanted so badly to look away, to stop all this from reaching him. Then he heard the other voice and saw that impossible smile. "Aww, come on, Georgie. Do the kid a solid, huh?"

George took a deep breath and stared at the thing looking up at him. Mickey's true voice spoke, "Please, make it stop."

George pulled back the hammer on his pistol. "I'm so sorry, Mickey." He leveled his gun and pulled the trigger. After George knew Mickey was dead and had taken that thing with him, he walked back toward the railroad tracks. He fell short of reaching them and landed hard on his face.

-CHAPTER 4-
THE CURSE OF A SECRET

George read the blood-stained note in his hand again for the third time. He tried to remember if Robert Holcomb had any surviving family. He was married once, a robust woman with a voice as voluminous as her figure. George recalled her leaving Robert some time ago.

He looked over the yellow envelope and remembered how his only friend and mentor Jack left the service and the world in a way too similar as Holcomb's. Not a day had passed that made George wonder if it was best he never shared what had happened to Mickey and his family with his friend. He would give anything if he could travel in time and take away that conversation after leaving the hospital.

"I should have never put this on you," George said to the envelope, sticky with blood and clinging to the interior of the plastic bag. "I'm so fucking sorry Jack. You deserved better than that."

# # # #

Jack suddenly became gravely silent after sharing the gossip around the department and the most recent calls worth discussing. George waited, knowing what would come next would be unpleasant for them both.

"Listen, George, I don't know what happened at the factory…or the railyard, for that matter," Jack started, eyes staring hard at George. "You were lucky that the engineer stopped and radioed for help." George lay there watching intently and playing out the worst-case scenario. How would he explain shooting Mickey lying prone in the grass without his legs?

"We found evidence of the fight next to the tracks, and you were beaten to hell and nearly dead yourself," Jack continued. George was about to open his mouth to say something about that night when Jack gave him his famous '*shut your fucking mouth and listen*' look. George clamped up and waited patiently for Jack to continue. After Jack was satisfied he would not be interrupted again, he continued the police findings.

"So, you were found nearly dead by the engineer, who said he found you unconscious and had no idea how you or Mickey wound up where he found you," Jack explained. "So, with all your blood everywhere and the signs of struggle, we found the department has concluded that you shot Mickey in self-defense, and he landed on the train tracks. The train hit him right after." Jack said this deliberately. George gathered this was more of a *this is how it happened* speech and kind of discussion.

George felt sick. Jack wasn't the kind of cop who hid the facts or the type to lie for any reason, and not the kind to cover up any wrongdoing by another cop. These were traits that made him unpopular at times with some officers. Not that Jack gave two shits about that. The lie George could tell was hard for him.

"So, we're clear then?" asked Jack.

"Sure thing, Jack," George replied.

"Now that we've got that out of the way, get some rest," Jack said. "When you get out of here and are ready, you and I will discuss what happened."

George cleared his throat and swallowed hard, not looking at Jack. He wouldn't tarnish this moment with his guilt or his tears. "Did you guys find the tunnels? Under the factory?" he asked without looking up.

Jack took a moment and then answered. "Seeing that you don't get much information here, I'm not surprised you don't know," he said cryptically. "Apparently, there is a series of limestone caverns under this town. They dug them to mine the limestone and later transported coal during the Civil War. Anyway, after years of wear and tear and erosion, the occasional sinkhole will appear," Jack said.

"Every now and then they collapse, creating a sinkhole," Jack continued. "Luckily, no one got hurt since the factory and those railways are mostly abandoned, but no one is allowed near the hole either."

Jack looked at George curiously. George's face had a strange expression. It was a mix of confusion, grief, and relief. George didn't ever want to go back down into those caverns again, but he wanted to retrieve the bodies of Mickey's family and investigate the nature of those tunnels and that room. He remembered Mickey's sister. Sarah? Samantha? Why couldn't he remember her name? George was shaken out of his reverie when he saw Jack stand.

"You get some rest now." He turned to leave. "Oh, by the way, congrats, papa." George looked confused. "Shit, I thought you knew. Cat's out of the bag, I suppose. Your baby girl was born last night. The delivery was rough…wife's probably sleeping it off after all that," Jack stammered. "All right, well, I'll leave you to it. See ya around."

As soon as Jack left, George began to sob. His whole body was racked with the weight of everything that could no longer be held back. He laid back down, knees to chest, and cried himself to sleep.

# # # #

George told Jack what happened that night in full detail after he was discharged from the hospital. He told Jack about the tunnels, the glowing veins of slime, the altar, the servants, and the girl. George gave his accounts of how Mickey died that night, Mickey's eyes, and that smile. He even told Jack about how he '*felt*' the danger and that something otherworldly was happening in that room. Jack patiently listened to his story without interruption. After a long silence followed by a glass of whiskey, Jack gave him some advice.

"Don't ever tell this story to anyone again," Jack said sternly.

"Figured you wouldn't believe me," George said with some resignation. "I probably am going crazy."

"That's not what I said now, is it?" Jack said bluntly. "I believe every bit of your story." He continued, "I've lived in this town for a long time. Hell, my whole family goes back for generations. There is a long history of weird shit going down in this town. The county, for that matter. People are disappearing, going crazy suddenly, or seeing strange things in the woods." Jack drank the rest of his liquor. He paused to allow the burn of his drink to pass from his mouth and throat. "What I'm sayin' is that if you tell people, they'll treat you like you've gone fucking nuts. Tell the *wrong* people, and you will endanger yourself and your family."

George considered his words. He sat in his favorite chair, his left arm in a sling to restrict the mobility of his healing shoulder. He thought of all the trauma his mind and body had suffered. Beyond the dislocated shoulder, pneumothorax, fractured wrist, and concussion, George knew that his mind and soul would never knit together the same way. He had a fresh scar on his sanity, added to the long history of abuse and grief he knew as a child.

"There's no coming back from this," George said quietly.

"What's that?" asked Jack.

"There's no coming back from this one, Jack," George said somberly. "I don't know how I'll ever recover from this."

"Well, you have to, and you will," Jack said sternly. "You have a wife and a baby who love you. They both need you to be there. You will have to do whatever it takes to be there for them. Copy?" Jack finished with that.

He excused himself politely when Amanda asked him to stay for dinner. Jack hugged and kissed her on the cheek, shook George's hand, and gave a sheepish wave to the baby in Amanda's arms. George somehow felt like he was saying goodbye. His warning system buzzed as he watched Jack drive away.

Not long after that night, Jack retired. The news came to George as a surprise because Jack had five more years left according to the plan. For the following year, Jack wasn't seen often in public. Even though George considered him his best mentor, he rarely saw or heard from him.

George invited him to a function or various parties, but he declined. He would claim to be too busy working on something. George discovered the truth that winter when he finally decided to reach out and find out what was going on with his friend and mentor.

He arrived at Jack's home and found him at his desk. Papers were cluttered and piled all around the house. Some were clippings of news stories about the misdeeds that occurred in the town, others were copies of old handwritten letters or journals, and each one told a story about the unusual nature of the area. Creatures were spotted lurking in the woods at night, monstrous things reflected in the lakes and streams crisscrossing the county.

In front of Jack was a large file, a manila folder with his name typed on the lip. George slowly took in the scene—the folder with photos of a mass in his lungs, intestines, and brain. Pamphlets to educate recipients about accepting terminal illnesses, and papers with local support groups and churches that try to dull the pain of knowing one's fate. George saw the blood spatter on the wall, on the desk. Then he found the revolver. It rested next to Jack's right foot in a puddle of congealing blood. Jack had a letter in his shirt's breast pocket.

The envelope contained Jack's last will and testament, bequeathing his benefits and pension to his ex-wife. He had also written her a letter. George found another note tucked in Jack's stiff hand. His fingers were wrapped tightly as if he was trying to protect its contents. On one side, Jack had written, *For George.* On the other side, he wrote simply, *Sorry, kid. I really tried.*

# # # #

Since that night at the railyard, George hadn't felt so much as a tingle or vibration. Whatever had tried to protect George had been dormant until tonight. Tonight, George's head screamed at him to stay away. His bones and spine tingled like he was holding onto an electric fence. His heart was tapping out a beat he felt in his temples and ears.

NO TRESPASSING

The large red and white sign agreed that George should return the way he came. George sat in his police cruiser and stared. His hands felt paralyzed, and he could not release his grip on the steering wheel. His knuckles were white, and the veins bulged on the backs of his hands.

"Come on, this isn't real. You're just suffering from flashbacks, anxiety, or some other PTSD bullshit." George took another slow, deep breath. Dispatch sent units to the Marcus quarry. Dr. Judge and Maria Marcus bought it up.

Maria's brother, Herman Montrose, was an absolute bear of a man in stature and intellect, and he managed the quarry with the grace and temperament of a bull. It supplied work for over a hundred citizens, and the pay was decent, but Herman believed in the adage, *The whipping will continue until morale improves.*

Due to the occasional disgruntled employee, a security system was installed to notify police if anyone had trespassed. The only thing that made the work environment bearable was the foreman, Joe Steiner. Joe ensured the crews were on schedule and making quota and matched Herman's heavy-handed approach with good humor and fellowship. That and the bonuses and beers helped too.

George had been out to this quarry several times, but this was the first time he felt the fear— the warning system. *Breathe*. Probably nothing, maybe a homeless person or drunk looking for a place to sleep. *Breathe*. Perhaps it was just a glitch, or an animal set it off. *Breathe*.

He had just taken another deep breath when there was a sharp tap-tap tap on his window. George looked out in surprise, nearly jumping out of his seat. His hand had instinctively found the holster of his pistol. There, smiling through the window, was Rook.

The same fresh-faced recruit who brought him Holcomb's note. The young cop waved enthusiastically from behind his flashlight, causing the torch to take on a strobe effect that gave George a headache.

"Hey there Sarge!" Holts said, his smile was audible as bubbly as a cheerleader's, "Fancy meeting you here!"

Rook was a nickname, of course, for two reasons. Firstly, he had only been in the department for six months. Secondly, he was gifted and cursed with a youthful visage. His cherubic features were magnified by the fact that his cheeks were always round and had a rosy hue.

His birth-given name wasn't much better. Robbie Holts. Blonde-haired and barely old enough to drink, he came to the department straight out of high school. He always wore a smile, and it reminded George of an old-time puppet show like Howdy Doody.

Holt's blue eyes were big, round, and still filled with child-like wonder. George thought he looked like he always seemed surprised by something. George glared at him through the glass as he recovered from his jump scare, which he once regretted when Robbie shined his flashlight into the cab of his cruiser.

"What the fuck, Holts?" George said as he held his hand up to block the light. He rolled down his window. "Are you trying to give me a heart attack and blind me?"

"Sorry, sir, I didn't know you were coming," Robbie said, obediently lowering his flashlight. "Officer Manns is on her way up, too. We'll take a peek and see what all the noise is about. If you want to go home, we can manage this for you, sir."

It had been a long day, and George was tired, but he couldn't ignore the electricity in his skin and bones. Something was more than not right. There was real danger here, and George wasn't about to let his people run in unsuspecting.

"No, Rook, I think I need to be here for this," George said.

"Sir?" Robbie asked, not understanding why.

"One of these days, you'll learn to trust your gut on certain things. I'm not about to let you two be the blue canaries," George said, with no hint of humor in his voice.

"Uh. Blue canary, sir?" Robbie said.

God, this kid is dense! George thought. "I'll tell you when you get older. Oh, and Rook?"

"Yessir?" Robbie replied.

"Fuck off with the *'sir'* shit. I'm not old enough to retire, and I'm not your dad. Now go get that gate open while I wait for Manns," George spat back.

"Yessir," Robbie replied with a somewhat hurt look.

"Blue canaries," George whispered to himself. There was something wrong with this. All of it. The quarry. This town. The whole fucking moonless, starless, darkest night he had ever seen. George would be damned if he'd have another Mickey Corners kind of night ever again. He wouldn't let this happen to anyone ever again.

-CHAPTER 5-
THE FORGOTTEN CHURCH

Sicily Manns had heard all the jokes. She was tall, stood at six feet and two inches. Many considered her half-Cherokee features attractive. Her tan skin, long brown hair, and bright green eyes gave her a somewhat exotic appearance.

Sicily was proud of her native features and heritage, but the ignorant always made comments that raised her hackles. Remarks like, "Wow, you're so pretty. Where did your family come from?" or "How do you get your hair so straight?" or "Your English is so good."

Then there was the usual sexist bullshit. She sometimes was treated as frail, weak, or dumb because she was a woman. It was one thing to hear from some random Joe on the street, but it was another matter when it was from a fellow cop— especially those who have seen less action than her. So yeah, Sicily had a bit of a chip on her shoulder.

She had to be tough, though; she had seen people do the worst and brutalize each other. Sicily fought to protect and serve while also contending with the public opinion that she was a fascist. She transferred nearly three years ago from Chicago after her mom had a stroke and needed care. She would need some help around the house, and the timing was perfect. Sicily had hit a rough patch in Chicago and needed a change.

Transitioning from Chicago to a small town out in the boonies was challenging enough; she didn't know how to do any other job besides police work. She took a chance and applied for the open position. Surprisingly, her captain back in Chicago vouched for her and praised her.

Sicily discovered she was the only female cop in the department. At least she was the only one not answering phones and getting coffee. She quickly established she didn't take shit from anyone, which didn't make her too popular.

Sicily hadn't been on a year before the handful of locals were calling her a lesbo or dyke. The public wasn't warm to her and her "big-city" attitude. These comments didn't bother her. In fact, they helped keep unwanted attention from men away.

Six months on the department, a drunk bigot who nearly beat his wife and four-year-old child to death, spit in her face. He followed his assault by calling her Pocahontas and grabbed her ponytail.

After that, Sicily's world was a blur. The next thing she knew, the piece-of-shit bigot was on the floor in cuffs nursing his swollen testicles, broken nose, and busted knee-cap. Henceforth, she was dubbed "The Sicilian." It was cleverer than she thought this place was capable of producing. Part of her wanted to find the person who came up with it first and demonstrate how exactly she broke that guy's knee. The other part wanted to give him a high five and buy him a round.

Tonight, she was glad to be on the streets patrolling. She loved her mom to bits, but the physical therapy hadn't been going well, so it put her in a foul mood. Sicily knew she would be extra needy after her lack of progress, so when work called and told her they needed her to cover a shift, she jumped on that grenade happily. She was even happier when she saw Sergeant Thatch standing outside his patrol unit on the side of the road, heading into the quarry.

Sicily flashed her lights and gave a short burst from her siren. He responded with a few pumps of his middle finger and mouthed the words "Fuck you." This guy always made her laugh. He was the only cop in the department who treated her like a cop, not as a woman in cop's clothes. He always had her back, even after she beat the shit out of the perp. He also let her know when she needed to check her attitude.

"I love you, too, Sarge!" Sicily said, laughing as she got out of her patrol unit. George gave the derisive snort for which he had become famous. "Where's Rook?" she asked, noting his unit.

"I sent him up to unlock the gate," George replied. They watched as Robbie tried to hold a flashlight to navigate a set of keys into the padlock.

"Hey, Sarge?" Sicily asked. "What do those keys go to?"

"Have to ask Paul, the school janitor. He lost them at last night's football game. I found them in the parking lot this morning," George said evenly. "I figured this would keep Rook busy for a minute until you arrived."

Sicily laughed deeply at this as she watched Robbie drop his flashlight for the third time. "When should we let him know I have the keys?" The quarry was part of Sicily's route when she patrolled. The quarry manager gave the chief two extra sets of keys, one of which was passed onto Sicily. When dispatch called about the disturbance at the quarry, Sicily jumped on the call. No use bothering the police chief since she had a set of keys anyway.

"I figured I'd let the kid sweat it out for a few more minutes. Besides, I'm not really in the mood to look at him right now," George replied with a smirk.

Sicily saw something in him just then. Something was in his eyes that she hadn't seen before. Was it fear?

"You good, boss?" she asked. "You look worried or something."

"The only thing I worry about is Robbie having children." On cue, Robbie dropped his flashlight again and let slip a few curses.

"Yeah, he is a big dumb animal, folks," Sicily said. "Shit, here he comes," she said with a mischievous grin. "Fucking hell, Rook, I hope you use more finesse than that when slipping off your girlfriend's bra."

"No, ma'am, don't have one," Robbie replied sheepishly.

"Figured that out, Rook," Sicily said with a laugh. "Give me those keys. Someone has to get us in there." She looked back to George with an evil glint in her eye as George looked over at Robbie. The poor kid was sweating, and his cheeks reddened when Sicily took the keys. She felt pity for the young cop.

Not even a minute passed before they heard the rattle of chains, and the padlock fell to the ground in front of Sicily. Out of the corner of his eye, George saw Robbie slump. Sicily turned and regarded Robbie with a look that was an even mix of "Bless your heart" and irritation.

"Alright, let's check this place out and return to the station. I want to get home at some point," George said.

Robbie and George returned to their units and pulled through the gate, followed by Sicily, who locked it behind them after pulling through with her unit. They drove up the brush-framed road to the large pit, where miners extracted the gravel and stone. The area was peppered with signs indicating where the drop-off was and warned against trespassing.

The patrol cars drove around the pit until they reached an access road. It was similarly gated and locked, just as the entrance to the quarry grounds. The vehicles stopped, and Sicily casually got out of her unit and walked up to the gate, flashing a mischievous wink at Robbie as she did so. He rolled his eyes and laughed off the small amount of embarrassment he felt. Sicily unlocked the gate and swung it wide. She returned to her car, and when she was ready, George guided the three units down the access road onto the pit floor.

The dirt road spiraled down into the quarry. It was wide enough for the large dump trucks to fit through but so rough that Sicily's teeth clacked together if she didn't keep her jaw clenched. They continued down the bumpy dirt road until it reached the bottom of the stone bowl ten stories down.

The base had several large piles of rock and dirt, presumably awaiting pick-up, and at the opposite end of the road sat the double-wide trailer house that served as an office for the foreman, administrative assistant, and Herman Montrose. In the very center of the quarry was a large pool of water, the quarry pond. This pool was built from years of rain and equipment digging into the underground water sources.

The pool looked turquoise in the daytime and, on a sweltering day, rather inviting. The foreman had to secure the area because a teenage boy was found floating face down in its cold waters two years prior. Reports on the scene stated he jumped into the pond on a dare from twenty feet above. He was drunk enough not to see this stupidity and dove head-first into the water. Only this water was barely ten feet at its center and about four feet deep where his head contacted the pond's rocky floor.

The three officers parked their vehicles and got out of the driver's side of their cars. They each stood there looking over the pond. Cold, black waters held as still as death and reflected only the quarry's walls.

Each officer turned on their spotlights, pulled out their flashlights, and scanned the area around the edge of the quarry pond. Finally, after feeling confident that this was all the result of an alarm sensor misfire, George instructed the others to stand down while he checked the control panel housed within the trailer. George wanted to use this moment for himself as well. The sensations crawled up and down his spine and churned in his bowels. Something was not right. As he approached the trailer, he immediately picked up the scent of something metallic in the air. The light breeze that bowled its way down into the quarry kept George from figuring out the exact location.

George used his flashlight to scan the ground before him and to his sides. George was so distracted by his early warning system that he hadn't noticed the drag marks in the dirt that led up to the trailer. With so little light in the night sky, he couldn't see the blood mudding the soil and guided his flashlight to the handle on the door. There were streaks of ichor on the door panel and frame. He noted a long, stringy black hair clump on the bottom step.

"Manns! Holts!" George called out. "Get over here." Whatever sniping conversation the two were having immediately ceased at the sound of George's voice.

"Whatcha got, Sarge?" Robbie asked.

George didn't say anything. He just tipped his chin at the evidence before him. Sicily was already moving into position to breach the trailer. She cued up the mic on her radio and gave a dispatch notification. Robbie moved to the door opposite Sicily. George moved instinctively as his hours-upon-hours of training muscles kicked in, but he also tried to fight off the vision of that terrible room underground. The poor girl in stitches, the beastly servants, the stench, and the pain. Mickey Corners.

George looked at her and let her know he was in the moment. She nodded back. George felt that respect is a precious resource among people. He respected Manns because she was tough and intelligent. Hell, George even respected Robbie Holts, now ready on his left. He knew the kid would go above and beyond to prove he was a good cop.

George took a quick look at his team. Each had their sidearm and flashlight ready. First, he tried the handle. It was unlocked. The hairs on his neck and arms bristled. He mouthed, "One…two…" and threw the door open on three. "Haven Shire PD! Hands where we can see them!"

The three officers entered with practiced efficiency, their weapons pointed in the same direction as their flashlights. Manns was the last to see the scene before her. She entered and quickly checked behind the door and part of the trailer concealed by it. When she turned, the look of surprise and horror matched the looks on George and Robbie's faces.

The interior of the trailer was pure eighty's decor. Faux wood paneling stapled to the walls, ashtrays filled to the brim with ash and cigarette butts, a velvet Elvis and pin-up calendars. If you took a picture of the room, you knew how it smelled by the image alone; old cigar smoke, burnt coffee, stale beer, and sweat. The room was equal parts locker room, lounge, and bar.

In the center of the trailer was a mock meeting area with a small pine-stained table with six chairs around it. Herman and Joe met with those who purchased the limestone from the quarry. They would also meet with Mr. and Mrs. Marcus' son, Thaddeus, to discuss the financial and profit reports.

Tonight, Joe Steiner sat at the head of the table. He was an older, lean man with skin so tanned it held a leathery appearance. At the opposite end sat his wife, Cherie. George always thought she was kind. She ran one of the few dining establishments in town. It was the only place that served tacos, so naturally, it was popular.

Around the table sat his four children. Each family member sat tied to their chairs, heads slumped forward, blood running down the front of their pajama shirts and nightgowns. All except Joe. He sat poised in his chair, looking proudly upon his family. The table was set for dinner, dressed with fine China plates, crystal dinner glasses, and silverware placed in front of everyone in attendance.

"Welcome, officers. If I knew you were coming, I would have set a few extra places for you," Joe said.

George's mouth seemed useless. "What did…di…what the fuck, Joe? What did you do to yourself?" was all George could get out before falling silent to the horror scene. Somewhere in the distance, he heard Manns yelling commands at Joe. Behind him, he heard Holts stumble and vomit.

All George's senses were attuned to Joe. He sat there with a smile, a thin carving knife, and a serving fork, peering at him from sightless eyes. Bloody tears streaked down his face from sightless holes where his eyes once were. His eyes gazed at George, unblinking and in a pool of blood, atop the China plate before him. The same meal was prepared for all those in attendance this night.

The rest of his family looked down onto their meals with sightless eyes and slack jaws. Pink frothy drool oozed from the corners of their mouths.

George tried to compose himself as he approached Joe, his gun trained on him. "What the fuck, Joe? This is your family!" Joe's sightless gaze and smile followed George as he made his way around the table toward him. Sicily slowly made her way from the opposite direction, her gun trained on Joe as well, as she checked the wife and children for vital signs.

"I couldn't let them take my family, George. They were going to steal their eyes and souls," Joe said. He began to laugh at George, the desperate laugh that comes with resignation. "I showed them, though. This is my family, not theirs. No one will take them from me." His laugh came faster now, more manic.

"Joe, who was going to take your family?" George asked as he checked Joe's youngest girl for a pulse. She was cold. The chill had set in her flesh and bones some time ago. "Talk to me, Joe." George was almost within arm's reach.

"You're a family man, George... you'll understand soon." With surprising speed, Joe thrust the knife and serving fork into his throat. He began to laugh madly as blood spurted from his throat and down the front of his shirt. His cackles were interrupted by the occasional fountain of blood that filled his throat and mouth. He coughed, spraying blood from his mouth onto the front of George's bulletproof vest and jacket.

"Fuck! Holts, get your shit together and get over here!" Manns screamed. Her voice cracked a little and sounded higher pitched than intended. George quickly holstered his weapon and grabbed Joe's knife hand, trying to prevent him from doing more damage, if possible. Sicily was on the opposite side and inadvertently pulled the fork from his neck. Blood sprayed on the front of her vest and in her face. "Fuck, fuck, fuck!" She tried to staunch the blood flow with her hand and control his left hand simultaneously.

Holts got to Joe and placed his hands on the pumping wounds. George and Sicily pried the utensils from his hands and threw them to the floor. When they turned to regard each other and Joe, they began forming a plan wordlessly. George nodded to the floor. Sicily nodded in agreement. Robbie picked up on the agenda and moved Joe to the floor. He wasn't resisting now. His face and arms were limp, pale, and sweaty. Robbie held his hands tightly to Joe's throat.

"Dispatch! Unit 110 is requesting additional units for this scene. Send EMS units, code 1 for a stabbing victim!" George commanded.

Dispatch acknowledged his request.

George and Sicily began fishing in their cargo pants for gloves and gauze. "Come on, Joe, stay with me, you crazy motherfucker!" George yelled.

"What the hell did he mean, George?" Sicily asked.

"What the hell would drive someone to do this, Sarge?" Robbie followed. "Seriously, this is fucked," Robbie continued with snot streaming down his face and vomit on his breath.

"Both of you focus on getting Joe to the hospital right now. We'll ask questions later," George barked.

Manns ripped open his shirt and quickly listened. She hissed a volley of cuss words and began chest compressions. George notified the incoming EMS unit they were now performing CPR and that the suspect had no pulse. The minutes felt like hours until EMS and fire units arrived. They took over compressions, and the medics attached their monitor. They worked on trying to bring Joe back, but everyone in the room knew that was not going to happen.

George, Sicily, and Robbie stood beside their units an hour later. The quarry manager, Herman Montrose, arrived with the coroner. As the grim task of collecting the Steiner family, Herman walked about the scene. It struck George, Sicily, and Robbie odd how jovial the man seemed. He patted the backs of the first responders and other police on the scene.

"You must be Sergeant Thatch!" Herman said as he turned his attention to George and his crew. As the man approached, George was surprised by the man's size. The man was a walking wall of flesh and muscle. He almost like a comic book villain. Broad, square shoulders topped his barrel chest. Herman's suit was not tailored to hide his frame. It appeared as though someone had to stretch the suit over his thick arms and legs.

"I want to thank you folks for you work tonight," Herman said in a deep thunderous voice. George's warning system was screaming at him as Herman's hand dwarfed his in an enthusiastic handshake. "It's a terrible tragedy."

"Any idea why Joe would do what he did?" George asked rubbing his hand, more to get rid of the crawling feeling Herman gave him then to recover from the strong grip. "Has he been acting out of the ordinary lately?"

"Sad to say I just recently had to let Joe go," Herman said grimly. "He started showing up to work late, even drunk on occasion. I think he had some family troubles as well. Well, I mean obviously, am I right?"

Sicily and Robbie glanced over at George as Herman laughed heartily at the comment. George and his crew felt saved when the Police Chief arrived on scene, drawing Herman's attention away.

"You folks take it easy and be safe out there!" Herman said over his shoulder. George watched the man walk over to Police Chief Joe Waters SUV and greet him with the same smiles and handshakes. George felt his alarms still ringing under his skin but less so now he had distance from that man.

"What the fuck, Sarge?" Robbie broke the silence, blowing his nose and rinsing his mouth with water. Sicily had already wiped the blood from her face and now stared blankly at the still quarry pond. Both were just as horrified by Herman's demeanor as George was.

The water was black as pitch under the moonless night. George stared at them both, at a loss for words. Something in his skin and bones told him this was related to that night under the factory. How could he explain it to them, though?

Sicily looked at George, seeing that there was something there. "What is it, George?"

George's eyes darted back and forth at their faces. Jack's words rang in his head. *"Don't tell a fucking soul about that night."* These were Jack's words to George that night around the fire. He thought about those words that ended their conversation. *"Not a single soul."*

"Fuck it," he said with a grim chuckle. "All right, I'm going to tell you something, but I need you to swear on your mothers that you'll never tell another living soul." Secretly, George was glad he could finally unburden himself of this story, of his secret. He told them everything that happened that night at the factory.

-CHAPTER 6-
LIFE IS A BIZAAR BAZAAR

Outside an abandoned aqueduct within the bowels of Kansas City, built into the bluffs near the West Bottoms, sat a polished and sleek 1965 Cadillac DeVille. Its black exterior cloaked itself in the shadows of the cliffs. It had been in the gravel parking lot for some time, waiting for the appointed time. On the other side of the lot was a cluster of local thugs occupied with their business in illicit pharmaceuticals or illegal weapons.

Phineas sat in the passenger seat, writing in a journal a list of needed supplies to replenish his stores of components used in rituals and curses. Beside him, Vincent sat anxiously drumming his fingers on the wheel. Vincent would alternate looking from his Rolex watch to checking his well-groomed blonde and silver hair and back again. For a man nearing his mid-sixties, Phineas thought of him as having the patience of a little boy in a hardware store.

In the back seat sat Phineas' best friend and partner, Mata. Silently, she looked out across the gravel lot at the gang of petty criminals. Her face bore a grim smile as she sized up all those in attendance among the dealers and thieves. Similarly, eying the cadre was Lizzy, a giant black mastiff. She occasionally issued a guttural growl in her throat, possibly in response to Mata's agitation.

Phineas finished his list, closed the small leather journal, and placed it in the folds of his long coat. "It's time. I wish you guys could join me, but they have rules at the Bazaar. Do you want me to get you anything?" Phineas asked, looking at the duo.

"Just a job, good sir. I think some work will do us all good," Vincent said.

"I'll see what they've got," Phineas replied. Looking over to Mata, he noted the intensity on her face. Phineas leaned in close and whispered to Vincent. "Hey, Vinnie, do me a favor and keep an eye on Mata. I get the notion that she is feeling froggy."

Mata, though deaf and mute, gave Phineas the finger. She pointed at the crowd of men to the largest in their pack. He was approximately six-and-a-half feet tall, with a head full of thick black curls and dark olive skin. Even in the dark, his amber eyes shone. Phineas looked over at the man, examining him.

"Yeah, I saw him, too," Phineas said with a smirk. "Not exactly human. Changeling? Lycanthrope?"

Mata shrugged and smiled back at him. She wore a pair of brass knuckles and looked eager to use them. Phineas chuckled, but then with all seriousness, he wagged his finger at Mata and shook his head.

"We're only here for business," Phineas signed to Mata. *"I don't think the folks here would appreciate you beating up on the locals. They don't want the attention, and neither do we."*

Mata rolled her eyes and threw up her hands in feigned outrage. Phineas put his hand to his chin and lowered it, palm facing up, to say *"thanks."* He then gave her a wink and turned to leave. Vincent grabbed Phineas' forearm, stopping him halfway out of the car.

"Hey, uh, see if the madam has any more of that powder you sprinkle on your dick, you know, to give it some girth. I have this special lady…"

Phineas didn't allow Vincent to finish his sentence and instead mimicked retching. "Fucking dirty old man," Phineas said with a laugh.

Phineas walked toward the aqueduct. Even though it was dark out, he wore a pair of blackout sunglasses. Phineas watched the local dealers as he journeyed across the lot; they, in turn, watched him. He was glad they didn't make a move, for their sake.

As he entered the tunnel, Phineas removed his glasses. He only wore them to dampen his sight and operate in public. Phineas would need to use his "gift" to find the Bazaar. Phineas was born with what he believed to be a curse for most of his life. He had been able to see and communicate with spirits since his early childhood.

As a bonus, Phineas could also see beyond our plane and into the land of the dead. Our reality and the land of Gehenna exist parallel to each other. One is a dark and shadowy mirror of the other. Perceiving the two simultaneously would have driven him mad long ago if not for a mentor he had met when he had crossed over to Gehenna during an attempted suicide.

Thanks to the education he received along those shores of the river Styx, he could attune his hearing and other senses to energies foreign to this reality. His sight, however, was doggedly seeking out stimuli from both the physical and ethereal planes. It wasn't until he experimented with various cursed items and enchantments that he came to the pitch-black concessions he now wore daily.

The spectacles were tailor-made in the Bizarre Bazaar, as it was called by those in the mystic community. The silver-rimmed shades allowed Phineas to focus on the physical beings on this plane. Without them, Phineas would have trouble telling the difference between the souls of the living and those who had moved on beyond the Veil.

The Bizarre Bazaar was enchanted, deterring any who lacked any magical or psychic talent. As Phineas walked down the tunnel, the sigils and glyphs led him to secret and disguised passages. Some of these turns and tunnels were mundane tricks of physical sight, bricks and mortar laid in a fashion to camouflage the path. Pathways were cursed, so anyone who tried to continue in a given direction would feel nausea or anxiety. Phineas had erected psychic defenses from such attacks.

The cobblestone path he walked along the tunnel floor turned into a concrete ramp that led to a multi-story book and curiosity store. The "door greeter" was called Granny. The title bestowed on the woman belied her disposition. Granny was a large, pale woman who sat behind a booth decorated with various blossoms and woodcarvings.

Even though she always wore the uniform of a sweet and gentle Midwestern grandmother, her scowl was less than hospitable. Above the booth was a large pastel sign, lit by chunky Christmas lights and adorned with chalk drawings of flowers. It read "Welcome," an ironic sentiment whose humor was never lost on Phineas.

"Good evening, Granny!" Phineas greeted cheerfully, in which she replied to Phineas' salutations with a sneer. She poked a bulbous and stubby thumb at the floor above. Her hands were peppered with liver spots and warts, and each digit ended with tobacco-stained fingernails. Phineas understood the meaning of her gesture and commenced to his predetermined meeting place.

Phineas could not be late for this appointment, so he made his way quickly to an ancient elevator and pressed the designated floor. Inside the elevator cabin, Phineas tipped an invisible hat at

Granny. The surly shopkeeper replied with a billowing cloud of blue-grey cigar smoke and spat on the already slick concrete floor.

The second floor was a dust-laden series of rooms, each with a numbered door and a symbol. Half the wall was covered in dark cherrywood paneling, topped with quarter round molding. The wallpaper continued where the paneling ended. It was a port-colored background with silver Fleur-de-lie prints running to the ceiling.

The paper peeled and curled away from the wall at the seams, and there were stains from water and smoke in several places. The hall's doors were stained dark and glossy, which was complimented by polished bronze handles and hardware. Phineas pulled a slip of paper from his many-pocketed trench coat. On it, written in smudged black ink, was the number "212" and the symbol of an eye with a spike driven through it.

"Cheery," Phineas smirked to himself. Of course, Phineas always seemed to be wearing a smile, crooked and somewhat mischievous. "I wonder if the room has an iron maiden or a rack," he mumbled.

Phineas walked down the hall and was impressed by how long the corridor was. Phineas recognized the use of magic to create space within spaces. He used such enchantments on his clothes to create pockets to hold more than what appeared to the naked eye. The challenge was remembering which pocket Phineas placed his components. He had to memorize the design of his garments and the pockets sewn within pockets or risk losing those essential items held in those spaces.

After walking for several minutes, he found the door indicated on a scrap of paper. He grasped the polished doorknob and carefully entered the room. It was blanketed in dust and cobwebs, just as the hallway was, but well-lit and warm. Phineas scanned the room and laughed out loud when he spied an actual iron maiden in the far corner.

"Find something that amuses you, Thatch?" came a deep and gravelly voice near the active fireplace on the left side of the room. Before the mantel sat two wing-backed red leather chairs facing away from the door. Phineas could make out the silhouette of his agent for this contract. Cassandra Ergos was a thin, seemingly middle-aged black woman. Her head was shorn, but Phineas noted her eyebrows were the purest white. He often wondered how spectacular her hair was when it had grown out.

"Oh no, dear, I just love the places you bring me to," Phineas replied with a touch of sarcasm.

"These traditionalists do love their conventions," Cassandra sighed. "If you are done sneering at the décor, I have a job for you. One that pays well and may entertain you."

"Sneering? I would never," Phineas replied with a mock pained expression. Upon seeing the lack of amusement on Cassandra's face, he let the topic go and got down to the business at hand. "What's the job?"

"Investigate, and if need be, exorcise a local," Cassandra said, handing over a large yellow envelope. "The client is a *mundane* who knows a few folks. Folks like us. You came highly recommended because of your discretion."

The term *mundane* was often used by those in the community that Phineas associated with for those who could not use magic or possess extrasensory talent. It was rare that a *Mundane* would employ the skills of someone like Phineas, or his crew, these days. This person was rare indeed.

The job interested Phineas. He enjoyed circumstances that were more than they seemed. Puzzles and riddles were a spice Phineas very much appreciated.

Phineas exited the room and walked down the narrow steps. As he walked over to Granny's booth, his attention got snagged on a portly man spying a jar of organs and smoking a comically oversized pipe. The man was pale and heavily freckled and had a thick, greasy beard. He appeared to have just emerged from his bedchambers, wearing a silk smoker's jacket and house slippers. Phineas immediately recognized the man as Jasper Boehns, pronounced "bones," Jasper would often say, then follow up the joke with some lewd innuendo. Phineas noticed how hard the man was working to appear as though he was not peeping on Phineas's movements.

Had Phineas had more time, he would have found some way to root out Jasper's reasons for being there, as he rarely left whatever hole he slid out of for anything. For the moment, he needed to focus on the case at hand. The others were waiting for him outside, and Mata was not the type to remain idle for long, especially if presented with a chance to exercise her hot temper and equally hot fists. Vincent was no doubt sweating bullets from the tension of waiting in his lovely car in a less-than-scrupulous neighborhood.

Phineas strolled to the booth and greeted Granny with a sickly-sweet smile. Granny rewarded his efforts with a look that spelled *fuck-you*. Those exact words were also tattooed on the knuckles of her bulbous fists. She made an effort to display the ink-laden skin often.

"Are you buying something or just here to creep me out?" Granny asked in a gravelly voice cultivated with whiskey and cigars over the years. Her yellowed teeth puffed cigar smoke in the direction of Phineas' face. He winced at the irritating clouds and the bitter stench they held.

"I can't tell you how I look forward to our tête-à-têtes, my dear," Phineas said with some dramatic flair. "How much longer must we do this dance around our true feelings? Come, leave this dark place, and run away with me!"

"First of all, you're too young, skinny, and unable to handle me, sonny-boy," Granny growled.

"Secondly?" Phineas replied, unflinching.

"Secondly, you can turn around, take a left, and fuck off," Granny yelled. With that, she roughly placed a burlap bag on the counter, the contents of which sounded somewhat fragile and caused Phineas to cringe at the idea of some of the ingredients breaking and spilling. He knew of the ingredients and chemicals held within, some volatile, while others were rare or expensive. Granny then held out her free hand for payment.

Phineas handed Granny the credit voucher that was given to him by Cassandra. She looked at the coupon and then spat on the floor. She tucked the voucher into her left bra cup and pointed to the exit with her chin.

Phineas picked up the bag, turned, and walked toward the exit. As he was about to leave, he noticed a gourd bottle laced in silver chains, obviously hollowed out to use as a container, judging by the cork. From the center of the hourglass curve, a twine shoulder strap suspended the bottle from a hook pinned to the wall. He pointed at the item with his cane and yelled back at Granny, "Add this to the tab as well, would ya, sweetheart?"

Phineas left the Bazaar and was nearing the entrance of the aqueduct when he heard the familiar baying of Lizzie, the Cane Corso. This bark meant that the dog had intended to cause harm to someone or something. He muttered curses and began to jog down the dark tunnel. Once the tunnel opened up to the night air, he breathed a sigh of relief. Mata stood over two drug dealers huddled across from where they had parked.

Both men were alive; one held a severely disjointed arm, while the other cupped his groin and moaned pathetically through swollen lips. Mata had an expression of a woman wholly unsatisfied. She always enjoyed a good fight.

Phineas looked over and saw that the few remaining thugs wanted nothing to do with Mata or Lizzie; the latter gave a low guttural growl from time to time as she stared them all down. Her expression was a dare and a warning. The few street thugs stood aghast, mouths slack-jawed in fear and amazement. Phineas looked over to the car he had arrived in, and to his amusement and bewilderment, he found Vincent negotiating the price of something with the large, curly-haired man.

Upon closer inspection, the man looked like he may be related to Mata. His skin held more olive hue than her caramel skin tone. Their facial features were similar; broad noses, angular cheeks and jawlines, and intense eyes.

Vincent looked up, found Phineas watching the transaction, and immediately beamed his self-proclaimed, award-winning smile. He held a pouch with some indiscernible ingredients in his palm.

"There's the man now!" he said to the dealer, pointing in his direction.

The more prominent man laughed warmly and said something in a Slavic language that Phineas couldn't understand. Vincent didn't understand either, but that never slowed him down during a negotiation. The man stepped forward and held out his arms as if to greet Phineas with a hug. Phineas held up a hand and nodded over to Mata and her fallen companions. The man's expression darkened, and he cleared his throat.

"My apologies. My customers didn't heed my warning about the girl," the man apologetically stated with his thick Eastern European accent. "I told them the woman was more formidable than she looked and was 'hands off.' I once saw her fight in an underground match, and I knew better than to make that one angry."

The dealer pointed to Mata with his bearded chin. Mata was now watching the discussion, no longer concerned with the two men trying to retreat and join the others. She asked Phineas something in sign language and indicated to the dealer. Phineas shrugged.

"It appears Vincent found himself some goods he wished to purchase," Phineas said vocally and in sign language. "What are we discussing, Vincent? If you don't mind my asking."

"Oh yeah. As it turns out, our street dealer is a purveyor of fine and exotic teas and tobacco," Vincent said with a laugh. "It a passion we share, you see, since Mata owns her own- "

With a glance, Phineas shut down further discussion. He looked over the dealer; he and Mata saw more about the man than Vincent could see himself. Vincent seemed somewhat perplexed at this silent exchange. The dealer began to catch on that they had seen his "true" face.

"What's your name, good sir?" the dealer said cautiously. "I'm Mihai, a simple businessman."

Phineas and Mata looked at each other and then back at Mihai. Phineas broke into his crooked smile and presented his hand. Mihai calmed at this gesture and shook his hand warmly. The tension melted away among the group as Mata and Lizzie returned to the car. Vincent pocketed the herbal bag he had been inspecting and returned to the vehicle. His expression reflected his disappointment that negotiations with Mihai were ending.

"So, I'm guessing you aren't from around here, yeah?" Phineas asked when he was finally alone. Mihai's eyes widened with feigned surprise. Phineas smiled back in mild amusement. Mihai nodded in resignation. He looked up at Phineas, and as he did, his eyes had changed from the amber irises and round pupils of a human to the glowing amber orbs of a cat. Phineas' smile didn't flinch from this display.

"I'm sure you have permission to sell your wares in this territory," Phineas stated.

"Teas and smokes? No," Mihai replied. "Information? Yes." He presented Phineas with a bag of tea. Phineas smelled it and turned his nose away immediately, disgusted by the odor.

"That is the scent of the man who will try and betray you. When you brew this pungent tea, you will witness your betrayal in the leaves," Mihai said with a greedy smile. "This is valuable to you, no?"

After a few moments, Phineas considered the offer and looked back at Mihai with a wicked grin. "How much?"

-CHAPTER 7-
UNEARTHING SINS

Phineas Thatch sat in a dark room with his journal a few nights later. The only light source emitted from the globe that topped his cane. He jotted down what he had discovered in the tea leaves in the diary.

It was a fascinating spell in that once the information was gleaned, it must either be acted upon or recorded; otherwise, the particulars were soon forgotten. For those who dealt with secrets, it was an efficient way to generate repeat customers.

He also used this time to write down the flurry of intrusive thoughts and emotions he was experiencing. He usually did this daily, and when he was alone, sitting in bed and slowing down at the end of the day. Later, he might review these entries and attempt to excavate some meaning from them. His mind and soul always tried to whisper to and warn him or sometimes to remind him of a lesson needing remembering.

Sometimes though, as was the case now, those little intrusive thoughts didn't come from him. Spiritual or psychic attacks often come in the form of painful memories, disturbing thoughts, or emotions not belonging to the victim. They also manifested in desires and addictions— a challenge for Phineas daily without the help of outside involvement.

Presently, he wrote down these intrusive thoughts. The thought of whiskey pouring over ice. The idea of its amber-colored solution, barley, vanilla, cinnamon, and malt aroma. He was swimming in the song of it dancing over ice globes and how the crystals refracted the light and seemed to make this promise of numbing come to life. Every sip was a salve for frayed nerves, a cozy blanket to curl up under and hide from the ghosts, a doorway into peaceful oblivion.

Phineas hadn't considered drinking for three years, eight months, one week, and five days. If he had to, he could count the hours and minutes. Even down to the second if pressed. That wasn't nearly as important as "why" he had these thoughts. It was a distraction, a crowbar to pry other feelings and memories long forgotten to swallow him and keep him away from the invoker of these intrusions. The weeping mother. A scared child. Misty hills and valleys. Feelings of guilt and shame bit at him. The images blurred between what was here and now and what was then.

He sat in a cold room; the white walls were dingy, and the paint cracked and peeled. Phineas could see mold growing in the cracked concrete bricks and corners that didn't marry as they should. The black rot sought out moisture and abhorred the light. Phineas could feel these tendrils growing toward him. Thick vein-like structures reached out to him desperately. Was this the spirit or prediction?

This place was perfect for the corruption to grow and spawn more corruption. The floor had a thick film of dust over it that insufficiently masked the bile-colored tiles. Phineas sat on a plastic chair near the center of the ten-by-ten room.

Little light entered through the small row of windows near the room's ceiling. They were just big enough to provide some illumination and inform whoever stayed in this room if it was day or night. That was all. There is no chance to escape, see the world outside, or foster a little hope. Isolation and despair was the theme. It was once a patient's room.

"No," Phineas said to himself, realizing that these were not his thoughts again. He quickly began to write down these notions and any ideas they gave birth to them. There was something else at work here. Not just his client, whom he'd come to see, but other spirits were trying to warn him of something. Coming from someplace he had forgotten and had vowed from which never to return.

Phineas was a thin, small-framed man with almost translucent pale skin. His hair was dark red with skunk stripes, parallel almost perfectly placed opposite each other. Phineas shaved the sides of his scalp, exposing a series of tattooed runes and ancient symbols. His circular pitch-black sunglasses entirely obscured his eyes with pure silver rims.

Next to Phineas' chair was a leather backpack and a black cane. A simple silver globe sat atop the rod, emitting a soft emerald glow. On the opposite end, the cane concluded into a silver-tipped point. The lacquer on the shaft was black, but those who looked within the images reflected in its polished surface could see a green hue in the right light. Those who knew how could look beyond the reflection and see another world's shadowy green structures and constructs. The world from which the cane was constructed.

He wrote and scribbled furiously into his notebook as he awaited his next client. As he punctuated his final sentence, he looked to see 'her.' She was so tall she bent her head to avoid dragging the top of her scalp across the ceiling. She was also woefully thin. She wore the standard uniform of a patient of this institution, with dirty white scrub pants, a tattered white t-shirt, and a pair of ashy-grey socks.

Phineas could see the pinpoint lights of her eyes and the pain within. Her arms were covered in sores and bruises, and even in the dim light, Phineas could make out rows of scars from the chronic needlework of drug abuse. He could even make out a few of the same marks on her neck.

His client, Eleanor Doe, was a habitual drug user and sex worker. Tragically, one habit facilitated the other. She was turned out to the streets at the age of ten by her parents, who also had a severe drug addiction, and had to "earn her keep" and help keep them high.

By fourteen, she had three STDs, two abortions, and two miscarriages. She had been admitted to the ER multiple times for fractures, lacerations, contusions, and overdoses. She had been arrested equally often for sex trafficking, assault, and possession.

The last time Eleanor was arrested was because she had overdosed. When the police officer had administered Narcan, the opiate antidote, she immediately attacked her saviors and bit an earlobe off. Her actions led to her imprisonment in this state-run, poorly funded establishment. Phineas discovered these details on yellowed intake forms and clinical notes filed away in mold-infested cabinets. Some pages held within the degraded manilla folder were illegible due to the black mold obscuring their contents.

How she must have suffered to escape this way, this often, Phineas thought as he looked over her wounds and scars. Phineas took a deep, steady breath and began his process.

"I've been assigned to your case," Phineas began as he put the yellow folder he had been reading onto the floor. "It is my understanding that you no longer need to stay here anymore, and I'm here to help you "transition out." So, could you tell me what I do to help facilitate this move for you?" Phineas asked dryly but warmly.

After he asked this, he knew he had to wait. He needed to give the spirit a chance to have her say. The more you try to push clients and take away their perception of control, the more they resist. Otherwise, it became a power struggle that could cause this assignment to go on for weeks. His specialty did not provide him with regular work, so he needed to "turn and burn" to maintain his semi-comfortable way of life. He awaited her response eagerly and was finally rewarded.

"I've been looking for so long now," Eleanor said. "I miss her so much… please help us."

Her voice sounded like dry leaves crushed in a palm. Each word exhaled was raspy and filled with so much pain and sorrow. Each syllable dragged Phineas over gravel and glass and scratched his soul. She never moved her mouth as she spoke but let her jaw fall open. The gravelly syllables poured into Phineas and touched on a longing he wasn't aware he was vulnerable to feeling. If Phineas hadn't erected his defenses prior, he would be dead.

"He won't let us go," she rasped.

"He?" Phineas replied quizzically. This was somewhat unexpected. Phineas thought there might be some issues with the client. His contract was only for Eleanor before him, not some other lost soul. If Elleanor was a prisoner, there were other challenges to consider.

"Please pardon my rudeness, but I need to make a call." He pulled out a flip phone. He only used it for moments like this— an emergency.

Smartphones would interfere with his work as they often invite distractions via the internet or social media.

He tapped a button to quickly dial Vincent, who facilitated meetings with those who hired out his services through the Bazaar. Vincent was aware of additional information thanks to their tall, olive-skin friend. Cassandra was an agent who found work for Phineas and his crew, so if there were complications, she would have tried to make him aware. No. This was someone acting outside the Magi community. Someone was trying to hide the details of this case. That also means that he and his crew were possibly in danger if they uncovered certain truths. Phineas felt this was all accurate, and if his band were threatened, the consequences would be most severe.

"Vinnie. No, the job isn't done. We were only contracted for one client, correct?" he started, the frustration was evident in Phineas's voice. "Yeah, well, contact Cassandra Ergos and tell her she needs to contact the client and tell them that I have expensive complications. No, Vincent, I get the feeling they knew about this." Phineas's anger was rising. All of this was unprofessional. It was also cruel. He thought how this poor woman had become some wailing spirit and had suffered. Then, some had been led here to end their lives. So much pain. So many souls.

"Look, Vinnie- "he paused and indicated to Eleanor with an outstretched hand and index finger he would only be a moment longer. "Let Cass know if the client doesn't want me to walk out of here, and then they will pay me triple the contracted amount," Phineas noticed Elleanor was walking away. "Take Mata with you. Just in case they try anything stupid. Good? Text me as soon as you get our money."

Phineas closed his phone, took a deep breath, and looked at Eleanor. She was no longer there.

"Fuck!" Phineas hissed. He quickly grabbed his cane and backpack and stepped out into the hallway. Phineas caught her just as she strode down the hall. He followed her from a distance, not too close, but just close enough to see where she was taking him. He slipped on the backpack and steadied the cane in his palm.

She came to a decrepit stairwell and led Phineas up. He watched as Eleanor climbed up the steps and felt profound empathy for her within him. He wanted to hold her up and help her to the next floor, but interactions like that didn't go well in the past. Best to just let her lead.

As they reached the designated floor, Phineas received a text on the flip phone in his pocket. He looked at it. "I'm coming with the goods." Phineas grimaced at the message.

Vinnie was also really shitty at slang. Phineas smirked when he remembered the month he let Vinnie invite everyone he knew to "Netflix and chill" at his one-bedroom apartment— got a good laugh when he asked a couple of fellas from the gym who took him up on his offer and got the surprise of his life later. He had to call in Mata to go and rescue him.

Despite Vinnie's poor use of modern vernacular and his chronic misuse of the word "literally," which he literally used to describe literally everything, he was great negotiator. Phineas could be off-putting for some people. His calm, almost cold demeanor, the fact that he would get distracted, or the crooked smile that seemed permanently etched on his face. These little facets that were the portrait of Phineas Thatch often made social interactions challenging.

Vincent was a rescue. He and Mata took him on as a client early in their profession and kept him on ever since. Now Phineas couldn't get rid of the guy. They both adopted him as a surrogate parent and loved him dearly.

Phineas and Eleanor came to a set of oak double doors. They were carved, and the door handles were gilded with a flaking brass finish. There were stained glass pictures on each entry. One showed a dove holding an olive branch, and the other was a glowing cross surrounded by clouds. Something lit the room from within; the light promised safety and love. It promised peace. It promised salvation.

Phineas turned to regard Elleanor. She averted her gaze to the floor as she opened the door. Phineas investigated the light within that chapel and slowly approached it. He entered the brightly lit room, nearly bowled over by the aroma of scented candles, the tones of an organ echoing off the walls, and the colored refractions of sunlight through stained glass depictions of 'the crucifixion.'

He looked around the room and found a small congregation in attendance. Eleanor took her seat in a pew furthest away from the pulpit. Below the obscenely sizeable wooden cross stood a thin cut of a man. His hair and beard, the same color as the wooden cross behind him, fell onto his chest and shoulders in tight brown locks. He wore a black suit and tie with a neatly pressed white dress shirt.

"Let us welcome another to our flock, brothers and sisters!" the preacher greeted warmly. "Welcome all who enter the house of the Lord!" He moved with the grace and energy of an over-caffeinated teenager. In Phineas' eyes, the preacher looked to be in his thirties. "Tell us, brother, what is your name so we may include it in our daily prayer today?"

His smile was infectious and broad. Then there were his eyes, bright, so very sunny, and warm, too. Beyond those eyes dwelled a hunger, some savage thirst.

"Fuck you…that's my name," Phineas retorted angrily. Angry because this promise of peace, love, and fellowship was a lie. The lie enticed those needing all these things, only to use them and destroy the soul seeking salvation. Churches and preachers like this reminded him of his childhood. It reminded him of his hometown's intolerance and bigotry against the strange and beautiful. He hissed these distractions away and focused on the enemy before him.

"Enough of the games. Show me who you truly are!" He punctuated his statement by slamming the point of his cane into the floor. It sounded like thunder, and the warm light and joyful congregation scattered like sand in a gale. Now Phineas stood in the truth. He stood in a dark room with corpses where a parishioner once existed. Each corpse was desiccated and clutching its own murder weapon. One corpse had a tourniquet wrapped tightly around its arm and a syringe still plugged into its elbow.

Another, a girl, sat in a pool of dried blood. The curdled remains of her life stained the wood and the once pretty sundress she wore. Lacerations were etched on her thighs, and long, deep cuts made into her wrists. Each cut was made so deeply that Phineas saw her severed tendons within those wounds. She couldn't move to find help even if she wanted. Another victim had no noticeable marks or injuries and seemed to have given up. No weapon, just time. The man appeared to have moved into the room, sat down, and died.

The pews were worn and rotting from days and nights of exposure. The windows into the chapel faded, and there was an inch of dust and cobwebs all over the room. The room was more extensive than Phineas initially thought. There were twenty pews total, with ten on each side. The corners were deep in shadow.

The stained-glass mural window shattered, and Phineas could smell the cold and the filth from the streets outside. The shadows were inky. They moved across the floor with black tendrils around Phineas' feet and ankles and back to the pulpit. The shadows clouded the rafters as they bellowed from the churning mass below them.

When Phineas turned back toward the pulpit, he found the preacher. He was convulsing and raging at Phineas now. Spit and drool flung from his lips and evaporated into the air. His body twisted and bulged, his face swelled, his legs and arms looked like they would burst, his flesh became thin, and his bones cracked under pressure.

The preacher howled, cursed, threw his head back, and his torso contorted into impossible positions. His flesh turned gray and blackened, then became thick black and green fog. Within that fog, the screams and howls were no longer of the preacher but of his many victims over the decades. Faces swam in the sea of putrid evanescence, their wails belching the odor of decades of rot and decay.

Phineas reached into memory to find the name of the creature before him. It was an entity that could entice its victims to come to this forgotten church in this abandoned hospital and lull its victims to end their lives. The face of the entity became many, constantly shifting and twisting. The multitude of mouths moaned and screamed and cursed all at once.

Within his mind, Phineas was assaulted with scenes from his childhood and his self-extrication from Haven Shire. He'd sought some place to blend in and disappear. Instead, Phineas had felt more alone than ever and began drinking and using. He drank to forget his father's many abuses, his mother's madness, and ultimately, her lonely death at the doorsteps of her own home.

Phineas gritted his teeth against the mental assault. That was the creature working its weapon- despair. It howled a song into Phineas' heart, offering him two choices. Live alone and suffer or give in to death and be free of this life. The allure of freedom from suffering was a trap. Once the victim died, their psychic energy and soul fed this creature. Eleanor was bait; he knew this now. She had to lure others in, and in exchange, something didn't devour her. She wasn't ever allowed to leave, though. Like in her living existence, she trafficked herself in exchange for an undead continuance of suffering.

Phineas felt something else at work here. "The Howling Darkness," as it's often called, isn't a specter born from the death of one being. This thing is more the result of one powerful spirit suffering. That suffering calls for the suffering of others in an attempt not to feel alone. The curse is that it never can feel a connection, isolated until freed from its trap. Then Phineas recalled Eleanor saying, "He won't let us go..." He quickly pulled his notes on Eleanor and found a clue.

Phineas steadied himself and began a mantra he knew to fight against such monsters. He learned the song from a disgraced Tibetan monk caught practicing the dark arts. The mantra was difficult because it required a low guttural throat sound that Phineas had not yet mastered. Still, the purpose of this chant was to focus his mind and anchor himself in the moment. Then, when he calmed his anxiety and feelings of depression, he went on the offensive.

Phineas opened his long coat and pulled forth an ancient tuning fork. The polished brass was eight inches long, and all along each tine were sigils and pictures of a man subduing beasts with sounds of music. Near the base of the fork was leather twine, at the end of which hung a small silver ball. The hilt was of the same metal as the fork and wrapped in leather straps. The grip ended with a four-pointed spike. The spike had an ancient Greek song written down its length in a spiral.

The shadows beneath Phineas coalesced into tendrils wrapped around his feet and ankles. Their touch was cold as ice water as they entered Phineas's skin and made their way up his legs, trying to steal his strength. He shivered from the chill and fought to keep his teeth from chattering or his tongue and lips from misspeaking a phrase or syllable of his mantra. He pointed the fork's spiked tip at the floor before him and held it towards the Howling Dark like a crucifix.

Phineas took his cane and began beating the silver globe against the fork as he sang the throat song. The fork sang a deep melodic tone that sent vibrations throughout the room. The tendrils began retreating from Phineas's flesh, and he felt himself filled with warmth and peace. In rhythm with his song, he began to drum the fork with his cane faster, sending a warm, soothing tone through the room.

The swirling mass of wailing was drowned out by the sonic and psychic attack from Phineas and his tuning fork. The mist and shadows became thinner. Phineas approached where the preacher stood and, as he did so, paused, beating the fork and pulling forth the silver-laced gourd jar. He pulled the cork from the jar and placed it before his feet. He still held the fork before him; even though he no longer drummed it with his cane, it now hummed a deep, warm tone.

"For you to be born, there had to be great suffering here. What better a birthing place than a state-run mental institution," he said, more to himself than to the spirit. "I've been inside my share of these cold and callous institutions of so-called 'healing,' I'm sorry for all your suffering." Phineas' eyes moistened somewhat as he heard the screams of rage turn into pleas for help. "I will cleanse this place so that no more shall have to know to suffer as you have. I hope you find peace."

Phineas took the tuning fork and raised it high above his head. He then took a deep breath, and upon exhaling, he drove the spike at the hilt's end into the pulpit's floor. With a broad stroke of his left hand, he stood straight and smacked the fork with the tip of his cane. The tones reverberated all through the chapel, through the floorboards, the plaster walls, and the glass. The apparition started to convulse violently and fold into itself. It tried to retreat, but the tuning fork compelled it and the spell Phineas had evoked when he opened the jar. It presented itself as a sanctuary from this awful tune that weakened it. The baleful host of agonized souls ripped themselves free from the corners and beneath the pews. The tangled mass of pain-filled faces swirled into a spiral, like a tornado in reverse.

Phineas struck the fork repeatedly, and as he did so, the funnel cloud grew tighter and tighter and began streaming into the jar's tiny orifice. The funnel cloud growled and hissed at Phineas as it retreated into the jar. When the last wisps of evanescence trailed into the container, Phineas rushed to the jar and plugged it with the cork.

Breathless, Phineas turned to retrieve the tuning fork. He was startled when he found a tiny wisp of a spirit still lingering. It floated around the tuning fork as if dancing to the humming tune. Curious about this last soul, Phineas carefully approached and knelt to see it closely. He felt it necessary to get down to his knee as if he was about to talk to a child.

"It's you!" Phineas exclaimed softly. It was the essence of a child. The little spirit grew and took on the form it possessed in its living existence. He looked at the child, a little girl, and realized the visage of the preacher, Elleanor, and this little girl had much in common.

"You're their daughter, aren't you?" Phineas asked. "Were you born here? Did you die in this horrible place?"

She replied with a smile.

"Where is your..." Phineas broke off, suddenly remembering Elleanor. She led him here. He remembered how she said, "He won't let us go." He initially mistook this to mean all those souls who suffered here. Phineas' heart sank as he realized that Eleanor was a patient, the preacher the father, and this poor lonely soul was their child.

"Will you come with me?" a soft, almost melodic voice said.

Phineas looked down at the little ghost, shaken free from the horror of this discovery. The little girl's eyes were large, begging for comfort and love. He knelt to face her.

"I'm afraid I'm not so lucky, little one. I brought you a surprise, though." Phineas looked back and, in his mind, summoned Elleanor. He felt her presence nearby. She heard his call, and from the last pew, she stood and began to walk in his direction. Her steps were less of a weak and tired shuffle but timid and fearful.

"It's your daughter Eleanor, and she needs her mommy." Phineas reached his hand out, palm facing up to her. He could sense her trepidation, fear, and shame of all she had done. Your crimes are laid bare for all to see when you are dead. Phineas could feel how she desperately wished to hide her sins now. "You've nothing to fear, Eleanor; she's asking for you. Won't you tell her how much you missed her? Show her how much you love her?"

He watched as she moved with purpose. Her wounds from all those years of addiction and abuse began to melt away. The filth and grime on her skin turned into wisps of smoke, and her clothes began to mend themselves. She moved to the glowing light that started to fill the little girl.

The child's spirit became so bright that Phineas had to shield his face. He didn't need to see the joy from this reunion with his eyes. Even though they both existed in the same space all this time, they were somehow unable to find each other. Eleanor's spirit, which led others here to their demise, was anchored here because she couldn't leave without her child. Her child was buried by someone under so much sadness, loneliness, and despair. She was lost, unable to understand what had happened to her or her mother. She only knew there was a moment of pain and was left in this place. Someone else's dirty secret, not a little girl who just wanted her mom.

Phineas let a single tear go for the mother and her daughter. He reached down, and when he touched the tuning fork, he noticed the rotting floor of the pulpit decaying from black mold. Phineas gripped the handle of the tuning fork and yanked hard, pulling up part of the spongey flooring with it. Reaching down, he moved the soft molding planks and discovered where the preacher had attempted to hide his secrets. His face contorted with anger as he looked down and found the remains of Elleanor. She was wrapped in plastic sheeting. Her body desiccated and withered. He reached and grabbed another plank; these came up quickly enough.

After Phineas had pulled up six planks, he found a child's blanket rolled up and tied with bungee straps. Phineas pulled a serrated knife from his leather boot and cut the straps. He unrolled the blanket, and there he found Eleanor's child. She was bundled up and placed at the feet of her mother. Someone then covered the bodies with the stage.

Phineas got up, walked over to the lead pew, and, mentally and spiritually weary, sat down. He reached into his leather pack, put away the fork, and pulled out a water bottle. Phineas took a long drink of its ice-cold contents. He drank until his mouth and throat burned from the cold. This was something Phineas did anytime he wanted to drink. Right now, he desperately wanted that cold promise to numb him. Instead, he focused on what needed to happen next.

Phineas pulled out his phone and made the call. "Hey, Vinnie, yeah, it's me. Tell them it's done," Phineas said. "What? They're almost here?" Vinnie sounded anxious. Phineas could feel the fear in his tone. "Well, good, to be honest, it saves me the trouble of finding them. Tell the client I'm in the hospital chapel." Before Vinnie could react or protest, Phineas hung up the phone.

He shut off the phone and tossed it into his pack. He reached in, fished out his leather-bound journal, and began to draft his report of the mission and details regarding his client, correction-

clients. He drew a picture of the little girl, Eleanor, and the preacher from memory and with as much detail as possible. He wanted to get the details right while they were still fresh in his mind.

-CHAPTER 8-
UNDENIABLE JUSTICE

An hour had passed before Vincent walked through the chapel entryway. Phineas turned to his old friend. Vincent was more senior than Phineas by thirty or so years. He always dressed as though he just walked in from a nightclub in Miami. Today, he wore his favorite khaki suit, leather loafers, and a bright pink dress shirt.

He wore a tie today since he was "on the clock," but it had been pulled loose and hung limply from his neck. The top button of his shirt was missing, exposing a tuft of gray chest hair through the top of his shirt. His ordinarily jovial smile was replaced with pain from a split lip. A droplet of blood dotted his left nostril, and dried blood was on his mustache.

"Vinnie, this is not the condition I left you in. What happened?" Phineas inquired. His smile cooled at the sight of the three men who followed Vincent into the room, two of whom sported handguns. Phineas immediately recognized the leader from commercials about spas and hotels built to pamper the wealthy. The man was also making a bid for the state senate. He ran a campaign based on the fears of the dissolving middle-class workers losing their jobs to immigrants, voting fraud, and evil government conspiracies.

"We had to persuade our friend here to give us your whereabouts," a round man said with a smile. Ronald Teach was sporting a spray tan that reminded Phineas of those creepy dwarves from "Charlie and the Chocolate Factory" as he escorted Vincent into the room. He did so as though he owned the place. Which, in truth, he did. He probed Vincent with the tip of a nickel-plated 9mm pistol. Phineas could make out the pearl handle as well.

Ronald Teach was the portrait of a salesman, no matter how much money he spent on his suits and watches. He was overweight but spent a lot of money trying to hide that. His spray tan only extenuated the plastic surgery scars that glowed white near his earlobes. Phineas could tell by the cut of his suits that they were tailored to steal attention away from his chest and flanks, but when he sat down, Phineas could still see the top of Ronnie's girdle. Everything about him said he would sell or take something from you. Every story or joke Ronald told, every pat on the back, even his smile, were all intrusive and a mask for some ulterior motive. Any legal complaints or allegations seemed to slide off of him, just like his cheap wig, which he constantly adjusted.

"Convince me nothing, you fat cock sucker!" Vincent protested. "I told you where he was. I even offered to lead you there. You went and ruined my best shirt and tie for nothing!" Vincent looked back at Phineas and gave an apologetic shrug. Phineas returned the gesture with a shrug and a crooked smile.

"Yeah, well, I felt you needed to know how important this meeting was for me. I didn't want to miss this chance to meet the infamous Phineas Thatch," Ronald said with his over-whitened, saccharine smile. Flanking Ronald were two employees, who looked to have spent so much time at the gym that their tailor couldn't keep up with their steroid-fueled muscle growth. They looked as menacingly as possible at Phineas. He just smiled at them in return.

Phineas looked over at Vincent. "How's Lizzy?" he asked so casually as if he was ignoring the other men in the room.

"Lizzy? Oh, she's just great. Mata is walking her now," Vincent replied in the same carefree tone as if they were catching up after work. "She'll need to be fed as soon as she's back from her business," Vincent continued. He looked down and moaned at the mess that had been made of his clothes. He vainly tried to wipe a spot of blood from his silk shirt.

Ronald looked at the exchange between the two men, and his face reddened. He did not abide by people ignoring him or not taking him seriously. He looked back at his bodyguards in astonishment and returned his look with bewildered shrugs.

"I'm sorry, but who the fuck is Lizzy?" Ronnie asked, looking again at his men as though this discussion was ludicrous. "Should I invite this special someone to our little party?" he solicited menacingly, with a slight chuckle.

Phineas looked over at him from behind his blackout specs, amused. "Oh, sorry. Lizzie is my lovely dog, a puppy. I named her after Lizzy Borden, the lady who butchered her family…" Phineas started.

"Do I look like I give a flying fuck?" Ronald roared, spittle flying from his lips.

"Well, you might, she's an amazing animal. I rescued her from a terrible man who wanted to use her in a dog fighting ring. Anyway…"

At this point, Ronnie's patience had run out. He raised his nickel-plated pistol skyward and fired three rounds. Plaster and pieces of wood fell nearby, nearly hitting Ronald on the shoulder. Phineas stopped talking, but his crooked smile never left his face. He lowered his gaze so that Ronald could see his eyes and that they rested intently on him now.

"Look here, you fucking weirdo. I went through a great deal of trouble and had to pull the right strings to get the church involved and get you out here to clean up this mess. So, all I want to know is whether or not you did what you were paid to do," Ronald said, trying to hide his boiling anger.

"Well, we need to address a couple of issues with this job first before I can give you a detailed report," Phineas began, pushing his glasses further up the bridge of his nose. "You gave me a file on the client you wished me to 'remove.' You failed to notify me that there was a whole other entity here, which was far more dangerous but required my attention," Phineas explained. "Now, I'm sure my associate here explained that this increased the price threefold. Correct?" He punctuated this statement by looking over at Vincent. Vincent nodded without looking while trying to wipe a drop of blood off his tie.

"Oh yes, Mr. Thatch. Your man, Vinnie, is a great negotiator. I would have him come work for me if I didn't think he was so loyal to you," Ronnie smiled.

"The fuck I am!" Vincent exclaimed, pausing his attempt to remove the blood from his tie. "Oh, and the name is Vincent, you dumb cunt."

Phineas chuckled. "There is another issue at work here, Ronnie," he continued. "You hired me to come out here and exorcise whatever apparition was in your report." Phineas paused for dramatic effect. "You didn't say anything about covering up murder or rape."

Ronald's eyes narrowed at Phineas at this. Phineas continued, "Such services come at a much, much higher price tag." Phineas's crooked voice and smile took on a more menacing edge.

Ronald began to shift from foot to foot, and a bead of sweat began to trail the side of his cheek. "I don't know what you are saying," Ronald started. "Where do you get the balls to…"

Before he continued, Phineas interrupted. "You see, before we accept a job, we do a little background check on our living clients." Phineas was smiling now, his eyes were wide. On the surface, he was calm, even soothing, but something was inside him was licking its chops. Phineas procured a small leather journal in a blink, seemingly out of thin air. Ronald's jowls shook from the display, and his face contorted in wonder and confusion.

"You are Ronald Teach Junior, son of a wealthy industrialist and real estate douchebag, Ronnie Teach Senior." At this point, Phineas opened up his journal and began flipping through pages. "Ronnie senior passed away thirty years ago under mysterious circumstances, and you and your mother inherited his estate." Phineas looked slightly accusatory at Ronald.

Ronald's face was beet red now. "Momma Teach was going to remarry and, therefore, possibly prevent you from getting your father's inheritance." Phineas was reading from his journal at this point. "Teresa Rose Teach committed suicide the week before her wedding to another man. Ronald Jr. set to get all of the inheritance." Phineas glanced up momentarily and showed a news clipping, pulling it out of the air like a card trick. The article is over two decades old and yellowed from exposure.

"Interestingly, before that, you had several failed businesses and restaurants, all of which required some financial aid from your daddy." Phineas looked down.

Ronald started to look uncomfortable now as if he needed to piss something fierce. He adjusted his toupee and wiped his cheek. Phineas eyed him intently. He enjoyed the spice of this man's discomfort, and his mischievous grin showed it. "You even dabbled in ministry work, correct? Tried your hand at tending a flock?"

"What can I say? God had been good to me. I thought I might return the favor," Ronald replied, attempting to appear pious.

Everything about this man revolted Phineas.

"To do so, you had to serve your community, and you were sent here by the ministry to meet the local criteria, correct?" Phineas continued, reading his journal. Before Ronald had a chance to reply, he continued. "How closely did you tend to this flock, I wonder? Did you tend to one or two sheep more than others? Were you a preacher? Minister? Not a priest, for sure. Vows of celibacy and all that."

"I don't know what you could mean by that. I also don't care for your tone, Mr. Thatch," Ronald said with a hint of menace in his voice.

Phineas closed the journal he held and stuffed it into his leather pack.

"My clients negotiated the terms of their release. They all agreed to leave so long as the one responsible for their torment came forward and repented for his transgressions," Phineas said, standing up straight, facing Ronald.

Ronald tightened his grip on the handle of his pistol.

"Oh? Who did they have in mind? What did this man do, per se?" Ronald asked with his smug smile, as though he had a secret he desperately wanted to share.

"Oh, come on, Ronnie. You recognized our client immediately, and even though she didn't present a threat to you personally, she was drawing a great deal of attention," Phineas began, his smile giving way to a look of boredom. "With the increase of suicides and overdoses in the area, it would only be a matter of time before the increased foot traffic would have dug up your secrets."

Ronnie looked at him and shrugged as if to say, "Go on!" or "So?"

Phineas was done with his plaything. "The woman, Elleanor, was a patient here." From within Phineas's sleeve, a small bird flew clumsily and landed at Ronald's feet. He looked down and saw it was an origami swan. He picked up the bird and carefully unfolded it. It was a photo of Elleanor. Young, clean, and happy.

"How? How the fuck did you...?" Ronald stammered.

Before he could ask any more questions, Phineas interrupted him. His voice took an angry edge as he was wrapping up his debriefing.

"She attended your so-called church sermons. She confided in you, and in return, you raped her. Nine months later, she had a baby girl. Cosette. A Les' Misérables fan apparently."

Ronald still looked puzzled by the photo he held in his hands. He looked down and dropped the picture as it changed to now include the portrait of Cosette as a baby, cradled in her mother's arms. He looked at the photo and back to Phineas, his face white and mouth wide with shock.

Phineas acted exhausted by the man and spelled it out to him like a dunce. "Hospital records were discovered in this basement, abandoned just like the patients who resided here. They had nowhere to go after you bought the hospital and closed it. Many were left homeless and turned to crime. Drugs. Death!" Phineas took a breath and continued. "Eleanor, thirty-four, gave birth to a seven-pound, four-ounce baby girl in the institution. Father unknown." Phineas glanced at Ronald with a knowing look. "One month after, mother and daughter were discharged from hospital. According to follow-up visits with her clinician, Elleanor was clean for two-and-a-half years. So she got a job and an apartment and did all she could to take care of her one true love." Phineas paused for a moment. Vincent looked up and saw something behind his eyes. A memory?

As if remembering his lines, he began again, "So, what happened? She suddenly shows up out of the blue on your doorstep. Or did you keep tabs on her, just in case?"

Phineas slowly walked toward Ronald. Ronald looked over at Vincent, who now moved away from Ronald and shared his blood-spattered smile. "After you obtained all your inheritance, you decided to buy up this property and shut it down. Eleanor and her daughter are reported missing around the same time, yeah?" Phineas took another slow step. Ronald slowly raised his gun.

"Stop right there, you fucking weirdo," Ronald demanded with a touch more anxiety than he intended.

"What happened, Ronnie? Eleanor asked you to pay child support, perhaps help her raise your child?" Phineas asked.

"Stupid bitch found out about my windfall and thought she could cash in," Ronald spat disgustingly. "Claimed that the girl needed the money for surgery or some shit. If I didn't help the little girl, she would go to the press claiming I raped her."

"Cosette," Phineas said with no amusement. Ronald looked confused. "The little girl whom you killed was named Cosette."

Ronald blew a raspberry and shrugged.

"So-the-fuck what!" Ronald contended. "You've had your fun, Mr. Thatch." Ronald steadied his gun and his gaze at Phineas. "So, what will you intend to say next that will convince me not to bury you and your friend here with them and then burn this whole place down? After I have my boys play with you first, of course."

Phineas's smile widened, and he replied, "Lizzie Borden took an axe/And gave her mother forty whacks. /When she saw what she had done, /She gave her father forty-one."

Ronald's face twisted in confusion for a moment. Then he heard a low, guttural, and wet growl behind him. Without having to look, Ronald felt the gravity of the beast that hungered for his life. He felt the stare on his neck. He slowly turned to see the most enormous dog he had ever seen. Her shoulders were broad enough to leave little room for Ronald to move around her.

The ears on the hound came to a point above her head, like ebony horns. The sleek, shiny coat was so dark that the dog seemed one with the shadows. The only color on the dog was a patch of bright white in the shape of an upside-down cross on her forehead. That and the murderous gleam in her eyes and bone-white teeth.

He turned slowly but quickly glanced around for his men. His eyes found the first at the back of the room, lying face down on the floor. The second looked back at Ronald, eyes wide in fury and fear, struggling to free himself from the grip of the woman who held him in a rear naked choke hold, her arms coiled around his neck like a snake. She seemed so small compared to his hired man that he first mistook her for a child.

As Ronald watched her overpower the man, he could see her powerfully built tattooed arms and her legs. Her thighs bulged through her black cargo pants. From what he could see, she wore a midriff black t-shirt, exposing her powerful flanks and abs. Her hair was thick on top of her head and tied in a large knot that flowed down almost to the floor. The hair was black and held a sheen; he could make out baubles and chains within the braid. The sides of her head were similarly shaved and tattooed, much like Phineas.

Her eyes were fixed on Ronald as her prey began to lose his will to fight, and his breaths came slower and ragged, sputtering with spittle. Her toothy smile matched the menacing hound before Ronald.

Ronald looked at the dog whose throaty growl culminated into a powerful bark that made him almost jump out of his shoes. He felt a trickle of fear and piss run down his pant leg. Ronnie was about to raise his pistol at the beast until a hand gently fell onto his. Ronnie froze at the touch and saw Phineas staring at him from behind those mirrored spectacles. He swore for a moment he saw something in that reflection. A pair of pale figures?

"I wouldn't do that if I were you, Ronnie," Phineas said, whispering in his ear. Ronald could hear the crooked smile in his voice. He could almost feel the gleam of his teeth on the nape of his neck. Ronald felt his spine tingle and his bowels drop. He breathed a ragged and shaky breath as Phineas moved the palm of his hand over the top of the pistol and gently tugged the gun out of Ronald's hand. Ronald saw the gun pass to Vincent, who was now within a breath's reach on his left side. He felt his eyes on him. He could smell the blood on his breath. Feel his smile. Ronald let his right hand drop to the side and watched the Cane Corso as she buried her eyes into his throat. The intent was clear. If he moved in any way she disapproved, she would sink her powerful jaws into his throat, crush his windpipe, and rip out his jugular.

"Wah-What do you want, man?" Ronald stammered. "I'll pay you. I already got your payment for this job here." He yelped a little when he felt a cold palm slide across his flank, crossing his chest and entering his jacket pocket. The fingers found the thick manila envelope hidden there and tugged it free. The bulging envelope, filled with the promise of payment, slipped quickly and was smoothly handed to Vincent.

"This is a start. What you promised," Phineas said, his voice a hiss in Ronald's ear.

Vincent then began to unclasp the very expensive Rolex on Ronald's wrist. "This is for my shirt and tie, fuckface." Vincent then grabbed and yanked the bejeweled ring from Ronald's small finger. The action tore the skin near the knuckle and caused Ronald to whimper in shock and pain. Vincent looked the ring over, looked at Mata, who was kicking away her victim, and tossed it to her. She caught the ring mid-flight without looking, turned it over, appraised it briefly, and then stuffed it in her pants pocket. She reached down and pulled on a small leather jacket. "Mata deserves a little something for coming here on such short notice," Vincent said to Phineas.

"I agree. Your attendance is a gift," Phineas said, exaggerating each syllable as he spoke. He winked at her and blew a kiss in her direction.

Mata bowed dramatically, and when she came up, her smile was playful, almost sweet. She mouthed the words "Thank you" and signed the response.

"Forgive my guardian angel. She doesn't have much use for words, and I suspect they would be wasted on you anyway," Phineas whispered.

Ronald felt a hand roughly grab his suit collar and yank him backward. He stumbled and tripped, even trying to fight the pull for a moment until he heard the growl of the hound padding behind him. He moved his hands where they were visible and walked obediently after Phineas. They all came to the altar.

"Kneel," Phineas stated coldly. His eyes were wild now, and his wicked grin seemed to glow in the night. The tip of his cane pointed to the bodies of Eleanor and her girl. Ronald looked down into the shallow hole beneath the stage on which he stood so many times before. He looked down at the burial site and began whining.

"I'm going to give you a choice, Ronald." Phineas moved to a squatting position, his cane in one hand, the tuning fork in the other. "You may repent here in this place before God and us. Or you can turn yourself in for rape and murder. For the heinous crimes committed against Elleanor and her child."

"If I repent here, you'll let me go?" Ronald asked, his tear-filled eyes drying immediately and filling with hope.

"Once you understand the pain and suffering you've wrought, you will be left to your own devices," Phineas said soothingly. "No rush, though. I want you to consider this moment fully before—"

Ronald started laughing, cutting Phineas off. "Here! Here! I want to repent. I want to repent for all my sins!" he shouted, laughing and crying simultaneously. Bubbles of snot billowed from his nostrils, and tears and spittle rolled down his chin and pooled in the folds of flesh in his neck. "I want to bare my soul to God and pray for his forgiveness!" He raised his hands in prayer and turned toward Phineas, prostrating himself before him. Phineas stood up straight.

Ronald began to scream a prayer, begging that God deliver him from evil and sin. Then he vomited promises of becoming a better man and becoming an example to others to be better.

Phineas threw his arms out high and wide. "I ask all of you who are in attendance today to help this man repent for his sins!" He screamed this aloud to some invisible crowd and with a joyful laugh. His cane and the fork held high. Then he swiftly brought the point of the tuning fork down onto Ronald's left leg, just above his knee. Ronald shrieked in surprise as the spike tip tore through the fabric of his pant leg and bit into the flesh.

"What the fuck! You said you would let me go!" Ronald screamed and started crying.

"Oh, shut the fuck up, man. It's just a flesh wound," Vincent said irritably.

"He's right, you know," Phineas said, crouching again before him. His expression was wild. "You must understand all the suffering you've caused here before you are allowed to leave." He flicked the fork, causing Ronald's slight hum and pitiful whimper.

Phineas suddenly spat out a prayer in the same throaty tones he used when he sang to the spirits earlier. The tuning fork began to hum and vibrate in response. Ronald, horrified, looked at Phineas, not understanding the words or their reason. Phineas walked to the gourd jar and popped the cork free from the top. He lifted the jar above his head with one hand and swayed back and forth.

Mata and Lizzie were the first two to react. Lizzie backed away from the altar and sat down next to Mata. Mata gazed up into the night sky through the broken stained-glass mural. Vincent turned from the altar and sat in the front pew closest to the pulpit. Green and black smoke from the jar began to shoot forth and swirl above the stage. The spike vibrated, and a high-pitched tune keened through the space.

The fork wasn't deep into Ronald's leg, but despite his best efforts to pull it free, it was held there by some other force. Ronald screamed as he pulled on the hilt of the fork. He pulled and grunted at it. It did not budge. Then he heard them. The screams and cries in the night. Ronald looked out into the night sky. Then he looked around the room and watched as the shadows grew deeper and darker, and small pale green lights began to flicker and move within those dark pools— the torrent of screaming spirits dismissed earlier by the tuning fork now summoned back to this place. The tempest began to form a funnel cloud over Ronald, whipping up dust, paper, and other debris.

Ronald knelt beneath the storm raging over him, unable to move out of terror and from being pinned by the cursed object in his leg. He began screaming and begging at the raging, swirling wraiths that shook the room with their pain and fury. The room suddenly filled with the odor of Ronald as he evacuated his bowels and pissed himself on the stage.

Phineas walked off the stage and turned to regard his work. Ronald looked over at him and his company, his face pleading and whining, streams of snot and spit, and tears glazed his pitiful visage. His toupee gave up its hold on his head and fell to the floor at Vincent's feet. Mata looked on with her sweet, playful smile and flipped Ronald the middle finger. The hound Lizzie had now laid down on her belly and was panting as if a little bored.

The fog of hate and sorrow slammed down over Ronald, the weight of decades of grief and despair shaking the stage and the rafters above. Dust fell from the plaster walls, and pieces of loose glass fell from the window. Then, it was all over faster than it had begun and certainly with less dramatic flair. There knelt Ronald Teach, mouth agape, eyes squeezed tightly shut, covered in his piss and shit.

"Wha-What happened?" he sputtered. Before Phineas had time to explain, it began. All those who died in despair, depression, and choking on vomit because they overdosed filled his mind. In his skin and bones, he felt every single one die. He gasped for breath over and over as he relived the final moments of every victim of the Howler. He felt the complete isolation and shame of every man and woman who died in this building. He felt Eleanor's violation and the longing and sorrow of a little girl who just wanted her mother.

Ronald felt all this, and all he could do was scream. He screamed so hard and long that he ran out of breath to fuel his wails, and his vocalizations became a series of squeaks. The pitiful sound spilled from his lips as he sobbed, wracked with the grief of those lost to this awful place.

He inhaled because his body was starving for oxygen and then began to scream again as he felt every piercing by a needle, cut by a razor, tear of a bullet. He gripped the sides of his face and clawed at his eyes and mouth. He began to rip off his clothes and tear at his chest and belly.

Finally, Vinnie walked up to Phineas and handed him the nickel-plated pistol. Phineas took the gun from him without looking away from Ronald. His eyes were fixed only on Ronald's atonement. He approached the wailing Ronald and laid the pistol beside his right knee. There was no magazine, just one in the chamber. Phineas removed the ancient tuning fork and wiped the tip off with Ronald's sleeve.

"You have a single bullet, Ronnie… use it wisely." Phineas began to walk away. "Oh! Thank you for your patronage and for paying in advance by the by." With that, he turned, leaving Mata, Vincent, and Lizzie in tow.

As they exited the building, they paused and heard Ronald's final scream and the gunshot crack resonated through the building. Phineas pulled the jeweled gourd he had purchased before leaving the Bazaar from his long coat. Phineas whispered the curse needed to activate the effects of the container. The Howler, and along with it, the new addition of Ronald Teach's soul, began extracting itself from the building. The screams floated through the night air and filled the void of the silvery chained jar. Phineas popped the cork back onto the jar, silencing the screams.

-CHAPTER 9-
HOME

Paul McConnel stood staring down at the sizzling skillet on the stove. Paul was a bland human being in every way measurable. He was the only actuary in the small town of Haven Shire. Paul was punctual, meticulous, and frugal. Some would also say he was boring, constipated, and cheap. None of this phased Paul in the slightest. He was married to the love of his life, Brenda. His wife was his mirror image, and they kept a tidy home together. Well, as neat as they could with their twin toddlers- Benjamin and Clara.

Paul and Brenda did not seek out risk or excitement. They compulsively avoided the chaos and played it safe. This was true when they relaxed, made love, or watched TV. It was all secure, free of violence, closed off as best as possible from the world's chaos beyond the Shire.

So why was Paul's wife tied to her chair and seated at the dining room table? Why was she screaming and sobbing through a tightly wound gag? Why was he standing over this hot skillet, frying flesh and animal fat? Paul couldn't remember how he got there, it all felt wrong. Yet, it also felt like something he needed to do.

Paul looked down and saw that dinner was nearly ready. He added the sizzling meat to a plate covered in similar offerings. God, his mouth was dry. He just wanted to sit with his family and enjoy a meal. Paul picked up the plate and noticed his hands were covered in blood. It was so thick that it felt tacky as he picked up the plate and serving fork.

"Oh dear, I need to wash up," Paul heard himself say. It seemed as if he was speaking from far away. Paul had difficulty hearing his words correctly. *I sound muffled or something,* he thought. He heard Brenda sobbing loudly from the table now. "Don't worry, dear! Dinner is almost ready!"

Paul couldn't wait to share his day with Brenda. Something strange and exciting occurred at the office. An exception in the day and life of Paul McConnel, CPA. He met with Judge and Maria Marcus to discuss their accounts. They owned several properties and had savings in several high-yield accounts. Still, he found they had several properties they forgot to declare on their taxes for the last ten years.

Paul explained that they needed to complete some amendments and pay back taxes and penalties before the IRS audited them. They should be able to avoid trouble. He, of course, would be paid for his services. Paul assumed the rest of the meeting had gone well, but his memory of what happened next was somewhat fuzzy.

I must be tired, he thought. He and his family need an extended vacation. After setting the plate aside, he washed his hands at the sink, cleaned off the blood on the serving ware, and proudly strode to the dinner table. There at the table sat Brenda. Her face besmirched by tears and streaked with mascara, upset Paul. He needed to get to the bottom of this. He sat beside her and removed the gag tied around her mouth. She coughed and sputtered.

"Brenda? What's the matter? Just look at the state you're in."

Paul wondered why his voice wasn't working. His tongue felt dry, and he had the damnedest time getting his lips to form the words he wanted. It was frustrating because he wished Brenda knew everything was well.

"Paul, wh-wha-why? Why are you doing this?" Brenda asked between sobs. "Where are the children? Please, Paul." Brenda was overcome with another bout of sobbing.

"Why? I just wanted to have a nice meal with my family?" Paul was genuinely confused. "I promise you'll feel better after we sit and eat together."

"Oh Paul, your face. Why would you do that to yourself?" Brenda questioned. Paul thought the query was silly and picked up a serving spoon to look at his reflection. She was right. Paul was curious as to why his face had been removed. It was cut away, exposing his cheekbones and the muscles that worked his jaw. His lips and nose were also gone, displaying a sickeningly white smile and the cartilage that formed the bridge of the nose.

"Wow, that is strange, isn't it?" Paul asked. If he had eyelids, they would be wide with surprise. "I must have done a real number on myself…shaving." Paul chuckled and paused for a moment. Brenda saw a large tear rolling down his cheek. Then, as if suddenly reminded by someone else in the room. He looked over to the plate of fried flesh and meat. "Oh yes! Dinner!" Paul picked up the serving forks and placed several strips onto Brenda's plate. Then his own. He pulled the linen napkin from beside his plate and laid it across his lap. He reached down, picked up the carefully placed fork and knife, and sliced off a small portion of the still-sizzling meat on his place. Brenda watched in horror as he took the speared bit on his fork and put it in his mouth. Paul savored the morsel he was now chewing in his lipless mouth.

"Oh man, that is good. You should dig in before I gobble this all up for myself," Paul said with a wet chuckle.

Brenda responded by retching and heaving the contents of her stomach onto the tile floor.

Paul looked at her curiously, as best he could without eyebrows anyway, then exclaimed as though he had solved a great mystery.

"Ketchup. I forgot ketchup, didn't I?" Paul asked with a mouth partially full. "I know how much you love your ketchup, sweetie, but you must try it."

Brenda heaved again, but she had nothing left to give. After a few steadying breaths, she lifted her head, and her face went pale in horror as Paul reached across the table with a piece of his fried facial tissue on the tip of his fork. He tried to make the same *Choo-choo* noise for the kids when challenging them at the dinner table.

Brenda realized through the fog of terror that she hadn't heard them cry or call out. Even as Paul tied her down and began cutting his face away with a carving blade, they never made a noise.

"Oh god, the children. Paul, what did you do with the children?" Brenda sobbed while trying to avoid Paul's offering.

"The kids?" Paul tried to remember. Brenda saw as he searched his memory, and another fat tear rolled down his bloody face. "Oh, yes! They went to stay with Marcus. They were so kind to take them off our hands for tonight. Isn't that sweet? They said they wanted to show the children their gardens and collection of pets." Brenda began crying anew. Paul reached up and gently caressed her swollen cheek, reddened by tears and covered in spoiled makeup. "Now you really must eat. Otherwise, you can't have dessert, my love."

Paul took Brenda's cheeks in his hand and pried her mouth open. She screamed and tried to fight his grip as he forced the forkful of flesh into her mouth. "Yes, that's it. Eat up, my sweet. Eat. It. Up."

Judge Marcus slowly opened his eyes from the dinner scene that had been playing before him. Paul had his instructions, and thanks to the curse Judge placed upon him, the dimwitted man would follow them without fail. He didn't have to check on Paul's progress, but he really and truly enjoyed how practical the spell was. Judge rarely had time to enjoy his work these days. He enjoyed viewing the suffering of his victims through their eyes. He was able to feel their fear and pain. For Judge, this was his aphrodisiac.

Judge used magic most often in service of more extraordinary beings these days. He had to conserve his strength to appease them. However, his time with Paul and Brenda was a rare blessing. He thought of checking in on the children's status but decided not to run the chance of using too much of his energy on such trivial matters.

He sat at the long dining room table within his church. His Forgotten Church. A large fireplace lit the room in a dancing glow. The bone-white granite that comprised the mantel detailed the denizens and beasts that lived just beyond the Veil. Judge fantasized about the world he could create with their power.

Oh! What a world it would be! Judge mused. He envisioned the gifts bestowed upon him and how he would remake everything. This world would have the chaos it deserved. Judge fantasized about the gifts he would receive and convey to those left under his rule. Pain and pleasure were enough for everyone, and it wouldn't matter how much wealth or political clout one would have amassed.

What lengths would people go to, and to what depths would they sink, to avoid being cattle to those who, even now, clawed at our reality? Judge smiled as he projected his thoughts onto those waiting outside our plane. The Veil was thin here, and he could communicate with the Formoria.

"Can you hear their screams, feel their pain?" Judge asked as he shared his vision of the world to come. "...their pain, their tender flesh, their madness, it all will be yours."

He could feel them salivate in his mind. Their desire ran down his spine and gripped his groin. They were pleased with his vision and sent him their approval with promises of knowledge and power. He felt their energies fill his muscles and give him vigor.

"Thanks be to the Ancient Ones! Praise the Old Gods!" Judge screamed gleefully as he tore off his clothes. He walked and stood before the altar of Yog-Sothoth. Judge placed his hands on the table to pay his tribute. A tribute in blood and pain and shame. "I give to you my suffering and humble myself before you. Please bless me with your power and wisdom."

Judge grabbed the ceremonial blade at the foot of the alter and began carving the sacred testament of the Elder God onto his bare chest.

Judge spent most of his life finding ways to please his masters. He initially fed them his pain, cutting and bleeding for them in his rituals. Then he discovered that he could give them more and receive in kind if he provided the lives of other creatures.

His first attempts met with disapproval and severe punishment. He learned that they required not just flesh and blood but intellect. He was taught harshly with his first sacrifice, a neighbor's cat, with months of agony and visions of the horrors that awaited him if he didn't atone for his insult.

Judge's next lesson also ended painfully when he killed a homeless man pickled on cheap booze. They ate the man's corpse and unceremoniously vomited it back onto him. His punishment lasted for months of nightmares and sores across his back.

Finally, he gave them what they wanted. He was attractive, and it took little effort to seduce a weak-willed classmate. She gave in to his gifts of drink, drugs, and promises of pleasures and everlasting love. He led her out into the woods to a cave he had discovered. It was his church, his holy ground, a place for him to escape his boring life in suburbia. He showed her his special place, plied her with drink and hypnotics, gently subdued her, and let her believe she was safe.

When she awoke, Judge listened and absorbed her fear and screams. He performed the ritual he had cast many times before and watched his studies finally pay off. He saw the Veil thin around the girl and watched as the Formoria reached through and devoured their prey, both body and mind.

They gave him his first reward. Knowledge. They spoke the words to the prayers and rituals he would need in his mind. They laid at his feet in his piss and the girl's blood, the circle he would need to maintain a doorway through which he could feed them more, and they, in turn, would reward him with their gifts. He provided his enemies to them first. A mutual pleasure for sure. No more school bullies, interloping teachers, or truant officers. It wasn't long before he fed his mother and father to the beasts.

These people didn't matter to him. They were his currency, nothing more. Their pain, screams, flesh, and blood brought him new strength. He learned their language but lacked the tongues to speak it. He discovered the truth of their imprisonment and how to open a doorway large enough to let Formoria enter his world and reign over the children of The First Tribe.

They were weak now, they explained. They were greedy and selfish and lost their old ways. Those spells that used to bind, hurt, or even kill them were weak. Very few owned those gifts. Very few were like Judge, who had the will to stop them.

Judge was ripped from his reverie by the entrance of Maria and their sons. His two sons, Thaddeus and Gerald, followed their mother, dressed in a black silk robe and nothing else as far as he could tell. From where he stood, he could smell her perfume of sweat and sex from across the room.

Maria's long black hair fell about her shoulders and the front of her chest. She had been working diligently, speaking to those on the other side of the Veil. The masters there had gifted her with the ability of possession and sight. Her body was the perfect vessel to funnel Formoria from beyond the Veil, and so long as she was in the scrying room, she could see through their senses.

Judge admired her beauty and power but hated it because it distracted him. He wanted all that power she had for himself. She was a cleric of their faith and served their mutual masters. She may have had the sight but didn't have his vision or knowledge. Despite this, he often wondered if they favored her more than him. The thought stoked fires of rage deep inside of him.

Judge could create bodies for the Former to inhabit. He knew spells and rituals to torment and kill, and those he worshipped bestowed the strength of ten men upon him. He had all this, but he wanted more. Judge often fantasized about killing his beautiful wife and stealing her power, but she was protected. If the gods beyond the Veil favored her and Judge allowed or caused harm to her, the Gods would punish him most severely.

Maria had the grace of an apex predator. She was nearly the same age as Judge Marcus, but she used her alchemy and spells to preserve her beauty. Judge noticed the sheen of her skin, voluptuous lips, and breasts and determined that Maria had recently applied these arts. Her hair was a short pixie cut today, which she often changed in style and color when it suited her mood.

Maria always walked with an air of superiority. Being chosen to be the cleric of the Formoria, and gifted with divine energies from their gods, constantly bolstered her confidence. She never doubted or envied. He hated this about her. She has no obedience to her husband, just her faith. He should be the one she worshipped.

As if sensing his malice just now, Maria stopped at the head of the table opposite Judge and looked coolly at him. The corner of her mouth curled with amusement and daring. She waited, staring hard at him, and taunting him. Behind Maria, a monstrous being obediently shuffled up to help her to her seat. Gerald was their second child and a gift from the Old Gods. He was also a constant reminder of Judge's inability to provide Maria with a strong child.

"Such a good boy, so beautiful. Now go and sit by your father."

He purred and moaned as she stroked him gently. Gerald was a lumbering and clumsy being. He would stand over seven feet tall if he could, but his spine was as bent and as twisted as his mind. The bony processes were visible from behind. The protrusions jutted out to the point that they might push their way through the flesh of his mighty back. A prominent hump bulged, swallowing his right shoulder and some of his neck and face.

Gerald's filthy skin was mottled with grey, brown, and white patches. His skin color was indeterminant due to the filth covering his body. Large, blood-bearing vessels could be seen throughout his exposed back and torso. The arteries pulsed, and when he became excited, they thickened and engorged to the point they appeared as if they might explode. He wore no shirt, he never needed to since he was not permitted outside the church. Tonight, he was primarily nude, with only a loin cloth, which barely covered his oversized and useless genitals.

He shuffled to his seat, his large pink eyes fixed on Judge. Drool poured from his mouth and ran down off of his jutting mandible. He licked the row of yellow teeth with his thick tongue nervously. As he pulled his chair away from the table, Judge growled at him. Judge often regretted praying to the Old Gods for this child.

The Formoria inseminated Maria, and along with Judge's contributions, she became pregnant. A full ten months went by before she gave birth. The delivery had to be without the support of pain control or outsiders. The Formoria desired Maria's pain, the blood, the afterbirth, and her screams.

Maria barely survived the ordeal. It took Judge's considerable resources and power to keep her alive. The child was powerful. Judge could sense this, but he was repulsive and nearly cost him a valuable asset in Maria. Judge still had to admit, Gerald was an improvement over Thaddeus, their first natural-born son.

Thaddeus was beautiful. He was brilliant and without any physical flaws. What Gerald lacked in his appearance and intellect, Thaddeus was gifted five-fold. What Thaddeus lacked was access to the Formoria and their gifts. Of all the flaws that could offend Judge, this was worse than any deformity Gerald possessed.

Thaddeus had barely entered the room, still standing at the entrance to the dining hall. He tapped furiously on his cell phone, texting those who worked for him and his family. Judge growled at the occasional ping that indicated a reply. The rest of the family became collectively frustrated as they could not proceed with their meal until he sat.

Finally, Judge slammed his fist on the table with enough force to shake the glasses and dinnerware. Thaddeus jumped at the explosive power of Judge's fist upon the thick oaken table. He quickly moved to sit between his parents. As he did so, he felt Judge and Maria's gaze fall upon him. Their withering glares caused Thaddeus to avert his gaze from the phone to the floor.

It didn't matter to them that Thaddeus could swoon a nun, intimidate anyone of any size with a look, and was an efficient killer. To them, he was just so fucking ordinary. However, this didn't keep Thaddeus from trying, and his parents enjoyed watching him suffer for his efforts.

From across the table, Gerald stared hungrily at Thaddeus. Thaddeus returned his look with one of boredom. "Now, boys, let's enjoy this time as a family," Maria said. "...and offer thanks for the blessings of The Veil.

"Food?" Gerald blurted out, drooling. He sniffed the air hungrily.

"The boy is right. I haven't all the time in the world," Judge said. "Bring us some goddamn dinner!" he roared, slamming his fist into the thick wooden table again. Off to the side, Gerald whimpered.

"Oh now, now, my dear boy," Maria cooed. "You know your father gets a little cranky if he hasn't eaten."

Gerald calmed at the sound of his mother's voice and shifted his focus to playing with his loincloth.

The servant's entrance to the kitchen opened, and a serving cart rolled in, pushed along by two young women. Three more servants followed them. The serving girls were recent acquisitions from Judge's contact in Hong Kong. They were bought fresh from the docks.

Each woman was young and made blind and muted with stitches to seal their eyelids and lips. The Judge branded them with two marks. One brand was the family crest, and the second was a Formorian sigil that would alert Judge and Maria if any girls tried to flee. Not that they would get far, blinded as they were.

Judge had them cleaned and vaccinated. Maria had their uniforms tailor-made, made sure they were kept fed, and even sewed their eyes shut herself. She kept the youngest and prettiest servant as her plaything and handmaiden. At the end of each day, the servants were led downstairs to the cellar and chained inside a single cage, barely big enough to accommodate all five.

It took a week of training. Thaddeus had the pleasure of using brutality as his teaching instrument. He hurt them when they tripped, spilled, or got hurt by anything other than himself. The pain stopped if they were perfect at completing their duties. They all suffered if there was even the slightest mistake by one. He prodded them where to go, where to wait to be called, and when and where to rest. Thaddeus instructed them where to evacuate their bowels or make water, which was close to where they ate.

Judge was pleased with this purchase and told himself that he would have to get more soon. Thaddeus had trained them well enough, and such activities tended to keep the boy out of sight as well. A win-win in Judge's book.

The servants maneuvered around the dining cart and moved several plates with roasted vegetables, bowls of soup, and bread. Gerald seemed uninterested in anything they put before him but eyed the covered serving platter on the top of the dolly. One servant removed the large silver topper by its handle to expose a large cut of meat beneath. The meat sizzled in its juices, crowned with roasted tomatoes and baby potatoes garnished with sliced pears.

One servant began slicing thick strips of the meat and placing them on a plate. Another servant grabbed the dish and served the course, starting with Judge. Gerald was the last to receive his meal, and by the time the server got to him with a plate, he was foaming at the mouth. The plate barely touched the table before Gerald, forgoing utensils, snatched up the cut of meat and tore it into it voraciously. The servant hadn't made it back to the serving cart before he was calling for more, holding his hand out whimpering like a child.

"Now, Gerald, you really must eat your vegetables first before asking for seconds," Maria said sternly.

"Yes. At least eat the bread," Judge said, as he cut into his meaty offerings.

Gerald began to growl, "I want more meat."

"No," Judge said simply and then pointed at his plate of vegetables. Gerald looked at the assortment of tubular vegetables and peppers in disgust. It was a look that didn't improve his appearance at all. He growled and dropped his plate of carrots and peppers onto the floor.

"Meat." His voice took a menacing tone.

The Judge stopped cutting into a potato and looked up at Gerald. A servant moved to remove the plate and food from the floor. They held each other's gaze as she did so, and as she began to retreat to withdraw the discarded food, Gerald snatched her wrist, causing her to drop the plate of food. She let out a muffled yelp in surprise, which then turned into a scream of terror as Gerald bit down hard on her hand.

The mutilated servant tried to pull away, but his grip was too firm, so strong that her bones began cracking in his grasp. The terrified and pained wailing of the servant increased in pitch. The others also began sobbing and whimpering. With a snap, Gerald bit off the index and middle finger. Blood spurted and splashed across his face and lap. His gaze remained fixed on Judge the whole time it took to perform this action.

Judge responded to the challenge with his fury. He stood quickly, walked over to the fireplace, and pulled from it a poker. The tip was glowing orange and yellow from absorbing so much heat from the flames. "Release her now, goddamn it!" Judge roared. Thaddeus turned to regard his father and the scene with great interest. He couldn't decide whether he wanted to watch his father beat Gerald with the white-hot poker or witness Gerald tear the old man's throat out.

Judge began slamming the poker down onto Gerald's back. Each strike issued a sizzle from his bare flesh and a howl of pain from Gerald. Gerald threw the servant girl to the floor. She hit the stone floor hard, still screaming and clutching her bloodied hand. The other servants did not move as they were trained to do in this situation.

Judge had struck at least ten times, occasionally catching a chunk of fat, pulling it away from Gerald's back or flanks, and sending it to the floor. Gerald fell from the table, covering his head and face as he crawled into the corner. He screamed, cried, and curled up into a ball as Judge walked after him, beating him with every step.

"Enough!" Maria's voice boomed throughout the dining hall. Her voice echoed off the stone bricks and mortar. Judge stopped his assault, and the poker raised high above his head. After a moment, he collected himself, took a deep breath, and turned to Thaddeus.

"You, stop grinning like a fucking idiot and get the girl. Take care of her," Judge commanded.

"Me? What the fuck? I didn't make the mess. Have that disgusting abomination clean up his mess for a change!" Thaddeus exclaimed.

Judge's eyes lit with fury once again. "I wonder how well you would fare to a poker across your back, boy," Judge threatened through clenched teeth, his voice guttural.

Thaddeus shook his head, stood up, and approached the servant. She was still lying on the floor, clutching her hand and moaning in pain. He reached down, grabbed her pressed shirt and tie, and dragged her from the room. New muffled screams came from the girl and continued as Thaddeus moved her into the kitchen.

The patriarch stared at the matriarch as though they were participating in a stand-off. The screams in the kitchen ended abruptly, the silence now intensifying the tension in the dining room. There was the sound of something heavy thrown into a large garbage can in the corner of the kitchen. Then, nothing. Just the sound of Judge's breathing, Gerald's weeping, and the fire crackling.

Thaddeus returned to the room, covered from head to toe in bright red blood. Judge scoffed at Thaddeus. Thaddeus shrugged both helplessly and unapologetically.

Judge shook his head. "Get out of my sight. Go upstairs and get cleaned up," Judge said, his voice shaky with anger. "I don't want to look at you for the rest of the night."

Thaddeus rolled his eyes and stormed across the room. As he reached the door, Judge yelled into his back. "Meet me in the surgical theater at first light. We will work on your piss-poor incisions." Thaddeus smiled somewhat at this but dared not let it show. He left the room and let the door slam shut behind him.

The remaining servants cleared the table. Judge replaced the fire poker and sat down. He picked up the napkin by his plate and wiped his brow. Gerald still lay in the corner of the room, sobbing like a child. Maria took a drink of wine and looked over at Judge. Her silk robe had fallen open when she spoke, but she did not notice or care. She looked over the top of her glass at Judge.

Judge looked back at her. She nodded to Gerald as if to say, "*Deal with the crying child.*" Judge scoffed and looked away. Maria gently put her wine glass down and sat forward in her chair. Her eyes, which generally seemed to hold a *come hither* look about them, flared in anger. Judge looked at her as she bore her look into his skin. He felt her mind in his. She projected her intent and her anger into his mind. Judge winced in pain from this.

"Fine!" he hissed at her. Her anger cooled at this, and her stare calmed as she turned toward Gerald. The corner of her lip curled upward, and "*Good boy*" slipped into Judge's mind. He rolled his eyes, walked over to Gerald, and knelt beside him. Judge reached up and put his hand on Gerald's shoulder. The monstrous man winced at the touch and began sobbing loudly. "Oh, come now," Judge said, trying to soften his tone and sound caring. "This was unfortunate. Let's see what we can do to make it right, shall we?" Judge stood up and thought about it. Gerald continued to cry, but now Judge could see his sobbing started sounding a little forced.

"Oh, what shall we ever do, Maria?" He feigned to be at a loss. She shrugged her shoulders and smiled sweetly at Gerald, who was now peeking through his fingers to look at her. She giggled a little. "Well, I guess we have nothing to eat with dinner ruined." Judge exaggerated his pain and sorrow. He heard Gerald chuckle as Maria made a silly, weepy face at him.

"My dear Maria, did our staff not make a lovely German chocolate cake this evening?" Judge asked.

"Why yes, dear, I do believe they did!" she replied, eyes wide with excitement as she looked at Gerald. The lumbering man's large head popped up.

"Cake?" he said excitedly, now drooling with anticipation. He began moving his massive bulk about like an animal, hooting and yelping joyfully. "Ice cream?" he stopped and asked, kneeling before Judge. Eyes pleading. Judge looked down at the creature. He hated this thing and the games he had to play to keep his family happy. Judge wanted to be free of this and return to his work. He wanted to reshape the world, not play father to his two failures and his wife's passions and desires. On the outside, he smiled and went along with it for now. Soon. So soon.

"Oh ok, fine," Judge said with resignation. Gerald began to dance and clap his hands. "I guess I do spoil you all," he said with a smile to his wife. Judge wondered what kind of noise they would make under his knife. Then, as he looked at Gerald, who now held his mother around her naked waist, he thought he might need a chainsaw, too.

-CHAPTER 10-
REVELATIONS

George, Robbie, and Sicily sat in silence around a firepit. After they washed the blood from their faces and exposed skin, they attended the critical incident debriefing concerning the Steiner family murder-suicide. The "hotwash," as they called it, was a review of the call and how the officers and EMS felt it went.

Robbie was a mess. It was his first time seeing something this bad; murdered children, suicide, mutilation. Hell, no one in that meeting had ever seen anything like that. Hardened by her time in Chicago, Sicily had dealt with gun violence, domestic disputes, drug possession, and the usual crimes. Nothing as weird as this. She tried to play it cool, but the tap-tap-tapping of her foot on the floor said otherwise. George was the only one impassive through it all.

George shared what had happened to him at the factory. He spoke of the murder he witnessed, his injuries, and Mickey. He talked about all the weird things and described them in detail. The only thing he kept to himself was his "advanced warning system." He didn't know how to explain it, and it wasn't something he entirely relied on anyway.

After he shared his story, he waited. The silence was killing him. He wanted to be free of the burden of this secret, but now he had to wait for the fallout. He was concerned about how either officer would accept his tale. So, he sat and waited and drank his beer.

Robbie sat with a beer and stroked the top of his head. He looked as though he was trying to massage his brain or something. Sicily's eyes reflected the light of the fire. She looked at George and finally spoke. George braced himself.

"I saw a girl once back home…no one knew what was wrong with her. She was only seven or eight," she began. "Her mom called us because she was suddenly acting violent and cussing and spitting," said Sicily. "Without provocation, she allegedly took a pair of nose hair scissors and nailed her mom's hand to the dinner table." She paused as the scene came into focus in her memory. "When we arrived, the girl locked herself in her room. She had moved every bit of furniture and barricaded the door. She had broken the glass from the apartment window and started cutting herself up." George could see Sicily's eyes begin to glisten. "By the time we got in the room, which took maybe two or three minutes, she had over fifty cuts all across her body."

"And?" Robbie prodded.

Sicily paused and took a deep breath. "Come to find out, she had been molested by a priest at her Catholic school." A tear scurried down Sicily's cheek. "I rode in the back of the ambulance with her and watched her fight and scream the whole way. She broke the medic's nose. The fucked-up part, aside from the priest shit, was at some point, I swear she began levitating off that gurney."

Robbie looked at her, his expression even more confused than ever.

"Levitating?" Robbie asked still in obvious confusion.

Sicily looked at him, slightly exasperated. "I'm just saying that here we had this sweet, innocent girl. She came into the world good and wanted nothing but to play and feel loved," her voice cracked a bit, and Sicily swallowed hard, fighting the tears, she blinked away the pain and donned a mask of rage. "Whatever was wrong with that little girl, that fucking priest put it into her."

"What happened to the girl? The priest?" Robbie continued to inquire solemnly.

"Fuck if I know. I never heard about her after that. The church did its church thing and removed the priest from that parish. Relocated his sick ass." Sicily looked away and took a long drink of her beer. "I don't know if I understand or buy everything you said, George. I think this whole town is sick, though. Mom keeps saying it wasn't always like this. I think someone put that sickness in this place."

"Fair statement," George replied. He looked over at Robbie.

"What? I don't know, man. I have never seen some shit like I did tonight," he started. "Do I think this is the work of demons or some weird fucking cult? I just don't know." Robbie rubbed his face with his hands.

It hurts to see Robbie like this, George thought. Part of him wanted to keep the rookie innocent just a little longer. All in a single night, the young cop seemed to age nearly half a decade.

"I don't know what you guys need from me, but I'm here. I'll do what needs to get done," Robbie said. "Just don't be surprised if I puke again," he said with a sad chuckle.

Sicily patted him on his shoulder and gave a heartfelt laugh. "Seriously, boy, how much did you eat?"

All three laughed at that.

"What!? I'm trying to bulk up!" Robbie tried to recover, but he knew he was in trouble now.

"Bulk up? You trying to look like George over there?" Sicily said with her evil smirk.

"What the fuck, Manns?" George retorted, looking down at his belly. "I earned this."

"See, Robbie! You gotta be a dad before you get the dad bod." Sicily roared as George and Robbie flipped her the bird.

George was glad to hear them laughing and busting each other's balls again. It sounded like hope to him. He knew the humor was a coping mechanism, but it felt normal. Normal was needed.

"So, what now, Sarge?" Sicily asked. "We just go on and do what with this?"

"Not sure yet. Maybe it's time we start looking into it deeper. Ask questions," George said. "I do know one thing. This town has always been weird, but ever since the Marcus family moved in, it sure as hell keeps getting stranger."

"I can check out what local dealings they've had, changes they've made," Sicily said, her tone changed, getting down to business.

"I can look at the history of the town. My dad is a fan of the local legends," Robbie added.

"Sounds good, Robbie," said George. "Focus on the occult and weird stuff. I think there's something there."

"Sir," Robbie said, suddenly serious. George looked at him, surprised by his tone.

"What's up?" asked George.

"It's Robert, sir. I always hated Robbie," Robbie said. George looked hard at him, his eyes narrowed. Robert didn't look away, didn't blink.

"How about this, Robert? You quit with all the 'sir' this or 'sir' that, and I'll work on calling you Robert. Maybe just Holts, even. I've always liked Rook. If you want me to call you Robert, that's what I'll do. And you can call me Sarge or George, but if you call me 'sir' again, I'll pistol whip you. Copy?" George asked, his eyes never leaving Robert.

"Yes, S—sarge," Robert said, blushing as he almost earned that pistol-whipping. He smiled and looked at Sicily, silently asking the same of her. She looked as though she was considering it. As if to change the subject and brush off the request, she looked over at George.

"What are you going to do?" Sicily asked.

George considered her for a moment. "I'm going to look over a few unsolved cases. The disappearances mostly. Maybe I'll find a pattern," he said. "If anything comes up on your end, give me a call."

Both officers nodded in agreement and started gathering their things. It was time to go to work, maybe not at the station, but certainly in this case.

"Hey, both of you." As they were about to leave, George spoke up. "Be discreet, watch each other's backs, and stay safe, yeah?"

They nodded in agreement and, in unison, replied, "You too."

-CHAPTER 11-
THE CALL

After dealing with Ronald Teach and his clients, everyone got into Vincent's car and agreed they needed to decompress. The drive was quiet, even Vincent lacked his usual quips. Phineas stared out the window, vacantly looking into the shadows. Mata tapped him on the shoulder and looked at him with concern. Phineas attempted a smile and signed the word *"tired."*

When Phineas and the crew arrived at Mata's teashop, he walked past the bar to the manager's office. Vincent walked behind the bar, scooped some tea into a strainer, and poured hot water into a cup. Mata was doing the same, but for two. Lizzie curled up on her dog bed behind the bar. Vincent began scribbling answers into the book, oblivious to a growing look of frustration spreading across Mata's face.

After a few minutes of intense puzzle-solving, Vincent felt a slap on his shoulder. He looked up, more startled than he wanted to appear, at the fierce gaze of Mata. She slid his teacup in front of him.

"What's up with Finn?" she signed. She noted Vincent's blank stare and narrowed her eyes in frustration.

"Mata, sweetie, I don't know sign language. Why do you do this to me?" Vincent asked irritably.

Mata responded with a light slap to his forehead.

Vincent winced. "Ow, dammit, Mata! What?"

She gestured to the office, where a brooding Phineas went.

"Oh, Finn? I don't know, maybe that last gig was rough on him. You know how he gets with moms and kids cases," Vincent said, hoping not to elicit another slap from the heavy-handed tea tender. "He gets moody every now and then, ya know."

Mata's bottom lip curled up in exasperation, and she stared at the man.

Vincent shrugged helplessly and held up his hands to guard against the next slap.

Mata rolled her eyes and grabbed the two cups of tea on the bar.

Phineas hunched over the bathroom sink. He breathed deeply and exhaled slowly. Phineas splashed cold water on his face hoping that the shock would get him out of his head and ground him in the present. The wailing spirits of the dead he was used to and fighting his need to drink was not new, either. No, tonight he struggled with the past. Maybe it was seeing that ghosts of that little girl and her mom reunited. Perhaps it was all the abuse and suffering they endured. Phineas hadn't thought about his hometown of Haven Shire in so long. So why now?

He could feel his guts churn, and his chest felt on fire. He had this feeling before. He named it *The thing with teeth* because it felt like some beast was gnawing at him from inside his torso. He felt on edge, and embers of rage popped to life. He reran cold water, aware suddenly that his breath had quickened. As he came back up, he took another deep breath. He could smell leather now, hints of sweat and steam. Then there were mint, lavender, vanilla, and cinnamon scents in the air.

"Hey, Mata," Phineas said with a relaxed tone. "That for me?" he asked, eyeing the tea. She knew him well, and when he seemed low, she would make him a lavender and mint tea. The vanilla and cinnamon of her lotion was a strange mix for the leather she wore, but for Phineas, it worked. She was always a calming presence for him. She handed him the tea, and he raised his cup in a salute to her.

"What's got you down, Finn?" Mata said in sign as she sat at the desk across the cot. Phineas grimaced at the nickname. It brought back more memories. George, his dad, and his mother. His poor, sad, dead mother. He shook the image and tried to muster a smile.

"Nothing," he attempted, but Mata quickly shot him down with a look. Phineas let out a deep, resigned sigh. "I've been thinking about home lately. Thinking about my mom."

"You never speak of that stuff. What brought this on?" Mata asked, her face softening. *"Was it the client?"*

"Not sure," he replied with a shrug. "Maybe I need to get outta my head for a bit and do something fun," he said more positively.

"You can come to the gym with me!" Mata signed excitedly. She put on a predatory grin and looked at him playfully.

"I said fun, not punishment," Phineas replied, returning his evil smile. Mata playfully slapped his leg and shot her middle finger. She rose with a smile.

"We run at five o'clock, all the way to the gym. No breaks," Mata signed with authority.

Phineas knew he couldn't escape this. He let out another sigh. *"Yay! Sounds great,"* he signed back, wondering if there was sarcasm in sign language.

Mata looked at him, and her expression transitioned from her severe and authoritative look to a sweet smile and back to a visage of caring and concern. Phineas caught the look and smiled and waved her away dismissively. She left the room, and now it was just Phineas alone on the cot. He considered why he might be feeling blue.

Since he could not pinpoint it, he shook his head and decided it may have been this last job. After all, the ghosts attacked any weakness in his defenses. The battle may have exposed a feeling, like a raw nerve from an old injury. He laid down on the cot and began to rest his weary mind and spirit. He then looked over at the clock. The blinking digital numerals repeated one o'clock AM.

He shot up. "Fuck! It's one o'clock?" He considered his deal with Mata about going to the fight gym in four hours, not driving but running the five miles to get there. He fell back into the cot with a groan. Well, so much for rest. Despite his protests and the knowledge that he would be sore all week, he looked forward to working out with Mata. "This is going to hurt," he whispered to himself, and then he quickly fell asleep.

All around him was fire and ash, the air thick with it. The trees were twisted black skeletons, still smoking and crackling. Embers floated in the air, and Phineas found it hard to breathe. He could taste it in his mouth. He looked and saw several piles on fire. There was the odor of burning wood, plastic, rubber, and flesh.

He tried to determine his location, but the smoke stung his eyes and made it hard to see. He tripped on a stone, maybe a root, and fell on his hands and knees. When he opened his eyes, he stared into the sightless face of a human skull. Looking behind him, he saw the exposed tibia and fibula, another skeleton, or maybe the same one, he couldn't tell.

He stood up and tried to make out some landmark, a star in the sky, or a body of water. He turned to the sharp, repetitive sounds of something moving through the mud. Then he heard singing. It sounded like hymns. He started making out figures walking in a march through the smoke. They looked like mourners, all dressed in black, faces shrouded in lace or dark hats.

They numbered in the hundreds. Phineas could see them more clearly now. In the middle of the marching congregation was a large black coach. Lanterns hung from each corner. They swayed to and fro, in rhythm with the parade's march and aglow with a sickly green flame. Each parishioner carried a lantern in their hand with that same pale-green light. Some held the lantern while comforting a child, holding a loved one, or supporting the infirm.

Each parishioner sang their prayers in low somber notes. Leading the caravan was a preacher, or Phineas assumed he was, shouting from a large leatherbound book. His proclamations and prayers brimmed with fury and warnings for those who did not heed his words. He raged and frothed at the mouth and commanded those within range of his voice to repent for their sins.

The preacher's white hair flowed wildly from beneath his hat. He looked up at Phineas, his eyes wild and fierce, as he screamed quotes and parables from a bible. None of the stories sounded familiar to Phineas, but it prophesized that the "The Former," those who lived before, would return to this land, spelling the demise of all that lived on the planet. His teeth gnashed and gnawed on each word.

"You sinner!" he said to Phineas and quickened his pace to get closer to him. "Your misdeeds and ignorance are what brought the Formoria here. They who lived before having been awakened, and now they hunger after their long slumber. Are you prepared to offer up your soul? Your sanity? Or will you choose to be a slave to their perversion?"

"Lived here before? Before what?" Phineas asked, confused. "What the fuck are you talking about, old man?"

The preacher spat on the ground. "I speak of that!" he screamed as he pointed toward the horizon. Phineas suddenly realized he was on a large hill, almost a mountain, and in the valley below lay the ruins of a town. It seemed familiar, but he couldn't place it.

On the hill beyond that stood four obelisks. They surrounded a compound or church. The structure appeared Byzantine in design. In the gloom of smoke and ash, he saw that the walls were black and trimmed in gold— the sides of the mansion illuminated by bonfires, which rose almost as high as the building itself. There was no logic in the building's design. It seemed as though it rebelled against the typical architectural ideas of any building Phineas had ever seen.

One side of the structure ended with a tower. This tower rose, only to birth another tower, like some tumor from the side of the tower's face. Each tower pointed inward with a golden spear growing long and coming to a needlepoint. From another side of the building erupted a dome. The roof had an eye-like design hand painted in gold and red with various runes and hieroglyphs. In no order, spikes rose from the crown. Phineas could make out shapes, maybe human, impaled upon them. They writhed and twitched violently.

"Listen, boy! Do you hear them?"

Phineas tuned his hearing to listen for anything unusual. From a distance, he heard screams. Hundreds of people were screaming. They seemed to be coming from all around the hateful black compound.

"What is that?" Phineas asked, revolted by everything he witnessed.

The preacher laughed hard. He was close now, and Phineas could smell his awful, hot breath. This man hadn't bathed in a long while, either. Phineas could tell the preacher had tried to cover his odor with spices or herbs, but it just made him smell worse, like trying to hide the shit smell of the toilet with a cinnamon-scented spray. It still stinks and is now worse because you want to smell the pleasant scent only to catch the hints of feces.

"That boy, is the Forgotten Church," the preacher said after catching his breath, only to fall into a fit of hacking coughs. He coughed up something thick and spat it on the muddy, ashy dirt. "The cult of the Old Gods rebuilt it. Now we are all properly fucked."

Suddenly Phineas heard a tearing sound in the sky. He saw the thick quilt of clouds begin to swirl above the obelisks. Green lightning lit up the sky so brightly that he had to shield his eyes.

Then came that tearing sound again, this time louder, so much so that Phineas gritted his teeth and stopped his ears with his hands. He could feel the vibrations of the sound and its echoes across his skin. He also felt them in his head. It seemed as though this was all true insanity. Absolute chaos.

The air became foul with the scent of decay and waste. The stench of it was so thick that Phineas could taste it in his mouth, feel it coat his skin, penetrate him, and he felt spoiled by its foulness. He doubled over and vomited violently. He tried to catch his breath and gasped in horror as he saw worms and maggots mixed in his vomit. They twisted and churned, some sought refuge in the nearby soil, and others seemed content in the filth.

"Taste that, boy? Taste that corruption? That's what is in store for the whole world now," the preacher cackled. "It gets inside of you and lays its eggs. Soon, you will be mad, or worse, you'll change into one of them!" He pointed to the funnel cloud above the four black daggers pointed to the sky. Phineas tried to accept what he was seeing. The funnel cloud was at least five miles in diameter.

Within the swirling chaos, eldritch lightning bolts fired. The clouds barely concealed their brightness. Another thunderous tearing sound erupted. He looked around and tried to find the source. In the distance, he saw the clouds moving as something monstrous moved within that Veil. It was like watching a giant serpent moving in water as it approached the funneling cumulus above the church.

The parade of mourners began screaming as they looked to the sky in disbelief. Some clawed at their Veils and revealed their pale and cracked skin beneath. Some threw themselves onto the ground, holding their hands up high, begging and pleading for it to stop. Others just started running, no destination that Phineas could see, just away from this inconceivable and beguiling dread.

The eye of the storm opened. Red light bathed the black church. The light turned everything it touched into the color of blood. The screams were pained and desperate before they turned into maddening cries and pleas. From the red eye of the clouds, a form oozed down toward the church and all those screaming below. A mishappen mass of flesh uncoiled from within the darkened sky and floated down in a serpentine path toward the collective wailing.

Phineas tried to cover his mouth and nose but was desperate to breathe. He fell to his knees, his gaze never leaving the thing erupting from the hole in the sky. The massive abomination slithered down and peered, at least it seemed to, at the four spires and the church. The tip of the snaking split open, revealing a maw large enough to devour the hillside and surrounding landscape.

The alien creature had skin, black and slimy, covered in warty bulbs. Not bulbs, he realized. Eyes.

The iris was hateful, and the pupil pitch black and thin, like an octopus. Then another bulb burst open, exposing a mouth filled with jagged yellow teeth. The maw opened, and six long, almost human appendages thrust out. The undulating, hulking worm was constantly changing, seemingly unable to maintain a single form for long.

Phineas gasped for air as he realized he had been holding his breath. He immediately regretted it and coughed and gagged. The preacher laughed beside him and likewise coughed and hacked up more phlegm.

Above the hill, the open maw let out a massive scream. The sound made Phineas swoon from the pain. His head swam, and his ears felt as though they were tearing. His brain screamed from the assault of those suffering.

The beast's tongue slithered forth, exposing the monster's true form. The bald head had two milky white pupils, looking from side to side, searching for a meal. Down the body of the fleshy protrusion, another mouth opened. The lips quivered in anticipation. Phineas could feel the joy coming from this thing.

It fed on the suffering and fear of its victims. The mouth opened, and thousands of tentacles erupted and pierced those surrounding the church. The screaming continued as the snake-like appendages drew in those impaled or caught.

The preacher suddenly grabbed him and pulled him to his feet. His hot breath on his face, saliva raining down his cheeks, as he cackled. "Witness what you gave birth to, boy!"

"What the fuck are you talking about!" Phineas screamed through his tears.

"Phineas," a soft voice called from behind him. "It's time to go." He looked over his shoulder. There a woman stood, her hair long and red. Even though there was no breeze, it seemed to sway gently. Her bright green eyes shone, and Phineas felt the fear and chaos of this world melt away. Love and tenderness filled Phineas, a feeling he hadn't allowed himself to feel in so long. He began to weep.

"Mama?"

She smiled so sweetly at him. He remembered that smile. It was the same one she gave as she wrapped him in her arms and let her hair fall around him. He felt the world crumble from behind him as the beast feasted on the morsels that writhed in fear and insanity. He turned and regarded the monster one last time, but his mother caught his chin and averted his gaze away from the horror.

She gently caressed his face and smiled. "Time to go, kiddo." She leaned in and kissed his cheek. Then suddenly, she raised the same hand that gently stroked his cheek and slapped him hard across the face. His eyes danced and sparks filled his vision.

When he opened his eyes again, he was looking into the fear-filled eyes of Mata. She raised her right hand again to deliver another sobering blow. His eyes shot wide open, and he raised his hands in defense. "I'm awake! I'm awake! Jesus fuck Mata!"

He recoiled from her, and when he felt safe, he peered out from behind his hands. She was breathing hard, and her face streaked with tears. She was also in her sleepwear. He crashed in the office of the tea house. Her grandmother's house was a block away. She ran here.

"What are you doing here!" he signed with shaky hands.

"I heard screams coming from here!" Mata replied.

Phineas' face screwed up in confusion.

"I heard like I do with the spirits," she explained. Suddenly fresh tears flowed down her face. Phineas had never seen her this shaken up, even when her grandmother visited her. *"There were so many people crying. So much pain. Then I found you here! You weren't breathing."* She continued, *"I thought you were dying."*

A cold sweat covered Phineas, and his heart felt like it would explode. "I'm ok, Mata, I swear. It was just the most fucked up dream I've ever had, was all."

Mata shook her head, grabbed him roughly by hand, and pulled him to the bathroom. He wasn't sure he was ready to move yet and was surprised at how well his legs worked. She stood him in front of the mirror and threw on the lights. Phineas gasped and stepped back. He was covered in soot, and drawing deep lines down his face were trailing lines of blood. His blood. He touched the gory tears that streamed down his face and the soot on his skin.

Mata looked at him, and her hands covered her mouth, her face a look of horror. Again, Phineas couldn't understand her reaction. He chuckled a little at the insanity of it all. She turned quickly and grabbed a hand mirror she kept in a drawer. She put it before his face and pointed to the mirror behind him. He looked into the reflection and once again gasped in horror. On his back, there were two words written in blood-

COME HOME

-CHAPTER 12-
THE PENITENT MAN

Vincent lay in his California king bed. He spent an entire day picking out the right mattress and evaluated each for twenty minutes. He practiced the positions he would lay, saw how the bed retained heat, and read each review. This foam mattress was a bitch to move into his house. It felt like the damn thing weighed almost four hundred pounds. It made Vincent sweat watching Mata and the movers squeeze it in. For as much time he spent thinking about the mattress and its frame, he agonized twice as long over the bedspreads.

The pillows were easy to match, but he wanted to ensure he felt and looked comfortable. He spent the better part of two weeks before he bought his first two sets, only to return them the next day because they didn't match his wall color. When he couldn't match the wall color, he decided to have the walls painted and then bought six sets of sheets to match. Vincent finally rested on his choice. Literally.

This early morning, however, he couldn't relax. He had tossed and turned all night and now saw a glow on the horizon, announcing the sun's return. He was anxious. It wasn't the last job. He had seen worse in his few years with the "kids." He laughed at that, remembering how young they were when he met them. He reached up and tugged gently on the silver chain around his neck. Clasped around the end of the necklace was a blood-red gem, wrapped in gold and silver with runes etched into the tendrils that held the bauble in place.

"Maybe," he expressed aloud, "I need a new bed. Maybe a new job." He considered these options for a moment. "Nah, new bed. Unless this gig is finally getting to me." He wondered just how long this relationship between the trio would last. He liked Phineas and Mata. He loved them like a little brother and sister, but they were growing and getting better at what they did. He wasn't going anywhere. He sat up and swung his legs over the side of the bed. He bounced a few times, testing the mattress out. How long do these last again?

"Fuck," he groaned. "Here we go again."

Every night he reminded himself that it was indecision that put him in this predicament in the first place. Like some bedtime prayer, Vincent relived the moments that ended his life of wealth and luxury and placed him in the service of one Phineas Thatch.

"Inde-fucking-cision," Vincent whispered into the darkness as the faces of his wives and children pushed forth to the forefront of his memory. Their loving faces, their drowning faces, their looks of shame and heartbreak.

This character flaw clung to Vincent throughout most of his adult life. Indecisive to a fault. Things had to be so, trying to ensure his standards were met. He used these tactics often and applied them to every part of his life. He would tell himself this is why he fell in love with two women. Indecision is why he had two families, two houses, and two lives. He loved both and didn't want to give either up.

It was shitty, no doubt, but he felt it unfair to have met two remarkable women and fallen in love. He had met them almost simultaneously; both gave him everything he needed, and he had money to afford them. He also thought it was so unfair that he had to hurt one of them to live by society's standards. Leave one and possibly be denied access to the children he loved. Just fucking unfair.

"Right on cue," Vincent remarked as he rolled over into his pillow trying to shut out the image of his families floating out into the sea, "…not that I deserve any less."

He thought back to that night. The night he met Mata and Phineas. They saved his life, sanity, and soul, and did so without asking a price. He remembered the pain, the suffering, and the demon. This was his penance after all, wasn't it? To relive his shame and be reminded what waits for him after he dies.

Vincent traveled for a living. He was a scout for professional fighters, and he had an eye for them. Not technique, muscle, or speed- he saw that easily. He could see how much fight they had in them, their character, and their flaws. He could look at boxers and assess which one would have future problems, whether legal, psychological, or physical. He had an internal algorithm determining their potential profits. That's when his true gift would kick in. Negotiation.

Vincent was both loved and hated when working out a fight contract. He always somehow came out on top. Very few times in his life could Vincent not find the angle, make a profit, scam some sucker, or get a better deal. He turned it around with every penny he won and put it into himself. After all, he was his best investment.

Despite having two lives, he never felt the stress. He always felt like he was winning at this game of life. That is, until something came along and wiped all the chess pieces off the board. Katrina. Not another woman, no. A fucking hurricane. His family lived in Louisiana and Mississippi. He happened to be in California when the storm hit. He tried to rush home to get to his family, but which one? Flights into both areas were a nightmare, so he rented a car and drove while calling and trying to contact everyone he loved.

Vincent told himself whoever picked up first he would swing by and check on. As he drove into Kansas City, he got the calls simultaneously. Both of his families died in the hurricane. His wives and children. The very things he worked hard to supply and care for, were just gone.

Vincent spent a week drinking and trying to work out the numbers. What were the odds? Something didn't add up. How could these people, who were innocent, and whom he loved dearly, be punished while he was left unscathed? His possessions were replaceable, most of them. Insurance would pay for all of it. He was going to receive payouts on his family too. He felt sick at this.

In week two, he gave up on figuring out the why and how of it all and decided just to say, *fuck it*. It was unfair to have everything he worked so hard for taken away. Something had it in for him. Something out there hated him. Not God, karma, or destiny, Vincent didn't buy into that crap. He didn't know what it was, but it cheated him out of his game, his chance to keep winning and going for the high score.

The point was it wasn't his fault. None of it was. He didn't like the rules that others followed, so he bent them, yes, even broke the shit out of them. No one was getting hurt, though. If that's how the universe played this game, he decided he didn't want to play it anymore. He hadn't left KC since the notifications. He didn't have a reason to go back. His score got wiped out, and it felt too late to start over. So, fuck it. He hung himself.

He couldn't even win at that! Vincent woke up in a neck brace and tied to a hospital bed at Research Medical Center. The nurses attended to him, and doctors asked questions, but he didn't know what to say. He got cheated out of all his winnings, and now he didn't want to play this fucking game. How could he tell them what he had lost? They would judge him because he didn't want to play the game their way. So, he lay there, silent and still, catatonic.

They kept him restrained and inserted a urinary catheter. He didn't eat, so they gave him fluids. Vincent stayed silent through it all and mainly slept. He just wanted to wait for time to do what he couldn't do for himself. He waited for death. It wasn't until his third day that the hospital staff heard a peep from Vincent.

Vincent awoke at three in the morning and immediately knew something was terribly wrong. He was freezing. The moon sliced the shadows in his dimly lit room. He went to turn on the lamp above his bed but found that his body wasn't responding to him. His muscles felt rigid. He couldn't open his mouth, His heart suddenly started pumping furiously in his chest, and his breathing quickened. He looked around. His door was closed, and the hall lights dimmed. There were small lights on the panels on the wall. *Breathe!* He commanded in his mind.

He had sleep paralysis, common after moving around too much and not sleeping well. The cold was different. It was still summer, and he didn't hear the AC unit blasting, but he could see the white streams of his breath. He looked up and saw that his saline solution had a layer of frost forming. Where was this coming from? How long was this paralysis going to go on?

From the darkest corner of his room, he heard something. He had a tough time placing the sound, it was so familiar. A memory thrust itself forward to the forefront of his thoughts— razor wire. As a child, he grew up on a cattle farm, and a mountain lion plagued the farm and stalked the livestock. So, Vincent Senior bought yards of razor wire as a deterrent.

When the razor wire unwound, it had a strange musical quality. The wire seemed to almost come to life, and the razors glided against it like a twisted violin. That's that sound. Why did he hear it here, though? He looked at that corner. It was so dark it felt as though it went on forever.

He tried to remember what was in that space when the lights were on. Door? Coat rack? Closet? Within the dark of the shadows, he could hear that awful chime of the razor playing against the wire. There was something else his ears were picking up on, breathing. Low and ragged, filled with a strange click noise.

Move, dammit! he shouted in his mind. *Yell! Call for help! Something!*

Some of those deep shadows broke, and a piece began to move independently. Vincent heard the padding of barefoot on the linoleum floor. He saw an arm stretch in the darkness toward him. Vincent saw something twist around the sleek arm and move like a snake around a fresh kill. He heard soft flesh drag across the floor and another naked foot padded into the moonlight. He felt his insides go cold, and his balls shrink into his abdomen. Vincent's heart pounded in his ears, and he felt like he was being smothered. Vincent knew he'd be pissing his pants if it weren't for the catheter.

He wanted to scream, but his lips wouldn't move. He could only release a muffled and pathetic cry. The thing was slender and tall enough that it had to tip its head to keep from dragging it across the ceiling. It moved slowly into the pale blue light shafts, and Vincent could make out details within that meager illumination.

What the fuck is this? Vincent's brain screamed against what it was seeing.

It appeared feminine, with curved hips and thighs, breasts, large full lips, and long black hair that nearly reached the floor. The rest of this creature was a grotesque patchwork of leathered flesh and metal.

There's no way! No fucking way this is real! Please God, help me! Tears streamed down the sides of his face. As if it heard his panicked thoughts, a dry cackle clicked from within the monster's face.

The creature's arms ended in long bony fingers tipped with filthy nails. The thing's arms and legs had long strands of razor wire caressing and entering muscle and exiting the wrists, only to return to the shoulders, the point of origin. Its torso split open, exposing its lungs, heart, and liver. The intestines and some of the other viscera were missing. In the core of the creature's chest was what appeared to be a spool of razor wire. It constantly turned, and from it, the wire moved through the limbs and torso. The creature's sex squirmed with the razor wire as well, which would arc out and undulate. The contents screamed and hummed with anticipation and hunger.

There was no face in this horror, just a row of jagged white teeth dripping with saliva. It dragged its long bony feet across the floor, and each step landed with a loud thud that echoed off the walls. By now, Vincent could smell blood and decay and something else. Vanilla?

The odor was overpowering, and Vincent wanted to vomit but knew in doing so, he would choke to death. His whole body trembled like prey facing its end at the jaws of a hungry beast. He may not piss himself, but his bowels released as the beast bore down on him.

The beast laughed. A clicking sound mixed with a wet gurgle filled its mouth as it licked its lips. It leaned over Vincent's prone body and swung its leg, straddling him. The thing's weight caused the bed frame to groan, and the plastic started to protest with a series of cracking noises. It put its face close to his, and the greasy black hair on its head draped over Vincent. He could see bugs he'd never seen before crawling in her rancid mane.

"Oh, Vinnie," it cooed. "You think that your luck will last forever?" it asked in a high-pitched voice. The head of the creature bent closer, inspecting him with sightless eyes. At this range, Vincent could see a pair of slits in its face where a nose could have been. They expanded and contracted, taking in his scent.

"You smell good. You are almost ready to eat," the creature said with a chuckle that sounded like gravel and piano strings snapping. "I spice you up. Make you ask for death. Make you tender." It knelt close and ran its cold, slimy tongue from the base of his neck to his hairline. Tears streamed down Vincent's face, and he moaned weakly.

"They told me you would ask for me, ask for pain," it whispered in his ear. "Before they moved on."

His eyes widened, and he looked closely at the beast with the question, "Who?"

It laughed in his face, grabbed his chin roughly, and turned his head to the side. His frozen muscles protested the action, but against this creature, they were helpless. The beast took so much pleasure in his fear and confusion that it started fondling its sagging, wrinkled breasts. Its hips gyrated above his groin, and her razor-wire-filled groin began to squeal excitedly.

"Ha...Ha-ha...Wives." It both laughed and moaned with pleasure. Vincent's eyes shot wide open. "I found souls floating down the river, out to sea. They called for me. I almost ate them there. They bargained instead. For you."

Suddenly, Vincent stopped resisting. They knew. They knew and said nothing. Why? What were they waiting for? They hated him now. Now and forever more in death. His stomach sank, and Vincent wanted to be sick. He couldn't make it right. Vincent felt he deserved this. He turned his eyes to look at the demon. Indeed that was what this was. Something infernal, summoned to punish him. He looked pleadingly at the beast, asking for it to kill him. Vincent silently begged for his sentence.

The creature stopped and sat up straight. It smiled at Vincent and wagged a finger. "No, not yet. Need you afraid. This spoils feast." The creature crawled backward off the bed, nearly tipping it with its weight. It stood up, tilting its head. "I come for Vinnie. Not when he wants. I come when you are scared. When you shit, piss, puke, and cry like a helpless fawn," it said.

With a low metallic growl, it turned away from Vincent and returned to the corner it emerged from. Vincent felt his muscles loosen, his breaths became manageable, and his jaw started to unclench. His moaning turned to muffled pleas. His lips were finally able to make the shape of the words, his tongue no longer thick. He began screaming.

"No! Come back!" Vincent screamed. "Please, come back! Kill me! Kill me now! Fuck! Kill me!" he cried and screamed. Nurses burst in, commanding Vincent to calm down. They began adding restraints in the fear that his others would fail. After what felt like the whole night, a nurse charged into the room and plunged a needle-tipped syringe into his thigh. Within a minute, Vincent began to drift back to sleep.

The psychiatrist held onto Vincent after that outburst. He began talking to her and the other healthcare workers. He told his story and didn't care if they judged him anymore. It's what he deserved. They needed to know that he deserved whatever punishment awaited him. The doctor prescribed anti-depressants and anti-psychotics. She explained that they would help calm him and maybe help with the hallucinations.

Every night for the next week, the creature visited him. It found fresh ways to torture him. No matter how hard he screamed or called out, the orderly in the room couldn't hear him or see the creature. It felt like a bubble around him, and whatever happened in it was hidden away.

No one would know his suffering. No one would understand or believe him. The creature knew it. Every night it bit him, cut him, and toyed with his groin. Every night it would threaten to devour his cock, violate him, and finally eat him, but it always stopped at the last minute before doing so. Every morning he would wake with fresh cuts and bruises, leaving the staff confused about their origins. He tried to explain, but no one believed him. Instead, his "treatments" grew more aggressive.

Doctors ordered scans, electroshock treatments, blood draws, and more potent medications. When the dawn broke, the staff member would stand baffled about how Vincent had hurt himself.

"We believe you," came a voice from the door. The night was about to begin its usual routine of pain and pleading. The orderly looked up in surprise to see a tall thin man with half his head shaved and covered in runic tattoos. Even in the low light, the young man wore dark round sunglasses and carried a large leather pack over his right shoulder.

The orderly was about to call for help when the man moved next to him so quickly that it appeared as if he had just teleported there. The stranger held his palm just below the orderly's chin, and mist arose from his hand. The nurse's aide slowly sat down, and his head fell forward within seconds.

"Who are you?" Vincent said. He was curious but not afraid. At least he looked human. Vincent felt something move near him, just to the right of the bed. He yelped in surprise when an intense tan-skinned girl stood with a long black braid on top of her head. She was short and feminine, but her muscles bulged beneath her knitted midriff red sweater. Her abs appeared chiseled, the lines of her hips cut, and her dark skin seemed carved from stone. She bent over, looking into his eyes and smiled with an innocent playfulness.

"Holy-fucking-shit. Who are you people?" He waited for a response as her eyes never left his face. Vincent looked over to the thin young man standing at the foot of his bed. He stood there with an almost evil, crooked smile.

"Don't mind, my friend. She doesn't speak, can't hear either," he paused and corrected himself. "Well, she just can't hear things in this world." He chuckled at this other information. "She can read lips, though. I would be careful what you say and keep things respectful," he said threateningly.

"Got it," Vincent said, glancing at the girl. He could tell from his years of scouting fighters that she was more than capable of hurting others. "What do you want from me?" Vincent started. "Do you work for the monster? Are you here to hurt me too?"

"Let's start with introductions. I'm Phineas; this beauty here is Mata." Phineas bowed theatrically, indicating to Mata. She silently scoffed at him and waved away his compliment. "We're here to save you, Vincent. You sir, have a demon problem as you are well aware of. I study planes of existence outside of our own. This one comes from the lower planes. It was somehow summoned, thus able to pass the Veil."

Vincent looked confused. "I'm sorry, but I'm not sure how two kids will save me," Vincent said with a slight chuckle. "How do you know about my, um, problem?" he stammered.

"You can say that I've got a sense for these things. Mata too," Phineas began. "We could hear this beast roaring all the way to the West Bottoms." The West Bottoms was a series of old warehouses recently turned into shops and a few haunted houses during the fall.

"How?" Vincent began but was interrupted by Phineas.

"There will be time for more questions later. First, this demon. We happen to know how to send these beast back from where it came." To his right, Mata put on what appeared to be a pair of brass knuckles. She tested them by knocking her knuckles together and stretching her neck from side to side. She calmly walked over next to Phineas. Phineas smiled eagerly at her and then at Vincent. He reached into his backpack and pulled out a bundle of dried plants. The herbs had black twine, wrapping them together into a stick. A silver chain with a cross dangled from the center of the knots. The metal glinted in the moonlight.

The room suddenly chilled, and their breath became steam in the low light of the night. Phineas pulled out an antique zippo lighter wrapped in gold. He lit the bundled stick of dried herbs and plants. "Sage?" Vincent asked. "You think you can fight this thing with sage?" Phineas and Mata smiled at each other and looked into the deepening shadow that the demon appeared from nightly.

The thing's stench filled the room; decay, blood, and rust filled the air with just a hint of vanilla. Phineas blew the flames out on his bundle, leaving behind red-hot embers and thick white smoke. The room was brimming with the smell of sage, tobacco, and cedar. There was something else. "Weed? I knew you had to be fucking high. What are you going to do? Roll a blunt for the thing?" Vincent asked in shock.

"Do you think it'll help?" Phineas said, looking over his shoulder and baring his crooked grin. "If you don't mind, Vinnie, I need you to stay quiet for now."

The sound of the razor wire played a tune on itself, and heavy footsteps approached. Phineas reached into his pocket, and Vincent saw he pulled out a corked vial with a strange liquid. Mata started dancing back and forth on the balls of her feet, her hands coming up to her face in a defensive position and her torso curling, bringing her into a stance that reduced her body size. Not that she needed that. Vincent had seen many fighters use this "turtle" stance. He was impressed with her or would be if there wasn't a giant fucking demon moving into the room.

"What this?" the creature hissed. "Leave here, or I eat you."

"Sorry, but Vinnie here is forever under my protection and indebted to me. So, fuck off and find someone else to con," Phineas said with a presence and command beyond his age. He waved the incense before him, and the monster recoiled from the smell.

"Fine, I play with you, then eat him." The demon lunged for Phineas and Mata, its long arms and clawed hands looking to grab their throats. Phineas threw the glass vial down, and a flash of light and smoke burst forth. The demon screamed and held its hands up to try and avoid burning. Mata moved in quickly, and with a powerful cross-hook, she smashed her metal-covered knuckles into the side of the demon's knee. Upon impact, there was a flash of blue light, and the flesh smoked and was left charred where her fist made contact. The bone beneath buckled awkwardly to the side.

The creature howled in pain and raised a clawed left hand back to swipe at the vicious girl who savaged its knee. Suddenly another glass vial broke upon its face. The liquid spilled down and into its mouth and chin. Whatever the elixir washed over began to smoke and sizzle, and the flesh peeled and blistered.

The creature reared its head back, clawed hands going to its face and tore at the burned and melted parts maddingly. Mata took a quick hop back and two steps forward, launched into a jump, and delivered a punch into the left hip of the demon. The bone beneath made a loud, wet crack, and the skin burned where she landed her punch.

The monster toppled over and began sliding away from its attackers, trying to avoid more damage. It blindly slashed at the air before it and hissed and shrieked at them. "I leave! I leave!" the demon screamed at them.

"See that you do," Phineas said. "Vincent is ours now. I'm taking him on as a client."

"Hey, wait! What the fuck does that mean?" Vincent demanded at this new turn of events.

"I return for him, you as well," the demon said. "We live forever, always remember," the devil continued.

"Yeah, yeah. Good luck with that," Phineas said dismissively. He turned and walked back toward Vincent, who sat in amazement at everything he saw. The demon roared at them all and suddenly vanished, taking its shadows.

"Well, shit!" Phineas said excitedly to Mata, who was jumping up and down and pumping her fists in the air. "That worked!"

"I'm sorry, what the fuck?" Vincent blurted out.

"Sorry, Vinnie, there aren't many occult instructors out there. Especially ones who deal with exorcisms. We weren't sure if this was going to work out."

"You could 'a got me killed! Yourselves, too!" Vincent shouted.

"Relax, Vinnie. This is a time to celebrate!" Phineas laughed. "So, let's discuss how you will pay us."

Vincent was shaken from his memory by his phone buzzing angrily. It was Mata. She texted an ambulance emoji and two words that sent a chill down Vincent's back for some reason.

PHINEAS. HELP.

Vincent arrived at the tea house and hurried into the building. He found Phineas and Mata sitting at a table in the center of the room. Lizzie sat close to Phineas, nuzzling his leg. Mata sat next to him, watching intently. Vincent had never seen these two look so frightened.

They faced the streets together. The pimps, users, thieves, and whatever sicko could be found in downtown KC. They witnessed horrible things and came out smiling. So, what the hell got these two rattled?

"Hey, Finn, what's the story? You dying or something?"

Mata banged her fist on the table and glared at Vincent.

He held his hands up apologetically. "Talk to me, kid. What's got you shook up?"

Phineas looked up as though he had just realized Vincent was standing there. His eyes were puffy from crying, and he was pale. More so than usual. His gaze seemed drawn to someplace far away. Vincent didn't see Phineas without his glasses too often. He always had an issue with light or something. His eyes were the palest grey he'd ever seen. What was strange about his eyes was the way they looked at you. He appeared to look through you, at your soul, and in your thoughts, all at once.

Vincent put his hand on Phineas' shoulder. "What do you need?"

Phineas took a deep breath, reached for the glasses on the table, and slipped them on. "I had a vision. My mother gave it to me. I need to go home. Today. Can you go to the self-storage?" asked Phineas in a shaky voice. Before speaking again, he cleared his throat and tried to compose himself. "I'm going to need to go to Granny's library and look over the books. I will head out to Haven Shire when I'm done there."

"Haven Shire? Where the fuck is that?" Vincent inquired.

Mata reached over and squeezed Phineas' arm. *"What about us?"* she signed. *"What do you need us to bring?"*

"I'm going alone on this one. If what my mother warned me about is true, I can't risk getting you guys into this," Phineas replied to Vincent and signed to Mata.

Mata at once shook her head.

"This is bad, Mata. End-of-the-world stuff, bad. I can't get you into—"

Mata slammed her fist on the table so hard that Lizzie jumped up in surprise. She pointed at Phineas forcefully. She took a breath and calmed down. *"You, Vincent, and Lizzie are all I have left,"* Mata signed. *"I saw that look on your face and the blood on your back."* Mata's eyes started welling up in tears. *"You're scared. I get it. I don't know what you saw. I don't care. We go together and deal with it. End of story."*

Phineas knew better than to argue at this point. Any further argument could end up with her putting him in an armbar or rear naked choke hold, forcing him to submit. He had lost multiple arguments with Mata when she used that tactic. Phineas was in no mood to get his ass kicked. He looked up at Vincent, not asking him to come but not asking him to stay.

Vincent looked down thoughtfully. "How much does this gig pay?" he finally asked after a long pause. He glanced up at Phineas with a smirk.

Phineas shrugged his shoulders. "Sorry, buddy. This is pro bono," Phineas replied. "If it works out, you'll be a hero who saved the world."

"Shit," Vincent said, laughing. "They at least have any pretty gals where you come from? If I'm saving the world, I might try and get the gal while I'm at it."

Phineas chuckled. "You'll always have Lizzie."

The Cane Corso looked over at Vincent and growled and chuffed at him.

Phineas spent the hour explaining in detail what he saw. On more than one occasion, looks of disbelief passed over the faces of Mata and Vincent. Most of the supernatural stuff they had dealt with so far was minor. It was maybe a little dangerous, but only if you are mentally unstable and don't have the right tools. What Phineas witnessed was straight out of Lovecraft's nightmares. After he detailed his vision, everyone considered their next move.

"You sure we can't get paid?" Vincent reiterated finally.

Mata stood up and tapped Phineas on the shoulder. *"Time to study then. Gather info on these things."*

Phineas stood up, and he, Mata, and Lizzie headed to the front of the shop.

Vincent gave out a dramatic sigh.

Two hours later, he was knocking on Mata's humble home. She was brewing up some potions Vincent had seen Phineas use when dealing with the ghosts and demons. Phineas was hunched over a large leather-bound book, muttering something in an old language. Lizzie lay curled up at his feet.

"What 'cha got for us, kid?" Vincent asked.

"Hastur, the god of shepherds," Phineas began. "Or zealots and cultists of The Great Old One or Yog-Sothoth maybe?" Phineas read and then, frustrated, slammed the old book closed. "I don't know, honestly. Most of this old god shit is unreliable at best." Phineas took off his glasses for a moment and rubbed his eyes. "Most of the people who wrote these things were bat-shit crazy. Leaders of some weird cult trying to end the world or something."

"Sounds like any church I've been to," Vincent quipped.

"Regardless, whoever this group is they don't seem to care about who they hurt. I saw the extent of death and pain they planned to rain down on all of us," Phineas said.

Phineas put on his glasses and looked Vincent, who stood looking incredulously at him. "I don't think the destruction will end just with Haven Shire. I think this will eat us all if we ignore it."

"Just like global warming, eh?" Vincent joked.

"You are awfully glib today," Phineas said as he packed the books into a trunk.

"Hey man, it's not every day I see something that scares the fearless Phineas and Mata," Vincent said. "I gotta get a look at this thing."

Phineas finished packing the texts and papers. Mata filled several glass globes with various elixirs, holy water, and even a few explosives. She carefully placed them in a case. She rushed into her room and turned on the shower.

Phineas followed her with his eyes, and when she was sure to be getting cleaned up, he turned to Vincent. "Hey, Vinnie," he said.

"Yeah?" Vincent replied as he grabbed an armful of books.

"Promise me something, would ya?" Phineas solicited.

"What's up, bud?" Vincent's tilted his head toward Phineas.

Phineas paused, considering his words. "If things become untenable, you gotta grab Mata and Lizzie and get the fuck out of dodge, okay?"

Vincent met Phineas's gaze. "Finn, you know I can't take her in a fight. Lizzie either, for that matter," Vincent started. "What could I possibly do?"

"Whatever you need to. Mata'll hate you for it, but I need to know she'll be okay," Phineas pleaded urgently.

"In that case, I need a bigger gun," Vincent said, half-joking.

After getting cleaned up, Vincent pulled up in a rusty, off-white van they used if they needed a lot of gear. He loaded the books, and Mata grabbed the case of elixirs and her bag of clothes. Phineas grabbed his overstuffed backpack and jacket.

Phineas looked over the gear and the books and saw that Vincent had packed his supplies. There was a large duffle bag, which Phineas knew was filled with a couple of long rifles, shotguns, and a few pistols, with plenty of ammo for each. He also brought a bible and a crucifix. Phineas looked at those with a smirk.

"What? I figured we would need every weapon we could get for this," Vincent said sheepishly.

He opened up a hidden storage space in the floor and tossed in his gear. Vincent then went to work securing various weapons to the interior walls of the van. When he was done, Vincent pulled on several straps that unfurled a heavy blanket to cover the van's contraband.

Mata threw in an extra backpack. Phineas recognized it as her collection of favorite knives, clubs, and a pair of brass knuckles she had blessed by the Catholic church.

"That's right," Phineas said finally. "Bring all your curses. Every blade. Every bullet. I think we'll need them."

-CHAPTER 13-
THE SHAKE SHACK

Thaddeus awoke in the early morning. He prided himself on being an early riser. It helped him achieve his goals as well as avoid his father. Since his arrival in this inbred town in the middle of who-gives-a-fuck Americana, he had to find ways to entertain himself. His singular pleasure in his miserable existence was power. Lust for power and control was the only thing he and his father had in common. That, and their way with people.

For the last two years, Thaddeus had been greasing palms, paying off union leaders, and, if needed, silencing those who got too close to the family. Today was a meeting with the local clergyman. Judge and Maria had caught a mother reaching out to the Vatican for help regarding her son's strange behavior. Even though the prayers and scripture didn't work on the eldritch beings of the Veil, they didn't need others poking around the town.

Thaddeus showered. He wanted to ensure that no one found evidence of his other appetites. He styled his hair in a way that suggested he wasn't too dapper and put on a suit that indicated that he was "one of the people." His target was Father Curry. He had been the Catholic priest in Haven Shire and was well-liked by many, but his reputation was not above tarnish. Given the media and political climate regarding the church, enlisting someone to claim he was a wolf among sheep, preying on children would be easy.

He would do what he did best- find the thing everyone was afraid of and use it. Homosexuality? Minorities? Religion? All these were good, but sometimes he needed more. Planted photos, paid hookers, a few grams of cocaine, and in the worst of cases, the target would give in to their shameful actions and die by their own hands. At least, it would appear that way.

He adjusted his tie, and when he finished, he looked down at the local paper. Within it held the details of the provincial election. Then, an article caught his eye.

Local Farmer and Herd Missing!

He thought back over the years and considered the state of affairs in this small town. *"Drug and alcohol abuse on the rise,"* or *"Death by suicide and domestic violence running rampant,"* and *"Missing person reports triple over the last five years."*

Not that his family had anything to do with it, he thought with a smile. So, he left the Forgotten Church and attended services of every conceivable variation of Christianity within the county to pour the venom of rumors about Father Curry's "misdeeds" into the ears of parishioners. By the end of the day, he used his considerable charisma to spread the seeds of fear and bigotry among the religious leaders and their congregants.

He needed a break after a long day of painting a pretty smile and lowering himself to touch those less than himself. The dusk was upon the small town of Haven Shire, and he needed a distraction. Typically, he knew every place where a community hid its dirty secrets. He knew every drug den, whore house, and den of sin. He knew where to find the nooks and crannies where debauchery festered.

There weren't too many options to feed his appetites when his father sent for him, he had to make his own. Since his arrival, he ousted the local mayor, who had started taking notice of his father's work. He had a successful den of boys he was training, and each was eager to pose with the mayor. At the same time, the man lay inert from a lovely concoction Thaddeus put together. The rest was just a matter of using the local paper, which more than welcomed a scandal to increase readership.

After the man killed himself, it was easy to establish a small drug operation and get some locals hooked. He used this weakness to extract favors and information. If anyone got wise, he had no trouble bribing, threatening, or killing them. His father, of course, knew of his operations, and as long as it didn't draw attention to him or his cause. He looked the other way because he didn't care.

Tonight, he needed something special. After his "family dinner," he needed to blow off some steam. His mother insisted on those dinners once a week. In part, he thought, it was some pathetic attempt to remind the family that they were still human and needed each other. The other reason was that she got off watching Dad torture him. Fucking cunt.

Enough of that, though, he had a party to attend. He could taste the pleasures now. It was already making him hard.

He arrived at his destination. He called it "The Shake Shack." He found it driving aimlessly while some local sucked his cock. Well, the local's head, anyway. He couldn't remember where he left the rest of his body. Thaddeus pulled around behind the abandoned diner with a sign out front. *"Best Shakes in Kansas!"*

When he first found the Shack, he entertained himself by torturing and murdering the squatters. When they stopped coming around, he had it cleaned out and considered turning it into a strip club. The name was appropriate, and he would have plenty to entertain himself. He was inspired one night when he witnessed one of his father's pets "mating" with locals.

Thaddeus captured them and brought them to the Shack, hoping they would entertain him again. As it turned out, the Formoria his father summoned reproduced quickly if they bred with something from this plane. Instead of waiting forty weeks, as is the case with human gestation, Thaddeus got to see the outcome within a couple of weeks.

The result was usually explosive for the man, woman, or beast. Whatever was born was usually hungry, too. If whatever was born lived, which was a rarity, he kept it. He discovered that each Formorian spawn that lived quickly grew more robust than the parent— evolution on fast forward.

He reached into his glovebox and pulled out a silver medallion and a nickel-plated 9mm Glock. Thaddeus specifically tailored each bullet to those who lived beyond the Veil. Each shell had runes etched into the casings. When they struck Formorian flesh, the creature would wither and become desiccated. Within minutes, the creature would crumble into ash.

He stepped around to the trunk of his sedan and opened it up. Within was a large duffle bag with his hazmat suit. He found it kept the gore off him best. The second item was tonight's dinner. Seventeen-year-old Casey Li. She was sitting outside getting rained on in front of the library. She was pretty, wearing her school uniform, and full of potential and promise.

That's what turned on Thaddeus. All that life yet lived. All those victories, mistakes, and choices will be his now. He will take them all for himself. Her screams of protest and begging will be foreplay to his final gift to her. His release will come later, as he watched the recorded action in high definition.

"I cannot wait to get you home and watch this over and over on my seventy-five-inch QLED screen TV," Thaddeus nearly salivated at the thought of watching these exchanges in his den.

He hefted her over his shoulders. He approached the door and unlocked the padlock on the chain that discouraged trespassers. He didn't care if someone broke in though. The creatures inside would take care of them.

Once inside, Thaddeus faced a bipedal beast that spawned just two weeks ago. At eight feet tall, it was the largest he had seen yet. It had the body of an athlete, its smooth skin constantly glistened in some oily coating, and the skin was a giant bruise. It had hair only around the writhing and twisting member that protruded from between its legs. It was about four feet in length, pulsing with muscle and blood, and it ended with a mouth with several rows of needle-like teeth.

It sniffed the air around it and tilted its bald head as if to listen with ears it didn't own. It was sightless; most of its face was a maw with teeth that rotated around and around in its mouth. It reminded Thaddeus of those mask-looking creatures his father used to replace key town members. Inside the mouth wiggled a purple tongue that constantly applied saliva to the teeth that moved about in its face.

"Get the fuck out of my way," Thaddeus said coolly and pulled out the medallion of warding. The creature hissed and returned to the dark corner from which it appeared.

Thaddeus walked past the front counter and into the kitchen. He walked past the row of large metal kitchen sinks. Some were a quarter-filled with a strange combination of fluid and garbage. He knew there was a dead possum in one. He sympathized with the creature only because he felt the same way about his existence in this backwoods, inbred town.

He continued to the back of the kitchen, past the refrigerator, and came to a short flight of stairs leading to the basement. It was dark, but Thaddeus had come here so often to check the progress of his work that he could walk this path blindfolded. He considered dropping the unconscious girl down the stairs but thought better.

Thaddeus couldn't risk killing her. He needed her alive and her brain intact.

The Formoria ate their victim's organs, but the brain was their primary source of sustenance. There was no biological need for it he could determine from the autopsies he and his father performed. Still, Judge explained that the Formoria didn't simply dine on their prey's tissue. They feasted on their souls. Thaddeus wasn't sure if he believed anything had a soul, especially his father.

Upon reaching the last step, Thaddeus heard hisses and gurgling noises from the room's corners. He listened to the rattle of chains emanating from the center of the room. There, hanging from her arms, was Jane. Jane something. Jane Swan-something. Fuck, it didn't matter. Judging from her condition, she was due tonight. He walked over and laid little Casey Li at the feet of Jane Who-the-fuck-knows' feet.

The things in the dark growled and licked their lips eagerly. Thaddeus could hear them padding back and forth on the floor, climbing along the walls and up to the ceiling. He pulled a folding chair from beneath a storage space under the stairs, the camera and tripod stashed next to it, and set it up approximately six feet from Jane and Casey. Thaddeus checked the camera and retrieved extra batteries.

He withdrew a leather journal and a slim gold cigarette case from his inner jacket pocket. Within were six perfectly rolled joints. Each one was laced with something to enhance the high and with different effects. He thought of them as a box of chocolates in that way. He placed them in no particular order so that when he smoked them, he would be surprised by their effects.

He reached up and turned on the lamp on the camera. A focused and pale, warm light fell upon this evening's subjects. The light was sufficient for Thaddeus to jot a few notes in his notepad-

"Casey, 15 yr. old female. Asian descent with long black hair. Jean shorts, white blouse. Wearing a candy scented lip gloss and some sort of vanilla perfume. Some cheap scent found next to body sprays for teenage boys. The subject is fit, but not athletic."

He lit his joint and then recorded his subjects' date, time, and condition.

"Fall of the year of Azathoth. 2345 hours," Thaddeus said out loud as he wrote in his journal to record the date on camera. Jane hung unconscious from chains bolted to the ceiling, ending at the thick iron cuffs around her wrists. The skin from beneath the cuffs was torn and raw, and streams of dried blood ran down her arms to her neck and torso.

She rotated gently from left to right, her belly bulging from whatever grew within her. So much so that the skin was nearly translucent, and the bulge hung so low that it passed her hips and groin and looked like it would tear open at any moment. Her shoulders were dislocated from bearing the weight of her body and the fetus. Her toes glided across the floor, tracing small circles in the piss and shit below Jane's suspended form. Thaddeus noted in his journal.

She smells ripe, and the fruit is ready to be plucked. I have offered a young classmate, Casey Li, to feed the spawn or bear the next in its genetic line.

He was interrupted when he heard a moan come from Casey. He began waging a personal bet to see who would awaken first; Casey or the creature within Jane. As if to increase the stakes, a squelching sound came from within Jane, and she shuddered with pain. It pleased Thaddeus to know she was still somewhat responsive to painful stimuli. He took a long drag from his joint, closed his journal, and watched the spectacle unfold.

That was the strangest dream, Casey thought. She was waiting for her mother outside the library when she felt a hand over her face, and something stung her leg. Surprised, Casey found she felt so tired suddenly. She must've fallen asleep outside because the concrete was cold, and the air felt damp. She fumbled for her backpack. Her vision and brain were still blurry as both adjusted to the situation. Something smelled acrid, and the stench made her nearly vomit.

Suddenly, fear took hold of Casey as her brain processed the information around her. She didn't just fall asleep, she was attacked. She also wasn't still at the library or outside. She looked around, trying to determine where she was. As she did so, her head spun with the motion, and she tried to steady herself on her hands and knees.

There was a bright light on a stand. Casey could smell weed, shit, and something that smelled like spoiled meat. She suddenly felt nauseous, and her head spun again. Casey couldn't hold back any longer and retched and vomited on the floor. After her stomach had calmed down, she slowly returned to work, trying to find a way to familiar territory.

A chair sat next to the light stand with a man sitting comfortably in a tan suit. He took a hit from the joint that Casey had smelled. He seemed curious but otherwise impassive. He didn't bother covering his face. The thought suddenly sank in, he wasn't worried if she saw him.

"Hey, I don't know who you are," Casey began, tears rolling down her face. "I never saw your face. I just want to go home. Please, let me go." She started to move to her feet, fighting vertigo and nausea as she did so.

The man continued to watch. Casey realized that he wasn't looking at her but through or past her. Just then, she backed into something and heard chains rattle above her. She turned suddenly to face whatever had snuck up behind her. Her eyes widened with horror. Jane Bueller. She was a cheer co-captain at school.

"What happened? Jane?" Casey stammered. She looked her over. She was unconscious, naked, and filthy. Thick chains suspended her awkwardly from a hook above her head. Where her arms met the shoulders, Casey could see bruising and swelling, and they were deformed, with bulging round masses where her upper bicep and deltoid are. Or were? Her skin was jaundiced, and her hair filthy. The notices posted across town said she had been missing, but those just went up about a month ago.

Looking down, she also saw Jane was pregnant. Casey couldn't reconcile this either. She just saw Jane right before she went missing. She worked as a lifeguard at the Haven Shire waterpark. That was less than three months ago. There's no way, right?

Just then, Casey saw something move around inside Jane's swollen belly. Jane moaned, and her eyes fluttered. Casey began to weep uncontrollably. Not just because she was terrified and confused by everything happening around her but because Jane was suffering terribly. She wasn't close to Jane, but that didn't mean she didn't see how much she hurt at that moment. Casey approached her cautiously and touched her face.

"Jane? Jane?" Casey probed, her hands and voice trembling. "It's going to be ok. We're going to be ok." She whispered the lie weakly. She wanted to give her some hope, maybe trick herself into believing it too.

Jane's eyes fluttered open. The whites of her eyes were no longer visible. Instead, Casey looked into two eyes that had hemorrhaged so much that they were completely red with the pooling blood. Any white that was still left was as jaundiced as her skin. Her irises were still that crystal blue but somehow accentuated by the red and black of her large pupils. She looked weakly at Casey, tears flowed down her cheeks. She began to moan and try to form words.

"What is it? What can I do?" Casey whimpered.

With all her strength, Jane whispered, "Run."

Thaddeus watched with interest over the next chaotic moments. Every birth of these otherworldly abominations was different, but each promised a rather explosive death. It reminded him of watching fireworks. First was the fire, the violent reaction as the gunpowder-coated wick lit, the shower of sparks, and finally, the culminating explosion. Every man and woman who birthed Formorian spawn differed in how they delivered these twisted and hungry things into this world. The birthing process is the part that Thaddeus studied the most and would later revisit in his bedchambers. He noticed the bulge in his slacks and readjusted for comfort.

Jane screamed. "RUN! RUN! RUN!" she shouted over and over. Each plea was more pain-filled and desperate than the last.

Casey stepped back and slipped on the pool of vomit she had made earlier. She was as transfixed by the scenario as Thaddeus was. They watched Jane's convulsions intently as she began to swing back and forth.

Jane's arms bent and twisted awkwardly as the mass within her belly shifted from side to side. From her hips and shoulders came wet popping and cracking noises as the fetus began its descent. Jane's head fell forward in a slump, and her hair fell around her breasts and belly. She started shaking and shuddering quickly, and piss and shit fell from her body onto the floor.

Something made a loud pop inside Jane's body, and a green viscous fluid spilled out of Jane's vagina. Then nothing. Instead of the explosion Thaddeus had longed for, he got silence.

"Fuck. I guess this one's a dud. No matter. I have the others down here. We will record the findings and start anew with our newest arrival."

Casey looked over at him, horrified, as his words took their meaning in her head.

Before Thaddeus could move, the transformation Jane had begun to undergo started again. This time, the opposite occurred; instead of swelling, it pulsated, and finally, an explosive crescendo of gore. The flesh around Jane's torso, neck, and face tightened and shriveled. The muscles, fat, and blood seemed to wither and shrink. The skin blackened as it appeared to desiccate, and blood-red cracks formed in various places.

Where Jane's sex once was, came a crackling noise as the skin between her legs stretched and ripped as something began to push its way out of her body. Jane's head fell back, and Casey saw that her neck bulged as something forced its way up and out of her mouth. A long tail-like appendage snaked its way from her mouth. It reached out to be about eight feet long, and when it reached the apex of its length, it split into four more appendages. Four tentacles, each covered in slime and blood, began to flail around, exploring the world around them.

Six thin spidery legs erupted from Jane's flanks, each approximately five feet long and segmented. Jane's legs, hips, and thighs suddenly started to kick and bounce violently in the air as something tried to descend out from her belly to freedom. The tissue where her thighs met her hips bulged and began to tear until each appendage fell to the floor with a sickening splat. Mucus, fluids, and feces splashed across Casey's face and chest. She barely registered this as she watched the horrific transformation before her.

A pair of tusks pushed through from the now-empty space that once occupied her lower extremities. Jane's groin tore open, all the way to her rectum. From that opening, a giant, jaundiced eyeball appeared. The eye rolled forward, and a red, cat-shaped iris appeared. It looked about and twitched as a mouth gaped open with long rows of teeth. The orifice's corner started below the eye and came together where the anus once was, forming a sideways maw.

The creature shook and kicked against the chains that bound it until the arms ripped from their sockets. The beast fell to the floor in front of Casey, who now sat in a pool of urine, her knees beneath her. Thaddeus looked at the pair on the floor before him, covered in filth and gore. Casey sat on her legs, arms hanging limply at her side, looking at Thaddeus almost as though she was praying to this abomination.

He was in awe of the violence he witnessed in this monster's becoming. Usually, these things take place in seconds, barely enough time to absorb the nuances of suffering and change that occurred. Yet, he felt as though there was still more to see. He picked up his journal, the excitement of what he saw had him shaking and with trembling hands, he took notes.

"Never had I witnessed a transformation such as this? What will be born from all my hard work?!"

Thaddeus wrote furiously into the pad.

Casey was lost. Not just because there was no escaping this basement or this god-forsaken town, but because her sanity could no longer bear this. This newborn horror was something Casey's brain could never conceive. Even in her worst nightmares, she would have never given birth to such a monster.

The creatures in the dark hissed and growled, and Thaddeus could hear them beyond his ecstasy. He watched intently as the beast hovered over a slack-jawed Casey. He looked at her empty eyes and her broken mind. She had disassociated from the reality of her plight, and who could blame her? There was no escape, though. Thaddeus could feel the presence of this thing in his thoughts, feel its hunger, its desires.

Casey looked up at the creature as it rose over her. "This isn't real, it can't possibly be happening," she said meekly, tears streaming down her face. The maw opened as the eye peered down at her, exposing several rows of teeth and multiple tongues whipping around, looking for a taste of that next meal.

The creature came down onto Casey's chest so hard that both legs broke under the weight of the blow. The pain in her legs and the teeth biting into her skin at once sobered Casey and ripped her from the safety of insanity.

The creature thrashed about with her in its teeth like a dog with a toy. It growled and screamed as it did so. It was a bestial scream, mixing with Casey's cry of terror and pain. Thaddeus wrote furiously. It didn't kill Casey, though. Thaddeus watched as it used its tongues and spindly legs to tear away her clothes. The tentacles spilled forth from the maw and pulled Casey's lower extremities into its mouth. Casey bellowed in pain and pleaded to Thaddeus for release, for death. Thaddeus observed as the flesh that formed the creature's lips molded around Casey and then began to melt into her flesh.

They were becoming one, flesh from both subjects are knitting together. Casey is not being eaten but absorbed into the newborn Formori.

He giggled like a child with a new toy.

Thaddeus started laughing at this new development. Casey's skin became pale and mottled as her organs, tissue, and blood became one with the monster. Her screams ceased coming from her and now joined with the atrocities as they assimilated her. The creature rolled over, and it transformed again.

This time when it rose, it still carried Casey's upper torso, her long black hair falling over her face. The sideways maw was now more immense, and it started from between her breasts and ran the length of three feet down the center of the monster's body. The rest of the body stretched, and the many segmented legs shortened and multiplied. The creature's tail ended with the remains of Jane's head gaping in an eternal scream with tentacles writhing out of her mouth.

Thaddeus approached the monster. The Casey's torso's arms reached out as if to embrace him, and the mouth cooed and moved as if to kiss him, but when it came with a foot of the medallion around his neck, it recoiled. It screamed in the voices of its victims and those beasts from beyond. He reached out and grabbed it by the wrists, and the flesh beneath his touch sizzled and burned, thanks to the power of his medallion.

"You are so beautiful. You are glorious! Finally, I have something that's mine. I'm going to feed you and give you what I never had. Love." The creature quit trying to recoil from the painful grip Thaddeus had on it, and with Casey's dead eyes and lips, it smiled back at him, accepting his promise.

-CHAPTER 14-
THE BREADTH OF SCOPE

George felt adrift.

He searched for the cold cases in Haven Shire and was horrified to find that even though he knew there were quite a few for a small town, he didn't know half of them. There were missing persons cases mostly, but also instances of murder and sexual assault.

The number of cases doubled over the last three decades. In the previous five years, the number of missing children in the county was as higher.

George also broadened his search to all crime in Haven Shire and the neighboring towns. The increase in violent crime and drug abuse had also doubled. He remembered the headlines about some of the strangest acts in the paper as he poured over the files.

"Teacher murders student in ritual during recess." He remembered some of the details of these headlines. A bright young teacher killed a little boy and claimed she was under the devil's instruction. Strangely, she denied having a history of mental illness or religious affiliation.

"Six arrested in orgy, one person found dead." He remembered this one. The group had a key party, and someone brought a horse to join them. They recorded the whole event. They didn't stop filming even as the animal fucked him to death. George would never forget that one, especially since he was assigned to review the footage for evidence of wrongdoing. "Everything about that call was wrong," he said then. "They had to put the animal down. Were they worried the horse would do it again? Did he have a taste for it now?"

"Three girls found slain in a treehouse, child to blame," George remembered many on the force were haunted by this one. Four ten-year-old girls made some pact to try and summon an urban legend. The fourth one convinced them all that if they slit their wrists and muttered some weird prayer, the being would show itself. Most took it as an internet challenge and blew it off until the fourth girl went blind and crazy three days later. She's now locked up in a

children's hospital psych ward, playing truth or dare with the ghosts of her dead friends.

In that same paper was a report on the increase in crime. He checked other headlines as well. There were strange stories of people going insane that struck George.

The most unusual of these was a story of the obese county commissioner who was found dead from shock because he tried to eat himself. The report said he was obsessed with fad diets but had trouble finding one that worked. He had come across auto cannibalism while fasting for a month. He spent a year cutting off slices of himself whenever he thought about cheating on his diet. The man was determined for sure. He went from weighing four hundred plus pounds to two hundred and six.

George didn't find anything that tied a crime, or the suspicion of one, to the Marcus family. His frustration mounting, he changed gears and performed a background check on them instead. No history of criminal action, not even a speeding ticket. George finally consulted the internet to see if the family was mentioned elsewhere.

There was a Marcus family that had lived in a small town in Pennsylvania. George couldn't find photos to confirm if they were the same people. This family had a similar M.O., though. Mother and father were doctors, bought up properties and businesses, and paid well for their purchases. Those employed were fired, rent was raised, and each community suffered.

George found several interviews and articles about people disappearing and mysterious illnesses, especially among the homeless and the vulnerable. The events involving psychosis were blamed on a new drug causing hallucinations. No direct mention of Judge or Maria. He continued to comb the internet and found other communities with similar stories. These events appeared to happen in clusters.

Finally, he found a link to a charity event to help families who lost loved ones in a mining incident. There it was. A picture of a man and woman who looked just like Judge and Maria. James Thurgood and Olivia Masterson. They looked almost identical to the Marcus'. They were seen together in the photo, not as husband and wife, but as co-chairs of a non-profit group— the Lord's Grace Fellowship.

George later found that the charity group and all its members met with an untimely end in a structure fire. A charity dinner to feed the poor and homeless population went sideways when a crazed man ran into the event with two Molotov cocktails. In addition to the flammables, he set several more incendiary devices, enough to level a city block around the building. Reports from the few survivors stated he set himself on fire shortly after throwing the bombs into the kitchen and the dining hall. James and Olivia had been counted among the dead.

"Wait, what the hell?" George felt his enthusiasm drain when he looked at the date of the article.

Some of the news clippings dated as far back as the early eighties. There is no way that Judge and Maria are as old as they are. That would mean they were nearly eighty.

Just as he was about to read further, George felt a tap on his right shoulder. The shock nearly sent him flying out of his chair. He turned and saw Police Chief Joe Waters standing next to him.

"How's it going, George?" he said grimly. "Working a case?"

The police chief was a good guy and well-liked by the community. He was nearly sixty years old and sported snow-white hair with a handlebar mustache. He played Santa for the kids every year. He was fair and calm. Today, he seemed out of sorts, George thought. He wasn't his jovial self. He had been on edge and quick to snap at the officers for the last few days.

"Just looking into the Steiner family and clearing some cases off my plate." George didn't know why he just lied. Something told him he needed to keep this close to the vest. It felt like Jack's voice was in his ear. *"Don't tell anyone else,"* rang in his brainpan.

"What can I do you for, Chief?" George asked, trying to sound friendly. Before he could answer, George's dispatch called for his unit on his radio. He was thankful for the save as they dispatched his unit to the Grey Farmstead. George listened to the details and found them almost too strange to believe. Except, there was no such thing now, was there?

"I need to head out to the Grey farm. Someone called in about something killing their livestock," George said, grabbing his coat. "Is there something pressing, sir?"

"Where's Manns and Holts?" asked Chief Waters.

"They needed the day off. That call last night was a rough one," George said. He had this lie in the chamber in case anyone asked. George felt that buzzing in his head again. Maybe Jack was right.

George stood next to Elmer and Martha Grey. Their family had lived in this town for nearly two hundred years. They even had a major country road named after the founding family. This road ran north to south from one end of the county to the other. They had seen or heard the stories of this place and are very much part of its history. George thought the brother-sister living arrangement was strange in itself. Neither married, had kids, or had ever been separated. That still wasn't as weird as what he was looking at here.

Every head of cattle, every goat, sheep, and chicken was dead. "They all been murdered over-night," Martha Grey said weeping.

"Anyone have a reason to do this? Has anyone threatened you?" George asked.

"Nah," Elmer said as he spat tobacco-laden saliva on the ground. "We been keeping to ourselves mostly. Just the way we like it."

"How many of the animals were killed, Elmer?" George questioned surveying the farmland. Corpses littered the fields for over a mile it seemed.

"Eighty-five cows, sixteen goats, and fifteen chickens," Elmer said flatly. He had been stoic throughout this ordeal— barely any perceivable emotion. Martha was emotional enough for both of them as she broke out in fits of sobbing during questioning.

"Eerie part is that neither of us woke in the night," Martha continued. "You think killin' on this scale would have raised a ruckus? Not a peep outta the lot."

"Notice anything weird going on around here? In town or around the county?" George asked. If anyone had noticed any strange activity, it would have been these two, he hoped.

"You mean around the farm?" Elmer replied. "Nah. All has been well, and nothing unusual we could see. The dead go back to my property line up in them hills."

George recalled the scandal about the Meyer's land and those hills. The Marcus' had contacted the Greys to buy their land. The

Greys declined their absurdly generous offer. Then the Marcus' tried to dispute the property lines legally and claimed they owned everything on the hills. This claim was also refuted by the Greys using extensive documentation and records that dated nearly back to when their family settled in the area.

"What about the Marcus family? They come onto your property or contact you?" George asked.

"Not a word from them for a couple of years after we politely told them to fuck off and get off our property," Elmer said with a yellow-toothed grin.

"How about in town? Notice anything unusual?" George left the question as vague as possible. This family had been here for a couple of centuries.

"Don't see many families walking the streets anymore. We used to see all the folks when Elmer and I went to church," Martha said. "The Shire has gotten quiet lately. Not too many talking to each other in stores or the square."

"Yeah, I've noticed that, too." George considered this observation as well. "Anything else come to mind?"

"I've seen more hobos in town. Strangers. Must be coming in from the tracks," Elmer stated. He jutted his chin in the direction of the railyard. The memory of that place put an ache in George's stomach.

"Would you folks mind if I checked out your property? Maybe see what could have done this?" George asked.

"Not at all," Elmer replied. "I'll get my cart and guide you." George smirked at the "cart" comment. Elmer was referring to his all-terrain utility vehicle, which he spent a few dollars on and was quite proud of having.

"Much obliged, Elmer. Lemme make a call while you get ready."

"Best do it now," Elmer said. "We lose cell reception the closer we get to them hills."

George made a three-way call to Manns and Holts. He wanted to give them the updates he found on the Marcus Family and what he found at the farm while he could.

"What'cha got Manns?" he asked standing next to the police cruiser. He wanted to prevent anyone from overhearing what they were uncovering. His instincts hinted that he needed to be careful about what they were finding.

"Not much so far. I'm meeting with Jonesy from The Herald" Sicily explained. "I bumped into her while I was asking around, and she said she had some info about the properties being bought up. Sounds important."

"What about you Holts?" George asked, "Does your dad have anything that might shed some light on this nightmare?"

"We just got started but he was pulled away for physical therapy. He'll be back in a half-hour. So far, all I got is that Haven Shire has all sorts of strange stories and legends that go back hundreds of years."

"Copy that, I have to go onto the Grey's property. I may lose cell service but you two look out for each other until I call later," George said a little too sternly.

Something was bothering him. His Warning alarms were buzzing. He had no clue who he should be worried about. Himself? Manns and Holts? All of the above?

George also needed to get back home at some point. Things still were rocky with the wife, and even though she was visiting her parents, he wanted to ensure his home was orderly and clean if she returned. The girls were with her, too, and even though he missed them, he was glad they were out of this town.

George felt something ominous was about to happen and couldn't shake the sense of that impending doom. Of course, that could just be the trauma talking. Fuck, he needed to see someone about this. Or get a drink. *Right after this gets wrapped up,* he thought.

George was quiet as he rode shotgun in the ATV. He checked in with dispatch and let them know his location. He called the station and requested a vet and county animal control to come out. They would need a ton of resources to come and collect the animals for testing and disposal.

Beside him, Elmer talked about the property and how his family had come to own it. He spoke of family scandals and legends passed down. George passively listened as he looked at the trail of dead animal flesh. The herd had broken up across the three-square miles of farmland. This activity was unusual since they are herd animals and typically stick together unless spooked.

"Something spooked them, I reckon," Elmer stated as if he read George's mind. "Whatever killed the cows returned to the farm and then killed my goats and chickens."

"And you didn't hear a thing? What could have done something like this?" George wondered aloud.

Elmer just shrugged helplessly. George found the older man's impassive demeanor rather amusing and strange.

"It even got my sweet Daisy. That's what chaps my ass," Elmer said, showing the first crack in his stoicism.

"Daisy?" George asked.

"My collie. She was old, but Daisy was still a worker," Elmer said proudly.

"You would think a dog would've barked or alerted you if something attacked the herd," George said.

"Shit, that dog was deaf and blind. She was always barking at all times a night, too. I could've missed it," Elmer said.

They approached the property line, and George saw the Grey's fence climb up the hills. The border was barbed wire and electric. The fence cut a large piece of the terrain into the Grey farmland. They stopped and trekked on foot into the forest-covered landscape.

"Just curious, why didn't you sell to the Marcus family?" George asked.

"This land has been in our family for generations. Some have been sold and bought over the years, but it is ours. I promised myself that I would not give anyone an inch of this property, and it would stay in my family name," Elmer said flatly. "I'll be damned if some rich folks from who-the-fuck-cares will just stroll in here and take it."

George nodded.

"Besides, they were rude," Elmer continued. "They threatened to take the land by law and then bankrupt us with legal bills. So, fuck 'em."

George chuckled at that as he began walking into the dense forest of Haven Shire Hills.

-CHAPTER 15-
STALKING PREY

Sicily pressed the red button marked END on her cell phone after George told her the plans for the night. She was waiting for her contact in the coffee house when he called. She had poked around public records and discovered that the Marcus family had bought up several businesses and properties around Haven Shire.

There hadn't been a specific connection between them that she could see. The Marcus' purchased some of these properties for much more than they were worth. Many who sold their land or property also quickly moved out of town.

On the list was the old dog food factory George spoke of, the quarry where they found the Steiners, and the land the railway ran through. Other properties included several acres of farmland around Haven Shire Hills, where their home was built. There was also the Jameson slaughterhouse, which remained in operation. However, the new owners hired new workers and fired all those working at that slaughterhouse.

There were also several storage unit businesses and a warehouse that was once going to be renovated and turned into affordable housing. The Marcus' had bought out rented space reserved for local businesses. Immediately following the purchase, the cost to rent the space tripled, forcing many shop owners to close.

"What the fuck are they trying to do?" Sicily remarked when she saw that all the Marcus' were doing was pushing people out. There was no profit or gain from any of this. She also spent part of the day asking the other store owners and some interested patrons if they ever had any run-ins with the Marcus family.

Nearly everyone had a story about how the Marcus family had somehow hurt them, a friend, or a business. Injuries ranged from legal to financial and, in a few cases, physical. Their driver, the large man who would drive to town occasionally to buy goods for the family, was especially notorious for his violence.

It was during her interviews that she ran into Jonesy Mickelson. She was a nice gal who inherited the failing business of the local newspaper, *The Haven Herald*. Her dad spent his life reporting the events in the town and county. He was a devoted newspaperman and hated how news was moving to something as cold as the internet. He honestly believed the words on paper connected a community to their First Amendment right of free speech.

Jonesy wasn't as rigid as her father in her beliefs and had set up a website to distribute the local news. However, to honor her father, she still printed the Sunday edition of the *Herald*. Jonesy had overheard a conversation between Manns and the owner of The Crow's Nest, the only bookstore in town. Maria had shown interest in some of the first additions the store owner prized. When the store owner explained that the books were not for sale, Maria became furious and even threatened her.

Jonesy told Sicily that there were several occurrences like this throughout the years. People didn't tell a Marcus "no" often, and when they did, it resulted in some form of misfortune. She wanted to go over the topic more but had to stop by The Herald and grab her files for Sicily to review.

Sicily was glad to know that someone had investigated the Marcus family. She had asked to meet at The Haven Herald later that afternoon. So, Sicily waited in the coffee shop and got a snack until the appointed time of four-thirty.

Sicily sat with her coffee and a turkey melt sandwich, looking across the street to the office of the Herald. It assumed the corner space on Main Street and Fischer. From the outside, it was just a plain, white building. Attached to the building was a locally owned auto shop and a tractor supply store. She reviewed the notes that she had taken throughout the day when she saw a large black SUV pull up in front of the building and park. The driver's side door swung open, and out stepped Roman.

From across the street, a vagrant stepped out from the alley and ran over to the large man. Roman listened impassively to what the homeless man said. Sicily noticed that the man nodded toward the coffee shop she was in too, or at least her direction. *Was this man an informant for the Marcus family?*

Her suspicions were supported by Roman when he passed something in a clear bag to the homeless man. The man then ran back to the direction of the alleyway where two more homeless stood; one a man and the other a woman. The man who spoke with Roman passed whatever contents were in the baggie to the other two and then the trio left in separate directions. *Who the fuck is Roman anyway? What is he up to?*

Sicily had seen him around town but always behind the wheel. She understood why he intimidated many. He was monstrous in build. Sicily put him at over three hundred pounds, and his hands were broad enough to make her head look like an infant in his palms. The thought of the man crushing her skull came to mind.

Sicily shook off the thought, ate her sandwich, and gathered her things. Roman walked through the newspaper's front door, only pausing long enough to look up and down the block. As she got closer, she noticed he had turned off the open sign and turned the latch that locked the door.

"Fuck," Sicily exclaimed as she reached into her purse and fished out her phone. She remembered the rumors of Roman's violent nature shared to her by Jonesy. The man was here on Marcus business, and Sicily knew that such transactions involved pain.

Jonesy promised her information, and she felt this guy would ensure it never saw the light of day. She ran down the street, hoping to find another way inside the building. She called the number that Jonesy gave her but only got her voicemail.

"Fuck. Fuck!" Sicily spat in frustration.

She hurried into the auto shop at the end of the block. "Is there another way into the newspaper?" she hurriedly asked while showing the manager her badge.

"Uh, yeah. Just walk on through to the back of the shop. Their loading dock is usually open, so we can use the pisser," the mechanic said, speaking in that slow country way that annoyed Sicily.

"Thanks!" she yelled as she ran to the back, past two mechanics arguing over a truck issue. Sicily emerged into the alleyway that led to the loading dock. She called Jonesy's number again. No answer. She then made a call to Holts. He answered.

"What's going on, Manns!" he chirped.

"I need you to get your ass down to The Herald, something is going down," Sicily said, blasting past any pleasantries. Before he could ask more questions, she hung up and pulled her Glock from her hip holster. She was in plain clothes today and considered calling dispatch to send units to her location. She was about to dial the number when she heard a scream. "Fuck!" she said and bolted through the open loading bay and into *The Haven Herald*.

Sicily entered the section of the building that was home to the printing press. It was running at the time, and she was glad for it. She heard another scream from the front of the room and the sounds of a struggle. Something thrown and crashing into boxes, things falling to the floor and breaking, grunts and growls.

Sicily sprinted, and as she rounded the press, she saw Roman holding Jonesy up against the wall outside her office with one hand. His massive fist held her by the neck, and Jonesy kicked and tried to punch him. Her blood trickled down from a head wound, and her face was reddening from the chokehold.

"Haven Shire police! Release the woman now!" Sicily commanded. Roman continued in his function as though Sicily wasn't there. Without further ado, she fired a volley of bullets into the large man. Each shot hit its mark across his torso and rocked him. Roman lost his grip as he stumbled back and fell to the floor. Jonesy fell to the floor as well and clutched her throat. She gulped mouthfuls of air, trying to catch her breath.

Manns kept her gun trained on Roman and got to Jonesy to examine her injuries. Her eyes were bloodshot, and tears streamed down her face. She looked up at Manns and started sobbing. She touched the top of her head with a trembling hand and winced when she felt the laceration that bled. There was glass on her clothes and in her hair.

Manns looked around and saw the source of the broken glass and the possible origin of Jonesy's head injury. Roman had thrown her through her picture-frame office window. There was some blood on the floor where she landed. Sicily peered into the office and saw that it was a source of struggle as well. Papers were strewn all around the office, and there were indentations from something or someone hitting the walls hard.

"My files," Jonesy said with a rasp in her voice. She swooned a little when she pointed to the desk. "The evidence is on my desk; we need it. Blue folder."

Sicily nodded and ran into the office. She counted her lucky stars when she found the file, thick with information. She snatched up the file and headed back to grab Jonesy. Just as she exited the office, something caught her hair and pulled hard.

The force was enough to lift her feet from the ground. Instinctively, she dropped the file folder close to her chest and reached for whatever had a hold of her. Sicily felt her grip on her sidearm slip as she went to grab whatever caught her hair. Suddenly, Sicily felt her body lift into the air and fell to the floor as if in slow motion. Time returned to normal when a massive weight came crashing down on her chest and slammed her into the floor.

Sicily felt all the air leave her body when the impact hit her chest. The blow hit with enough force to fracture a rib. Sicily was surprised it didn't shatter her whole ribcage. Fireworks exploded in her eyes, and electricity ran down her spine when she hit the concrete floor. She felt the world float away for a moment. Sicily coughed, and the pain was enough to sober her up. She took a deep, desperate breath and opened her eyes, looking for her attacker. The mountain of Roman stood over her with a bloody grin and a murderous gleam in his eyes.

Sicily tried to roll away and move to her feet, but Roman was surprisingly fast for a man his size. He grabbed her by the face with his large palm and pressed her head down into the floor. He intended to crush her skull, Sicily realized. She kicked frantically, sacrificed her hold on her firearm during the initial attack, and was limited to punching at his wrist and elbow. She felt the bones in her nose and jaw creak against the pressure of the man's grip. She heard him chuckle as her scream reverberated against his palm.

Suddenly, Roman's head rocked forward from a thunderous explosion behind him. His hand came up off of Sicily's face, and she could see that part of his face was now torn open, his right ear and cheek gone. She could see his cheekbone, jaw, and teeth were exposed, gleaming white in the light. He turned slowly, stunned by the injury, and came face-to-barrel with Sicily's pistol. Jonesy held the gun in two trembling hands, her breath came in fast.

He growled and moved to lunge at Jonesy. With a scream of fury, she pulled the trigger in rapid succession, emptying the magazine into his face. The skull that once belonged to Roman exploded, and his face, eyes, teeth, and brain matter flew away, unable to withstand the storm of bullets. He fell to the floor hard on his knees and prone in front of Jonesy. Blood and gore splashed onto the floor and at her feet.

Sicily scrambled to get on her feet, but her legs felt weak and unsteady. Jonesy stood over Roman's body, still pulling the trigger repeatedly. Her eyes were wide with anger and horror. Sicily made it to the file folder and shakily made it to her feet, her knees still wobbly. She slowly reached over to Jonesy, who was now trembling and put her free hand on the pistol.

"It's ok," Sicily said calmly. "You got him. He's not getting back up from that." Sicily realized this may not have been what Jonesy wanted to hear. She did just kill a man, even if it meant saving Sicily and herself. "You had to do it, otherwise, we would both be dead."

Jonesy began to cry quietly, lips trembling, a line of drool rolling off her lower lip. Sicily pulled the gun from her shaking hands and moved it to her hip holster. She moved to stand before Jonesy and looked her in the eyes. She put her hand on her shoulder and gave a firm squeeze. "We gotta call the station and meet up with my partner."

Sicily supported Jonesy and led her out the back of The Haven Herald. By the time they appeared in the back alley that connected the newspaper and the mechanics' shop, Jonesy could walk alone. She held herself as she trembled. "I'm so shaky. I'm not cold…why am I so shaky?" she asked.

"Adrenaline, dear. You've been through a lot in a short period," Sicily said. She was feeling the effects of the adrenaline dump into her system. Her body was beginning to register pain and fatigue in places. They needed to get somewhere safe. She hoped Holts would show soon.

She noticed Jonesy was also starting to feel the emotional impact of shooting someone. It didn't matter if it was in self-defense that she killed someone. She still killed someone, which would be a permanent fixture in her mind. Sicily slowed for a second at the rear entrance of the garage. The two garage doors were wide open, and she could see Main Street on the other side of the shop. She reached over, took Jonesy by the hand, and pulled her gently.

"Hey, Jonesy," she said, getting the trembling woman's attention. Jonesy looked at her. Tears streamed down her face and smeared makeup down her cheeks. "You saved my ass back there. Thank you, you did well."

Jonesy looked at her, fresh tears filled her eyes, and she quickly pulled her close and hugged her. Her injuries pained Sicily, but she also knew Jonesy needed this. Jonesy held tight until the trembling began to settle and then pulled away. She wiped away her tears and further smudged her eyeliner. She nodded at Sicily and gave her a brief smile.

"We're going to find that dumbass Robbie Holts and," Sicily's words were lost when a heavy sledgehammer came from behind Jonesy and smashed against the top of her skull. Her head exploded with blood and bone as the blow forced her skull into her chest. She fell instantly onto her knees and down to the ground on her left side. Blood splattered over Sicily's face, and she fell back against the wall.

Sicily saw the broken body of Jonesy, her blood pouring out into the alley. Behind her crumpled form, the three mechanics from the shop stood. All stared out at Sicily with impossibly wide grins and inky black stares. The one in the lead held a long wooden handled sledgehammer. The head of the hammer still dripped with blood, and a clump of tissue and hair clung to its end.

Sicily roared in rage and grief, clutching the file folder to her chest again. The three men chuckled wet guttural laughs and slowly began to approach her. Sicily pulled her sidearm and pulled the trigger.

Click! Empty magazine. No spare clips. *"FUCK!"* That was all Sicily could think.

Sicily steadied herself and looked around for a weapon. There was nothing close by. She would have to make a break for it and hope she was in shape to move quickly. She was usually quick on her feet but hoped her injuries wouldn't slow her down. Just as she was about to break for the newspaper loading dock, Sicily jumped as shots rang out and echoed off the alley's walls. Suddenly, for the second time today, time slowed down again for Sicily as she watched the bullets tear into the trio.

The man with the sledgehammer was the first to fall as a bullet tore through his temple and dropped him instantly. The other two turned and met with several slugs to their faces, necks, or torsos. The man directly behind the lead mechanic with the sledgehammer took the first bullet to his neck; it exited and struck the man beside him in his right shoulder. The following bullet hit him just below his left eye, and the impact sent him spinning before he fell to the ground. The mechanic beside him took three more shots, all center mass, each striking his sternum.

Manns saw Robert standing on the loading dock, his gun drawn. He jumped off the dock and ran to her, his weapon still drawn on the three men. "Manns, you ok?" he said, breathing hard.

"Jesus, Holts, I could fuck you right now," Manns said, trying to compose herself.

Holts looked at her, eyes wide with shock. "Really?" he asked with a huge grin, his voice nearly cracked.

Sicily laughed at his eagerness and goofy smile. "No, fuckface, but I love you forever for saving my ass."

Robert tried to hide his disappointment but failed. Embarrassed by the playful rejection, he quickly turned to check the men he shot. Sicily walked over to his side. The three men's eyes were no longer inky black, and their wide-open stares showed that the color of their eyes had returned to normal. They each still had that strange smile on their faces.

Holts stood back up and looked at her, his face filled with confusion. "What the hell is going on, Manns?" He seemed somewhat helpless when he asked this. "We got uniforms coming this way. What's the story here?"

Sicily looked at him and finally realized how out of her depth she was. She also understood George a little better now. "I have no fucking clue, Holts," she said. "We have to get to George and tell him what happened here."

# # # #

George and Elmer had spent most of the day looking through the hills to find anything that might explain the mystery of the lost herd and farm animals. So far, they had come up with nothing. No tracks, animal or otherwise, were found. There were no cattle corpses in the woods. The woods seemed utterly innocent and even inviting.

So why was George's early warning system going nuts? Ever since he met with the Chief and was dispatched to the farm, his skin and guts crawled. He felt like a tornado siren was going off in his head and rattling his bones. It had worsened since he left the farmhouse and walked into the woods.

"Hey, Elmer, let's head back. It's getting late in the day, and I will need a few more hands out here," George yelled. There was no reply. He repeated the old farmer's name louder this time. He looked around the woods and listened for footfalls. Silence. "Elmer?"

"Down here!" came a reply from a nearby ravine. George let loose a sigh of relief and headed toward the call. He got to a gorge that carved into the hillside. It was rocky, and a small creek cut down the middle of it. Elmer waved at him from the canyon of rocks and vegetation.

"What 'cha find there, boss?" he asked as he approached the old man. Elmer was somewhat out of breath by now from trekking through the dense woods and now this wet and rocky terrain.

"There's a cave this way," Elmer said between breaths.

"You take it easy. I'm not about to be dragging you out of here," George said with a chuckle.

The old man waved him away, dismissing the verbal jab.

The two carefully walked along the creek bed. The rocks were slippery and jagged. The ravine was narrow, so they had to wade into the water a couple of times. It was deep, and the water trickled out of the hills and into the connected farmland. George still wished he wore his waterproof combat boots, not police-issued steel-toed shoes. His feet started getting cold and damp from the occasional step into the depths of the brook.

The ravine snaked around the corner and into the side of the hill. In the rocky limestone face of the hill was the mouth of a cave. George looked at it and wondered why he had never heard of it. He walked closer to it and examined the walls and entrance. The opening was nearly a perfect circle in the stone. There were no grooves or signs that something bit into the rock. It was smooth. The walls told the same story.

"Hey, Elmer, you know anything about this cave?" George asked. "It doesn't look natural, but I have seen a tunnel like this."

"The cave is new for sure, hollowed out by something. I've never seen its likeness anywhere in this world," Elmer said.

"How the hell would you know? You've never been outside of Haven Shire," George said jokingly. His warning system was screaming now. George froze where he stood, trying to understand from where the danger might be coming. "How often do you come back here, Elm?" George asked, his mouth suddenly dried, and sweat began to run down his back.

"Been here only once. Never left…" Elmer replied.

George screwed his face up in confusion. "What the hell does that mean, Elmer?" he asked as he turned. He stopped dead in his tracks when Elmer was no longer Elmer. His head was shaking violently from side to side and back and forth. His movements were so fast that, at times, all there was of his face was a blur. With a loud crack, Elmer's lower jaw fell open and dangled with a wag. His eyes, once a sharp blue, were now completely white. His tongue blackened, rolled beyond his lips, and down to his navel. The serpentine organ came to a point and began pointing in George's direction as if trying to seek him out.

George watched in horror as the tongue split fourfold, and each limb or feeler began to move independently. They each turned and pushed against Elmer's head or pulled at his scalp from behind as if trying to extricate themselves from his skull.

Each extremity grew to the length of Elmer's torso, approximately four feet, and was as thick as his legs. The underside of each tentacle sprouted tiny hook-like barbs leading to the center. A bone-white protrusion appeared from the center of each limb that broke open and snapped shut. An octopus or bird-like beak hungrily bit at the air between itself and George.

The creature used the Elmer-like arms, tore the shirt off the body, and began pulling at its pink flesh. It grabbed hold of a paunchy bundle at the base of the neck and started tearing. Beneath the skin was a purple and black mass of meat with two rows of suckers. The ribs broke open outward, forming a row of spikes coming from its chest.

The human hands split down the center between the middle and ring fingers. From each division, a long, serrated, sword-like hook erupted. The shoulders and elbows snapped and stretched until his arms looked like those of a praying mantis. Elmer's flesh still hung from the outstretched appendages and torso like dirty rags.

Ribs turned into spikes that snapped like pinchers, and the spine tore through what was once Elmer's lower back. It lengthened into a scorpion tail. Aside from a bit of flesh and muscle, the only other thing that remained of Elmer was his voice. When the thing hissed, screamed, or roared, George could hear Elmer's voice through the din.

Then it spoke, not from the razor-sharp beak but in George's head. "I couldn't wait any longer," it said in a distorted Elmer voice as if a hundred different Elmers were simultaneously speaking from underwater. "I haven't feasted for so long, not since eating Elmer's brain. Well, there were the cattle, but we need substance."

George felt nausea as he felt this thing's voice in his head. It felt like someone repulsive whispering in his ear while they licked his ear canal at the same time. The invasion made him angry, and he growled against it. George's psyche bucked and fought against the sight of this abomination. He felt like someone could go mad if they looked for too long at this monster, much less listen and feel its repulsive voice in their head.

"Just what the fuck are you?" George spat, his gun now trained on the beast. "Where did you come from?"

"We were summoned. Commanded by our gods to come here and reclaim our world," the horror said. George could feel its loathing for him. And it's hunger. Always hungry. "We come through the Veil, and the priestess gives us form so we can stay awhile," the creature chuckled in George's head. George tried to inch his way into a defensible position.

"Those meaty animals on the farm smelled so good. I couldn't resist. The goat wasn't enough. I needed something with thoughts and feelings. The cows fed me for a time. You'll feed me, too. I wonder how your brain tastes. Your fear."

The creature drooled visibly and psychically. George began to maneuver away from the mouth of the cave and around to the monster's right. He wasn't sure where the cave led and didn't want to find out yet. He needed to reach higher ground and find the way back to the ATV.

The creature crouched low, the bony protrusions that once were ribs became spidery legs, and the once-Elmer legs twisted and popped until they formed grasshopper-like appendages. George watched the monster as it stalked toward him, its tail curling up and the tailbone now a stinger. George slowly moved to the right of the beast in case he could make a run for it. He doubted this was a possibility with its many legs. The creature roared an otherworldly noise that intermingled with the voices of Elmer, and it charged. It moved fast but was clumsy, as if it were still getting used to its legs.

George aimed his gun at the thing's tentacle-adorned head. The first few shots struck the writhing appendages, blowing chunks of flesh free. The next group of bullets struck the bony beak within the writhing appendages. The first bullet did not affect the monster, and the shot deflected off the beak. The second and third bullets struck hard the chomping mouth, and the upper half of the mouth cracked and then blew apart.

The monster roared and screamed in pain as black fluid flowed. It thrashed its head from side to side as though trying to shake off the bullets biting into the flesh and bone of its maw. George's confidence swelled when he saw this thing's pain and blood. He fired again, intent on emptying the remaining magazine into the beast.

Bullets screamed into the beast, striking its legs and torso. One of the spidery legs broke off. The mantis foreclaw fell to the side; both were now useless. Several wounds opened up on the torso, and black blood spilled out onto the stones of the creek bed. The creature shrieked in pain and horror as it tried to find cover from the barrage. The monster's surprise and fear flooded George's mind.

"Didn't expect a fight, did ya, you ugly fuck?!" George screamed in his mind as he reloaded a fresh clip and fired rounds into the retreating beast. The bullets pelleted the thing's back and tore the flesh and bone. The thing turned and hissed at George, projecting hate into his mind. Then, as George was about to reload his sidearm again, the monster scuttled into the cave's darkness. George could hear the screams of rage and pain deep into the tunnel.

George thought about pursuing the monster but considered it unwise for various reasons. If he were going to come back to the cave, it would be with bigger guns and an army of police officers. Hell, maybe the military. Either way, George knew he had to return to the station and report.

"What will I tell the chief?" he mumbled aloud, maybe if he had evidence. George began looking for something he could take back with him to prove that there was something alien there. As he looked on the ground for something tangible, he saw that every drop of blood, piece of flesh, or fragment of bone was disintegrating into floating motes of ash. Each flake of evidence then vanished into the air.

"Shit!" George holstered his sidearm and trekked back the way he came. He had to contact Manns and Holts. He hoped they were okay and hadn't run into a similar problem. They were the only ones who would believe him. He knew they were loyal to a fault, and maybe, with their help, they could convince others. He looked at the sky, it was getting dark from what little he could see beyond the forest canopy. Clouds were starting to thicken overhead.

There was a storm brewing in Haven Shire, and the dark clouds above reflected the storm roiling beneath the ground. George could feel it in his skin and bones. Everyone in the Shire was in danger.

-CHAPTER 16-
SKIN AND BONE

Thaddeus fell hard to the floor. He could feel his right cheek swell from the blow. Gerald towered over him with a malicious smile, spittle drooling from his lips, and his eyes were wide with excitement. Thaddeus tried to collect himself and get to a defensible position. His hands were kicked out from beneath him by Judge, who had been standing in the corner of the dining room watching with passing interest as Gerald executed Thaddeus' punishment.

"Tell me, boy, do you think I am stupid?" Judge spoke, his voice nearly a growl with rage. "Do you think I'm blind? That I do not have eyes all over this village?"

Gerald gave Thaddeus a powerful kick to his ribs, blasting the air from his lungs with the blow. The force behind the kick was powerful enough to cause Thaddeus to slide across the room. He hacked and gasped as he tried to catch his breath. Gerald gave a demented chuckle and imitated the noise Thaddeus made. He stepped forward, licking his lips and clenching his large hands into fists. Judge stopped him with a raised hand. Gerald followed Judge with a pout across his face.

"Your appetites were none of my concern so long as you were careful! I don't care what you did to whom, so long as you are not stupid enough to leave a trace of evidence. I raised you better than this! How to be careful and disappear if needed. But this…" Judge reached into the corner, pulled out an old shoe box, and threw it to the floor. The contents spilled out toward the helpless Thaddeus. "You were stupid enough to record your disgusting exploits!" Judge roared at him.

"No one saw but me," Thaddeus choked out.

"Worse yet, you went into the catacombs and took a Formoria with you! Such blasphemy! The heresy!" Judge spit the words venomously at Thaddeus seeming to ignore anything his son muttered. Gerald whooped and hopped in excitement and raised a massive fist to strike the prone Thaddeus again. He was stopped cold by Judge's fiery glare. Gerald shrunk under his gaze and backed away. Judge knelt by the cowering man, who was now holding his hands up in an attempt to escape more beatings. Judge's lips curled in disgust as he noticed that Thaddeus was hurting but also secretly enjoying the pain. His eye was swollen, his nose was broken, but there was no denying the hint of a smile. If he was going to truly hurt this man, Judge would have to hurt the only things he cared for- his toys.

"Here's what you will do. I can't find Roman, and your mother is tasked with gathering the congregation, so you will take your brother back to your little shack and burn everything in it to the ground. If there are any witnesses, you will dispatch them." Judge spoke coldly, reached out, and grabbed Thaddeus by his blond hair. Thaddeus moaned in pain and ecstasy. "When you return, I will already have prayed to the Formoria on which punishment would best suit your transgression. Pray that I am the one to administer your re-education and not one of their emissaries."

He jerked Thaddeus' head sharply to the left, stood straight, and walked toward the room's exit. Gerald stalked toward Thaddeus, preparing to torment the man further. He was stopped cold by a sharp snap of Judge's fingers in the next room. Gerald's face turned sour at being denied further pleasure in causing his pretty brother pain. He snorted and hocked a massive ball of spittle and snot onto his bowed head instead. He laughed heartily at Thaddeus' flinching at this and the following look of disgust. He then lumbered out of the room like a child on the way to play.

Thaddeus thought of composing himself and going to wash but found that his body would not move. Several of his ribs were fractured, his eye swollen shut, and his head swam in the attempt to move. He slumped to the floor and laid his swollen cheek on the cold dining room floor. For a moment, he began considering how he would exact revenge for this attack. He could not consider this long as the room became dark, and unconsciousness took over.

Maria watched the exchange between Judge and Thaddeus from the summoning room. The room was large, as big as a gymnasium, and cylindrical. The walls were perfectly smooth all around where a giant mirror stood. Maria sat cross-legged on a smooth, polished, circular obsidian space on the basement floor of the Marcus mansion. The mirrored surface was trimmed in gold runes and symbols. She was completely nude as she regained her focus and chanted the mantra that would open a line of communication between her and the Formoria.

On the wall behind her stood a twenty-foot-tall by ten-foot-wide mirror. If one tried examining their reflection in the mirror, they would only find a pale, smokey white representation of themself. It would not reflect the viewer but was a representation of the Veil itself. The mirror functioned as a door for those who existed beyond the Veil.

"When will my boys get along," Maria sighed heavily. "Now come my pretties, come and collect souls for me."

Maria could open the door to their world just long enough for one of their kind to slip into our plane and take form. However, the pilgrim would quickly disintegrate and die painfully if the ritual failed. Soon, with the help of the ancient-cursed gnarls of roots and vines beneath Haven Shire, she would have obtained enough life and spiritual energy to open a permanent door to unite our world and that world beyond the Veil.

Maria felt within her breasts the pangs of motherly sorrow at seeing her Thaddeus suffer. She fought hard against her maternal reflex to rush to his side and protect him from his punishment for his transgressions. Not because Maria feared Judge turning his ire onto her, but because Maria was so close to the Formoria right now. When communicating with those beyond the Veil, she could hear their thoughts and feel their desires. They, in turn, could sense hers as well. The Formoria were not creatures that possessed feelings such as pity or compassion, even for their progeny.

"Give me the power Great Gods of Old," Maria began imparting her thoughts into the Veil. She began to entice them with images she held onto from her own childhood. Her memories of pain and hunger for power.

The Formoria knew only chaos, hunger, and lust, nothing else. They were intelligent by many measures since they had existed before there was light in the universe. They had knowledge of rituals and spells, ways to access the limits of the mind and break them, and power to give to others. Their only weakness was their carnal desires. They lacked physical forms or a cohesive shape, they could not engage senses outside their memory. They lost this ability when they were exorcised from this reality by the first people.

"I give thee my offerings of sensation, my Lords!" Maria cried out in pleasure as she began touching her body. She sipped the ceremonial wine as she reached to the floor and retrieved the cat-of-nine tails. Maria threw the glass of wine across the room and began flogging her shoulders, breasts, and thighs, "I offer my body for your pleasure!"

"We bless you human child," A watery voice spoke into Maria's mind, **"...we bless you with our strength and magic!"**

The first tribes brought light, fire, and order, along with rituals and spells of their own. Though the battle lasted several hundred centuries, the Formoria were unorganized and relied on fear and madness. They forced them to take shapes of things with vitals and biological needs. The Formoria became flesh and bone instead of the stuff of nightmares and madness. And, Oh! The sensations!

The Formoria immediately became addicted to what they could touch, taste, hear, smell, and see. They felt emotions before the change, but now those emotions had physical sensations. The experience was overwhelming for them, and when they broke free of their physical shackles and the desire for them, their memories continued to plague them and torment them.

The Formoria fled from the light that blinded, the fire that burned, and the intoxication of sensation. The long-standing war between the descendants of the first people did not end there. They prodded the Veil for weaknesses and sought out servants on this side to serve them, willingly or not.

To lay the groundwork for their return, some of the Formoria cross-bred with members of the first tribes. The offspring resulted in monstrosities gifted with powers and abilities and the hunger for revenge. Those who survived bred again, and their children grew weaker as time passed, just as those born of the first tribe forgot their spells and rituals and became reliant on technology.

Unlike those born of the first tribes, the children of the Former still maintained their abilities. Some had the ability to see the spirits of the dead, some were born with innate influence or the power to bend wills, and others had other gifts. Those blessed with blessings from beyond the Veil were also subject to insights and the wisdom of the Formoria. Sadly, the human mind usually lacked the fortitude to withstand this information. Maria knew this acutely. Even though she was born with gifts of sight and could speak with the Formoria, she was the only blessed child in her family in over five generations. The memory of humans is short, and with no one to understand her gifts, she was considered insane by many with whom she shared her insight as a child.

This world is unworthy of me, Maria thought as she felt the power swell within her. *No one is. Not Judge, my parents, or the rest of this sick and filthy race.*

Maria shared her memories of how she caused her blasphemous parents to suffer to the Formoria. This offering she gave up to them, not because they demanded it, but because it pleased her to do so.

Maria's parents were devout worshipers of the Christian faith and prominent members of their religious community. Her younger brother, Herman, was always by her side. As a boy, he was always quiet and rather portly. Maria's parents often speculated that Herman had a disability or disorder, but Maria always knew better. When they were alone, she shared her visions and lessons she had learned from the Formoria. Herman would often ask Maria about that place beyond our reality.

Maria's parents had caught her communing with those beyond the Veil. At first, they thought that she could commune with their God and His hosts. That is until Herman told them what Maria had shared about those beyond the Veil. After that, they called their preachers in for an exorcism.

Maria smiled as she remembered fondly the screams of shock and pain when she summoned those beyond the Veil to dispatch the exorcists and her parents. They sang their hymns and prayers as she funneled Formoria into them and had them all torture each other. They continued to sing as those beyond the Veil took over, forcing the preachers to kill each other as her parents watched in horror.

It took a whole day for the two exorcists to die and another day for her parents. Herman eagerly participated in preparing his parents for their sacrifice. After Maria and Herman murdered their parents and those loathsome priests, they put their home to the torch. They had packed food, a suitcase, and whatever money

Maria could find. Their company for their travels was each other and the whispers from those beyond the Veil.

When Maria met Judge, the voices of the Former told her to kill him and steal his knowledge and power. For some reason, she couldn't. It could have been because he was probably the only human she would meet who fully understood her. He saw her, peered into her, and didn't judge or think her ugly. She confessed with glee how she murdered so many through her travels, and he admired her.

In time, the voices forgave her for not killing him. They came to acknowledge his usefulness. They felt her desire for him and grew intoxicated by her passion. They also appreciated Judge's hunger and ambition. He wanted to unmake this world and remake it in his vision— a vision supplied by those ancient eldritch gods of the Formoria.

Soon, the plans, the pain, and the death would bear fruit. Judge used his considerable resources to build an army of Formoria. The tunnels and caves were lined with roots that oozed the toxins secreted from an alien plant. This viscous substance cursed the soil and allowed those beyond the Veil to keep their physical forms on this plane.

Judge chose from his flock those intelligent enough to ensnare human victims and perform the ritual to give some of them a human form. These mimics could then walk on land without risking being evicted beyond the Veil. This act was painful and considered blasphemy, but they functioned as agents through whom Maria could communicate. Those who went through this process would be honored for their sacrifice by offering up their bodies to be consumed by their gods when they arrived on this plane. Their consciousness would feed the eldritch deities and be the first of many to meet this fate.

Maria communicated with the Formoria and remotely viewed all the pawns at play. She also used her gifts to remove interlopers who were too close to discovering the truth about the Veil and may wish to stop the ritual. Maria had dispatched Roman to deal with the so-called journalist. When he failed, she projected her consciousness onto others to succeed where he had not.

"Poor Roman," Maria whispered as she thought about the now dead servant, "I will miss you services. You were faithful and strong, blessed with an amazing cock, and sang so beautifully when I bled you. I will avenge you." Whoever killed him would be aware that the Marcus family sent Roman, and they would need to be silenced. The first attempt failed to kill the police officer, and now she had an ally. She could not decide whether they had received the journalist's information.

No matter, she could not allow for any loose threads. Loose threads would reflect poorly on her, possibly jeopardize the ritual, and the Formoria do not accept failure kindly. Then, there was Judge to contend with. She could feel his desire for her power.

It's a shame he didn't have that same desire for my body, she thought with a wicked smile.

The floor on which she sat functioned as a lens to stalk her prey or allies remotely. With the pool, she could find an unsuspecting victim to pour in the consciousness of the Formoria. The possessed individual would do whatever she bade them to do, even killing someone they loved. The most delicious part was that they were still aware of and watching what was happening.

Maria would use this gift now to rid her of the two police officers who grew closer to discovering her family. She had already wormed her thoughts into several townspeople, and now she would use them to erase those who would stand in the way of the Former. Maria might even enjoy it a little.

She would use her power on the two cops directly, but something interfered with her ability to reach into their minds. Some imprint or barrier. A mystery worth investigating later. For now, there were plenty of others up to the task.

-CHAPTER 17-
DESPERATION

Holts and Manns stumbled toward the car that Holts had driven. They scanned their surroundings in case there were witnesses. The sky had darkened, and the clouds were swollen and grey. Sicily's could feel electricity around her, and the air was eerily still. It would be just her luck for a tornado to touch down.

Just as Holts got to the car's driver's side, a thunderous boom split the air, and the driver's side window exploded. They both drew their guns and pointed them toward the gunfire. Approximately three hundred feet away stood the hardware store owner, Craig Hoager. He was an older man, nearly seventy, wearing a button-up flannel shirt and overalls.

Craig held a sawed-off double-barreled shotgun in his right hand and was reloading the gun with his left. His eyes were pitch black, and his face broke into a wide, insane smile. With a loud *crack,* he reloaded the gun and aimed it from the hip in their direction.

Holts jumped behind a trash can secured by a chain to the light pole on the side of the street. As he ducked for cover, the shotgun thundered again, spraying buckshot all over the driver's side door panel. Manns ducked behind the car for cover. She glanced down the street behind the vehicle for an alternate escape route.

"You pigs will suffer for what you did to Roman!" voices rang out from behind Sicily. She turned to see people coming out from alleyways, a few homeless and citizens of the Shire alike, walked onto the sidewalk and into the street. In unison they spoke in the same wet, hate-filled voice. The spiteful choir sent a chill down Sicily's spine.

The employees of Dale's pharmacy and soda shop walked up the street. Each had a knife or a blunt instrument in their hands. Even Dale's ten-year-old granddaughter held an aluminum bat. Each bared their teeth in an insane smile with pitch-black eyes.

"Shit," Manns said. "Holts! Watch your six!"

"What the fuck is going on with them?" Robert yelled back. "Is this what George was talking about?"

Manns wasn't sure and decided to focus on the one person, other than she and Holts, who had a gun. Craig stalked closer with his shotgun. Suddenly, from behind him, Julie Hoager, his wife of twenty years, came running out the front of the store screaming.

"Craig! What on Earth are you doing? Why are you shooting at Sici-

Before she could finish her question, Craig spun on her and unloaded both barrels of 12-gauge buckshot into his wife. The force of the blow picked her off her feet and knocked her to the sidewalk. She died instantly as several buckshot rounds tore into her face and neck.

Sicily screamed in rage and horror as she looked upon the dead body of Julie Hoager, her hair still smoking from the blast of the 12-gauge shotgun.

Craig turned slowly, still wearing that awful smile and growling. His eyes were still black, but thick tears flowed down his face.

Even as they hid behind the car doors for protection, a small mob was stalking them from behind, armed with whatever they could find. Manns watched as a candy striper from the pharmacy took some buckshot to her shoulder that missed the car. She reeled momentarily and then looked back at them with that strange smile and chuckled as her white button-up t-shirt turned red with her blood.

"What the fuck are we going to do, Manns?' Robert asked, his voice higher pitched than he intended.

Manns thought and finally said, "When he reloads, we return to the paper. We'll go through to the alley and run for cover. Got it?"

Robert nodded his head in agreement.

Manns didn't know if it was the best idea, but it was the only thing she could come up with. Sicily didn't want to shoot these people unless she was forced to do so. She knew they were not in control of their actions based on what George said. Something else was in control, and as soon as they were safe, they could figure that out. Sicily nodded at Robert to come through the car's cab while she covered him.

He dove in as she fired a round into the store window, hoping the glass would distract Mr. Hoager. It didn't. He didn't flinch as he stalked closer, aimed his shotgun, and pulled the trigger.

"Click!"

The empty chamber sounded like church bells to Sicily and Robert. Sicily grabbed Robert roughly by his shirt and pulled him toward the paper. She saw where Robert had made entry when he came to her rescue. A street-facing tempered glass window popped and fell on the sidewalk. They had less than a minute before Mr. Hoager reloaded the shotgun and began his barrage anew. She prayed he would wait until then and not fire when he inserted the first round. Her luck wasn't total shit, she guessed.

They jumped through the broken window. They took cover behind a counter when the first round of the shotgun thundered and blew apart several papers and decorations on the countertop. Shrapnel from the fake potted plants and plastic signage rained down. Manns and Holts covered their heads as they crouched low to the floor and duck-walked toward their next refuge. The printing press in the rear of the building would supply the most cover, but they needed to duck between desks and tables to get to it.

Sicily heard several clambering footsteps, as the mesmerized mob charged into the building entrance. The report of the shotgun's pump action sounded at the front of the office. She knew Hoager would stay where he was and let the others flush them out. That's what she would do, too, in their place. They had to move quickly.

"Holts! To the back! Stay low! Move fast!" she shouted to Robert.

"You, too! We're both getting outta this!" Robert replied over another shotgun explosion as it tore through the office and destroyed the PC sitting on top of the counter.

Suddenly, she heard Robert shout and curse as something crashed into him. It was Dale, the pharmacist. He had tackled him and was trying to wrestle Robert's gun from his hand. She saw store patrons, people she recognized, running up to the scuffle.

"Fuck!" Sicily swore. She whipped out from behind her cover and fired into the patrons running at Robert and Dale. Her heart sank as she saw the bullets tear into more than one citizen. She knew at least one of the four or five was fatally wounded. Right now, she had a partner to worry about.

Just as she was about to fire on Dale, she heard Robert's pistol fire. For a moment, she feared the worst until she saw Dale's white shirt filled with blood and his lifeless body slump to the floor. Holts quickly pushed him off, his face filled with revulsion and horror.

"Come on, Holts! Move your ass now!" Sicily commanded.

Robert pulled himself up to his feet and started running.

Sicily quickly followed suit and fired three more shots at Mr. Hoager. One bullet missed and struck the picture-frame glass window behind him, but the other two hit their mark and knocked him onto the sidewalk outside. She didn't check if he was alive; she just ran.

The pair jumped over desks and ducked the occasional thrown object from the pursuing mob. Once they reached the door to the print shop, they jumped through it and turned immediately to slam it. Just then, someone blocked the door, preventing it from closing. Sicily and Robert looked down and saw Dale's granddaughter, her right arm and head stuck between the door and the frame.

"We will find you both, and we will eat your guts!" the little girl said, smiling at them with her huge polished black eyes. Sicily saw the door cut into her cheeks, and her arm contorted awkwardly at the elbow. The little girl's wet, throaty chuckle shocked Manns awake.

With a scream, Sicily wrenched open the door and kicked the girl in the chest as hard as possible. The ten-year-old flew back into a desk like a ragdoll and slumped to the floor. Sicily slammed the door hard again and turned the double bolt lock. Several bodies on the other side of the door hit hard against it.

"They'll figure a way through," Robert said. He was visibly shaking.

Manns knew they had to get out of there and meet up with George. "Let's make a run for the station," Sicily replied. "How far is it? Two miles?"

"If that," Robert replied. "You don't suppose the whole town is like this, do you?"

Sicily shrugged at this. "I just know that I'm low on ammo, and since we're not on duty, neither of us is wearing a vest," Sicily said. "Plus, if there's any chance there are others on the force who can help, we need to enlist them."

Robert thought about it for a moment and nodded in agreement. They ran toward the loading dock, and once through the open door, they were relieved to find that the bodies of the men who attacked them were still down. Sicily took only a moment to look at the body of Jonesy, editor-and-chief of the local paper. She felt a stab of grief for the poor dead woman who was so brave.

Just then, Sicily realized she still had the file folder. She had folded it and crammed the package down the lower back of her shirt and into her blue jeans. She checked to see if it was still there. Upon touching the folder, she felt a small measure of comfort. She promised she wouldn't let Jonesy's death be in vain.

Somehow, Sicily will use this information to burn down whoever did this. Sicily had a feeling she knew who it was. After all, Roman worked for the Marcus family, and he never acted without orders. They will answer for all this, Sicily swore.

Just as Manns and Holts made it through the mechanic's shop, they ran around the corner, opposite the way they came. Once they turned, they found four officers walking in their direction. Each had his gun drawn and walked low in a defensive formation. Sicily saw their faces, and she couldn't suppress the smile when she saw their eyes were clear.

Sicily pulled her Haven Shire police ID from her pocket and held up her gun. Roberts took the cue and did the same. They announced themselves individually to the approaching officers. The four men seemed to relax somewhat upon hearing their names and IDs. They had each begun to holster their weapons.

Manns and Holts approached the incoming team, and Sicily shouted details of what was following them. She explained the situation in a way that would keep the police from immediately using deadly force on the entranced civilians. It was a perplexing task under the circumstances. Robert let her talk as he guarded the rear in case anyone ran around the corner.

As Robert backed toward the incoming reinforcements, he backed into Sicily as she suddenly stopped. He turned to ask what the situation was until he saw her frozen in her tracks, her face a mask of despair. He followed her gaze and saw the four police officers standing in place, convulsing. When the gyrations ceased, their smiles grew wide, and their eyes filled with inky black pools.

The four policemen raised their firearms and leveled their aim in Sicily's and Robert's direction.

Time slowed down for Robert; he looked at Sicily. A single tear rolled down her face as she shook her head in disbelief. He watched as all hope was carried away with that salty drop that fell from her chin.

He didn't want to look at the four police about to shoot them. He didn't want his last memory to be his friends' guns pointed at him. He only looked at Sicily, the only person he knew he could trust besides George. The woman he secretly cared for more than a friend. The last friendly face he might ever see.

-CHAPTER 18-
YOU CAN NEVER GO HOME AGAIN

Phineas, Mata, and Vincent gathered every literal and spiritual weapon, but this brought little comfort to Phineas. Even with Lizzie resting comfortably in her well-furnished pen as backup, he felt they needed an army. He drove as Mata snored sweetly on the passenger side. Vincent lay uncomfortably in the remaining space in the second row beside the dog pen.

He looked to the horizon of the Kansas sunset. He tried to focus on its beauty rather than try to inventory the pain and trauma he had experienced in Haven Shire. There were two things he had learned from his recovery- you can never go home again, and the more you resist facing your fears the more they grow. The anxiety building within him now was testament to that.

Phineas was terrified not just of the horrors his dream had portended, but also of the fact he was returning to the painful backdrop of his childhood. On the surface, Haven Shire was just a charming village that many would picture from some Norman Rockwell portrait of Americana. Phineas had thought he would never see this cursed place again.

The townsfolk were kind and warm, and they truly appreciated the ideals of community. If someone needed help, the village would come together. Offers of food, clothes, and prayer were always in abundance when someone's family suffered a tragedy or if farming was not bearing fruit.

But there was the other face of Haven Shire. The judging faces, the looks of shame, or the outright sneers if you couldn't find a way to assimilate into the ideal community. As a child, Phineas saw this side of the Shire; his father- the drunk, neglectful and abusive and his poor, insane mother. Even then, as a child, Phineas could see too much.

Oh, mom, Phineas thought, *I hope you escaped that shithole. I wish I could've done more for you.*

Phineas' mother had the sight, he shared it, but she didn't understand her power. Her life and death were all the more tragic to him now that he understood his gift. She knew the spirits and ethereal beasts were real, but no one would believe her. Instead, they locked her away, poisoned her with medication, and left her to waste away. Phineas could have shared this fate if he had stayed in that quaint village.

Because he was a child, Phineas could not look away at the evil worming its way into the roots and foundations of his hometown. He turned into it, eyes wide, and faced it head-on with all the curiosity gifted to a child. That is how he came to learn about the evil in Haven Shire.

He could sense some ancient heart beating in the hills outside of town. To Phineas, those flint hills, thick with brambles and trees, were a leviathan stalking the unaware citizens of the Shire. The mounds of rock and stone whispered to him, as they did his mother, and with every breath, it wove a tapestry displaying the town's fate.

Phineas had thought as a child that he was just as crazy as his mother until he watched his father die from liver disease. He watched the man's soul depart his jaundiced, piss-stained body and begin to travel to some promised hereafter. Instead of going to the "next life," Phineas watched as his father's soul wailed as it got snatched up by unseen hands and dragged screaming into those hills.

He followed his father's spirit, hoping to catch it and find some way to give him peace. He chased it all day until he found a cave that no one ever spoke of in town, wedged between a chasm carved into the side of limestone cliffs overlooking a creek. As he stood before the mouth of that hollow, he heard the screams and howls of every soul that ever died in Haven Shire.

Phineas discovered the truth about Haven Shire that day. Even in death, those who dwelled in the Shire never left. They were doomed to haunt those hills and valleys. The revelation that all those whom he'd ever loved were never granted an afterlife of peace broke him. It broke him again when he realized his mother never left this place to be free from suffering.

Phineas was barely thirteen, but he was not about to spend another day in this town. When he got home, he waited for George to return and packed what he could. Phineas then remembered his mother's final year here. He desperately wanted to explain things to his brother.

Still, George might think of Phineas as he did his mother, some poor soul who had gone mad and listened to voices rather than be there for her children. Or he would hate him, just as their father hated him, for being too much like his mother, and lock him up until he died from neglect.

George didn't see the world as Phineas did. His world was black and white, with little room for grey. Phineas was the empath; George was the fighter. He took the brunt of their father's ire. George was the one who punched and kicked those who would speak ill of his family. He was the one who refused to back down from any challenge.

Phineas remembered the note he left his brother back then. Whenever he thought about how he left, the guilt would begin to creep up from the depths of his being. "Why do I do this to myself every fucking time?" he murmured.

He knew that this was how his helix of shame began. First, there was the guilt of leaving without saying goodbye. Next, there was the embarrassing fact that he didn't even get that far from Haven Shire, not physically anyway. Then it was the shame of homelessness, trying to earn money, food, or shelter any way he could.

Final stop, addiction. Alcohol mostly, but Phineas did anything to numb himself. He saw phantoms in the shadows, windows, and mirrors hanging around those about to die. After some time, it all became too much. Phineas couldn't drink enough, smoke enough, or fuck enough to get away from the visions. So, he killed himself.

"Dammit boy," a stern voice said to him as he lay in restraints in that hospital bed. "Why on God's green Earth would you go and do something so stupid?"

When he awoke, a nurse was looking down on him. She was broad-shouldered and wore rainbow earrings, jewelry, and the brightest red lipstick he had ever seen. Antoinette Baker was the most formidable lady Phineas would ever meet until Mata came along. She was gifted just like him. Phineas felt that at once. Antoinette Baker, formally Anthony Baker, looked at Phineas and didn't see a junkie or homeless kid, she saw a survivor.

"A pretty thing like you, with all your gifts," she said as she hung another bag of saline on the IV pump, "...and you would go and waste them. I see you are hurting but this is not the way, you hear?"

"You wouldn't understand, lady," Phineas croaked.

"Well, I'm the one who gets to babysit you, so sing me your sad song and I'll sing mine," Antionette sad firm but warmly.

Finally, he wasn't alone, and neither was she. She introduced him to a community of seers, prophets, magi, and healers. He met teachers of demonology and witchcraft and learned how to defend himself and bring his enemies to their knees. He was an adaptive learner and still a novice today compared to the scribes and instructors he'd met. Phineas finally accepted his gifts, himself, and was humbled by his role in the universe; this one and the next.

All his confidence shrank when he saw the signs indicating he had crossed into Haven Shire. The air around him immediately told him that his hometown was gone. It was now a place of corruption and madness. Phineas removed his dark glasses and looked at the scenery unfiltered.

The sky was a blanket of smoky, grey clouds. Motes of tiny red lights floated like lazy fireflies in the air. The clouds swirled and rolled, some threatened to funnel down and grab all they could of the Earth below.

He tapped Mata, who he had just now noticed was having a nightmare. Maybe the environment inspired the dreaming, trying to warn her. Even Lizzie began to whine uncomfortably. Vincent rose, bleary-eyed and rubbing his sore neck and shoulders.

-CHAPTER 19-
KNITTING AND TEARING

Thaddeus drove the utility van. He had awoken and cleaned himself up just before Gerald met him in his room. His muscles and bones still ached from the beating Thaddeus had taken from Gerald. His eye was a swollen purple lump, and he could barely see through the throbbing contusion.

"Come, we go clean up the mess," Gerald said with a malicious grin. They loaded the van with several five-gallon jugs of gasoline. Thaddeus moved to the driver's seat when they loaded the tools. Gerald sat on a bench in the cargo space of the van. The van served dual purposes- transport of Judge's "purchases" from human traffickers and the disposal of such resources when they had served their purposes.

Gerald adorned himself with the only clothing he wore besides the loin cloth. He wore a long leather butcher's apron, which had seen so much gore and blood to make the garment stiff with dried blood. When he moved or bent the right way, the apron would crackle, and remnants from his victims shook loose.

The apron was adorned with several blades, cleavers, and spikes from the torso to waist. At his waist, Gerald carried a hand axe and a tenderizing hammer opposite each other. Most, if not all, of these utensils were rusty, bent, or still covered in dried blood from Gerald's last kill.

Thaddeus hated Gerald for many reasons; his persistent need to be liked by his mother and father, his disgusting appearance, his smell of weeks gone without bathing, and a loin cloth he never changed. Most of all, that stupid apron and his total disregard for the tools it contained. Thaddeus would never allow his tools to fall into complete disrepair. It was sloppy.

Thaddeus cringed as Gerald let loose a fart that lasted at least thirty seconds and was punctuated by him partially shitting himself. The stench was enough for him to roll down his window. Even over the cool wind in his face, he could still hear Gerald chuckling like an idiot.

"You are a pig," Thaddeus yelled.

At that, Gerald's childish laugh stopped abruptly. "Yeah, and you are jealous," Gerald pouted.

"Jealous? Of what? Certainly not of your looks," Thaddeus replied.

"Mommy and Daddy like me best. They let me kill your pets. They might let me kill you," Gerald said with a sneer.

"Doubt it," Thaddeus said, dodging the threat. "They need a pretty face to run their errands outside the church. You know, the building you can never leave in broad daylight."

Suddenly, Gerald began to roar in laughter.

"What the fuck is so funny, you freak?" Thaddeus asked, irritated.

"You don't know Daddy's plan, do you?" Gerald replied. "Mommy said they are going to turn everyone into people like me. I will be a king!" Gerald resumed his laughter. "Maybe you can be royal cock-cleaner!" he said and began to laugh again harder.

"Don't be ridiculous. What's the point of having a bunch of imbeciles like you shambling about in their shit? What's the point of ruling over that?" Thaddeus sneered bitterly.

"Not rule, he gives," Gerald said, wiping a line of snot off his face. "He makes all the world ready for those who come before," Gerald said almost dreamily. "He makes it perfect for the ugly to rule, eat, and shit."

Thaddeus looked in the rearview mirror and could tell Gerald wasn't lying or crazier than usual. Their parents told Gerald more of what was to come than their perfect son. His head spun with fury. He did everything his mother and father wanted, and they kept this from him but shared it with his twisted, ugly, stupid brother. Thaddeus felt bile rise in his chest and his teeth grit so hard, they could've cracked in his mouth.

They pulled up to the abandoned diner. Thaddeus exited and opened the back door to pull out two five-gallon gas cans. Gerald grabbed two in each hand and flexed his muscles at Thaddeus with a big, toothy grin. Thaddeus rolled his eyes and walked toward the diner. Just as he approached the dilapidated building, he stopped dead.

"What?" Gerald asked, irritated. "Why did you stop?"

"I didn't leave the door open," Thaddeus said, his face screwed up in confusion. "I always lock up."

Together, they approached the diner. Thaddeus saw that copious amounts of blood had spilled from within and onto the concrete steps leading into the building. Thaddeus set down his gas cans and pulled out his medallion.

"What that?" Gerald grunted, eyeing the amulet.

"Just a precaution. Nothing you need to worry about. Your stench is enough to scare away the devil," Thaddeus replied.

Gerald scoffed, set down two gas cans, reached into his belt, and pulled out the large meat tenderizer. He showed Thaddeus the spikes on both sides covered in dried blood, flesh, and hair. "This all the protection I need."

Gerald walked up to the door and threw it open. Thaddeus had grown accustomed to the smell of death and decay. The hum of blowflies was typically a soothing white noise to Thaddeus. Upon opening the diner entrance, the usual gentle buzz of flies was absent.

Thaddeus pulled a powerful flashlight from his belt and shone it across the room. As Thaddeus called it, the "doorman" was not there to greet him and Gerald. He had looked forward to seeing how well his brother would fare against his security measure.

The collar that at one time tethered the beast in place lay broken, and in its spot was nothing but a large pool of blood and some articles of flesh. The blood spatter was across the floor, and whatever bled appeared to be dragged toward the kitchen.

"What the fuck?" Thaddeus spat aloud.

"What happened to the pet? It breaks free?" Gerald asked, looking and sniffing around curiously. Thaddeus considered his brother at this. Did he know of the Formorian spawn? Or did he assume it was an animal?

"No idea," Thaddeus said with a shrug. He nodded to the kitchen. Gerald led the way through the kitchen, following the slick trail of gore on the floor. At one point, the course ended on the floor and then resumed on a countertop. Then it stopped again but finished its trail along the wall. At several points, Thaddeus noted claw marks from whatever was dragged, trying to escape its predator.

"Your pet downstairs?" Gerald asked. His voice sounded like a mix of anticipation and something else. Perhaps fear.

Thaddeus swallowed hard and hated the thought of letting Gerald touch his work. He left her alone with those other aberrations. Thaddeus left her unchained since he didn't anticipate her trying to escape with the defenses in place. Now he was forced to betray her in exchange for his life and let this disgusting cretin kill her. He was too stupid to appreciate what she was, just like his mother and father.

They descended the stairs to the meat locker. The odor of death and decay was so pungent that Thaddeus put on a mask he kept in his pocket. He always brought one when he came here, and tonight he was glad for it. The stench of blood and shit was overpowering in the basement. Even Gerald, who usually enjoyed the odor, recoiled somewhat.

The room was pitch black as usual, but when they stepped off the final stair onto the meat locker floor, Thaddeus felt the slick remains of not one of his prizes but several. What could have killed them all like this, though? One of the beasts was powerful enough to take down a grizzly bear. He had four pinned in the basement last he counted. This didn't include his newest addition. His masterpiece.

Gerald and Thaddeus heard something moving in the corner. Several clicks tapped across the floor and on the wall in the room's far corner, along with a considerable mass dragging its bulk itself. Whatever it was, it coiled into a pile, filling half the space. Even with Thaddeus' flashlight, it was impossible to make out the dimensions.

The air suddenly hummed, and Thaddeus and Gerald felt the hair on their bodies bristle. The bulb inside the flashlight held by Thaddeus suddenly popped, and smoke trailed out from behind the lens. Both Thaddeus and Gerald looked around for some other light source.

Pure white lights appeared in the darkness, pale as moonlight. The luminescence shone onto the blood-caked floor in front of Gerald. On the edges of the light, Thaddeus could make out armored-plated segments and insect-like legs. Thaddeus realized he and his brother were surrounded by the body of this monster as the soft light shone around them. His imagination barely touched the actual size and magnitude of the creature.

The segmented body was like a centipede; each segment had three legs on each side. On the back of each carapace segment were several quill-like protrusions. The body wrapped around them filled the stairwell exit behind them and continued up the wall and onto the ceiling. Thaddeus followed the segments until they terminated into what looked like a tail. The end of the tail retained a twisted image of Jane's face, now stretched out to encompass the final segment of the beast. The jaw still hung wide, and from within erupted a bone-white pincer.

The pincer lifted and slowly hovered over Gerald, flanking him and poised to strike. If Gerald knew it, which Thaddeus was sure he was, he didn't seem concerned. His focus was on the other half of the creature. The segments coiled in the far corner, and Thaddeus followed them with his eyes, adjusting to the darkness until he found a torso emerging from the center of the multi-plated mass.

A muscular humanoid form straightened up, its flesh grey with lesions blotting its surface. The abs were chiseled, and the flanks were perfectly cut to reveal strength and grace. Four thin arms, powerfully muscled and long, ended in lithe, slender hands tipped in long black needle-like claws.

The creature retained some of the feminine qualities of its previous hosts; breasts, thin lips, and long black hair. The hair ran down to the humanoid waistline and swayed in rhythm with the monster as it danced back and forth, eyeing the two intruders. The thin, delicate lips parted to reveal sharp teeth like a shark's and a smile broad enough almost to reach its ears. The source of the soft, pale light emanated from the creature's eyes. They focused now on Gerald like spotlights.

"She's beautiful," Gerald said in awe of the monster. He began to chuckle lewdly and turned to look over his shoulder. "I think it likes me."

"If you had access to a mirror, you may reconsider that," Thaddeus said to Gerald, his anger rising. The creature was his labor of love, his most significant work, his sculpted and magnificent achievement. She had evolved into something more beautiful than he could ever imagine. He was disgusted by this simpleton's jeering and base appetites.

"You think it fucks?" Gerald prodded again. "You think I can before I kill it?" he chuckled. A thin line of drool rolled down his chin.

"Fuck you, you fucking pig! Keep your hands off of her!" Thaddeus roared as he charged at Gerald. With the speed that belied his size and shambling stride, Gerald swung a backhand across Thaddeus' jaw, stopping him mid-stride. With his right hand, he brought a mighty fist into Thaddeus' groin, doubling the man over in pain.

While Thaddeus coughed and gagged, Gerald stood over him, smiling. "Sorry. Father says he doesn't need you. You are weak, powerless. He wants only strong in the new world to come," Gerald said grimly. "First, I kill the pet; you watch. Then you. Then I go home."

Gerald turned to face the creature, who had now risen twice his height. Through the pain and his gasps, Thaddeus heard his creation hiss at Gerald. Above him, the pincer-like stinger clacked at such a rate it made a rattling noise. He realized his creation was not mindless and barely self-aware like his other abominations. This creature was fully aware of Gerald's intentions.

Gerald moved with a flash, his hands pulling the mallet and tomahawk from his waist. To his surprise, his opponent was much faster than her size projected. She slithered quickly away from the first swing of the hand axe and slithered behind him.

Gerald sneered at the creature, swung a powerful right cross with the spikey mallet, and struck the humanoid hip of the beast. She rocked from the force of the blow and let loose what sounded like a chorus of screams and bestial growls and hisses. The sound pained Thaddeus' heart, and he wanted to run to her and protect her. Thaddeus could only shake his head in dismay at the sight of the battle. The outcome of which would change the course of his life.

As Gerald leaped to follow the last attack with a chop of his axe, pinchers struck out from the shadows. The blow to Gerald's forearm was glancing but carried sufficient strength to knock the weapon away and force him to drop it to the floor with a clang. He roared in rage and pulled forth a massive, blood-spattered cleaver. The blade's edge was wickedly chipped and broken, giving it a serrated quality.

Gerald squared off again and tried to mimic the serpentine sway of his opponent. The creature hissed again and dove at Gerald; claws cut into his thighs and flanks as it attempted to slam him into the wall. The monstrous man hugged the beast and gritted against the pain, his feet barely moving a few inches from where he stood. The two titans wrestled, clawing, biting, and cutting into each other. Thaddeus watched his creation coiled around Gerald as the big man dug in with his blade and bit into her shoulder.

With terrifying strength, she rose quickly and slammed his body into the steel and concrete ceiling, causing dust to rain down and massive cracks to form on impact. Thaddeus clamored up the stairwell while still nursing his swollen testicles. If he didn't escape this building, he would die here.

"Come on, baby, you got this!" he cheered as he ascended the stairs and hobbled through the kitchen. The floor rocked from another blow to the basement ceiling, and cracks formed across the kitchen and dining area tiles. Thaddeus suddenly smelled the distinct odor of gasoline filling the room. One of the gas cans must have tipped over. No matter the outcome of this battle, he would ensure his brother died there.

As he made his way through the Shake Shack's empty and rot-filled dining room, Thaddeus opened up and spilled the flammable liquid onto the floor. Sounds of battle continued to rumble through the diner's basement, and further clashes caused dust to fall and the foundation to shake. Just as he reached the exit to the restaurant, the floor exploded, and rubble and steel flew into the air, throwing him through the air and outside the building entrance.

Thaddeus hacked and coughed as dust tickled his throat and filled his mouth. He slowly stood up and surveyed the damage from the explosive battle. Gerald erupted from the rubble and crashed into a heap next to Thaddeus. The force sent shockwaves across the ground. Thaddeus held his breath to see if there was any sign of life from the behemoth. He jumped with a start as Gerald pounded the ground with a fist and began to raise himself to a knee.

"Brother…" Gerald said. Thaddeus was in shock. Not just from the fact that Gerald was still alive but from his physical state. Across his face were long gashes, deep enough to leave part of his right cheek flayed open, revealing bone and tendons beneath. His speech was slurred, and several jagged teeth were missing. His apron was in tatters, and the contents were all missing except for the mallet in his right hand.

"I kill…I kill…" Gerald said between gasping breaths.

"You killed her? You piece of shit! You killed that beautiful creature?" Thaddeus screamed as tears filled his eyes and streamed down his face.

Gerald chuckled at this display of sorrow and pulled himself to stand as straight as he could. Thaddeus felt exceedingly small now, standing before him. He couldn't kill him even if he wanted to, he realized. With tears in his eyes, he fell to his knees and began to beg for his life.

"Please, Gerald, we're brothers!" he cried. "I will serve you and father and mother faithfully! Please spare me!" He was blubbering now, seeing the sadistic joy Gerald was getting from this. His sobbing increased as he watched his brother raise his arm, holding the mallet above his head.

"Bye, brother," Gerald said as he licked his lips and brought the hammer down with enough force to crush Thaddeus's skull easily. Thaddeus clenched his eyes shut and raised his hands in a pathetic attempt to protect himself.

Then there was nothing. No bone-crunching force slamming down onto him. No pain or release. There was a loud thud and the sound of meat tearing and blood spilling, but not from him. Thaddeus looked at his hands and arms and then examined the rest of his body for damage. Nothing. He looked up at Gerald in complete shock and disbelief.

Through the muscle and bone of Gerald's right shoulder, a bony spike from the two-pronged stinger punched through, stopping the forward motion of the attack. Gerald's face was a look of confusion and horror. He tried to continue the task of killing his brother but found he was unable to move his arm. Graceful, long, clawed fingers wrapped themselves around his wrist and elbow. From behind Gerald, the face of Thaddeus's creation rose from over his shoulder.

Her long, segmented body rose from the hole made by their battle in the center of the diner. Her body snaked around Gerald as it coiled around his waist. Her other two hands grasped his other arm and pulled them outstretched to his side.

Gerald howled in pain as Thaddeus's creation lifted him off his feet and spread his arms wide. He kicked and twisted, trying to shake himself free of her mighty claws. Thaddeus looked in awe at her power and the twisted scene that reminded him of some sick version of the crucifixion.

With a violent jerk, the creature ripped her tail out of Gerald's shoulder, and blood spurted and flowed heavily down his chest. Gerald began screaming and crying like a child now. Tears and snot streamed down his face.

Two of the creature's arms reached down, gripped Gerald's ankles, and pulled his legs tight. She held him high from the ground and then looked down at Thaddeus. Thaddeus could now see the damage done to his masterpiece. Several large gashes dotted the landscape of her torso. A spike protruded from her back, and her left eye began to swell shut. If she was in pain though, she didn't hint at it.

"Oh, poor dear, what did he do to you?" Thaddeus asked tenderly. Gerald was crying and screaming now but with less vigor as his life continued to pour out of him and onto the soil beneath.

"Mommy! Daddy! Save me!" Gerald cried. Thaddeus looked at the giant of a man with disgust. Maybe a drop of pity, too. He returned his gaze to his only love. The creature returned his look with an impassive stare. Thaddeus wondered if this being felt emotions like love. He saw she could exhibit rage. He pondered if she could return the feelings that stirred within him for the first time. As if to answer his thoughts, she spoke.

"For you," she said, offering Gerald to him. Her voice was a choir of hisses. "For the Veil, for our Gods," she continued, each word seemly taking significant effort to form with her alien tongue. She bowed briefly, lifted Gerald to the sky above, and then lowered him as an offering to those below. This sacramental offering fascinated Thaddeus. Questions flooded his mind as he watched this brief ceremony.

Then the creature concluded the rite by opening her massive jaws, exposing her shark-like teeth, and raising Gerald's screaming form to her face. With the tenderness of a ravenous bear, she began tearing into the man's flesh. Her mouth worked with the same speed and efficiency as a school of piranha.

Gerald's screams and cries increased in pitch and volume until the creature opened her mouth wide and bit down on his head. With a twist and a jerk, she tore it off and chewed the contents in her mouth. Thaddeus sat on the ground and watched the creature work until she had entirely devoured the man, bones and all.

When she concluded the meal, Thaddeus stood up. It had occurred to him that he may be next, but he didn't care. He swelled with pride in his work. He would happily die if she decided to eat him, knowing that this was his most outstanding achievement.

The creature looked down at him, and Thaddeus watched as the wounds from her earlier battle began to sew themselves shut; the swelling dissipated from her eye, and he could hear bones mending beneath her flesh and within her segments. The meal that was Gerald now healed her and renewed her strength.

"You are amazing," Thaddeus said. He stretched his arms out wide and presented himself to her, ready to accept his fate. The creature leaned in closer and, in a surprising act, pressed her forehead to his.

Thaddeus cupped his hands around her face. Her skin was cold, and he could feel the muscles of her jaw. Her breath was hot, like steam, and carried the scent of blood and decaying tissue. Thaddeus heard her take in gulps of air and watched as her powerful torso expanded with each breath. Her hair was a deep black and as delicate as a spiderweb.

He could also hear a purr emanating from her throat. She slowly reached up and caressed his face. Thaddeus felt the tips of her long, needle-like talons gently stroke his skin. The touch was gentle, but the claws were so sharp she still cut the surface of his skin. Beads of blood began to form where they had traced, but Thaddeus didn't care. The injuries were far from him as he stared into the pale lights of his creature's perfectly round, lidless eyes.

"We will be one," the creature said soothingly to Thaddeus.

Thaddeus smiled, and tears rolled down his face. "Yes, my priestess. My Goddess. My love," he said through his joyful tears.

He tore off his clothes with the enthusiasm of a teenage boy lying with his first lover. Thaddeus even found himself giggling. The creature watched him intently and patiently. When he finished, he threw his arms wide. He didn't know how to articulate himself or what to expect from his love.

The creature came forth and took him in her arms. She licked the blood from his face and then turned him, his back to her. Two of her limbs reached down around his waist and grabbed his thighs, the back of his legs and buttocks pressed against her hips and the first segment of her centipedal body. Her other arms draped over his shoulders and chest, hugging him close and stroking his abdomen.

Thaddeus sighed with her touch and reached up, caressing her face and stroking her hair. She looked down at him with expressionless eyes, and he could feel her purring through her chest. Then he felt the skin across her belly begin to ripple and move. It felt like thousands of tiny ants crawling across his flesh. Thaddeus couldn't suppress a laugh as it tickled the skin across his flanks and legs. Then suddenly, Thaddeus felt pinpricks across his back and legs.

Thaddeus gasped from the sudden shock of pain and looked down at his flesh. His eyes grew wide as tiny threads shot out from his priestess's skin and began to knit itself into him. The pain increased, and Thaddeus began to moan as his flesh meshed with the creature. The pain intensified as he felt the tearing going deeper into his skin, muscles, ligament, and bone. He didn't recoil or try to jerk free; he began screaming.

This union's burning pain was terrible, but Thaddeus knew he was becoming something. He knew this pain and torment would be his baptism, and he would be reborn anew, not as a man but as the culmination of his work. Perfect and terrifying.

# # # #

Maria screamed in rage at the image she saw on the black obsidian floor from which she scried. She watched in horror as Gerald fought and died at the hands of Thaddeus's beast. Judge stormed into the room to see his wife on her hands and knees, sobbing and raging into the mirrored black floor.

"What's the meaning of all this!" he shouted as he approached her.

"Our son is dead! Our beautiful boy has been murdered, Judge!" Maria screamed through her tears.

"Of course he is! Thaddeus was nothing but a complete failure. I grew weary of his disgusting appetites and failures," Judge said coldly.

Maria's eyes went wide at this. She knew Judge had punished him by destroying his pets, but she had no idea Judge had intended to kill him. This only compounded her grief now, and she began to cry anew. Her Gerald was dead because of Judge, she realized, killed by his brother, whom he charged with the task of murdering.

"You bastard," she said. "How could you murder your son?"

"I don't have room for his weakness. That's why I sent Gerald. To kill him as soon as Thaddeus' pets were dispatched," Judge said. He seemed somewhat confused as to why Maria was so upset about this. "So, is the deed done? Can we get back to the rituals?" Judge asked impatiently.

"No, you fucking idiot," Maria said venomously. "Thaddeus isn't dead. Our sweet boy, Gerald, is! Look for yourself!"

Judge approached the scrying glass and looked down on the scene below. He watched with some interest as Thaddeus finished merging with his last experiment. He watched as there were now two torsos, two heads, and six powerful arms. From the twisted amalgamation's back sprung a pair of fleshy wings.

"Why are you smiling, Judge?" Maria screamed at him. He didn't even realize he had been enjoying this moment. "What will you do now? That disgusting creature murders one son, our other son is now mated with it! How do you intend to repair this?"

Judge watched as the creature's wings beat rapidly like a hummingbird or insect. He witnessed the strength of those wings lift the massive beast and its long, segmented body off the ground. He saw it snake its way into the clouds above. His eyes narrowed in interest at these events, and his smile grew wide over his face. He looked over at his grieving wife and the mask of fury and hate she wore.

"Repair? Why would I want to repair that? It seems our Thaddeus has finally made something of himself," Judge said coolly. "Notify me when he gets home. He'll undoubtedly be returning soon."

Judge turned and walked out of the room, leaving Maria standing alone and sobbing on the polished obsidian circle, kneeling before the Veil and all of its hungry witnesses.

-CHAPTER 20-
COLLUSIONS AND CURSES

No shot. No pain. No release from it all. Instead, the scream of tires and the smell of burning brake fluid. Sicily winced from the noise, her mind trying to piece the scene together. She was facing down four of her fellow officers, each with weapons drawn and about to end her and Holt's lives. She had no more escape plans, no bravado, nothing left to use in the fight. So, what kept her alive then?

Sicily opened her eyes and blinked several times, then there it was, their salvation. The ugliest van she had ever seen barreled past her and plowed into the unit of officers. Two of them took the full force of the vehicle and were thrown down the street. The other two dodged to the side and clamored for cover.

The van's back doors opened, and a man began screaming at her. It took her brain a moment to realize what was happening. Robert must have caught on before she did. He gripped her wrist and tried to pull her toward the van and the stranger shouting at her.

"Come on, honey! Get your skinny butt in here before they regroup and start blasting holes in all of us!" an older man said. He looked like a Miami car salesman. Her body seemed to move out of instinct, and she followed Robert into the back of the van. When she collected herself, she looked up and was face-to-face with the largest dog she'd ever seen. It stared at her, assessing her, then, as if accepting her credentials, it licked her cheek and returned to its bed inside a pen.

The van's tires screamed again, and they drove backward away from the pile of cops, who were now collecting themselves and preparing a counteroffensive. Upon hitting the four-way, the van swung around hard, throwing Sicily, Robert, and the car salesman to one side of the interior.

"Fuck!" Sicily screamed.

"No doubt, man. Give us a break back here, would ya, Finn?" the salesman called out.

Why did that name sound familiar to Sicily? She heard it recently.

Sicily looked over to check on Robert and saw how shaken the young cop was. This was nearly overwhelming for her, a seasoned cop from Chicago; she couldn't imagine what he was going through right now. Robert's gaze was fixed somewhere far away. Every so often he would shake his head in denial. Who could blame him? Sicily was still having a hard time believing this wasn't some nightmare too.

"Everyone still alive back there?" the driver yelled back.

Sicily couldn't see the man's face well but caught a crooked, devilish grin in the rear-view mirror. A woman peered from the passenger seat. Her face was sweet and kind, and a long braid hung from her shoulder. Oddly enough, this woman seemed to be enjoying the chaos. She quickly scanned Sicily and Robert and looked as though she might say something, but all she did was wave and give a thumbs-up to the driver.

"All right, thanks for saving us, but who the actual fuck are you?" Sicily yelled to the driver or any member of this strange troupe that could explain their involvement. The van's back doors slammed shut, and the car salesman sat down, adjusted his tie, and looked at her and Holts.

"Don't worry, sweetheart, we're just the people who came to save the whole fucking world!" The hound seemed to second his statement with a howl, and the troupe began to laugh like lunatics, aside from the lady in the passenger seat. She just smiled sweetly and gave Sicily and Robert a playful wink.

Sicily wasn't sure what that meant as she sat on the bench seat of this van, but as she looked around, she noted several storage cases and large duffle bags. With another sharp turn, her head hit something hanging from the interior wall of the vehicle. She winced and saw several weapons hanging from clamps and hooks.

The thing that caught her eye, though, was the large metal canister that her head had struck. There were two straps and a backboard so someone could wear it backpack-style. A long hose connected to the back of a wand with two pistol grips and a cone-shaped head at the end ran from a connection at the canister's base.

"I'm sorry, but is that a fucking flamethrower?" Sicily shouted in disbelief.

The salesman laughed and gave her a look and said, "You bet your sweet ass!"

"Why?" Robert finally spoke, and his eyes were wide with wonder and fear at the collection of weapons on the wall.

"Well, son, nothing on our planet survives fire. We all burn. So, we keep that around just in case the conventional stuff doesn't work," the older man replied. "Name's Vincent, the gorgeous gal with the braid is Mata, and the young man driving is Phineas," he said. With the second mention of his full name, Sicily recalled where she heard it before.

"Phineas? As in Phineas Thatch?" Sicily shouted to the driver.

"Uh-huh. Have we met?" Phineas asked, not looking back.

"We have a mutual acquaintance," Sicily started, "You're George's little brother?"

From the mention of George, she saw that grin falter. "How's George these days?" Phineas probed, his voice accented by something. Was it concern? Pain?

"Not going to lie, bud, we need to get to him quick. If we ran into that much trouble just for asking questions, I imagine he is ass deep in shit right now," Robert replied.

"Where is he?" Phineas asked.

"He's at Meyer's farm…" Sicily said. Before she could explain why he was there, Phineas took another sharp turn and headed in that direction.

# # # #

George made it out of the limestone canyon carved back into the hills. His lungs felt like they would burst, and his legs were well beyond their limits. Not that he immediately realized any of this. His fear and adrenaline pushed him beyond his usual limitations. He remembered how horses could die from overexertion, but he couldn't stop.

The monster in the canyon may have fled into the cave, but what if it came back? What if it hunted with others, like in packs? What if there were more out there? He needed to get back into town, regroup, reload, and maybe even puke.

"Fuck, fuck, fuck!" George huffed as he ran. Suddenly, his cell phone vibrated against his leg several times. He must have gotten reception. "Oh shit! Oh, thank God!" he said between breaths. He stopped and leaned against a tree and looked at the screen. A thought balloon with an "8 missed calls" message appeared on the screen. He received three text messages— one from Holts and two from Amanda.

He pulled up the text messages and read Amanda's first. *"Hey, the girls stayed with Mom and Dad, and I'm on my way home now."* His eyes scanned the following text, *"I hate fighting with you. Can we talk?"*

George's eyes filled with tears. He needed his family so much right now, and this message filled him with so much love he couldn't hold back his relief. He was about to reply when he realized his fear. It's not safe here. He needed to stop her.

George frantically tried to call Amanda. He quickly dialed her number. "Please pick up, babe. Pick up!" The phone rang again and again.

"Hello? George?" Amanda's voice came through the phone. George sighed in relief.

"Mandy, where are you right now? Wherever it is, you gotta stop! Go back to your parents, get a hotel, whatever—" George was cut off.

"George? Can you hear me? George? I can't hear you." George got cold and felt nauseous. *"Well, anyway, I'm about fifteen minutes outside of town. How does pizza sound tonight? Sorry, you probably can't even hear me. I miss you."*

George was screaming now. "No! Amanda, stay away! Fuck! Please stop!"

George fell to his knees, roaring into the phone as Amanda disconnected. He filled his lungs again and screamed as he started punching the muddy floor of the hills. Dirt clods flew as he punched repeatedly, ignoring the pain of the rock and twigs digging into his knuckles. Out of breath and tears streaming down his face, he gasped for air and tried to center himself.

"Okay, I gotta stop this," George said shakily. "We're going to get to the bottom of this insanity, and I'm going to burn it down." George's resolve returned. Holts. George read his text message next.

"Manns needs help. She has a new lead. Going to the paper. Call us," the text read.

George considered texting back but decided against it due to the poor reception in these hills. His best bet would be to return to the ATV and ride hard for the farm. He could call on the way or something. Right now, he needed to get out of these woods.

George finally got to the ATV and checked his phone. Nothing. No matter. He needed to return to his family and ensure they were safe. After that, he would get to Manns and Holts and tear this down. He jumped on the ATV, started it up, and booked it as fast as possible. The drive to the hills from the farmhouse wasn't long. With the "thing-that-wasn't-Elmer" driving, the speed was slow and almost meandering. He would take the fastest, most direct route. It should only take ten minutes.

George's optimistic assessment died when the ATV began to sputter. It took only a few seconds to assess the reasons for the mechanical failure. Fuel. If you planned to kill the passenger, George supposed, then you didn't bother to fill the gas tank.

"FUCK!" George shouted. He quickly determined the distance from his location to the farmhouse. George drove the ATV as far as he could and then ran. He figured he could make it in twelve minutes if he ran balls out. "Fuck!" George yelled as he began to run. God, he hated running.

As he approached the farmhouse, a wave of relief washed over him as he spotted the police chief's unit parked next to his in the driveway. Maybe he could think of a way to get Joe into calling backup units to investigate the cave with every available weapon ready. He could do that, right?

One thing at a time, George. First, catch your breath. Then you call for reinforcements, George thought.

As he approached the farmhouse, he saw Martha and Joe standing near the vehicles and talking casually. It suddenly hit George like a right hook to the jaw. If Elmer was a monster-in-human-clothing, what if Martha was, too? How could he warn Joe? George received an answer when his alarm system suddenly started blaring again.

"Hey, George! What did you find?" Chief Joe Waters shouted.

Martha looked at him curiously and scanned the horizon to look for Elmer. "Where's Elmer, George?"

George began to conjure several excuses as to why Elmer wasn't there. "Oh yeah, Elmer found something. His ATV broke down a ways back," George said in between breaths. "Hey Joe, can I ask you something?" George feigned bending over as if to take a breather. Well, half faked his need for oxygen.

"What's up, George?" Chief Waters shouted. He began to stroll over, each hand on his belt and holster.

"Is Elmer ok?" Martha asked, concern in her tone.

"Yeah, yeah," George said, trying to dismiss the question with a wave. "Remember when we found the meth lab in the limestone caverns?" George shouted, lying about his findings and hoping he was wrong.

"Uh-huh. Is that what we're looking at?" Joe Waters said.

Fuck! George thought. There was no meth lab that they had found. This was not Joe. How much time did he have? What could he say? Could he escape?

As if in response to his thoughts, Joe Waters stopped in his tracks. Martha stared hard at George and looked over to Waters. "Well, George, out with it! What did you find?" Chief Waters asked.

"It's hard to explain, Chief. We will need extra units, maybe county sheriff," George stammered. He tried to hide the absolute terror in his voice. Just be cool. Function as if nothing were wrong. Put on that same mask you've worn since the day you shot the Corners kid.

Chief Waters looked George over. Martha walked up next to him. Between the two, George saw a silent conversation and knew at once he was fucked. He quickly took inventory of the bullets in his sidearm.

The two forms in front of him began to convulse and contort. Chief Waters' head looked up to the sky, howled into the dark grey clouds, and vomited forth a spike of flesh and bone. The tip of which split like the petals of a tropical flower and bent over to view its prey. Within the center of that strange bloom was an iris shaped like an octopus.

The petals around the bulb were filled with thorns, or teeth, which shook and rattled like a rattlesnake's tail. The torso of Chief Waters bent backward until the stalk that ended in a four-petaled bloom became a tail. The tail curled toward George to regard him with that baleful iris. The creature crab-walked from side to side, no longer resembling the man George had worked with for over a decade. The crotch of his pants ripped open, and a sideways maw of teeth appeared between his legs. The toothy hole drooled hungrily, and when the spittle hit the ground, it sizzled and steamed.

Martha took a cue from the creature next to her and squatted low. Her belly split up to her neck, and rows of teeth open and closed. Tentacles shot out and whipped around her squat form. Her neck lengthened and stretched to four times its original length and waved back and forth as the eyes rolled around until nothing, but the whites were left, and the mouth fell open, slack-jawed. From the sides of Martha's head protruded pinchers, four in total, opening and closing with sharp, clacking strikes.

"Come now, boy, you may as well give up," the Martha-thing gurgled mockingly.

The two creatures shambled forward toward George. George loaded the last magazine into the sidearm and bared his teeth. If he were going to die, it wouldn't be here, he swore silently. He had to escape and get his family to safety.

Just as George prepared to make a violent retreat, a column of flame rolled through and enveloped the two monsters before him. Waves of heat forced George to shield his eyes and back away a few steps from the scene. Screams filled the air as he looked for the source of the attack.

Next to his SUV sat a rust-spattered van. In front of the van knelt Sicily, wearing a Vietnam-era flamethrower, raining napalm-like hate down onto the two abominations. She screamed like a Valkyrie as she poured hellfire onto the otherworldly beasts. Her eyes were filled with rage, sending a chill down George's spine. This didn't stop a smile from creeping across his face, though.

The two monsters screamed and writhed on the ground. Their heads and limbs whipped wildly about, trying to escape the pain.

Suddenly, one of the beasts leaped out from within the rolling cloud of heat and fire and tried to reach George. The hands and feet now were prehensile claws looming for him.

George stumbled backward, trying to escape the attack. There was no way to escape this unscathed; George knew this. He pulled his pistol and aimed center mass, hoping the damage he would cause would stop it from killing him at least.

Before he could get a shot off, a black form slammed down onto the back of the shambling monster. The force of the blow was like a construction beam falling from twenty stories above its head. The strike nearly severed the creature in half. It didn't have time to scream, curse, or even breathe. George blinked and looked at what crashed down into the twisted thing. Before him stood a man holding a cane. He wore a long coat, his red hair in a mohawk with glowing runes etched into the sides of his scalp. His hair was bright red, and he wore a long black coat that flowed behind him. The place where he struck suddenly erupted in blue flames, and the beast screamed and writhed under the thin black wood that made up the body of the cane.

The creature writhed for a moment until the man placed a leather boot atop the head of the beast. He took the cane's tip and plunged it deep into the torso of the creature. The monster screamed horribly momentarily, convulsing from the pain of the stabbing, and then fell still.

George looked at the back of the man before him. The rest of the world vanished as recognition lit the form before him. His collar was flipped up, and it seemed as if he didn't want to turn and face him. Deep down, George didn't want him to see him either. Both of these men knew if they faced each other, their past would flood over them both, and they would have to admit it was all real. Not just the horror of their world but the past they both had been haunted by their entire adult lives.

"Hey, George," the thin man finally said. "It's been a minute, but I hoped you would save the world with me. What do you say?"

"Finn?" George posed shakily.

George's little brother wasn't little anymore. When he regarded him, his bright green eyes peered into George.

George, rose on shaky legs, still working to catch his breath, and looked at Phineas in amazement.

Phineas reached his hand out to help George, who then responded with a hard right hook to his face.

-CHAPTER 21-
SACRILEGE

Judge stood in front of his congregation. All the Formoria rescued from the Veil and inserted into human forms stood and watched patiently as he donned his robes, amulets, and rings. They each wore ceremonial robes of black with gold runes stitched down the length of the sides. Each rune represented the name of a god from beyond the Veil. Abhoth, Atlach-Nacha, Hastur, Ithaqua, Nyarlathotep, Shudde M'ell, Yig, and Cthulhu. Their offspring were also embroidered along the hem of the robes and the long, pointed hoods they wore.

In one hand, Judge held a four-foot-long ornate club, at the head of which was the carving of a bulbous head of an octopus with three pairs of eyes running along the sides. Each eye socket was encrusted with tiny marquise-cut rubies. The tentacles caressed the shaft of the club, and each one was adorned with small round emeralds. The shaft was carved to look like a formless monster, the gold plating displaying a variety of teeth and eyes spiraling down to the hilt.

As Judge put the final additions of his vestments, he began to chant the sacred prayer of the Eldritch Gods in veil-speak. It took him nearly a decade to master the language and even longer to learn how to write it. The speech was the oldest known, and only a handful of people spoke it. Half of those who did speak it were driven mad from the knowledge they obtained as a result.

"Ehyeahog Y'vulgtlagln, ahiloigehye goka ya ymg' blassing!" Judge cried out. "Please grant me your blessings so that I may cleanse this world for you, Anhoth! Give me your knowledge Cthulhu! Grant your servants wisdom and strength, Yog-Sothoth!"

The congregants bowed their heads in reverence and repeated the words he spoke. He needed to complete the ritual soon; the Veil had nearly thinned enough to tear open, thus allowing the Formoria to return to this realm. Those gods who waited beyond were patient but not forgiving.

Many more of the congregation were gathered beneath his feet as well. The room floor was made of thick, black wood. In the center of the chapel was a large hole cut into it and a heavy iron grate covering the gaping hole. An iron cage secured several victims acquired from Haven Shire, purchased by Judge, or taken from farmlands and towns nearby. That pit was now half full of the unholy communion that would feed the Formoria.

The prisoners writhed in the iron cage below Judge. The bars lining the cage had spikes that protruded inward, their points poking, prodding, and biting the crowded enclosure. The mass of men, women, and children appeared as a single roiling mass. They moaned, screamed, and pleaded with their warden to release or give them mercy. Their pain was the retort to Judge's prayers as he praised the eldritch lords from beyond the Veil.

Just as Judge's protestations and proclamations had reached a fevered pitch in veil song, the shambling mass of the Elmer mimic burst into the room. It was bleeding from several wounds, and it limped on broken appendages. The hooded congregants parted and made room for the shambling creature to pass. It rushed to the dais and fell to Judge's feet.

"What is the meaning of this intrusion! Sacrilege!" roared Judge as he ripped his robe away from the creature's reach.

"We are discovered! The police officer knows of this place!" the creature cried in the chorus of Elmer's voice, and the Veil tongue of the beast mimicked him.

"I assume you failed to dispatch him since you are here bleeding on this holy podium and interrupting our prayer?" Judge shouted, looking at the creature with disgust.

"He is strong and has been given gifts, your eminence. I sense them," the creature squealed.

"I'm sure your appetite to feast on living flesh had nothing to do with his being on that property. Or was it because you lacked the intelligence to bury the rotting animals you ate upon?" Judge grilled knowingly.

"No, my lord, I—" the Elmer-thing began pleading, but before he could finish begging, Judge plunged the head of his scepter into the center of the beast. The creature instantly exploded; flesh and gory entrails washed onto the congregation. They hissed, screamed, and applauded joyfully as they were bathed in their fellow Formorian's flesh and blood. A couple of the parishioners fell to lick up the blood or feast on the offerings on the floor.

Judge looked down upon them with little interest as he considered his following action. When ready, he threw his arms out wide, holding the scepter high. Immediately, those in the temple bowed their heads in reverence. Judge pointed out beyond to the town.

"Find and devour this officer, his family, and those with whom he has aligned himself," Judge commanded in a voice that carried like thunder. "Destroy any who get in your way."

The Formoria feared the wizard priest, but their hunger was greater than their fear. They burst forth from the room, hissing and growling. The mimics ran, crawled, and scaled the walls out of the Forgotten Church to hunt those who threatened their masters.

Judge watched them leave. This one man was becoming troublesome. This is the second time he has interfered, and Judge regretted not taking his life before. In addition, what were these gifts the Formorian spoke of?

Before he could ponder this officer any further, Maria sent Judge a telepathic missive. He could feel her disgust and hatred for him through the empathic link they shared at that moment. The suffering of her grief and betrayal gave him a pleasant respite from today's other annoyances.

"Our son is soon to return. What will you do?" Maria spoke in his head.

"I shall welcome him home," Judge replied aloud and in his mind. He reached over to a lever on the wall on his right. Below the floor, within the pit, heavy metal doors slammed open, and chains, pullies, and gears roared to life.

The spiked cage suddenly began to glow hot and rotate and rock. The prisoners began screaming in pain and terror as they clamored over each other to avoid burning or being impaled. Judge closed his eyes and took in their pain and suffering. Their cries gave him not only immense joy but powered his magic.

Judge knew Thaddeus was coming; he felt the power from the entity his son had become. He wanted to see this being with his own eyes. Judge wanted to grasp its life essence with his hands and crush it with his power.

When Judge opened his eyes again, the cage was quiet, and its contents had given him all he needed. With the pull of a heavy lever, the cell was opened, and the lifeless contents were dumped into a large chute leading to the basement furnaces used to dispatch them like so many in the past.

Judge could not deny the excitement he felt for the inevitable confrontation with Thaddeus. Maybe Thaddeus would finally be worthy of the Gods. It was also possible that this was a trial set forth by his masters to test his own strength and resolve. Part of Judge also considered the possibility that whatever Thaddeus had become may kill him. Judge thought how proud he would be if his son finally proved himself worthy to their gods and to himself as his father.

-CHAPTER 21-
THE HARBINGER

When the creature was born and met its creator, Thaddeus, it saw admiration and love in his eyes. It knew from the moment they met he would worship it. Deep within the creature's consciousness and from what it could glean from its creator's mind, it knew it was not of this plane but a denizen of the world beyond the Veil. It began to remember through its genetic memories that it was an ancient creature and had not known death. Only the maddening cycle of birth and rebirth.

Soon after feeding on the minds and bodies of others, it remembered its purpose for its pilgrimage to this plane. It was born to be the mouthpiece of the Old Gods. When it sang the hymns and prayers of the Ancient Ones, it would spread madness and force those of the first tribe to bend the knee. Thaddeus called it a priestess because it took a female mortal's flesh. This being liked the name and his admiration, but it was no longer needed. Now that it and Thaddeus were one—both body and mind—it would not be a mere priestess. It was now something greater.

"We are now a harbinger of the Old Gods. We sing the songs of their great power. We will prepare this plane for their arrival. We are *Ebumna'romnyth*, the tongue and mouth of the Ancient One," the creature spoke aloud as it swam in the ever-darkening clouds above Haven Shire. It called for a storm to wash this dirty, tiny town and prepare it for the coming. Heavy rain began to pour, and the clouds came alive with blue and green bolts of electricity.

"We are the tongue and the voice and..." the creature stopped and looked down to a pair of people below. "We are hungry."

Jerry and Mike Allgood were newlyweds who had just moved into town. Since their arrival in this quiet town, they had been miserable. They moved from East St. Louis, grew up together, and fell in love in high school. They knew coming out to their parents and sharing their love with their family and the black community would be challenging. Still, they underestimated the pain of their rejection.

The couple didn't have much money or established credit, so when they found a small house in this quiet town, they worked their asses off to put down enough for a loan. The price of the home sounded too good to be true, but anything was better than the high crime and poverty of East St. Louis. So, they agreed.

Tonight, the two practically skipped merrily to the annual Haven Shire Harvest Festival. They had set up the booths, but with this new storm rolling in, they wanted to ensure they were sufficiently covered and protected from the elements. Father Curry was already on the streets of the fair, double-checking the tarps and covers and helping the vendors. They were a block away when the rain started to fall. The pair went from a skip to a full run, laughing at their luck. What else could one do?

With the downpour and thunder, Mike couldn't hear the creature descending on him. Jerry was by his side for a moment, holding his hand, and then he wasn't. Mike looked over to see where Jerry had gone, and he simply wasn't there. Mike looked around slowly to see if Jerry had tripped or if they had got separated. When he looked down, he felt cold as fear gripped him and wormed its way through his guts and up his spine. The street at his feet was a puddle of diluted blood. His left pant leg was red from his hip down.

"Jerry? Sweetie?!" Mike said confused. His mind couldn't make sense of it. He was holding his hand but where was- "Oh my God! Jerry!"

Mike screamed as he realized the arm holding Jerry's hand was gone. It was severed so neatly and quickly that his mind wasn't yet aware it was missing. Reality came crashing down for Mike when what remained of Jerry and his arm crashed onto the street before him. The bloody water splashed onto him, startling him, and forced him to stumble back two steps. Mike's hand was still being held by Jerry's, leaving Mike's severed limb clutched in his dead hand. Jerry's broken body lay headless on the street, his blood pooling around him. His entrails were torn out and had been removed from their visceral home.

Mike's scream increased in pitch and grief at seeing his love's mangled body. He turned to run and suddenly felt something heavy punch him in the gut. All breath left his lungs, and he felt his legs go weak, but he didn't fall. He looked down to see a fleshy appendage that ended in pinchers. Each tooth of the two-pronged claw came together at the tip of the tail and met with what appeared to be a giant human skull.

Mike's remaining arm was pinned to his side as the tail lifted him from the street. He didn't have the breath to scream now as the jaw looked like it was opening its mouth. Suddenly, he felt something sharp punch into his stomach, and everything inside of him erupted in volcanic pain.

Father Curry and the dozen vendors had come together at his call. He needed this festival to go well for this town, her people, and himself. Someone had tarnished his name and spent considerable energy spreading a nasty rumor about him. It hurt him deeply to see his parents, who once trusted and put faith in him, look at him with disgust and fear. He couldn't for the life of him understand why someone would do this to him.

This recent accusation was a painful reminder of why Curry was assigned to this strange little hamlet. Someone had been spreading rumors that he had committed an act of impropriety with one of his parishioners.

Matthew Curry's faith in God was tested early as a newly appointed priest. The only person he had loved in this world, his beloved sister, Hanna, committed suicide shortly after his first assignment as a priest. Ever since she had been date-raped in college, Hanna had suffered symptoms of post-traumatic stress. Matthew Curry did everything he could to help Hanna. Even when she turned to drugs and alcohol, when she would call for bail, or when she stole from him.

Matthew swore he would never give up on her. So, Hanna gave up instead. After her latest stint in rehab, it was agreed that Hanna would check in every day at first. Then, every few days. Curry hadn't heard from his sister for over a week and worried she may have relapsed. So Matthew came up with an innocent reason to visit her and decided to surprise her with breakfast.

The image of his sister's pale, nude form on those blood-soaked sheets will be carved into his soul for the rest of Matthew's life. Matthew fought so hard to save her, only to fail. His faith deemed her suicide a sin, and to compound her afterlife sentence, she had also committed murder. Hanna confessed to aborting a pregnancy. The pregnancy was the result of her rape in college.

Matthew hated himself for his failings as her brother. Hanna had carried the abortion alone for all those years. In her suicide note, she begged him to forgive her. Without question, Matthew knew he would, but his religion would not be merciful. The ruling Pope, and therefore the Catholic faith, would not budge on the resulting punishment laid in wait for Hanna.

The inability to reconcile the edicts of the Church, and his love and grief for his Hanna, broke Matthew. He coped the best he could. Thankfully, Father Curry was Irish, so no one seemed to mind running into him at the local pub. Given what he had gone through, people looked away when he stumbled out those barroom doors. They looked away when his hands shook during communion.

It wasn't until he showed up to Sunday mass, his left eye swollen from a bar brawl the night before and vomit on his cassock and breath, that the Bishop called for an intervention. Father Curry was ordered to go into rehab, talk to a therapist weekly, and pray. Even after he paid the prescribed penance, Curry was subjected to one last indignity. He had to transfer to another parish. A punishment usually reserved for priests found guilty of pedophilia.

Father Curry accepted his assignment without protest, though. It was the least he could do after failing the only person he cared about. No amount of therapy or steps, be it twelve or otherwise, would absolve him of his guilt. He intended to come to this small town in the middle of nowhere, a place that, for reasons unknown, people would forget soon after leaving, to also be forgotten.

Then, Father Curry was blessed with something unexpected. Love. The more he became involved with the community and those who dwell in Haven Shire, the more he loved them. Which was why his heart broke as the community seemed to slip into quiet despair. Father Curry saw it on the faces of those who still attended mass. He recognized the oppressive shadow cast on the souls of his parish as the same as the one that snuffed out his Hanna.

So Father Curry decided this was a sign. A chance to atone for the life he couldn't save. A way to earn forgiveness. Not in the eyes of the Church or almighty God, but from Hanna and himself.

So he would fight, he decided. Father Curry vowed to not be distracted by these unfounded rumors and instead show the community he loved the type of priest he was. He had faith that righteousness would win the day.

Father Curry decided he would still hold the Haven Shire Fall Festival. It wasn't just to give him something to do to keep his mind off of the scandalous accusations but also because this town and its community needed to come together. Father Curry hoped this would offer some respite from the unexplained disappearances, increased violent crime, and the palatable fear in the air.

As he was securing a rope to the stake that secured a vendor's tent, a shrill, mournful scream cut through the darkening storm. He stopped and listened to find its source, but the sudden heavy downpour drowned out much of the ambient noise. He stood to look for someone in distress and found that he wasn't the only one. Several other vendors walked into the center of the street and began asking each other about what they had heard.

From behind Father Curry and the accumulating crowd, a loud, sorrowful moan cut through the storm. Father turned and found the source, though it was hard to make out. It looked like a person shambling toward them. Blood covered the man, and he held his hand over his stomach. Father Curry couldn't see well, but it appeared as if he only had one arm. The scene reminded him of the zombie movies he watched as a child, which would later guarantee a night stay in his parents' room as he retreated there from the ensuing nightmares. The vision now still gave him the chills.

"Oh, my God! It's Mike!" someone behind Curry said. He squinted at the approaching figure, and the identity was confirmed. Others recognized him, and the crowd rushed to help the injured man.

"Jesus, Mike, what happened? Oh, God, your arm," Curry said in horror. "Someone call 911! Get something we can dress his wounds. I need some folks to help me move him to a tent." Father Curry dished out instructions to the crowd of people rushing to help. For a moment, despite a man dying before him, he felt a swell of pride for his parish. Each person was doing something. Calling, bandaging, praying, or preparing a tent to help this stranger. He was sure they knew about Mike's lifestyle, but none of them stopped to consider it.

"Father?" Mike said weakly. His skin was looking so pale. Curry reached down and felt his cold and clammy hand. He saw the wound he held onto and was grateful it was no longer bleeding. He didn't know if that was a good sign, but the smell from the wound was awful. Father Curry held onto Mike's hand as firmly as possible.

"I'm here, Mike. What happened? Where's Jerry? Can I call him for you?" Father Curry asked, fighting the tears that threatened to pour from his eyes.

A new wave of sorrow struck Mike briefly, and he began crying. Then, he quickly recovered. "A demon, Father. Something flew down, killing Jerry, Father... it ate his insides..." Mike began between sobs, "It got me, too. It put something in me. I can feel it growing."

Curry looked down on Mike, unable to hold back the tears. The poor man must be in shock from grief and blood loss. "Shhh, don't talk anymore, Mike. Save your strength." The priest turned and looked at the people moving about him. Two men had assembled a make-shift litter basket with broom handles and a tarp. A woman tightly held blankets to her chest in the tent's doorway like it was her own infant.

"What's the ETA on that ambulance?" Father Curry called out.

Before anyone could reply, Mike began screaming wildly. His high-pitched wailing forced Father Curry to cover his ears, and others ran to help him. Mike's body convulsed, and his arms and legs flailed. He suddenly arched his lower back and thrust his hips upward until the top of his skull and his feet were planted flatly on the street. It was such a violent reaction that those near him heard his spine crack.

Then, as suddenly as it began, Mike fell to the street limply, and his head rolled to the side, looking at all his witnesses with lifeless eyes frozen in terror. The bystanders gasped in horror. Others wept, and others still prayed. Father Curry reached down, felt the man's neck, and shook his head somberly as he did not locate a pulse.

Then, from the corner of his eye, Father Curry saw something move under Mike's bloody shirt. He was about to reach for it when the body's abdomen inflated quickly like a balloon. Curry could hear the corpse's ribs pop and break and its internal organs crunch and shift. The swelling continued into his chest cavity, where ribs broke free of the sternum. Whatever process was wracking Mike's body moved through the body to his neck, swelling and distending it to the point of breaking. The head rolled around on its own with Mike's horror-crazed eyes rolling around.

The skin stretched to the point that it became more translucent, and he could make out something wriggling under the flesh. Then Mike just popped. His skin burst with a tearing sound, and liquids shot from his upper body. The flesh burst and ripped apart, and the smell of shit, blood, and infection spread. The audience screamed or jumped back in astonishment or horror. One person began vomiting.

From the remains of the body erupted thousands of winged arachnids. Their abdomens were long and thin and tipped with wicked black stingers. On their backs were long wings that twitched and rumbled. They were equipped with foreclaws, and two rows of sharp teeth were seen. They screamed in unison as if to protest having been removed from the warmth and safety of their nest.

The vendors and Father Curry all screamed and tried to run immediately. Many fell or ducked into the tents to hide. None of this mattered, though. Father Curry watched his parish wail and flail as they tried to bat away the ravenous monsters. The two men who created the make-shift litter basket got overwhelmed first by the plague of arachnid-like creatures. He watched as the men's faces were picked clean, leaving just glossy white bone, and they slumped to the ground. More of the spawn crawled into their mouths and ate through their bellies.

The fate of those others who braved the storm today to bring their community together met similarly terrifying fates. His tears streamed down his face, and he moaned as he saw their gory demise. Then, from above, he heard a buzzing and a gust of wind. A shadow of a monster darker than the clouds above hovered over him and descended to the street.

The Herald of the Ancient Ones, Ebumna'romnyth, landed before Father Curry. The surging drum of its wings was so powerful that it displaced the pooling water on the street's surface and knocked over nearby tents. Father Curry shielded his eyes, and when the force of the water and wind had stopped, the Herald looked over at Father Curry.

"Pray, Father," the creature said with Thaddeus' torso bowing in mock reverence. "Pray, Father, for we have come. We are Legion!" the harbinger screamed. "Pray to the Gods through me! Within me!"

"Lord, Jesus Christ, what are you?" Curry asked in shocked horror.

"What have I become?" Thaddeus replied, raising his clawed hands up before his eyes. He acted appalled mockingly by the sight of those razor-sharp talons. Then, a menacing smile broke Thaddeus' theatrics. "I have become a God amongst man! The Herald of the end of days!" Thaddeus roared above the drum of the rain now. He raised his arms to the sky, and the creature did the same. "I am now complete and perfect!"

The creature threw its head back in laughter as it called forth its plague. Those killed by the animals were spawning grounds for more of the forever-hungry swarm. All the Father could do was pray as a cloud of creatures fell upon him.

"Do you see pretenders! We will devour all in our path until you become my communion as I feast!"

Ebumna'romnyth beat its wings rapidly, and it rose into the air. Behind it swarmed a black cloud of death and rebirth, leaving nothing behind but death.

-CHAPTER 22-
REUNION

Phineas sat in the passenger seat of the police Explorer, rubbing his jaw. He looked over at George and stared hard at him, trying to think of the words that would open up his heart or mind to a conversation. He couldn't stop looking at his right eye, though. It was swollen and angry. George noticed him looking, which gave Phineas the opportunity he wanted.

"Fuck, if I knew how hard your girl got punched, I might have hugged instead," George said, touching his swollen eye, which issued a wince of pain.

"Yeah, she can be a bit protective, even when I deserve to be hit," Phineas said wryly.

Silence. Phineas didn't want to rush this. He just retrieved his glasses and put them back on. Phineas had decided after his punch in the face that it was best to let George come to him. When he was ready.

"So, what is she anyway?" George started.

"Who? Mata?"

George nodded.

"Oh, well, she's deaf and mute. Don't call her deaf and dumb. Not a fan. Don't let her silence fool you, though. She sees and understands more than she lets on."

"No, I mean, what is she?" George started over, sensing his misstep here.

"Oh, that. Well, from what I gather, Mata's family were gypsies. The real deal, not homeless beggars. They were part of a community all over Europe and then..." Phineas excitedly began explaining.

"No, asshole! Is she your girlfriend or what?" George yelled, exasperated.

"Ah, yes. Let's say that we take care of each other and leave it at that," Phineas said in resignation. "How's that eye?"

"Fine. Just needs ice. How's the jaw?" George retorted.

"Fine. Been clocked by Mata harder than that," Phineas said with his patent evil grin.

George chuckled at this. Silence. The car and the road seemed quieter than usual, as if it were giving them space to talk. Phineas looked out over the town he grew up in, absorbing the past and the present. George drove in silence, every now and then, taking in Phineas' appearance. He was still the Phineas he knew growing up, but much had also changed. Not just his mohawk, tattoos, and dark patchwork clothes.

Phineas looked as though he had a light inside of him, that he saw the world differently, just like their mother. The difference was Phineas wasn't driven mad by what he saw. Even in their few minutes together, he saw that Mata was also different. George couldn't put his finger on it; it was just a gut feeling.

George had so many questions, but they would have to wait. His family was in town, and he needed to protect them somehow. Whatever their past was, they would have to deal with that later. Phineas finally spoke as if reading the room correctly.

"So where are we going, George?" he asked cautiously.

"My wife and kids are in town. They need to go somewhere safe," George said. Just as he was about to elaborate, the portable radio squawked.

"Manns to George."

George had set the radio to a talk-around channel that only Manns, Holts, and himself could communicate.

"Thatch here, go ahead," George responded to the radio summons.

"Hey, George, Holts and Manns here. Listen, not to be an asshole, but Holts has a cousin, Jackie something-or-other, and his dad, and I have my mom and...well..." Suddenly, George felt like an asshole. He worried about his family; he hadn't even considered anyone else.

"Look, I get it. Check on your families and then meet at my house," George replied. George looked at Phineas, who seemed to be scanning the horizon for something. George was angry at him for showing up unexpectedly, but he also felt this was the perfect time for them to reunite. It kind of pissed him off that it took the end of the world for Phineas to return. As if he had read his mind, Phineas spoke up first.

"I'm sorry I never called," Phineas began. He looked out the window at the town, both past and present, at once. "Every time I picked up the phone, I would remember all that we went through here, and I found myself calling my sponsor instead."

George considered that. How did he deal with it? Did he actually deal with everything he and Phineas went through? How many beers or shots did he drink? Hours worked? Or arguments had with the wife? All because he didn't even want to think about Mom and Dad. Or that day by the tracks? How many times did he bury the memory and pain, just as Jack said?

"We all have our way," George said after a pause. "You couldn't call because it would be real, right?"

"I often thought that it was just part of my delusions, the things that I saw," Phineas said. "I thought it may be better to be insane than have all we went through be the truth."

"What changed?" George asked.

"Lots of things. Sobriety, Mata, Vincent, even Lizzie," Phineas replied. "Each of them accepted me, what I saw and could do, and everything I had been through. Maybe because they went through some shit, too."

George went silent at this. He felt more alone than ever. Not even those closest to him, until Sicily and Robert, knew what he saw that day. Yet, Phineas could find his own tribe or family, or whatever-the-fuck they were, to help him cope with his pain. He flinched at this pain and tried to shake this thought away before he started crying due to this revelation.

As if seeing his pain and feeling it, Phineas looked at him and nodded with a tight grimace instead of his usual knowing grin. George realized that he had that same look, even as a kid. He always knew some secret no one else did. It always put people off, including him.

-CHAPTER 23-
COMMUNION

Maria sat cross-legged and naked on the polished black surface of her summoning room. She saw what had happened to the Formoria, who was disguised as Mrs. Grey and the police chief. She saw the attackers and how they made short work of them. One of them especially was supremely talented in the magic arts. His artifacts and use of enchantments were masterful.

His cohort, a short, beauteous woman, also had a natural ability. She was surrounded by some blessing or curse that enhanced her senses and body. She wanted desperately to have time with these two, but she had to focus on the ritual. This next step required her to focus on every remaining soul within the town. She needed their lives to finally open the gate and call forth the Ancient Ones and those who lived beyond the Veil. To fail here would mean forfeiting her mind, body, and soul.

She had already alerted Judge of their son's approach; even now, Judge was preparing to meet Thaddeus. Maria prayed with all her might that the two of them would kill each other.

Maria hated these men, and all men, for that matter, hated them for their greed and gluttony. She was disgusted by their need to feel powerful by taking the power away from others. She had her own designs now, and soon gender and form would mean nothing. All would become formless and one with the Ancient Ones.

First, she had to prepare the sacrament. She had to channel and focus every ounce of power and will to be stored within the church to ensnare the minds of all those who remained in Haven Shire. Their nightmares and pain will serve as a beacon for the Old Gods. They will rip into this reality and devour the minds and bodies of every person on the planet.

Those who serve will join them, become one with them, in their pilgrimage, devouring realities for eternity. They will feast on every sentient mind in this plane, then the next, and so on, until the multiverse is returned to the dark chaos from which it was born.

Goosebumps rose across her flesh at this thought. From beyond the Veil, the Formoria hummed their pleasure at her visions and gave her the energy to perform her rite. Maria sang their hymns and the magic words needed to capture the minds and wills of those within the town. The church amplified her song like a radio tower. From outside the church, those who lacked any gifts still felt an unusual vibration in the air and a tickle at the base of their skulls. They wouldn't even suspect astral tendrils worming their way into their brains and wrapping themselves around each consciousness.

If anyone had the gift of "sight," they could see these tendrils. Long and skinny, they wrapped themselves around the spine like a noose. The dark skies cloaked with those thick clouds also signaled a change in the atmosphere. The clouds took on a dark green hue, forming small funnel clouds. The gifted would see that the eye inside each funnel projected a small red beam onto the victims of this ritual.

As the ritual climaxed, the descending tentacles pulled at the astral cords of the unsuspecting, and their physical forms gripped in place. People walking down the street were suddenly overcome with rigor, and their eyes glazed over with inky blackness. They muttered the prayers' words and screamed the ancient hymns' chaotic notes.

The Old Gods showed their pleasure by etching giant, impossible smiles that sliced their way across their faces. The faces of the enslaved rose to look to the sky, where they saw the countenance of their new masters. The victims of the ritual were lifted up off the ground and hung by their own astral cords.

-CHAPTER 24-
NO MORE MASKS

Amanda Thatch left the girls with her mom. She wanted to spend time with George alone. They had been together since high school, and she must admit they had changed over time. Neither thought they would still be in this shithole town for as long as they had been.

At the age of nineteen, Amanda got a call from George. She had never heard him sound the way he had when he spoke. His voice sounded so sad, and she wondered if this was how he consoled victims who had lost a loved one. That's when it hit her. He slowly explained that her father had shot himself in the driveway. Her mother found him when she got home from teaching at the elementary school.

Amanda saw the same pain in George, the same distance, and maybe that's why she left after their last fight. Perhaps it wasn't just George's hurt and distance. Amanda finally realized she was running away from her father, too. She couldn't save her dad but promised she wouldn't let George go like that.

"George please, call me when you get this," she said into her phone. She had texted him and called him several times. It's not like George to at least text back. "Where are you?"

She tried to call George a few times, but the reception was spotty in most parts of the country and on the road heading into town. She was nearly a mile from the city limits when, as if she had driven into a strange dream, the sky blackened with thick, swirling, almost sickly green clouds. She saw electricity dancing in those billowing blankets above, each flash of light threatening to strike the earth below. There was something ominous about this cloud cover. Amanda could feel its spite for all those below.

Amanda spent so much time looking up at the sky she nearly ran one of the few red lights in town. Not that it mattered, it seemed; there wasn't a soul in sight. The town was sleepy but not dead yet, and strange weather usually caused people to go outside the shops and homes to gawk at the power of nature. Or whatever this was. Amanda turned on the radio in hopes that there may be a weather warning or report. Only static. On every station. Amanda felt hairs on her arms and neck stand up, and goosebumps crawl all over her.

She needed to get to George and get the fuck out of there. There was enough animal instinct left in her to know when a threat was stalking her. Right now, she wanted to get back to her family in a safe place. Just as the light turned green and she began to pull out into the four-way, Virgil Hanson walked out in front of the car. Virgil was the girls' teacher at school. He seemed somewhat confused or maybe drunk. Amanda wasn't sure.

"Hey there, Mr. Hanson! What's going on? You ok?" Amanda asked after rolling down her window. Virgil just stood there looking at her, an almost vacant expression except for a strange smirk on his face. "Hey, Virgil, you ok? If you stand there, this storm may come and get you," Amanda said, trying to appear somewhat amused by this scenario. "Virg?" Amanda said, this time louder.

Virgil Hanson opened his mouth as if to speak or cough, and much to Amanda's horror, dozens of thin tentacles shot forth like vomit and splashed against her windshield. Several whipped about and tried to enter the car's cab. Amanda's shrill scream of terror almost matched the pitch of her wheels as she slammed her car in reverse and peeled away from the nightmare in front of her.

Amanda got out of reach of the worm-like tendrils and watched as they retreated into the Virgil creature's mouth. His eyes blinked, and she saw nothing human about this thing in front of her. Two inky black orbs stared into her with pure malice.

The creature's torso violently twisted as it bent forward at the hips. The knees seemed to break and invert, and the once-human appendages twisted in their sockets. Now it was in a crabwalk position. The clothes started smoking and melting off the creature, and Amanda could see blood-red flesh beneath.

A tail erupted from between its legs from the groin. Or was it the ass? Amanda couldn't tell anymore, and her mind reconciling the truth of this nightmare. Amanda felt disgust boil up in her as she realized this was the thing's cock. The phallic tail whipped back and forth, and a cluster of needle-like spikes protruded from its bulbous tip.

Amanda began to peel away when the four-foot-long tail whipped in her direction, and several spikes shot through the car's windshield. Amanda screamed as she felt the projectiles scream past her face, slicing her right cheek. Her right shoulder erupted in pain as another found its mark. Her left hand raised to protect her head just barely fast enough to catch the needle tip in the center of her palm. Even through her tears, she could see the quill tip had pushed through her palm and out the back of her hand.

The pain from the attack had Amanda screaming like a wounded animal. Amanda slammed hard on the accelerator, forgetting she was still in reverse. The window's spiderweb fractures made seeing what was in front of her nearly impossible. She never saw the monster scuttle down the street with otherworldly speed and leap at her car.

Amanda gasped in shock as the creature's weight caused her to stray slightly from her reverse path. The tentacles erupted from its mouth, and this time, they wormed their way into the holes left by the projectiles. Amanda screamed as she began to whip the wheel back and forth. A few tendrils snaked toward her face. Her motions were senseless and frantic. All Amanda wanted to do was shake this terror off of her and wake up someplace safe.

The car suddenly seemed to explode from behind, and Amanda's head slammed hard against the headrest of her seat. The monster on her hood suddenly pitched over the vehicle. Amanda's ears rang as her airbags exploded, catching her head and face. Even over the force of the small grenade-like balloons, Amanda heard the creature give something that sounded like a scream as it crashed into a storefront window.

Amanda didn't take the time to assess her injuries or the car's condition. She threw the car into drive and slammed on the gas. She had never heard her once-quiet hybrid car make so much noise between the tires squealing and various pieces of her vehicle dragging on the street behind her.

Amanda looked for her phone as she navigated the quiet streets of Haven Shire. As she scanned the seat next to her and the cup holders, she heard fat drops of rain slap the roof and windshield of the car. Amanda tried to peer through any space of her windshield that wasn't obscured by webs of fractures. That's when she saw the thing in her rear-view mirror.

The monster's legs moved so fast that its movements made her think of a fly's wings vibrating above a swollen thorax and bulbous red eyes. Except these eyes were black, and its mouth was a slimy mop of tentacles. Amanda could hear it roaring as it pursued her.

It disappeared from sight suddenly, and just as quickly, a clawed hand smashed into the rear window, exploding it into shiny pebbles. Amanda quickly made another turn onto a familiar street. Her street. George's street. George was a good cop and loved his job. He also appreciated the value of a gun.

She cursed him so many times in the past for the money he spent on his guns and bullets. Right now, she prayed she could make it home to a safe room he built for them, with wall racks full of small arms that she had spent so many weekends dusting.

Their front yard was in sight when the car's roof caved in, the blunt force hitting her head like a baseball bat. Fireworks danced in her vision. She felt shadows creep into her sight. She was pulled back by another crushing force slamming onto her hood, causing her to swerve slightly. Her vision cleared as she saw talons reach into the shattered remains of her windshield and, as simple as ripping a piece of paper, tear the glass away.

The knee-jerk reaction of slamming on the brakes took over, and the creature was ejected from the car and crashed through the white picket fence she always wanted as a child. The monster rolled and was up on two feet in seconds. It threw back its head and shrieked as its tentacles and spiked cock slammed the ground triumphantly. It pointed at Amanda, and a wet chuckle emanated from the center of the mass that filled the creature's mouth. It started to stalk toward her as if it knew she was running out of room to run; with the monster between her and her sanctuary, she was.

"Fuck you! You disgusting piece of shit!" Amanda screamed, and she slammed on the accelerator again. The car wasn't known for its horsepower, but it had torque. The speed at which it could accelerate surprised the monster and Amanda. The car slammed hard into the creature's waist. Amanda felt part of it; the spiked dick, hopefully, rolled under the front driver-side wheel. She laughed maniacally as the creature fought for purchase on the wet hood of the car. Then it changed tactics. The many spaghetti tendrils shot forth and reached for her face. Amanda gasped as one or two of them slapped her nose and cheek,

Then the world exploded again. The car bucked and hopped as it hit the curb, ran over the fence remains, and ripped through the front lawn. The screaming, violence, and chaos culminated when the car slammed into the century-old oak tree in the front yard of her home.

The mimic screamed in pain and rage as it was pinned between the car and the mighty tree. Amanda watched, her eyes filled with the hate one can only harbor for a natural enemy, as the creature writhed in pain and struggled to free itself from the metal and the tree. She gritted her teeth and growled as she held her foot to the accelerator. The beast's blood oozed from its abdomen and spilled the foul-smelling contents of its viscera onto the grill of the hybrid car.

With a final gurgling and sputtering that nearly sounded human, the monster fell onto the car's hood. Amanda didn't release the vehicle's hold on the beast for what felt like several eternities. The foul odor of melting rubber and acid filled her nose, and she began to cough. This attack on her senses was enough to shake her from her stupor. Amanda pushed open the car door, her whole body shaking from adrenaline and fatigue. She took a couple of steps out of the car to review the actions that seemed to consume her evening, but in truth, may have lasted only minutes.

Amanda looked at the creature, its mixture of human flesh and some perverse and profane abomination. When she was satisfied it wouldn't move, she turned and stumbled toward her home. Amanda reached into her right pocket and fished out the keyring, which was home to her house key, mace, and other trinkets and tools she had collected over the years. She was within a few steps of the house when her body began to process the trauma it had just endured.

Amanda fell to her knees and vomited as the smell of the burned tires and acid filled her nose. She spasmed there on her front doorstep for a couple of minutes. As the adrenaline began to wear off, the pain of her injuries registered. Her right arm and left hand felt swollen, and nerves burned anew with the pain of quills that had yet to be removed from the monster's attack. She rose on shaky legs and turned to walk into the safety of her home.

She slid her house key into the lock and unlocked the doorknob and then the deadbolt. She turned the handle with a weak right hand and, with a whimper, pushed open the door. The interior of the home was pitch black. The darkness felt tangible, like walking into a thick fog and just as cold.

Amanda just remembered she had a small but powerful flashlight attached to her key ring, and with a clumsy hand, she found the button that turned it on. She shone the small light into the cold dark of her home. Her face screwed up in confusion as the lumines of her torch seemed unable to pierce the black Veil. Amanda's skin began to chill, and she felt an ache in her abdomen.

Amanda turned to run when a pair of strong hands reached out of that darkness and grabbed her. A powerful arm slipped around her abdomen, and a second hand grabbed her hair. She screamed in pain and desperation as her head was roughly jerked back.

Amanda looked up at her attacker with tears streaming down her face. The older man was well known to her, to anyone in this town. His marbled features, cold eyes, and well-groomed face stared down at her. His smile was malicious as he looked into Amanda's eyes.

"You are a remarkable woman, Amanda," Judge said with a smile. "I need you, my dear. Come along quietly, if you will, so we may change the world together."

Before Amanda could protest, his eyes took on a pale blue hue as he stared into hers. She suddenly felt so exhausted, and her brain demanded sleep. She wanted to resist, but her body began to give in to the comforting thought of sleep. Amanda felt her world and the recent events dissolve as the frames of her vision grew black. She felt her body grow heavier, and it seemed as though she was falling now, falling into the darkness that held her like a mother.

Judge stood there in the doorway, alone. He looked into the shadows at his feet and then into the night. His impassive mask melted as he looked at the dead congregant pinned to the tree. His smooth features gave way to rage. He was weary of these distractions. As if on cue, Judge looked up into the sky and saw what had become of Thaddeus flying lower overhead. It was now cloaked in a swarm of vermin, a plague of insects, as it flew toward the Forgotten Church.

"It is time to come home, boy. Let's see if you are finally worthy to be called my son," Judge said with disgust. He turned into the darkness and walked back to the church through that umbra. Back into the deep darkness that he would soon be unleashed onto the world.

-CHAPTER 25-
THEY COME NOT AS SINGLE SPIES

Manns and Holts sat in the back of the van again with Mata, Lizzie, and Vincent. The ride was as awkward for them as it was for George and Phineas. After arriving at the Grey farmhouse and saving George from some twisted, nightmarish version of Chief Waters and Martha Grey, George hauled off and punched Phineas. This issued an answer not from Phineas but from Mata, who moved to his side and hit George with the force of a two-by-four to his jaw.

The following moments were a blur. Sicily dropped her flamethrower and tried to tackle Mata while Robert pulled his gun and aimed at Vincent. Then Lizzie jumped from the van and tackled Robert. Nearly blasting Vincent's head off, Robert screamed shrilly as he tried to fight off the two-hundred-plus pounds of muscles and teeth. Sicily and Mata began to grapple in the dirt, neither giving quarter. The fight would most likely have ended with one of them dead if there wasn't a sudden blast from the flamethrower that broke up the entire scene.

Everyone jumped and was on guard, only to find Phineas holding the flamethrower.

"Everyone needs to calm down now!" Phineas said with his crooked smile, now painted red from a cut in his mouth.

"Manns! Holts! Stand down!" came George's voice following.

Even though the fight broke up and neither brother wanted to fight the other, there was still plenty of tension to go around. Mata sat in the back to keep an eye on the pair they had rescued and was now regretful of doing so. She and Phineas had poor luck with the police while living on the streets together. They often had to steal or beg to eat, putting them on law enforcement's radar. Some were understanding, even empathetic, while others wanted to dispatch them as if one would be a piece of trash.

This was especially true for Mata, who was not only often a person of interest due to her skin color, but her interactions were made even more difficult because she was also deaf and mute. The inability to communicate with cops was sometimes mistaken as non-compliance. Phineas had saved her on more than one occasion as her advocate.

Robert stared at the floor. He didn't even nurse the injuries he had received from the dog that pounced on him, superficial as they turned out to be. Robert felt like a child thrown into a lake without knowing how to swim. He had never seen Sicily in a physical confrontation before. Still, now he understood why she had been nicknamed "the Sicilian."

Then there was this other woman with her elaborate braid, tattoos, and those muscles. He had seen plenty of fit women at his gym, but this lady was carved from stone or something. Her strength coursed through her, and yet she kept her femininity. He tried not to stare, because if he looked for too long, the Cane Corso would issue a low, menacing growl at him. He got the message.

Sicily and Mata sat straight across from each other, locked in some psychic brawl, neither willing to back down. The quiet in the van was oppressive. It would have remained so if Vincent, who now drove the van, hadn't finally broken the tension.

"Seriously, let it go, you two. Maybe just kiss and make out. I mean, makeup. The sexual tension is killing me," Vincent shouted from the front seat. Sicily pulled her gaze away from Mata, who instantly looked in the same direction.

"Hey! Screw you, you dirty old prick!" Sicily replied and flipped him the middle finger. "Your girl here started it when she hit George."

"Who punched Phineas," Vincent retorted. "Who shares much history with your man. That is between them, not us."

Mata looked back at Sicily after reading his lips through the rear-view mirror and Sicily's responses. She relaxed visibly and, after a brief moment, reached her hand out to Sicily. Sicily looked at her, weighed her offer of a truce, and finally reached out and shook her hand. Everyone, including Lizzie, seemed to relax at this.

"How's the arm, kid?" Vincent called back to Robert, who was now nursing his forearm that had been savaged by Lizzie.

"A little sore, sir. That's one hell of a dog you folks have there," Robert replied.

"You have no idea, kid. Oh, and you can quit with that 'Sir' shit with me. It's Vincent," Vincent said. "Now that we've all made up, can one of you tell me where the fuck I'm going?"

Sicily gave him directions to her home. She needed to check on her mother. Even though she had made strides in her recovery, Sicily needed to be sure she was safe and could get out of town.

Robert was less concerned about Jackie. He wanted to see if she was safe but needed to get his dad out of the rehab facility that also functioned as the town's nursing home. It would be difficult to move him, but like Manns' mother, it was better to get his family far away from this place. As long as his dad was safe, Robert could fight as hard as anyone to save his home. He didn't want the distraction of worrying about others.

Within a few minutes, they were coming up to Sicily's neighborhood. Or what was left of it. When Sicily looked through the van's windshield, she had trouble understanding what was happening. All she saw for a whole block was fire and smoke. She looked through the other windows, trying to check the geography. With each glance, her breathing quickened, and slowly, a low moan built in her throat.

Sicily's home and every other house on her block were burning or had been burglarized. If the home was not in flames, then the doors were smashed inward, or the windows broken. In the yards and streets of each house lay the bodies of her neighbors. Many were disemboweled and mutilated, several torn apart. Without waiting for the van to come to a complete stop, Sicily opened the rear doors and jumped from the back of the van with her sidearm drawn.

"Momma! Mom! Where are you!?" Sicily cried, her black hair falling down around her face. "Mom!"

Robert exited the van with his weapon at the ready as well. "Manns! Sicily?" he cried out into the night. The rising flames and smoke made it nearly impossible to find anything. Robert spied into every shadow, each one deep enough to house any number of horrors. Before he knew it, Mata was beside him, looking as well. So silent was she that when Robert finally saw her, he let loose a yelp that sounded almost comical.

Mata didn't notice his start at her appearance. She seemed focused on a target concealed in the smoke. She pointed toward the engulfed home that Sicily indicated was hers. It only took a moment for Robert to understand why. From beyond the flaming pyre that was a house once, he heard a moaning wail.

"Sicily," Robert said, and he sprinted in the direction of her screams. When he could navigate between two burning houses without getting singed too severely, he found Sicily on her knees in her backyard. The heat from the blaze had melted the lawn furniture on the back patio, and embers had caught some of the leaves and branches of the large maple tree on fire. Sicily knelt in front of the burning tree. The same tree from which her mother hung by a rope, her body grossly mutilated and broken, her eyes wide with terror.

Phineas' simple flip phone rang. It was Vincent. Something in his core told him this was terrible news. He took a deep breath and answered the call. Vincent gave the details of what they found at the female cop's home and neighborhood.

"Fuck me. This is just so fucking awful. What's the next move?" Phineas asked. His heart grew heavy at the news of the woman named Sicily's loss, not just because her mother was murdered but also because of the knowledge of what happens to those who die here in this town. Each soul becomes trapped, and each one feeds something that has been growing like cancer for centuries.

Vincent stated that he and the two cops would gather reinforcements at the police station. At the very least, grab more guns and ammo. Phineas took all this in and decided to return to George with the tragic news. They had pulled up to George's home just as the call came in, and George charged at the vehicle at the sight of the car.

George was scouring the car, looking for Amanda. That was her car pinning one of those things out front. It was her phone and purse on the passenger floorboard. It could also be the blood he saw on the front porch step leading into their home. Then where was she?

"Amanda!" George called out as he ran through the open door of his home. He hurriedly checked the saferoom, the basement, and now the closets. She was nowhere to be found. His mind was already imagining what those things could have done to her. He rounded the corner leading into the hallway outside the master bedroom to find Phineas standing there. He wasn't wearing his trademark grin. He looked sick.

"What is it?" George asked.

"The lady cop, Sicily, she found her mom. They killed her, George. They butchered everyone on her entire block," Phineas said. His face was sorrowful but unbroken. He wore the look of someone who had seen so much tragedy and pain, and this seemed to add to a stack of woes he carried with him. He gave George the details of the next step.

"Ok. That's fine. I gotta find Amanda real quick, and then we'll join them," George said. It seemed he was a mile away from what happened, and Phineas knew he had to return him. Not just for his team's sake but his own as well.

"George, she isn't here, man," Phineas started. George looked at him and walked away. "Look, George, she was here once, I can tell you that much, but she's gone now."

"Gone where Finn?" George spun on Phineas and grabbed his collar, his eyes wet with tears. "How can you be so fucking sure, huh?"

"I don't know where she is, but you know I see things," Phineas said, almost pleadingly. "I can sense people. Even where they had been. She was here, but something took her away. That's all I can tell you."

"What does that mean, 'something took her away'?" George asked, still angry but becoming more focused on the problem.

"Something just appeared. It used magic I'm not familiar with. It opened up a bridge or door, and I think whatever it did, it took your wife," Phineas said.

"Judge," George said flatly. When he looked up and saw that Phineas had no idea what he meant, he took a deep breath. "The Marcus family moved in shortly after you..." George paused as if to consider his phrasing, "you...left."

"Ran away," Phineas retorted.

"His whole family moved up in those hills. I get the feeling they are behind this and every awful thing that's happened to this town since they showed up," George said, venom building up in his voice.

"Since you left, there have been murders, disappearances, and the slow death of this town," George continued. "I don't have much to go on as far as proof, just my gut."

Phineas looked at George, understanding what he was trying to say.

"Ok, let's get this piece of shit, kill him, and save the town. Maybe the world," Phineas said, a crooked, evil grin returning to his face.

George looked at him. As mad as he was at Phineas for showing up without an apology or explanation, he was glad to have him here now. Phineas had grown up, and he grew up strong. Part of George wondered if he could be that way, too, one day. Healed. George looked up to find Phineas looking at him.

"We'll do this together. I'm sorry as hell I didn't reach out before," Phineas said.

George nodded. It was all he could do. He didn't have the words right now to express his feelings. There were too many vying for his attention. He then took this big problem and looked for something he could control.

"I have guns," George felt a little foolish about how simple he sounded. "I mean, I have lots of guns and ammo."

"Well, that's something," Phineas said with his smile. "Let's get all we can in five and divert the crew to meet us here. I need a place to prepare, too. Mind if I set up in a room?"

Pain. That was the only thought Mata had when she looked at Sicily right now. After a brief mourning period, the woman stood up and turned away from her mother's corpse. To Mata, it appeared as though Sicily was singing a song in her native tongue. At least, that's what Vincent told her.

Mata looked at Sicily, whose eyes were red from crying and now wild with rage, and she wanted to console her somehow. Her inability to speak frustrated her at times like this. The feeling of being locked out of the world because of her deafness and lacking the tools to even give condolences. Not that "I'm sorry for your loss" could bear the weight of grief. The phrase felt as impotent as Mata did.

Finally unable to take the silence more resounding than her deafness, Mata moved to sit next to Sicily. The motion surprised the officer, and she looked at her as though Mata suddenly sprang horns from her head. Mata looked at her and held up a finger. She always carried a notebook with her just in case she needed to talk to someone, mostly Vincent. Mata scribbled a few words down, looked at Sicily with sweet sincerity and kindness, and then passed the note to her clenched fist. She pointed at the message with her chin, and Sicily opened it up. Immediately, she started to cry a little, but then a smile crossed her face.

"What's it say?" Robert asked sheepishly.

Sicily straightened the note out, so it was easier to read. In dark bold letters, the message read, "We will make them scream." Robert looked over at Mata, and she looked back at him with a beaming smile and an innocent nature that belied the seriousness of the note. When he looked into her eyes, he saw the truth in them. There was something monstrously potent about this woman. Whatever sweet smile she wore, however beautiful she was, she was also a predator. An image of a tiger appeared in his mind suddenly.

This sent a shiver across his skin because Robert was now sitting across from two dangerous women. He felt smaller somehow, useless, and weak. Robert wished he could have comforted Sicily somehow. Instead, he was doing everything he could to keep it together.

This shouldn't be happening. This is some sort of nightmare, maybe. Or maybe I lost my shit. What if I'm not really here, and this is what happens to people after they get thrown into the looney bin, or... Roberts's thoughts began racing, and his gaze turned inward as he fought to reconcile this new reality.

Robert nearly jumped out of the van when Lizzie the Cane Corse gave a "woof" from her cage. He looked over at the hound and saw that her eyes were fixed on him. The Cane Corso cocked her head slightly and gave a whine.

"I think she feels bad about your arm," Vincent yelled from the front seat.

"Aww, girl, it's ok." Robert reached forward, palm facing down, to let her sniff his hand and possibly let him pet her. Lizzie's ears flattened, and a low guttural growl brewed in her throat. Robert stopped his motion and looked over to Sicily and Mata. Each woman's face was tight with a grimace and eyes that reflected Robert's poor choice of actions.

"Yeah, son, I don't think she's there yet in this relationship," Vincent said with a bemused chuckle. "You may want to give her more time to come around."

Robert pulled his hand back before agitating the large dog any further. He wanted at least one good arm for the upcoming fight. He slipped his hand under his thigh and stared at the floor. Sicily gave a slight chuckle, the sad laugh that can only come from a moment like this while experiencing her grief. He looked up, a small smile of his own breaking this awkward feeling.

"Jesus, Holts, you have no luck with any girl, do you?" Sicily jabbed, her eyes still pregnant with tears, each fighting the gravity of her sorrow.

"Hey folks, sorry to ruin the moment, but we're diverting," Vincent called out from the front seat. He was reading a text from his phone. Everyone looked up in confusion. "We're heading over to George's place. I was told one of you knows the way?"

-CHAPTER 26-
HATE HAS TEETH

Across the dense, forested hills surrounding the sprawling Forgotten Church compound, the strange monotone prayers of the Veil reverberated. Maria sang her hymns, and those beyond the Veil retorted through those they now owned within the homes and streets of Haven Shire. Only the cops and these new interlopers seemed immune. This was a detail that frustrated both Maria and Judge. Neither of whom could spare any further attention as the time to begin the ceremony to tear open the Veil was about to start.

Maria commanded all those locked in the red eyes of the Veil, singing with her now, unknowingly giving up their souls. Beneath her, trapped in the obsidian floor, were the souls of every person who had died on these lands since the first tribe. Ironically, this characteristic of the hills and valleys was initially created to keep this land fertile and bountiful. The land was hidden and intended only for those blessed by the gods of the first tribe.

Gradually, the barrier between this plane and the poisoned lands beyond the Veil began to weaken. After intense study and research, Maria and Judge discovered the tree that grew in the chaos beyond the Veil, which had now poisoned the land and fed on the souls of those trapped on this plane. The twisted network of roots came from that tree, each seeping a putrid yellow slime that desiccated the body and withered the soul. It was a parasite and only served the purpose of weakening the walls that separated our planes.

The veiny roots of the tree now extended all across Haven Shire. So evil and corrupt was this alien plant that anything dwelling near it also suffered its corruptive influence. Not all of those who lived in the community were affected, though. Those whose ancestors settled in these lands seemed untouched. Even though they were not affected by the blight of the tree, they still provided sustenance for it. The alien plant fed on the quiet and secluded community's pain, suffering, and death.

The twisted and gnarled abomination bore fruit that fed the Formori's desire to consume all life on this plane. When the nutrients that gave birth to that fruit upon which the Formoria dined, they grew more insane with hunger. They were desperate, too. Little did they know that Maria siphoned energy and fueled the ritual to open the doorway and allow her gods to return to this plane and wipe humanity, and all their gods, from existence. It also made the Formorian servants more pliable to suggestions and comments. There was still so much to do, and the ritual's timing had to coincide with celestial factors.

First, she needed to kill those not under her siren call. It was only a handful, and Judge's creatures would be able to dispatch them. She simply guided them to their location. The challenge came from performing the ritual and hunting these heretics simultaneously. Judge was too consumed by his own hubris to be of any use. No matter, Maria had trained for this day all her life. Her faith sustained her. These distractions would not stop her, she assured herself.

"Work quickly, children. Feast on those who defy us," Maria whispered to them, sending rage into their thoughts. This sent the creatures into a frenzy, much like chum for sharks.

"Work quickly and be rewarded by Azothoth, Tamash, Cthulhu, and all who wish to return to this plane." Maria made this promise without any intent to fulfill it. All life would be corrupted or consumed as soon as the door opened. All would be used as food for the Formless, the Formoria.

Judge Marcus stood at his pedestal praying to those beyond the Veil. He focused his energies on the upcoming battle. Judge knew his son would soon come home.

Thaddeus is unworthy of the power he now has, thought Judge. He would take it for himself so it could be used for the glory of his lords and masters.

Judge's clairvoyance ritual tracked Thaddeus. With a telepathic call, he summoned the remaining Formoria, who awaited his bidding to protect the mansion. Maria had her own guards to defend her. Upon reflection, Judge decided he would need to be more congenial to Maria in the future. After all, they would be Adam and Eve to the new world.

Judge felt the telepathic responses of the Formoria in the church, each eagerly awaiting his orders. Judge hissed commands in Veil tongue, sending the abominations to defend the church. He heard each one accept their order and begin the tasks set before them.

After taking a moment to collect himself, Judge looked upward, his eyes not in the room but on the skies above. Through the black clouds and rain, he saw the slithering mass of claws, teeth, and the plague swarm that escorted Thaddeus. Judge exited the room through a secret corridor that led to a set of stone stairs that would give him access to the roof of his church.

"Time to finish this boy," Judge said to himself. He pulled his ceremonial robes close as he ascended the stairs, holding his scepter tightly. He prepared added spells of protection. "Let's see if the gods find you worthy."

-CHAPTER 27-
FATHER AND SON

Ebumna'romnyth flew over Haven Shire with its plague of *grah'n,* the flesh-eating insects, bellies forever hungry. The destination was only a short distance, but like its offspring, it hungered and made several stops to feed. The storm washed over the town, forcing its prey to take shelter. This meant having to feast on pets left outside or sully themselves to eat on the homeless. *Ebumna'romnyth* wanted to feast on those minds not yet spoiled by drugs or insanity. When it absorbed that flesh and digested those astral bodies, it enjoyed the sweet suffering and torment they endured within itself.

The harbinger of the Veil vowed it would have its feast when it dined on the pretender and his whore. Just as it was about to look for another meal, *Ebumna'romnyth* sensed a great mind below. It was familiar with the pretender's scent and confident he was close. The harbinger of the Veil flew to inspect the spot where it felt his presence, only to find the pinned corpse of one of his congregation. It breathed in the sullied remains and hissed in disgust at the adopted human features this thing wore.

Ebumna'romnyth stared out at the Flint Hills that hid the true church of the Veil. Not the disgusting structure the wizard-priest built his home, but the true church dwelled in those hills.

Ebumna'romnyth growled at the thought of this human and his mate desecrating that root system, born from the tree native only to the Veil, that somehow grew into this plane and suckled on the souls of the dead. It could spend eternity nourishing the twisted tree that bore fruit only for the eldritch gods. Instead, these humans sought to steal its power for themselves. This sacrilege was too much.

With renewed focus, *Ebumna'romnyth* launched itself into the air and flew toward those hills. It would find all those who served the wizard-priest, this Judge, and devour them all. Then make him watch as it would violate his wife and force her to give birth to its larva, then it would feast on Judge's mind and body.

The creature was so intent on vengeance that it didn't see the incoming police vehicle. Despite its many eyes and other senses, it couldn't see anything but Judge and Maria Marcus. This obsession was no doubt fueled by Thaddeus's mind, still active and working in concert with the entity *Ebumna'romnyth*. It had not yet realized there were new players on the stage.

It only hungered.

Above the church, *Ebumna'romnyth* circled the only access to the roof. This would be the stage of their glorious battle. The beast drooled in anticipation of this moment. What little remained of Thaddeus' psyche was engulfed with hatred. These emotions empowered the creature and made it focus on its prey.

It called the swarm of ravenous insect-like creatures to encircle the only door to the roof. It was a small concrete structure, built for this purpose only, with a heavy steel door and handle. As soon as the mage-priest entered the rooftop, the creature's spawn would bite, sting, and envenom. All that would be left would be a whimpering old man begging for it all to end. An end that would not be granted until *Ebumna'romnyth* had taken its pleasure in his screams.

Unfortunately for *Ebumna'romnyth*, the entrance Judge made was not as pedestrian as it had predicted. The small concrete and steel structure exploded in every direction in a massive burst of blue fire. The stones and metal cut through the circling cloud of venomous vermin, and the flames bit at their flesh. A high-pitched squealing issued forth from the swarm as the flames did not simply dissipate but began to swirl about the roof access like an infernal halo.

From the stairwell, Judge appeared untouched by the heat around him and walked out coolly. His hands were outstretched with his club-like scepter in one hand and a wickedly curved dagger in the other. His eyes were aglow with magic as he infused his body with the power of the Veil.

Ebumna'romnyth hissed as it watched the plague-spawn burn like dry autumn leaves, each floating pitifully away into ashes. No matter what it thought, this battle would not be as delicious if it were easy. It began its dive toward Judge, bringing every claw, tooth, and venom to bear. Within its torso, what was left of

Thaddeus roared, his arms stretched out before him. The shared spite these two had brought howling winds infused with electricity and black rain.

"Father!" *Ebumna'romnyth* heard Thaddeus's scream. "Your favorite son is digested and now spoiling someone's lawn!" With that, he laughed maniacally as the beast rushed at Judge.

Judge looked at the rushing beast and simply smiled. Atop the forgotten church, Judge and *Ebumna'romnyth* fought for the upper hand. Judge was no mere human as he was blessed by the Gods beyond the Veil with strength, speed, and stamina. He enhanced these traits with concoctions he created from ancient texts he found, written long ago by the cultists and clerics of the Veil. He tested these formulas on many townsfolk who grew too curious or outspoken.

Many didn't survive these experiments, but those who did had to be put down because they had gone insane with pain. Using the syringes filled with corrupted alchemy came at a high price. Infertility, for one, not that he cared or needed his own seed to reproduce anymore. Then there was the pain. Searing white-hot pain that rampaged through his organs as he injected the viscous contents with a large bore needle right before the battle began.

Any average person would be crippled or even dead from this intensity of pain. It took decades to train his mind, and he soon realized that pain and suffering empowered his spells. His suffering was the main component of his curses and evocations. He used suffering now as he spoke a baleful curse and spat a glob of black mist at the incoming onslaught of *Ebumna'romnyth' s* spawn. The last of the creature's plague swarm fell victim to Judge's corrosive attack that enveloped them in its mist. They screamed as each one melted and disintegrated before hitting the church rooftop.

Judge had no time to gloat, though, as a massive, clawed hand crashed into his right side and sent him sliding nearly to the edge of the rooftop. If Judge was hurt, he didn't show it; he simply stood up calmly and smiled at his opponent. This only incensed the Veil beast. With a chorus of screams and roars, it thrust the tip of its tail at Judge, hoping to impale him.

Judge spoke a word of power, *"Y'ai'ng'ngah!"* and thrust his scepter out before him. The tip of *Ebumna'romnyth' s* tail slammed hard into the forehead of the octopod representation of Cthulhu and went no further. A shock wave and pale blue light emitted from the eyes of the golden idol, and, in a blink, several feet of *Ebumna'romnyth' s* tail exploded and turned to ash. The monster screamed in rage and pain.

Judge continued his momentum and spoke another word, "*Ch'nglui'ahog!*"

From within the thick clouds above the church, a flash of lightning crashed down on top of *Ebumna'romnyth' s* segmented body. A report of thunder followed, and then another bolt slammed into a different part of its body. Instead of striking and burning or exploding whatever they hit, the shafts of electricity stabbed and pinned the monster. The beast screamed in agony. Judge smiled wide at the sounds of anguish that came not only from the creature but from his son as well.

That smile faded as the monster suddenly started laughing. Judge saw the sickly bust of Thaddeus cackling with his pitch-black eyes burrowing into him.

Before he could react, *Ebumna'romnyth* tore free from those segments pinned down by Judge's electric spikes. It seemed unfazed by the injuries it sustained, and thick black gore spilled out over the rooftop. The beast's size belied its attack's speed as it leaped onto Judge.

With one massive claw, it grabbed Judge's face, lifted him above its head, and slammed him onto the roof's surface. Thaddeus reached down and began pummeling his father repeatedly in his stomach. Each blow sent out shockwaves, and fractures formed across the rooftop. The massive claws and teeth of the monster began to ravage Judge's arms, torso, and legs, but not his face. It wanted to see the face of this heretic when he fell. With a final strike, *Ebumna'romnyth' s* hand formed a spear of claws, thrust deep into Judge's torso. It pierced through his chest and into the rooftop under him.

-CHAPTER 28-
A STRANGE COLLECTION

The cargo van arrived with Mata, Lizzie, Sicily, Robert, and Vincent. They each exited the vehicle and surveyed the damaged vehicle in the front yard, along with the broken body of the Formoria pinned to the tree. At least what was left of it. Most of the creature was rapidly decomposing, like the one George faced before the cave that led into the hills beneath the Marcus compound.

Both George and Phineas met the troupe outside. Sicily walked up to George, eyes full of tears and a face withered by her grief. They didn't say anything; he just grabbed her and pulled her in close. He whispered his condolences as she sobbed into his shoulder.

Vincent and Mata walked up next to Phineas, their faces expressing the horrors they had witnessed. Robert stood next to the van; the look of pain on his face was for Sicily's grief and loss, but Phineas saw something else there, too. Love? Jealousy? Regret? All those emotions played across the young cop's face.

"Come on," Phineas said to Mata and Vincent, "We have to get ready."

The trio walked into George's home, carrying a bag from the van. Robert was pleased he had a moment with his people. George looked up at him and gently set Sicily aside, giving her a nod. With a resolute tone, he said, "We're going to catch these bastards. They will pay."

She understood and stepped away. George walked up to Robert, and before Robert could speak, he grabbed him up in a firm embrace. Robert had not realized how much he missed this connection, this kinship. When he opened his eyes, he saw Sicily looking at them warmly. His face flushed at once at being caught in this moment by her. He broke off awkwardly.

"So, um, what the hell are we doing now, George?" Robert stammered. His face was still hot from embarrassment.

"Finn says he has to prepare us for what's about to go down. I get the feeling he's seen some pretty weird shit since I last saw him," George said to them.

"Can we trust him?" Robert asked.

"Dunno. All I know is that he also said he brought a shit-ton of hurt with him, weapons that can kill these fuckers," George replied, and then, as if hearing himself speak about this for the first time, he shrugged helplessly and rubbed his head.

"Well, let's take stock of everything we have and go from there," Sicily finally spoke, wiping away her tears.

"Sarge… I mean, George… what about my dad… my cousin?" Robert asked.

"We'll get to them, do what we can, and show them the way out," George said. He put his hand on Robert's shoulder, trying to reassure him.

"The faster we end this, the better everyone will be, Holts," Sicily said with a touch of grief spiking in her voice. All of them would have to learn to live in a whole new world. All except Phineas and his crew, it seemed.

"Let's get inside and talk over the plan with Finn's team," George finally said, hoping this would be a good excuse for him to consider the situation and how best to continue. They all walked in and found Vincent sorting various glass orbs on the kitchen table. Some were filled with liquid, others strange powders, and some with metal fragments.

Vincent looked up at George and the others and gave an award-winning smile. Something one might find on a billboard or bus stop photo. He pulled a duffle bag from a chair and tossed it at George. George opened it and looked inside.

"What the fuck, man?" George blurted out with wide eyes. Sicily and Robert looked over his shoulder, and their eyes followed suit. "Are you trying to kill us all?"

The duffle bag was filled with dynamite and plastic explosives. They both gasped audibly and looked back up to Vincent, who returned the look with laughter.

"Think that's scary? Wait till you see what's in the van," Vincent said between chuckles.

"Where's Finn?" George asked. Vincent's smile grew a little more serious at this. He pointed to a room at the end of the hallway. George looked down, and his skin and bones tingled a little. Something warned him to be careful here.

"Best to leave the two alone right now. This is how those two prepare. I'm not like them. I'm as boring as you folks. They call us 'The Mundane,'" Vincent said, trying to sound sincere. "What they can do is beyond my understanding, but I know one thing..."

"What's that?" Sicily asked impatiently.

"What they can do has fought off demons, monsters, even a small host of angels once," Vincent said. His eyes seemed far away now, somewhere or sometime else.

"Fuck this!" Sicily said as she stormed toward the room closed to them all.

"Manns! Wait!" George said. His voice betrayed him and showed how anxious he felt at this moment.

Sicily walked up to the master bedroom where Phineas and Mata were sequestered and banged on the door the only way a pissed-off cop knew how. She could hear some muttering, maybe a song, and she could smell incense. When no reply was offered, she shouldered the door open, splitting the frame, and banged the doorknob hard against the wall.

Sicily stood there, wide-eyed and silent. George and Robert walked up to her quickly in an attempt to collect the impatient cop. They also froze in their tracks at the sight before them. Mata stood in the center of the room, five feet of sinewy muscle and light brown skin. She sported her braid that ran down to her knees.

She looked like she was carved from a richly stained and polished wood, her skin free of blemishes and glistened with sweat and oil. Along the entirety of her body were tattoos. Runes and hieroglyphics ran along her arms and across her shoulders. Down her back were lines of kanji. On her powerful legs, lines resembling circuitry ran from her buttocks to her feet. Her shaved scalp also had detailed tribal markings and words. This script was Hindu in origin, possibly, each tattooed to encircle her head like a halo.

It wasn't just the intricate nature of the tattoos that amazed the witnesses or the strong and beautiful form they had been etched into, but the fact that they glowed. Each one shimmered and pulsed with energy, throbbing with an inner light and power. Some of the scripts even appeared animated, while others crackled and sparked. The writing on her scalp seemed to float around her head, displaying every spectrum of colored light.

Phineas was brushing her skin with a ceremonial wand adorned with feathers. He peered intensely at his work, each brushstroke drawn in careful detail. The face Mata wore, however, was one of pure ecstasy. She gasped audibly as the brush touched her body and traced the curves of her powerful form. As she silently sighed and giggled, Mata caught Sicily's eyes staring at her. Mata smiled knowingly, forcing Sicily to blush.

Phineas was performing the rites on himself as well. He was nude from the waist up; his chest, flanks, abs, and shoulders were also tattooed. Lay lines ran down his arms and back like Mata's legs. His hair was pulled into a topknot, exposing runes tattooed on his scalp. Instead of Hindi scripture, his head had some ancient formula that seemed almost alive as it swam over his skin.

Like those heard by Tibetan monks, Phineas sang a low and throaty song. Despite the grave tone, his voice was still soothing and warm. The words sounded ancient yet familiar to George. Almost as if he had heard them once in a dream.

"Well, are you folks going to get to work, or do I have to start charging admission for the show?' Vincent chuckled lewdly from behind the three stunned police officers. "Or, if you like, I can ask Phineas to bless you as well?"

George and Robert quickly and quietly turned around and backed out of the room. George was halfway down the hall when he realized that Sicily still stood in the doorway and seemed she may take Vincent up on his offer. Trying not to disturb whatever it was Phineas and Mata were doing, George quickly stepped to Sicily and tugged gently on her arm, snapping her out of her trance.

Sicily returned, still blushing, and joined Robert and Vincent in the kitchen. Vincent tried not to be amused by the looks of shock on their faces, but his crooked smirk could not hide the fact that he was enjoying this moment.

"So, uh, yes, we need to take stock of the guns, right?" George tried to compose himself.

Sicily and Robert nodded, their eyes still fixed on the image in their heads. They seemed to stumble toward the door. George turned and looked at Vincent, his face screwed up in confusion.

"What-the-actual-fuck did we just see in there?" George asked finally.

"It's how they prepare for every assignment," Vincent said plainly. "Your brother meditates and chants something to protect his mind and soul. Then together, he and Mata draw runes and shit with smoke over every inch of their bodies. It protects them from magic and curses. Hand to God, I've seen it work for myself. Those tattoos burn bright red or white when they take on demons and ghosts."

Vincent suddenly seemed haunted by a memory. "I've seen them fight some of the scariest shit, and they never seem to stop laughing and smiling while they do it. It creeps me the fuck out, and yet I feel lucky to see their work firsthand."

"And you?" George asked, letting the whole question hang there.

"Oh, me? I obtain the goods they need to do their job," Vincent said proudly. "If you are ever in the market for ancient occult works of art, books, weapons, or just some obscure ingredient for a trippy concoction, I am at your service."

"Weapons?" George asked, his eyebrow arched at this. "Have anything with you today?"

Vincent's response was a gleaming smile, and the man seemed to come alive fully. "Oh boy, just you wait. I got some real beauties for you!"

The conversation suddenly turned from a casual inquiry to Vincent's full sales pitch. As he preached about the benefits of dealing with him, George led the way to his garage. It was spacious enough for three cars, but a third of the room was home to several workstations for making ammo and modifying his firearms. George was secretly proud of his collection but more proud of the spacious shelter.

Sicily parked the van and had the back doors open in front of the garage. The contents were exposed, and she pulled out the duffle bags. Robert had pulled George's Explorer into the garage shelter so they could work out of the rain. He and Sicily laid out the weapons they recognized from the van and placed them next to George's personal inventory.

The table was covered by an assortment of shotguns, custom-built AR-15 assault rifles, a handful of pistols, and a variety of ammo suited for each weapon. Next to the rifles also sat half a dozen flash-bang grenades. Sicily and Robert looked at the collection approvingly.

"That's cute, kids, but if you want to exact some real damage to these slimy motherfuckers, you'll need something that really penetrates!" Vincent punctuated this with a dirty smile and a wink at Sicily. Her scowl put Robert and George, who were half expecting her to launch an assault on the older man, on guard. Vincent seemed oblivious to the threat.

"I present to you every tool professionals like me use in such cases." He lifted a handle on the van's floor with a touch of theatrics and threw open the floorboards. All along the space beneath the trap door were various weapons and tools. They ranged from the benign to the wicked.

George looked at Vincent's "wares" and felt a vibration in his palms as if he were holding his hands on a speaker. He wasn't sure why, but some of these relics called to something within him. They begged to stab, crush, and kill.

Sicily and Robert didn't pick up on this, but Vincent showed his approval with his broad smile and bright eyes. George caught Vincent looking at him curiously, forcing him to straighten. Sicily picked up a thick hammer, and her face displayed only frustration.

"So, we will fight demons with tools from my dad's shed now?" Sicily asked and looked over at Robert, who reflected her confusion with a shrug.

"Tools?" Vincent retorted with feigned pain, holding his hand over his heart. "I'll have you know, young lady, that each of these 'tools' has a history. Take that 'simple' axe there." Vincent reached down and picked up what appeared to be a standard wood-chopping axe.

Vincent took the axe, walked over to the tree to which the car was pinned, and took a swing. The axe's head screamed as it slammed hard into the side of the oak and bit into it. Vincent swung the axe with such ease and cut effortlessly into the wood. The axe buried itself to the hilt. When Vincent removed the axe, the damage went a foot farther than where the head stopped. The tree shook and groaned from the injury, dropping leaves onto the yard.

"Hey, fucker! That better not fall on my house!" George shouted angrily.

"So sorry, sir! I am simply displaying the true nature of these items. Each one's history is a curse. That curse is transferred onto whoever should suffer your wrath," Vincent said, mildly apologetic. "No other than Lizzie Borden herself used this axe. Her rage and hunger were so great that it left its mark on the blade's edge."

"Are you telling me that every weapon you have was involved in a murder?" Robert asked.

"That's why they're called weapons, genius," Sicily said, chewing her lip. She looked in the van and found something that caught her eye. "What about these?" she said, pulling out a pair of revolvers.

"Aces and Eights," Vincent said with a wide grin. "It's true about what they say," Vincent continued with his pitch, "...the weapon chooses its master."

"What do they do?" Sicily said, curiously inspecting each six-shooter.

The military-issued colt seemed to glow from the polish on the ivory handles and steel. Sicily felt an energy course through her hands and arms. Her mind and body hummed with the energy, and suddenly Sicily felt confident, strong, and capable. Sicily did not consider herself graceful, but she found herself involuntarily flipping and spinning the pistols in her hands easily. She looked up at Vincent and George with a giggle and a look of amazement.

Vincent chuckled and tossed the axe to George, who caught it. The head of the axe was larger than the standard wood-chopping instrument. Upon further inspection, the edge had strange chips in the metal. No, not chips, teeth. This axe literally ate whatever it cut; he felt that now as he held her in his hand.

"Her?" George asked to himself. He thought of the gender of a weapon and not intentionally. It imparted that to him. He felt the handle purr in his hands as he looked at it.

"Yessir! You are holding a piece of Lizzie. Therefore, the weapon identifies as female. It seems she likes you, too," Vincent said with a raised eyebrow. "Normally, only people like Phineas and Mata sense these details. I guess you are family."

Vincent walked over to Robert and was about to continue his sale when an explosion suddenly reverberated through the rain. The party turned to see a bright blue flash just beyond the trees in the Flint hills outside the town. Another flash lit the night sky, and a high-pitched roar tore through the forest.

"Finish your pitch on the way to the police station, Vincent," came a voice behind the group. They turned to see Phineas.

He stood in the doorway wearing black sunglasses, a black flannel dress shirt left untucked, a dark grey houndstooth vest, and a long coat. Around his neck hung a silver talisman with a dark blue sapphire. He pulled on black leather gloves and walked toward the van.

From behind Phineas, Mata stepped into the garage. She wore a white dress shirt, leather corset, skin-tight leggings, and combat boots. She sported a talisman similar to Phineas. Sicily looked at the enigmatic pair curiously.

"Are we making this a formal affair?" Sicily asked aloud, drawing a chuckle from Robert.

Mata didn't seem to notice and walked toward the table with grace and confidence as she pulled on a pair of black leather gloves that extended to her elbows. Running down the length of the gloves were black leather straps covered in silver spikes, each one a third of an inch long. The knuckles were covered with a metal band, and at each knuckle was a silver stud. She assessed the fit by throwing a few jabs as she finished pulling on her glove. Finally, she evaluated the knuckles by cracking them together. Blue sparks popped from the impact of the studs hitting each other, and small arcs of electricity crawled around her fists.

She and Phineas walked up to the van and looked over the cache of weapons. Sicily suddenly thought of the last image of Mata and Phineas. Mata's smooth dark skin, her muscles, and tattoos. Phineas' grace, intensity, and sleek, muscled form. She hadn't realized she had been staring until Mata caught her attention with a knowing smile. She looked at Sicily with a mixture of sweetness and play. Sicily blushed at her gaze, even more so when Mata gave her a frisky wink before getting down to the business of stowing the deadly parcels.

"We didn't expect to be lucky to have so many to help us in our endeavors tonight," Phineas said. "I know George has his own collection of weapons, and they will still be helpful. Sadly, I don't have enough charms for each of you."

"So, you're not going to paint me?" Robert asked with a chuckle.

Phineas looked at him with his usual grin, but a dangerous gleam lit his face. "Oh, I could paint you, sir, just like one of my French ladies, but it won't help you against those from beyond the veil."

Sicily chuckled slightly at this. "We still need to stop by the station and grab more ammo," she said. "We'll just grab our vests, too."

"That will help you against some physical threats, at least," Phineas mused. "I can't guarantee your safety against the dark arts or psychic attacks, though."

"We're cops, man," Robert said with a bit of challenge. "Nothing is guaranteed anyway, right?"

"That's the spirit, lad!" Vincent said, handing him a massive knife. The foot-long blade had a cross hilt and had skull and crossbones stamped where the blade ended, and the handle began. The weight and balance of the blade showed it could be easily used for chopping or thrusting.

"How's it work?" Robert said, curious.

"Well, son, that's easy. You take this pointy end here and thrust into something you would like dead," Vincent said with a laugh as he walked away.

Another report of thunder and fire sounded from just beyond the tree line. The group looked toward the sound.

"Well, are we going to play grab-ass all day or get on with it?" George grilled impatiently. "Let's hustle to the station, grab gear, and get to work!"

The party moved quickly to find their places in the vehicles. Sicily jumped in the passenger seat of George's patrol unit. Robert moved into the backseat. Vincent hopped into the van with Mata, who seemed almost giddy at the idea of the upcoming fight. This left Phineas and George alone for a brief moment. They stared at each other momentarily, trying to find the words to fill the years between them.

"I promise I will use every curse and weapon to get your wife back, George," Phineas finally said. He stuck his hand out. George looked at it, measuring this moment.

"Let's get through this alive. Get my wife. Save this fucked up world. Then, after all that, let's figure out where we are." George took Phineas's hand in a firm grip. His face screwed up in confusion as he found something had been passed to his palm. He saw a silver talisman with a dark blue sapphire in the center. It looked similar to the one around Phineas's and Mata's necks.

"What's this?" he said to Phineas.

"I brought one extra for the person I wanted to keep safe. Wear it if you would. It would be a kindness," Phineas stated rather sheepishly. Before George could reply, he turned and walked to the van, hopping into the rear compartment.

Another explosion sounded from the hills, and George looked at their target. He only thought of two things at that moment. First, save Amanda, his high school sweetheart, and mother to his daughters. Secondly, find Judge and part his scalp with the axe he held. The axe head seemed to respond to this with a vibration and a hiss that emanated from the blade.

He looked down at the weapon and felt an evil grin cross his face. "Just you wait."

-CHAPTER 29-
THE PILGRIMAGE

The two vehicles drove through the town carefully. Every person in town seemed to be held in some form of stasis, some floating in the air in strange positions, others standing on the streets or sidewalks. Each one was bathed in a red glow and seemed to mutter something to the sky as if praying to whatever was listening. The prayers and hymns were audible physically and mentally for George, Phineas, and Mata.

George struggled the most against this since he was unaccustomed to psychic intrusions. To him, the songs were a siren call to join the congregation. He felt invited to just give way to insanity and embrace despair and death. Sicily and Robert seemed horrified by the suspended citizens but otherwise unaffected.

He let Sicily drive as they grew closer to the hills outside of town. The police station was near the only road that led to the quarter-mile drive to the Marcus estate. George was visibly sweating and shaking from resisting the communal prayer.

"Hey, Boss, you ok?" Robert's voice broke through the noise and momentarily pulled George back to the moment. George looked up into the rear-view mirror and found Robert looking at him. His face was marked with sincere concern.

"I'm fine, Holts, just tired, is all," George said unsteadily. He rubbed his head, reached into his jacket for a handkerchief, and found the bejeweled talisman Phineas gave him. George slipped it on delicately so as not to draw too much attention. He felt the weight of the chain around his neck, the chill of metal against his skin, and then the world went quiet.

No, not the world, the hymns and singing. When they were silenced, it felt like George had gone deaf momentarily. Then, the mundane sounds of the world came crashing back. The rev of the engine, gravel under the tires, and explosions from a distance.

"Holy shit, it worked," George muttered to himself.

Just as his senses seemed to attune to the physical world, he caught a scent of burned rubber. His peripheral vision saw the glow of a nearby flame. He looked up and saw they were now approaching the station. Several patrol units were on fire in the street in front of the station. The front-facing windows to the station were broken. They led this brief supply run and pulled over to use the unit as a shield for the oncoming van.

Vincent saw the Explorer suddenly pull a hard right and take a cue from the police vehicle beside it. Everyone exited the cars; George and his team had their weapons drawn and ready. Phineas and Mata snuck in and used the police unit for cover. Sicily took cover as well and looked to George for some plan.

George turned to Sicily and whispered something in her ear. She nodded enthusiastically and moved to the rear of the unit. Sicily opened up the tailgate, reached in, and pulled out a long case. Phineas watched as she removed the contents of the case with practiced ease. It was a fifty-caliber sniper rifle. She then moved behind the van and assumed a post in the shadows of a large elm that grew just outside the parking lot. It gave her a flanking position if something came at them and allowed her to watch their back.

Robert moved around the front of the unit carrying a standard police-issue shotgun. He crouched down and looked back at George. They talked briefly to each other. They were too quiet for Phineas to hear. After a quick nod of agreement from Robert, George turned and confronted Phineas and Mata.

"We're going to go in and secure the station. You and your people stay here until we give all clear. Copy?" George said with all earnestness. "Sicily will give us all cover from..."

Phineas and Mata turned to see what had caught George's attention. A police officer was scrambling out of the front entrance of the station. George could see he was hurt, even in the dark. From behind him, two other figures exited the building. They stalked the injured officer, savoring his cries for help.

"Jackie?" Robert said quizzically. George and Phineas turned and saw that Robert had broken from his assigned position. They followed his gaze and saw that he was trying to talk to one of the hunters who walked behind the injured officer. George immediately recognized Robert's cousin from her posters around town as the area's number one realtor.

The injured officer had been working the front desk due to recent knee surgery. Matt Ruthus was always jovial and kind. Most of the officers in the department gave him grief over his weight, including George. The man took the jokes in stride, and in truth, every member of the force appreciated him because of his sense of humor. It hurt George to see him suffering as he was now.

The large man's high-pitched screams were like a child crying for his mother. Matt tried to stand and run, but in his panic, and due to a bleeding wound on his right knee, he fell straight onto his stomach. He desperately began low crawling. Anything to escape the couple.

"Jackie! What's going on? What happened?" Robert made a move to help Matt but was suddenly grabbed by George.

"Holts, those things aren't your cousins," George said firmly. Robert looked at him in confusion. Just then, he heard his cousin's happy, bubbly voice.

"Oh, look, honey! Robert is just in time to join us for dinner!" Jackie-thing said to her mate. "It's rude to bring company without telling us, Robbie." At her feet now, Matt was crying and holding his hands up to his head, trying to cover up from incoming assault.

George began dragging Robert back when suddenly the man fell onto his back. George turned to see what fell the young cop. Jackie's husband, James, arched his head back and opened his mouth wide. So wide that George could hear his jaw popping and cracking, and the corners of his mouth split open.

The neck of the James-thing bulged as something erupted from within him. From its mouth, a bulbous red tentacle shot forth. The end of the blood-red appendage opened like a five-leaved carnivorous plant, and each fleshy leaf ended in serrated hooks. The center of the appendage was a gaping hole with sickly yellow thorns.

Matt tried to push off on his good leg and low crawled toward George and Robert. Through his tears and spittle and snot, he cried out for them. "George! Holts! He... hel... help me! Please!"

Before he could issue another plea for help, the plant-like tentacle snatched the top of his head, one petal stuffing his mouth while the others dug their barbs into his skull. Matt tried to scream, but his mouth and throat filled with blood and flesh. Behind him, the Jackie-thing cackled and looked at the action with hungry anticipation. So aroused was this creature that it drooled and licked its lips. Matt's body shook and jerked from pain and shock as the monster gave a quick twist and a jerk.

With horrifying ease, it separated the top of Matt's head, his upper jaw, and his skull and let the rest of the corpse fall to the street. It lay there, thirty feet or so, twitching and spurting blood. The tongue rolled out like a dying snake whose body hadn't realized it had died yet. The creature that had murdered him began gulping, and the meal it had made of Matt's head descended to the monster's bowels.

George screamed in terror as he wrestled with Robert, trying to pull him away from the grizzly scene. Phineas began chanting a strange incantation, and an energy surged around him and Mata. Vincent looked on in horror and cursed several times as he raised his massive pistol.

"This form, Jackie suffered like that too, Robert. Her pain was so exquisite and long-lasting. I can still hear her screams if I lay still enough." The creature no longer needed to pretend and began to tear away the costume it made of Jackie. From its fingertips, long black claws protracted. It took the tip of the index claw and ran it down the center of its own face. It sighed in the pleasure it took from ripping away its mask, from the black blood that ran down its cheeks and neckline.

The clothes it wore peeled away and fell away like dried leaves, and beneath stood a bipedal, black-skinned creature. From the crotch to the top of its head were two rows of long teeth and a sideways mouth. It opened its maw and roared, squealed, and hissed while a thick purple tongue licked the air. Both of the monsters stalked toward the party, still hungry.

On the rooftops behind the two abominations, four more of their kin had crawled out of windows or simply made an exit of their own. They first appeared as the city council of Haven Shire, but now all pretense was gone. They screamed and hissed as they threw away their human forms to adopt their true selves in front of their prey. They were all masses of teeth and claws; tentacles wagged obscenely at George and his party.

From the shadows of the police station, transients emerged. George recognized them from around town and wandering the surrounding hills. He saw a few he had even taken into custody for public intoxication or disturbing the locals with their strange behavior. Now they each stared at him and the others hungrily.

George backed up to his unit and reached for his sidearm. From the corner of his eye, he caught Phineas and Mata, each walking with terrifying confidence, each smiling at their enemies. Mata pulled a sickle from the back of her black corset. George saw at the end of the handle was a long silver chain ending with a weighted ball. Phineas strode with his onyx cane topped with its silver globe.

How Phineas saw at night was beyond George, but this was a minor thing puzzling him in the context of the horror that was beginning to unfold. Phineas reached into the folds of his coat and pulled out a double-headed, foot-and-a-half gold spike. There was a hole large enough to slip two fingers into, which Phineas did and added a spin of the spike around his index and middle fingers.

From behind Phineas and Mata stood Vincent and their hound, Lizzie. Vincent held a nickel-plated .50 caliber Desert Eagle pistol by his side; a massive chainsaw with a thick leather strap was slung over his shoulder. The Cane Corso next to him was primed for great violence as she gave a low guttural growl, and the powerful muscles across her body rippled.

Almost as if it were the starting bell of a ring match, the report of a sniper rifle tore through the tension and set the battle ablaze.

-CHAPTER 30-
AT THE TONE OF THE BELL

The bullet from Sicily's rifle blasted a hole through the long tentacular appendage that murdered Matt. The beast squealed and howled in pain from the devastating trauma of the large caliber rifle. The other Formoria immediately rushed at the small group of interlopers. Phineas and Mata charged their chosen targets, moving with mystically enhanced speed and grace. Vincent took a stance next to the van and fired shots from his hand cannon. Lizzie bared her teeth and snarled next to Vincent, ready to attack the nearest threat.

From the shadows vagrants, or at least that's how they appeared, charged at the team. The Formoria held back, George felt it was a way to test the them and see how they each reacted in a fight. If the Formoria were hoping that George and the team were going to run or be overrun, then they were sorely disappointed.

A hail of gunfire from George and Vincent tore through the first wave. Four of the crazed street urchins made it to Phineas and Mata's position in hopes to have an easier time since neither had a gun. In less than a second they may have wished for a quicker and more clean death.

The first of the attackers swung an axe at Phineas in an effort to cleave his skull. He was surprised and horrified when the axe head stopped inches short of reaching him. For a moment, the tool was held suspended. George saw that Phineas was muttering something and then with a snap of his fingers the weapon decayed and turned to dust.

As if whatever happened to the axe was contagious, the decay didn't stop. It moved up the vagrants arms , blackening his flesh and rotting the filthy clothes he wore. The man tried to stop the chain reaction, at first trying to dust of the curse, and then by clawing at the necrotizing flesh and clothes. Within seconds the man fell onto the ground in a withered heap of flesh and bone.

The second turned and ran instead at George and Robert, after witnessing what had happened to the first attacker. Before the man was halfway across the battlefield, he was laid low by a beast of shadow and muscle. A black Cane Corso tackled the man and began to savagely tear into his face and throat. His blood-curdling scream unnerved George but he was grateful the hound was on their side.

The other two charged at Mata and he was about to shoot them down when something metal glinted in the lamp light of the parking lot. It moved so quickly George had no way to see what it was or how it seemed to move through Mata's attackers. That was until he saw that she was whipping the chain and sickle around herself furiously. The light caught on the silver chain and the blade of the sickle, which was now bathed red in blood.

Both of her attackers stopped in mid-stride before falling lifeless to the ground several feet from Mata. George saw a red line drawn across their throats and blood pumped onto the sidewalk and asphalt beneath them. Mata never slowed in her movements and began marching forward to support Phineas' flank.

George was impressed by how aggressive Phineas' crew was in the face of such horrors and knew that if they were to survive this, he and Robert needed to do the same. Unfortunately, Robert was frozen in shock. His sidearm was raised, but he mentally was not set on attacking. George decided the best recourse now was to take up a defensive position. He would do his best to protect Robert himself, and possibly provide support for Phineas and his crew. He hoped that Sicily would help cover the best she could without giving away her position.

He picked up the shotgun Robert had dropped and aimed it at the Formoria nearest him. The creature was bloated and covered in quivering pustules. Its head was broad and devoid of discernable eyes but had a giant toothy maw. The loathsome thing jumped from the roof like a toad, smacking the muddy ground beneath it with a sickening splat. George fired slug after slug in quick succession. The first two struck one of the creature's flanks, and the third blew off its arm. The last two blew a massive hole into its head.

The creature exploded and splashed gore and blood around it, narrowly missing George and Robert. George was horrified to discover that the creature's blood was also a potent acid. One that Sicily's first target wasn't immune to as the Formoria suddenly began howling and writhing in pain. It fell to the ground as the caustic fluids swiftly melted half of the creature, killing it. The thing that impersonated Jackie shambled toward them, moving surprisingly quick.

"Fuck you, you slimy piece of shit!" George cursed. He fired off the last round, which whizzed past the thing's head. George dropped the now-empty shotgun, pulled out his pistol, and peppered the monster. Each bullet slowed it just slightly, but it seemed to George that the creature was amused by his attack.

"Oh, Robert," the creature cooed in Jackie's voice. "I know you're scared. You aren't alone, though. Jackie is here, inside me."

"Fu … fuc … fuck you!" Robert screamed with tears streaming down his face, his hands shaking fiercely now.

"You can join us. Your father, too," the monster taunted with a wet, throaty chuckle.

"Dad?" Robert's eyes went wide. "You're lying."

"Oh, I'm afraid not, boy. His pain was delicious. He fought to the very end, though. He struggled in his piss-soaked bed in that old folks home that you sent him to. Everyone there sang songs of praise to the gods as we cracked open his skull and ate your father's…"

The monster was interrupted by a rain of 9mm bullets as George and Robert fired furiously into it. Its slimy, black skin was torn off in small chunks, and holes poured black blood from the gunfire damage. The mimic staggered and fell backward onto the wet asphalt of the parking lot.

Both men emptied their magazines into the creature. Robert was so enraged that he repeatedly pulled the trigger even after his ran dry. George calmly put his hand on Robert's forearm.

"Robert, pull yourself together…It's done," George said calmly. "You need to reload man. We need you back in this fight."

Robert looked over at him; his eyes were wide and filled with so much pain that George had to resist hugging the man. Before he could say anything else, a thick, muscled tongue smacked George hard in his torso and sent him flying. Robert saw him land hard enough to bounce and roll. Then he was still.

Robert looked at the creature that attacked. The Formoria had taken everything from him. Despite its injuries, it stood and seemed unfazed by the many holes and tears caused by the multitude of rounds fired into it. Robert watched as it retracted its tongue and then opened its mouth wide. It stalked toward him, and it occurred to Robert he would die here. Die scared and alone, with piss running down his leg.

Mata's deafness was both a blessing and a curse in such fights. When she fought one-on-one, she became laser-focused, and her senses heightened. In a chaotic melee like this, all the motion and muzzle flashes were a distraction. Luckily, she was trained in ways to remain calm and use her gifts to their fullest. Mata was not only gifted as a medium, but she had been physically blessed as well. What she lacked in hearing, the rest of her senses made up for abundantly.

Her sense of smell was sharp. She could smell the sickening stench of these abominations. Their scent of old feces and decay was almost overpowering to her, so she attuned to her other senses. Touch, for instance. Mata's sense of touch was strong enough to detect immediate air pressure and airflow changes. She could sense changes in temperature and feel vibrations from sound waves.

All these blessings allowed her to survive in the world Phineas and she had made for themselves. This was especially true now. Mata felt the explosion produced by the sniper rifle when it fired that large shell from the barrel. She felt the shockwave and air pressure of the bullet tearing through the air, sensed its vector, and knew its intended target. Mata could feel the heat of the shell as it superheated the air around it. Finally, she could smell the scent of blood, shit, and decay when it tore through the creature that murdered the police officer.

Mata felt the creature screaming across her arms and face. This was the bell that started the fight for her, as it was for the others, too. She was faster than the monsters and moved into range with her sickle and threw it toward one of the monsters jumping from the station's roof.

The creature apparently lacked binocular vision; its eyes were set on the side of its face instead. A set of purple quills ran down the bridge of a short, stubby snout, covering its head and back. Its mouth was small, but when it screamed, sharp, jagged rows of teeth were visible.

The curved blade caught the bipedal creature through its lower extremity. The eyes on the sides of the Formorian's head grew wide, and it squealed in pain and surprise. Mata smelled blood as the blade tore through the putrid flesh of the Formoria. She held the end of a thin silver chain in her other hand. The chain ran a length of six feet, at the end of which was the sickle she had just thrown.

As soon as the sickle had impacted the monster's flesh, she felt a tug on her chain, much like a draw on a fishing line. She grabbed that line with both hands, and before the monster even hit the ground, she pulled it with enough strength to force the beast to slam hard on its back.

The monster was confused, as it had never met resistance from a human before. The Formoria were more accustomed to humans screaming, trembling in awe, or defecating themselves in the face of their nightmare. This alien being was expecting a chase, a hunt, not two feet of steel piercing its flesh and forcing it to fall supine on its back. It was further surprised by the speed of the next attack from this tiny human.

As soon as the creature had landed, Mata moved with incredible speed and leaped on top of the monster. She quickly used the chain to tie the creature's clawed hands together. Mata didn't know these beasts' anatomy, but if they had a mouth or a neck, they possibly had a trachea and lungs.

Mata wrapped the thing's neck twice and pulled with her left arm. With her right hand, she reached behind her to grab the sickle from the monster's leg. Mata felt her hand catch hold of the end of the handle just as the beast bucked beneath her. She expected the creature's movements but was still taken by surprise by its strength. Mata was nearly thrown by its kicking and thrashing. The monster decided to forego its hands and began gnawing at its fingers so it could slip the chains.

Mata switched tactics from decapitating the creature with the sickle to resorting to the cestus she wore on each hand. She straddled the monster and began elbowing and punching as fiercely and quickly as possible. Mata aimed each strike so that a spike dug into the neck or head of the beast. With every crushing and piercing blow, she tried to avoid the quills on its face and head. The creature snapped at her hands, never minding the spikes.

Mata was so focused on her opponent that she hadn't sensed another attacker approaching her flank until it was within a meter of her. She looked briefly at the incoming attacker. It was a wounded monster that Sicily had shot. The Formoria was sputtering and spitting black, putrid blood on the ground with every step. Its clawed hands reached for Mata as it stumbled forward, committed to killing something before its life ended.

Vincent moved to back up George and the rookie but was intercepted by one of the Formoria that had gotten past Phineas. The stench from the creature was enough to make him vomit, and everything in his brain fought to reject the sight of it. Where it once had two human arms, it now had six insectoid sickle-like claws. It maintained some of its human mask, but Vincent could now see that, much like many insects that camouflage into predators, the human face was just a disguise for its true visage. The lower jaw split open and revealed mandibles beneath. The tongue rolled out and then curled up behind the pincher-like jaws. The eyes widened until they were two giant, black orbs with angry, red pupils filled with hate and hunger.

"Holy fuck, you *are* weird!" Vincent screamed as he raised the large caliber pistol and fired. He didn't have time to set himself against the recoil of the powerful pistol, and the shot tore through the dark over the monster's right shoulder. It paused just long enough for Vincent to try and get some distance between himself and this alien being.

"All right, Lizzie, let's turn this freak into a chew toy!" He turned to give the Cane Corso her target but was shocked she was gone. "Aww, fuck!"

The Formoria had closed quickly, and now all six scythe-like limbs came at Vincent. In a panic, Vincent pointed the barrel toward the creature and fired rapidly. He tripped as he backpedaled and landed on his ass.

The first shot blasted through the Formorian's hip, causing the left leg to suddenly go limp. The second shot chewed through the abdominal cavity, and the third through the right side of the chest. The last two bullets flew over its head, narrowly missing Phineas and his massive opponent.

Vincent's breaths came rapidly, and he quickly checked himself for injuries. As he took stock, he saw one of the injured monsters approaching Mata. She was punching and ripping at the bucking abomination she had pinned down. She was so preoccupied with her fight she couldn't see the predator stalking her now. Vincent moved to a sitting position and aimed his hand cannon at the shambling creature. One shot, miss. The second shot was too high.

"God dammit, Vinnie, breathe," Vincent chided himself. He took a deep breath, and on the exhalation, he fired. The bullet tore into the creature's flank. The force of the blow turned his body and forced the monster to face his direction. The creature looked down at its injury and then back to Vincent. Blood poured from its mouth, and with a throat filled with frayed tissue and blood, it gave a gurgling roar. Vincent responded by pulling the trigger again. He should have little trouble hitting his target at this range. Vincent's heart sank when the hammer came down, and instead of the thunderous explosion of a bullet being launched, he got a sad *"click."*

"Aww, fuck my life," Vincent said.

A bullet buzzed angrily past Phineas' head. Knowing his position, he wanted to take a moment to yell at Vincent. Still, Phineas was preoccupied with the largest of the Formoria. It was as big as a grizzly, its head flat like a toad's, and its mouth filled with rows of sharp teeth. It had eight white orbs that functioned at its eyes and three pairs of slits opened and closed while it breathed. It walked on two legs, and instead of arms, it swung at Phineas with two powerful tentacles.

Whenever Phineas got into a fight on the streets, he fought with his brains and agility. A larger opponent would try to grab him and become frustrated as Phineas slipped quickly from their hold and was on his feet in no time. He was a decent striker who focused on quick kicks and punches. His hits lacked the potency of Matas but were still devastating. It was because each hit was tactically sound. Every punch or kick thrown at him was dodged or ducked, and Phineas followed the attack with his counter. He used the trajectory of his opponent and turned their weight or power against them. He was also adept at using his cane, like a fencing sword.

The creature was too dangerous to get within Phineas's punching range, so he had to use the cane, the end of which had a sharp, silver spike. He nimbly sidestepped large swings and followed the unbalanced monster's attack with a stab of this point.

The Formoria was too large for his attacks to cause considerable damage. They did make the monster angrier, and its attacks came more rapidly but sloppier. Phineas knew he had to end this soon because his stamina was not limitless.

Phineas placed his double-sided spike in his mouth, reached into his long coat, and pulled out a small bag. The Formoria took another swing at Phineas, and upon missing, he roared at him. This act of frustration was met with a powdery substance exploding in its face and mouth. The Formoria began to gag and cough; its tentacles reached up to its mouth and throat. Something in the concoction reacted, and an acidic odor erupted from within the beast's maw.

Phineas took this moment and stepped in toward the Formoria. He pulled the spike from his mouth and launched it like a spear. The golden point drilled into the creature's leg, just above the left knee. The Formoria screamed in pain and fell to the injured knee. Its mouth had a red foam pouring forth as it tried desperately to breathe. Phineas took another step and, with a two-handed swing, smashed the other knee with his cane. The force of the blow broke a bone, and a crack resounded through the chaos. The monster sought Phineas with his arms waving back and forth just as the man took a jumping two-handed chop from behind with his cane, crashing down on top of its head, caving it in all the way down into the center of its chest.

The injured Formoria, slowly dying from multiple gunshot wounds, went into a berserk rage and rushed toward Vincent. Its progress was stalled by another shot from a .50 caliber sniper rifle from behind the stone signage with "Haven Shire Police Department" scrawled across it.

Sicily had a good vantage of the battlefield, except for Robert.

"Where the fuck are you?" she hissed. She peered through the scope and was thankful they had sufficient lighting from the outdoor parking lot lamps. There were still so many shadows, and she hoped Robert wasn't fighting one of these creatures alone somewhere in the dark. She knew Robert was a capable police officer, well-trained, and usually kept his cool. However, this was not the usual run-in an officer would have to face. She saw how these strange events were taking their toll on him. When he thought no one was looking, she saw how his hands shook and the distant look in his eyes.

"Fuck this!" Sicily abandoned her position to get a better vantage point. She liked Robert more than just respected, and part of her hated herself for this. She told herself she would never get involved with another officer after what happened in Chicago. The allegations, the sideway glances, the whispering and gossiping all left a scar on Sicily.

Sicily shook her head free of these ghosts and took a deep breath. That breath was lost when she saw the once-Jackie creature spinning and thrashing with a massive black beast latched to its left arm. Lizzie had a powerful grip on the monster's forearm, and each time it reached for her, she would backpedal and thrash. Sicily knew only one fact about the Cani Corsi dog breed. Their bite strength was superior to that of a lion.

Sicily's face beamed at the damage this good dog was doing to that creature. Her smile dimmed quickly as she saw that Lizzie had a few gashes in her flanks, and her sleek coat was slick with blood and mud. Cane Corso was known for its strength and stamina, but they still had their limits. Lizzie needed help and fast.

She looked over at Robert. He was sitting on his ass against the van, his gun was drawn, but she could see that the clip was empty. Robert was trapped there; his fear pinned him to the ground like a stake. His eyes were wide in terror, and his pants were soaked in piss. Part of her was furious. Not at Robert so much, but what these things have done to a man she had come to respect and care for.

The Formoria threw Lizzie away; the dog managed to tear its arm off just above the wrist. It fell several feet away with a loud thud. To her credit, the Cane Corso didn't cry out or whimper; it simply grunted. It rolled and stood up quickly, spitting out the limb and trying to tongue away the taste left by the monster's flesh in its mouth.

The monster turned onto Robert, its massive maw opened and poised to devour him. Robert was slowly rising to his feet at this point. Sicily aimed and fired and hoped she wasn't too late.

Sicily reloaded the rifle and raised it to fire but stopped when she heard hissing and growls from her right. Separating the police station from the local fuel depot was a tall fence topped with barbwire. Barbwire did nothing to slow the advance of four more disgusting monsters. They crawled over the tall chain-linked fence, ignoring the barbs, and landed on the other side. The first two began scrambling immediately to the ensuing fray.

"Fuck!" Sicily exclaimed as she bolted to get in position to fire on the reinforcements. *Click!* Sicily's face screwed in alarm and confusion. The gun jammed. Sicily didn't take the time to figure out why. She ran toward the lead monster and drew the pistols that Vincent had lent her. She prayed they gave her the luck he promised. Otherwise, she was fucked.

Robert was standing on his feet when the Formoria turned to face him. The creature's mouth opened and displayed all of its sickly teeth and a thick purple tongue. Robert felt the paralyzing fear creep through his body. Rather than succumb to it, he screamed at the monster. It was something deep and primal within him, something Robert never knew existed in him. Before he knew it, the Bowie knife that Vincent gave him was in his hand.

Just as the Formoria was about to launch into an attack, the report of Vincent's pistol and an angry hiss split the distance. The monster's leg exploded at the hip. The creature fell to the ground like it was hit by a car and landed hard on what could be called its face. It screamed an animal scream, a cacophony of bleats and squeals.

Robert didn't think, he just dove onto the monster's back and began stabbing furiously with the long blade of the Bowie knife. The edge was hungry, and so Robert obliged. He felt his confidence bolstered with each vicious stab, and a distant part of him wondered if this was the knife's doing.

Jackie's doppelganger screamed with each stab, the human voice now mixing with the piggish squeals. It bucked desperately to remove the crazed man from its back. The arm it used to push itself off the ground suddenly came under attack from the powerful hound. Lizzie savaged and tore, wrenching her head back and forth while also ignoring any of her own injuries.

Finally, the monster fell forward onto the ground, the creature's screams and howls now gurgling with its own blood filling its mouth. The knife screamed with glee in Robert's hand, mixing with his own berserker roar of rage and pain.

After what felt like an eternity, the creature's thrashing became nothing more than an occasional twitch. With a loud thud, Robert slammed the knife once more into the head of the beast and twisted the blade viciously. The creature would have laid still if not for Lizzie gripping it in her powerful jaws and thrashing it about.

Just across the parking lot, another battle had started. Robert turned to see Sicily standing before a stampeding monster, firing shots from her pistols. He reached out to her, trying to will the universe to save her from the incoming attack.

Sicily roared as she peeled her pistols from their holsters and fired bullets at the new attackers. Her voice was cut short by surprise when she saw how quickly her hands seemed to move. It felt like some unseen force was guiding her shots as each one struck its mark. Knee, hip, throat, face. The targets exploded from the power of the bullets and dropped the leading monster. The barrage rocked the monster mid-run, causing it to fall face first, slide, and stop dead at her feet.

She looked up and saw three more monsters begin their advance. Sicily continued her assault, hurling bullets in the direction of the creatures. Luck must have been on her side as the last shot struck not a monster but something metal on the other side of the fence line. The ensuing force of the explosion that followed was strong enough to knock Sicily flat on her back, belatedly reminding her that there was a large propane tank stored there.

Sicily caught her breath, and beyond the ringing of her ears, she realized the creatures were all screaming now. They were engulfed in a massive ball of flame, and pieces of their flesh were torn away by the blast. She whooped and began laughing at the dying monsters. She looked down at the pistols and her hands and told herself that Vincent would have to pry them from her cold, dead hands if he wanted these beauties back.

At the same time that the tank exploded, another battle concluded as Mata landed a solid blow to her opponent's neck. The cestus' spikes pierced deep into the monster, and with a tearing motion Lizzie would have been proud of, she ripped out the Formori's throat. Any strength it had left had nearly dissipated, and this coup de grace had punctuated the brawl. Mata rose, bloody and sweaty, and turned to see everyone staring at Robert and Lizzie. Robert had stepped off his opponent's back and crumpled down next to Lizzie.

His back was to the others, but everyone could see his shoulders convulse as he sobbed silently. Sicily had rushed around the SUV to find Robert in his state. She moved toward him but was stopped when he suddenly threw his head back into a primal scream. This scream was of pain and grief. Mata could not hear his pain but could feel it in the air. She walked up next to Phineas and gripped his hand. He looked at her and pulled her closer, arm reaching around her shoulder. A groan caught his attention as he turned to see George staggering to his feet. Phineas and Mata rushed over to him and helped him stand.

George looked up to see Robert kneeling, Sicily at his side, and Lizzie nuzzling him. George looked around at the corpses of the creatures. Each one was now dissolving into putrid puddles, just as the ones did at the Grey farmstead. His ribs ached from being hit and thrown across the parking lot.

"That was quite the tongue lashing you took there, sir," Vincent said with a hint of humor. "You hurt bad?"

"I'll be sore tomorrow if there is one. Right now, we've got a job to do," George said determinedly. "I'll cry about my scrapes and bruises when this is over and Judge is in the dirt."

"Let's do what we came here to do. Help your man out, get him in the fight, or send him home," Phineas said this, not coldly but with the recognition that they needed everyone to be in fighting shape. Mata stood by him, looking at Robert, Sicily, and Lizzie. The hound lay next to Robert, panting and licking a few of her wounds.

"I'll worry about my team. I know them, and we will be ready." With that, George marched toward Sicily and Robert. He whispered something to Robert. Sicily nodded as she listened to the words as well. She stood up and waited.

Slowly, Robert shook his head as he took in George's message. He looked at Sicily and then George, who both gave Robert a hand. When Robert was ready, he accepted their offer to help him up. Robert wiped his eyes and shook away the tears.

"That a boy," George said, patting him on the shoulder. Sicily gave him a pat, pulled him close, and gave Robert a light headbutt. Then she pulled him in hard for a hug. They held onto each other just as Sicily and George had earlier. Consoling each other for just one moment. When they broke, they turned toward the station and entered.

George turned to his brother and his crew. "Let's gear up, get vests and ammo, and then use everything we got to burn that fucking place to the ground," he said, pointing to the Forgotten Church. Lightning and fire ceased exploding over the tree line, but the party knew a fight was still waiting for them, and that was their only focus. Burn it all down and kill everyone in that forsaken place. Win it all. Nothing less.

-CHAPTER 31-
VIDE NOIR

Ebumna'romnyth roared with victorious laughter at the sight of the impaled Judge Marcus. That was until its throat filled with blood. The beast looked down and saw that its clawed hand had not impaled the wizard but instead pierced its own abdomen. It withdrew the claw, and its black blood coated its arm to the forearm.

From behind *Ebumna'romnyth*, a low rolling laughter began. The confused creature turned to find Judge Marcus standing with his scepter out to one side and his hand to the other. A sickly green glow surrounded him, and waves of magic poured from his body like a cloud of heavy smoke. Its wisps snaked out from the wizard and crawled around the Veil beast. The momentary victory was robbed by the massive creature. It roared in rage and lunged once again at Judge.

Judge sidestepped the attack this time, and with a twisted word of power, he clubbed *Ebumna'romnyth* in its flanks. There followed a crack of eldritch lightning and an explosion. The Veil beast tumbled forward and nearly off the church roof. Its segmented thorax and legs gripped the corner of the building and pulled it back upright. With its language, the creature turned and called forth lightning from the above pitch-black clouds. Green bolts rained down onto the building.

Judge reacted just in time to lift his hands above his head and speak a word of protection. The lightning crashed down on him and the structure. Pieces of the church exploded and melted from the assault. When the smoke cleared, Judge stood facing the monster, his eyes alight with hate and disgust.

"You dare come to my home, the Church of the Old Ones, and desecrate it with your pathetic temper tantrum?" Judge spat the words directly at Thaddeus. "Was it not enough to murder your own brother?"

"Brother…" Thaddeus said with drool dripping from his lower lip. "He was not worthy. Neither are you, Father."

"We'll see who is worthy, my upstart," Judge said. He called forth a new spell, and a pool of darkness formed beneath his feet. The inky pool expanded across the distance of the roof and below *Ebumna'romnyth*. The creature leaped into the air and flew, calling down more rain and lightning. The eldritch bolts slammed the spot where Judge stood, but they missed their mark this time. The creature scanned with its senses for the wizard's presence. It caught Judge's scent in the wind behind him and turned to face its nemesis.

Ebumna'romnyth began to fly toward its target but pulled up suddenly in horror. Judge now stood upon a growing mound of massive tentacles. Each one was black and oily. All across the tendrils were eyes and teeth and gaping mouths. The mound lifted the human into the air so that he was now staring at *Ebumna'romnyth's* eye level.

"Cthulhu is angered by your defilement of this church," Judge said imperiously. "Your punishment will be executed by me and his children immediately!"

Judge pointed his staff at *Ebumna'romnyth*, and a pair of massive tentacles shot forth and reached out for the beast. It tried to dodge and roll away from the powerful grip of the octopoid limbs, but it was too injured, and as a result, it was slow in the air. The tentacles coiled around the segmented thorax and gripped *Ebumna'romnyth* tightly. With the ease of swatting a fly, the arms slammed the beast to the rooftop. The tentacles lifted the beast and slammed it down again once, twice, three times. The two tentacles tightened their grip around a pair of segments and began pulling in opposite directions.

Ebumna'romnyth screamed and howled in agony as its segmented body was torn asunder, and it watched in horror as pieces of its body were tossed casually to the ground below. The torso and upper half of *Ebumna'romnyth'* 's body fell and crashed hard onto the rooftop. Blood and gore flowed from what remained of its monstrous form.

The monster whimpered like an injured fawn as it felt itself dying. It clawed at the rooftop's surface, trying to pull itself to safety, dragging its entrails. Beneath the still massive torso of the beast, the broken and bloodied bust of Thaddeus was dragged across the torn and cracked rooftop surface. His screams were muffled by the girth of *Ebumna'romnyth* as his face was scrapped across the rough surface of what was once a shingled rooftop. Now, it looked like some infernal battlefield.

Behind *Ebumna'romnyth*, Judge Marcus walked down the length of the tendrils as they crisscrossed themselves to create a living staircase. The final tentacle slowly lowered him down just behind the injured veil beast. He looked upon the wounded monster with disgust. The creature saw him approaching and hissed in a final attempt to scare away the wizard.

Judge didn't notice or care. He walked next to the monster and kicked it hard in the flanks. The beast flipped over onto its back as though it was kicked by a man ten times Judge's size. There was a little fight in the monster as it looked up at Judge. It wasn't until this moment that it had noticed that Judge wasn't stalking it. He was searching for what remained of his son.

When the creature was thrown onto the rooftop, it was Thaddeus who took the brunt of the impact. This was visible by his smashed limbs. Shards of bone stuck in several places in his arms where he had tried to brace himself against the strike. His right shoulder was severely deformed, and his left arm flapped limp and useless to his side.

Thaddeus's face looked more like a fractured mirror; the skin had split into several places, and blood oozed from open lacerations. His left eye had exploded, and blood and the eggy contents of his eyeball ran down his cheek. The man's perfect nose was smashed and bent awkwardly to the ride side.

"Admiring your work, father?" Thaddeus sputtered through missing and cracked teeth.

Judge said nothing as he looked upon the wreckage of his son and the beast he had become paired with. He lifted his boot, gritted his teeth, and brought the heel down onto Thaddeus' face. And again. And again. Finally, as Thaddeus' skull had split wide open and blood and grey matter spilled out, Judge stopped and stepped back to view the creature as a whole.

Ebumna'romnyth stared in wide-eyed horror as Judge seemed to consider the creature. "Why were you chosen? Why were you given power?" it hissed these words at Judge in the Formorian tongue. Judge looked at the creature as though the question was too silly to have been asked.

Judge replied, "Why are we humans the apex predator? How is it that this world and the creatures on its bow to us? We are not the strongest, fastest, or even born with natural weapons like fangs or claws. Our spawn is incapable of escaping predators. Why was I chosen?" Judge was irritated by the question itself now. "The Old Ones value lineage, you stupid animal. Within my and my wife's veins run the bloodlines of the first tribe. We are directly descended from those same beings that forced your pathetic species from this plane."

Ebumna'romnyth stared in disbelief at this. It began to shake its head in an attempt to dismiss the words. An almost human moan of grief poured from the creature's lip. Did this human wizard speak the truth? Had the gods denied it the power to kill this man?

"You lie, wizard!" it screamed at him.

"You believe the Gods care for you?" Judge asked, nearly laughing at the beast. "They only love chaos, suffering, and killing each other in their feud. You are nothing more than fodder, food, or amusement."

"You are only human," *Ebumna'romnyth* stated not only as a fact but in an attempt to insult Judge.

"Who better to wipe out those who exiled your kind beyond the veil?" Judge said flatly. "We've been murdering ourselves since our conception. Who is better equipped to murder the human race than a human? Instead of doing so sluggishly with fire, pollution, or a pandemic, I shall do it swiftly and with greater suffering. I will bring the Gods here to battle on this plane. They will wipe out all life, and I will, in turn, use their destructive power to create a new world. I will wipe the slate clean and start anew."

"Blasphemy!" *Ebumna'romnyth* hissed at him.

"Possibly. Maybe those same gods we worship may punish me as they did you, but I doubt that. Whether they approve of my machinations or not, they will be too preoccupied with their warring to be concerned with me. By the time any of the Old Gods, Outer Gods, or anything beyond the Veil realize what I have achieved, it'll be too late to stop me." Judge looked down at the broken creature at his feet with disgust and growing boredom.

"It's time to end this… I have preparations to deal with," Judge said. "You have something of mine, though, and I'll take it back. My flesh-and-blood."

Judge raised his hand to the massive coils of teeth and tentacles still standing behind him, patiently waiting for his command. The mass of limbs hungrily groped for *Ebumna'romnyth' s* broken body. The Veil beast screamed in rage and terror as it was pulled into the writhing mass. Teeth bit into its flesh, venomous thorns and spikes pierced into its hide, and a thousand eyes wept in pleasure at the monster's suffering.

Two of the most prominent tentacles snaked themselves around the busts of the now-dead Thaddeus and a wailing *Ebumna'romnyth,* pulling them in opposite directions. A squelching and cracking noise was audible beneath the skin and bones of the creature as the limbs tightened their grip. Then, as effortlessly as tearing a sheet of paper, the two beings were ripped apart. The skin made a wet ripping noise, and entrails and organs fell to the rooftop below, just a few feet from Judge.

What remained of Thaddeus was laid reverently at Judge Marcus's feet with more tenderness and respect than what Judge had ever given his own son. The remains of *Ebumna'romnyth* were held high above the mouths and limbs. Screams, screeching, squeals, and roars of victory and joy erupted from the tangle of tentacles.

"I am done with this business. Leave me," Judge commanded. Instantly, the animal sounds ceased, and with what may seem like an act of petulance, the tentacles tossed the body away as a child might a broken toy. The limbs and gnashing teeth receded into Judge's pool of summoned darkness.

Judge waited briefly to ensure he would not be spied upon. When the moment had passed, he looked down on the broken corpse of his son. Not a hint of emotion akin to grief, anger, or loss colored his stony features. If Judge had any emotion about this battle, it would be a disappointment. He had felt nothing but regret since Thaddeus was born, and he had hoped that his son would have proved more formidable, more cunning, more of himself.

Judge saw nothing except his own failures in how he raised the man. He pulled a wicked curved dagger from his robe and placed the blade on his palm. Whispering words of power into the edge, he dragged it across his hand. He closed a fist around the wound and held it, palm down, over Thaddeus' body. A few drops of blood fell onto what was left of his son's corpse, and with a single word of magic to finish the ritual, the blood burst into a green flame.

Judge opened his palm, and instead of blood, a line of green liquid bathed in flames splashed onto the corpse's chest. The molten fluid cooked the skin, and the fire hungrily devoured the tissue and bone. The tender flesh bubbled and peeled away and then blackened. Fat hissed, and the organs popped, expressing shit, bile, or whatever remained within their cavities.

"Your soul shall be spared from being devoured by the Old Ones," Judge stated, looking over the growing flames now becoming a bright green conflagration. "This is the only kindness I will offer you. Your soul will not be devoured as the others will. You simply will go into nothingness."

Without another word, Judge turned on his heel and walked away from the black ashes swept away by the breeze. Within moments, nothing was left of the once human, once monster and speaker of the Void. There was no evidence of the unloved child of the Marcus family. In the distance, an otherworldly bell tolled, signaling the end of this world and for those who were going to partake in its destruction to prepare themselves.

-CHAPTER 32-
INTO THE OPEN MAW

Robert pulled on his uniform pants and tightened the black leather belt around his waist. It was such a mundane act; putting on clothes and ordinary was precisely what he needed right now. After witnessing living horrors birthed from a science fiction movie, Robert needed to beach himself on the shores of something typical. He looked in the mirror and inspected his uniform.

All was back in place, the shirt was pressed and starched, and he brushed his hair free of any remains of the battle just outside the precinct. Robert Holts closed his eyes, took a deep breath, and slowly let it out.

He was shocked out of his reverie when a strong hand slapped him on his ass and then squeezed viciously. He was confident that one of those fingers was dangerously close to his asshole, and he yelped in surprise. He turned to see Sicily standing there with a big shit-eating grin on her face.

"Fuck, Manns! You scared the shit out of me!" Robert snapped back, his body suddenly became hot, and he knew he was blushing.

"Oh no, not again!" Sicily said teasingly and immediately regretted the jibe when Robert's face darkened. "Sorry, I'm not used to any of this either. The fact we're alive right now seems like a miracle or something," Sicily stammered.

"It's good, Manns. I just need a second longer, and then I'll be ready to go," Robert said. He wanted to steer the conversation away from the weird world they had just come from and would undoubtedly return to in a few moments.

Sicily looked at him and nodded soberly. She looked like she wanted to say something and thought better of it. She patted Robert on his shoulder and started to walk past him to return to the others. She stopped suddenly and whispered into his ear, and her breath on his ear sent pleasurable goosebumps across Robert's skin.

"Nice ass, by the way."

Robert could hear the evil grin in her voice. She followed the tease with a kiss on his cheek. Just as she was about to pull away,

Robert caught sight of a look on her face that he had never seen before- tenderness. As long as Robert could remember, he had a schoolboy crush on this amazing woman. She was the funniest, strongest, and smartest woman he knew, and he had always promised to get the courage one day to tell her how he felt. Why not now? Before the world ended.

Time slowed for Robert, and he saw that Sicily was just as scared as he was, and she began to pull away. *No more thinking, or planning, no more waiting for the "right time!"* Robert felt this as much as he thought it. Time rushed back into real-time like air filling a vacuum.

Sicily squeaked as Robert's hands found her hips, pulled her close into him, and kissed her fiercely on the mouth. Robert could feel the mutual relief and joy as they turned in their embrace and he pressed her against the lockers. Sicily pulled away just long enough to show off her hungry smile and a playful giggle. Then the pair crashed into each other again.

With all the pain and suffering and insanity of this night, this moment swept Robert and Sicily away to a safe harbor for just the two of them. Sicily let out a moan as Robert traced her neck with his lips and tongue and pressed his hips hard against hers. In response Robert felt her hands grab his butt and grip his ass, her nails biting into the tender flesh and muscle beneath his pants. Robert gave a tiny flinch that popped across his body like a firecracker. He pulled back to see her looking back at him, biting her lower lip playfully.

The pair were suddenly shocked when the lockers shook from a fist pounding heavily on the last door in the row. Vincent stood at the end of the row of lockers with a knowing, and rather lewd, grin on his face.

"Come on, sweethearts! You can do that all you like off the clock. Right now, we have a job to do," Vincent said with a wink.

Sicily swallowed hard and took a deep breath. Robert felt her gently push him away and he watched as she straightened her shirt and pants. He felt his face burning bright red and sweat beading across the nap of his neck. Seeing his fear and discomfort, Sicily planted a tender kiss on his cheek and walked away without a word. Instantly, Robert felt himself cool. That was until his eyes met that sleazy salesman, Vincent as he watched Sicily walk by and then return Robert's gaze with a wicked grin. Without another word, Vincent walked away after Sicily. Robert could hear the man's deep chuckle echo off the locker room walls.

"What a douchebag," Robert muttered to himself.

When Robert had come out of the locker room, he was surprised by how quickly the others had gathered the gear. Unless he had just lost track of time getting himself together. George had a duffle bag with shotguns, AR-15s, extra magazines, and ammo. Robert also spied a few flashbang and teargas grenades. On the table next to the weapons cache were three vests and some riot armor. Sicily was in a chair next to the table, applying a vest. George had already suited up in nearly full riot gear armor, minus the helmet and shield. Slung over his shoulder was the axe that Vincent offered him.

As if on cue, Robert felt a tap on his shoulder. He turned to see Vincent holding the sheathed Bowie knife out for him. He looked somewhat amused, but didn't he always look that way? Just another thing Robert found irritating about the man. Robert took the knife and swore he felt a vibration from the handle. He looked up at Vincent and his bemused expression.

"It likes you," Vincent said. "It suits you, my man. Mind if I borrow some armor from you folks?"

"You don't have something in your box of tricks?" George asked, overhearing the brief exchange. "No ring of protection or amulet of resistance?"

"Well, since there are real monsters with teeth and claws and God knows what else, I thought it better to be safe than sorry," Vincent returned. "I'm not afforded yours, Finn's, or Mata's gifts. I needed more on this go around. Normally, I'm not on the frontlines like you folks."

"What is it you do, anyway? Aside from being a porter for their weird roadshow?" Robert asked, pointing his chin at Finn and Mata.

Mata had taken off the shirt she had put on just before the battle. It lay on the floor, covered in stinking black blood. She and Phineas were having some conversation about the garment in sign language. She wore a black sleeveless shirt and a sports bra. She still wore the leather corset with a cross-body belt and pouches.

Phineas still wore his black suit shirt, tie, and trench coat. He wore the same silver-rimmed dark spectacles.

"I told you, boy, I negotiate and procure goods needed for their work. We also find items of interest for similar parties, and I'll sell them," Vincent said with a little dramatic flair.

"It's just that you don't seem to quite fit in with them, no offense," Robert said.

"None taken." Vincent looked over at the pair, who were now in a full-blown argument mixed with playful banter. Seeing them do this in sign language always made him chuckle. He knew the discussion would end as it always does, with Mata giving Phineas a sharp jab on Phineas' shoulder or ribcage, maybe a headlock, followed by a hug. Phineas would, of course, play the victim in the exchange.

"They saved my life; more than that, my soul," Vincent said, admiring the pair. "I owe them and will do whatever I can to help."

Robert digested this intense and somewhat cryptic moment. He nodded and walked over to the table where Sicily and George were finishing up their preparations. Vincent looked after Robert and his troupe. He thought how much they mirrored his own crew.

George, Robert, and Sicily met outside and loaded the van with the extra gear. George found a keycard that would get them past the security gate in the chief's office, and he began to go over what little plan there was. The torrential storm had come to a halt, and now it seemed Haven Shire was blanketed by fog.

"I'm not ordering you two to go along with this. I don't know what we're up against, but it will likely be worse than we've seen. I can't ask you to risk your lives for—" George began.

"No disrespect, Sarge, but it's not like we can go anywhere," Robert said. "Phineas laid it out for us all in there."

"Yeah, we're the only ones who know about the end of the world, and there is zero time to fuck around and call in the military," Sicily continued.

"Even still, you are two of the few people I trust worldwide. My wife, being somewhere in that shithole, is the other," George said. He looked like he wanted to say something more but struggled with the words.

"Yeah, yeah, George. We love you too, blah blah blah," Robert said, surprising Sicily and George with his audacity. "What?" Robert blurted out when he saw the looks.

"Boy's growing up," Sicily ribbed him.

Phineas walked up to the trio. Mata and Vincent had pulled Lizzie out of the van and moved her to the K-9 pens. All were empty, which was typical as they were rarely used. The K-9 units usually took the dogs home with them, and the cages were for those dogs in training or needing medical attention.

Lizzie was in good spirits but had suffered a few lacerations during the last fight. Phineas and his crew asked George if they could put her here to rest until this was resolved. He agreed and even helped with supplying bandages and gauze to treat her injuries.

"We're almost ready to go, folks," Phineas said.

"I gotta know, what's with the glasses?" Sicily asked. George and Robert nodded. They appreciated that she was also asking what they had wondered all this time.

"Well, George can attest that I've always had 'the sight,' some may call it," Phineas started. "Though we didn't know that was what it was. We both thought I was crazy, like Mom."

George looked thoughtful, his memory coming back to him. His mother had been haunted by her visions, the voices, the nightmares. Everyone in the family just thought she suffered from schizophrenia. Everyone except Finn, that was. George had just thought it was Phineas's way of dealing with the craziness of it all. He thought he was just playing along. George felt a sharp pang of grief and shame at how she was treated in her final years. He was angry, too, at himself and others for what they said about her and how they treated her.

"Anyway, I see spirits and souls all the time. I see our world and the world of the departed. For me, these realities exist at the same time," Phineas explained. "Gehenna, the land of the dead, is a busy place, and bright souls appear to me as lights. Dark souls, the souls of those who are damned, appear as disembodied shadows. The specs allow me to "tune in" which reality I wish to see whilst filtering out distractions. Make sense?"

"Abso-fucking-lutely not, but thanks for explaining it. Fuck, this is all so fucking weird," Sicily said. "Can we please go and kill the Marcus family and maybe find some way to escape all this shit? Like over a bottle of whiskey and some boring-ass serial killer docuseries?"

Fully loaded, the two teams left in the van and made their way to the Marcus estate. Once they made it to the gate, George got out and swiped the keycard that would initiate the gate to swing wide and allow them to pass. It was heavy and reinforced, and the group held their breath momentarily when he scanned the keycard.

At first, nothing happened, but then the door awoke and slid away to reveal a paved blacktop stretch of road. Everyone present let out a collective sigh. No one wanted to waste time trying to find a way to destroy the gate or determine the best way to hike up the stretch of road to storm, from the reports anyway, a literal castle.

The drive up the road was quiet and made eerie by the encroaching shadows of the forest and darkened skies. They had thought to try to drive up without the headlights, but without any ambient light, they would find themselves in a ditch or tumbling down the hill. There was no sound of life in the woods, only the occasional clap of thunder and a streak of green lightning that silhouetted the tree line.

Everyone in the van sat quietly or rechecked their gear. All except Mata and Phineas. These two were discussing something in sign language and looking around outside the van as Vincent drove the paved surface. Only they seemed to be able to see what lay beyond in the darkness. George snuck up to Phineas and tapped him on the shoulder.

"Hey, Finn, care to clue the rest of us in about what you two are seeing out there?" George whispered. "We're all pretty nervous here. Even your boy Vinnie is quiet."

Phineas looked around at the party with a smile. He seemed almost excited by what it was he could see. He looked about without his spectacles, and George saw how his irises glowed in the dim light of the dash. Mata was interested in something out there in the woods as well. She cupped her ears, attempting to capture the sound. It seemed like a child listening to music in headphones. After taking a quick glance around and taking a moment to consider how to answer the question, Phineas replied.

"The ghosts of every person who had died on this land float around us right now like fireflies," Phineas said with some wonder. "They flutter about like moths and sing some song. I don't understand the language, but it's all so beautiful." There was a touch of sadness in Phineas's voice.

"Yeah? Any of them singing a ditty about how to kill monsters?" George said.

Phineas looked at him, amused at first, and then a realization hit him.

"You can't feel them? Those same spirits have always seemed interested in you," Phineas said flatly, and then he continued, "You have spirits with you now. Keeping you safe."

George wasn't comforted by this revelation. "I only feel like my skin is crawling, and the closer we get to the Marcus family, the more my insides buzz like a hive of pissed hornets," George said.

"That's them. The spirits help you stay out of danger. They always have. You feel it when pulled away from harm or alerted about potential danger, right?" Phineas asked.

The thought of spirits or souls or anything looking over George unnerved him. Were they always there? Did they only protect him when he was in danger? *They haven't kept him from doing anything stupid, that's for sure. Otherwise, he wouldn't be here right now*, George thought.

"We're here," Vincent said. Vincent spoke in the same manner as one who had hiked an entire day to a mountain, only to find that the mountain was an active volcano.

The Forgotten Church was a place of worship for chaos, fear, and pain. The structure the crew saw as they drove up to it was a monument to the Formoria and a symbol of their ideals. Looking at the building itself inspired feelings of revulsion. The edges, angles, and windows promoted sensations of inhospitality and discord among the visitors.

The winds whipped around the building and created bursts of currents that struck the van from every angle. Lightning snapped above them with sickly green light, and the ensuing thunderclap sounded more like the rumbling insides of a hungry beast.

There was no symmetry, singular style of architecture, or chosen décor, to determine its origin. The vegetation that grew wild around the building was untended, either heavily overgrown or completely dead, without attempting to create a uniform landscape.

The circle drive surrounded a dry fountain, upon which stood a ten-foot black marble statue of an armor-clad woman. Her lower extremities were nude except for pearl white tentacles coiled around her legs, thighs, and buttocks. The woman's face was a mask of pustules, scars, and barnacle-like growths. In her left hand, she held a hefty tome; the stone was so well carved that it seemed the wind may actually turn the pages. She had a wickedly curved dagger in her right hand, pointing to the empty place where water should pool.

"Lovely," Vincent said dryly. "Well, let's get our seats to the end of the world, shall we?"

Mata gave the man a slug in his shoulder, which evoked a yelp of pain and a scowl. The party evacuated the van and immediately scanned the surroundings for danger. Everyone was on edge as they surveyed the exterior of the building. Each of them expected monsters or ghosts to attack them.

Even the flora expressed a foreboding threat to any who got too close. Thorned plants grew without ever bearing buds, trees bent toward the earth in twisted agony, the grass grew in chaotic patches, and the grounds smelled of the wet decay of vegetation and something else. Something rotting and feeding the maggots. Everything around them groaned as if in perpetual suffering.

The team gathered their gear, secured additional ammunition in pockets and belts, and slung weapons that lacked holsters over their shoulders. Phineas and Mata placed various vials and what looked to George like homemade bombs in their pockets. He watched as Mata slid several throwing knives into her belt. Each blade had a hoop at the end with a cloth tied in a tight knot. He caught strange symbols or words written in some iridescent ink. Phineas still held on to that double-headed gold spike.

George's early warning system warned him away from the weapon. George trusted his instincts, but it didn't diminish his curiosity. George was snapped back to reality when he heard Robert and Vincent arguing over an item with the van's cargo space.

"Come on man, I know how to use a fucking chainsaw. What's the big deal?" George heard Robert say.

"Look, son, this 'thing' is a little more than a chainsaw. It will chew you up and spit you out." Vincent stood between Robert and what looked to George as an old, rust-spattered chainsaw. The teeth on the chain looked custom-made and wicked as hell.

"What's going on here?" George asked.

"Nothing. George, I figured we would need something to breach a door. I saw the saw and reached for it, then Vinnie here got squirrely," Robert said.

"First of all, fuck you kid; the name is Vincent. Second, nothing in this van is 'just' a thing," Vincent snapped back.

"I just don't get it," Robert began until George turned him around and leveled him with a glare that hit like a smack across the face. Robert blushed a bit and then threw his hands up, ending the discussion.

"That young man needs to respect his elders," Vincent grumbled.

George glared at Vincent, who held his hands up in surrender and grabbed the saw. George then realized that the spatter pattern on the saw was not rust but something else entirely.

The ensemble walked up to the front doors. George and Robert took the lead, and Sicily brought up the rear. Phineas and Mata walked behind George. Both seemed energized and excited for this adventure. George remembered how Vincent spoke about the strange duo and how they always wore a smile when going on adventures like this.

Vincent was the exception to the trio. His "salesman shtick" only ended when he was with Finn and Mata. When no one was looking, Vincent treated them with a respect that bordered on reverence.

The doors to the building were unlocked, which was much less a welcoming gesture and more like an invitation to the den of a predator. The interior was polished and lacquered in thick, rich shades of black that reflected undertones of green, brown, or purple. On the walls of the anteroom hung oil paintings depicting strange beings. Some were without shape, just a mass of greenish-brown flesh with several eyes and mouths. No two were alike.

Within the building, the air was the opposite of the environment outside. The air was sterile and absent of the typical odors found within any home. Not even the wind outside the open door permitted entry. The house felt oppressive and heavy, as though at any moment, the gilded wallpapered walls or the black and gold tile flooring would gather those who entered and squeeze them into a jelly.

Each officer turned on powerful flashlights attached to the ends of their shotguns or rifles. Vincent carried his pistol and a flashlight in the opposite hand. Sicily followed close behind with her shotgun, her eyes constantly scanning the shadows for threats.

The oppressive atmosphere felt surreal to Sicily. Within the halls of this building, there was little to no breeze or lighting, yet it seemed the shadows were constantly growing and shrinking. There was no sound of movement, but she felt eyes on her from every corner of the room.

She scanned the empty spaces, looking for something caught in her peripheral vision. She wondered if the others were feeling this or if this was just the result of her anxiety. Considering everything Sicily had experienced in the last twenty-four hours, maybe she was finally losing it.

Sicily shook her head, trying to free herself of fear and doubt. She needed her focus more than ever, and these intrusive thoughts would distract her. She held on to the vision of everything she lost because of the Marcus family. Her mom. Her fellow officers and friends. This town. Her whole fucking world was broken into pieces because of the Marcus' and their freaks. She tempered her resolve with the fires of her rage now.

Phineas broke off from the group to check the rooms off to the left of the front entrance. They led to the dining room. Tall, single-hung windows were stained with depictions of alien lands and plants. These images ranged from the breathtaking to the grotesque. On the opposite wall sat a large brick fireplace. In the center of the room was a long, elegant dining table. Its dark surface was so polished that it appeared liquid and still, like a pool of inky black water.

Phineas pulled his head out of the room, and as he did so, he swore he caught movement in the shadows. He stared into the darkness. Even with his gifted sight, Phineas saw nothing. This was somewhat disquieting since he could see into both the living plane and the land of the dead. It felt as though Phineas was only seeing with one eye now. He felt a soft tap on his shoulder. He spun to see Mata. She looked anxious.

"I can't hear anything," Mata signed to him. Phineas looked at her, confused, then realized she was as gifted as he was. She could always hear the spirits he saw, even see most of them. This confirmed Phineas's fear that someone was using a curse or ward to remove this place from magical detection.

"I guess we'll do this the old-fashioned way," Phineas signed to Mata and shrugging helplessly.

-CHAPTER 33-
CREEPING DOOM

A massive staircase in the center of the entryway rose, lacquered in the same near-black polish. Each spindle was carved intricately, and each supported thick banisters. Down the center of the stairwell was a gold-trimmed, deep purple rug. There was no visible exit out of the room outside the dining room doorway but a hall extending beyond the room, past the stairs.

"So, up or down, boss? Officer George?" Vincent asked either George or Phineas. George looked over to Phineas, who replied with a shrug. George tried to focus and attune his senses, but all he felt was an uncomfortable stillness. Just as he was about to ascend the stairs, the party heard a chittering sound followed by shuffling from the ceiling above them. Everyone who held a firearm aimed their weapons at the space above.

Mata stuck close to Phineas, but her typical battle smile was gone. Phineas saw that she was unnerved by her sudden loss of perception. He playfully bumped her shoulder. When she looked up at him, he gestured in a sign, "You are more than your gifts. You are Mata, the five-foot force of nature."

Mata smiled at this and pulled her kusarigama, the sickle and chain, from her belt. Phineas also patted the pouches on their belts, reminding her they have other means to combat otherworldly creatures.

Mata nodded in agreement, wrapped her left cestus in the chain of her weapon, and gripped the sickle in her right. She took a deep breath and followed the group of police and Vincent. Phineas patted her on the back, letting her know he would bring up the rear and comfort her that he was always watching out for her.

The scuttling noises continued as the party ascended the stairs toward the second floor. Everyone who could hear the sounds suddenly realized they now came from above and below them. George looked down at Phineas, who was already peering up at him. He nodded his awareness of their situation. They were surrounded.

Just as they reached the landing separating the first and second floors, the noises ceased. George and Robert checked the space above them and saw that the stairwell continued to the third and fourth floors. The party paused and strained to hear if there was movement anywhere at this point. After a moment, George gestured to his fellow police officers to continue up the stairs.

George reached the second floor with Robert, and both assumed covering positions, waiting for the rest of the team. The second floor opened up into an expansive foyer. The stairwell continued upstairs, but beyond the threshold was a hallway, at the end of which was a sitting room with a table in the center. From that room, it was unknown if there were other corridors.

George communicated to Robert that he would cover the next flight of stairs and the ascending stairwell while he watched the foyer. "Check the doors and tell us what's past that sitting room. Manns, you give him some cover."

The foyer had two doors on opposite sides. Robert inched to the doors and tried them. Both were locked. He continued to the end of the hall and found that the sitting room had two hallways and several doors lined the paths. The sitting room had a luxurious couch along the far wall and a table at its center. On the table was a circle with strange markings and a water bowl. The sitting area was round, with no other forms of decoration aside from the large tapestry on the far wall.

The picture on the tapestry depicted a great storm destroying some ancient seaside marble city. Within the clouds and ocean waves were scores of strange creatures. Robert felt himself drawn to the details of the tapestry. He felt as though the scene was alive and in real-time. He could hear the thunder and crashing waves in the distance. His eyes tried to focus, to see deeper into the inky black water. He began to see a shape. Something massive commanded the invaders beneath those swells. Here and there, he started to make out bits and pieces of some colossus being.

Tentacles, eyes, wings, claws. Whenever Robert seemed to catch a piece of it in his mind, it slipped away, daring him to look deeper. Robert tilted his head, peering at the scene from different angles. The titan leading the apocalyptic charge seemed to follow him with a multitude of baleful eyes. Robert felt those angry orbs look into him, revealing his weakness, fear, and shame.

A swift slap across his head snapped Robert's attention back to the present. He turned in surprise, expecting some creature to await him with its open jaws and yellow teeth. Sicily stood there with an expression of both frustration and concern.

"What the fuck, Robert?" Sicily hissed. "I've been calling you. George, too. What are you doing?"

Robert blinked in confusion. "Sorry, I don't know what happened. I just looked at that painting for a moment," he stammered.

Sicily looked beyond him. "Of the naked chick? Come on, man, get your head in the game."

Robert turned in confusion. There was no painting of a storm. No invading army of water-born fiends or screaming citizens of some marble city. Just a woman lying partially nude in a meadow, a thin, nearly translucent gown draped across her. Robert felt his skin burn with embarrassment. He turned to explain, but Sicily was already walking away back toward the group.

Phineas and Mata had just reached the landing when a booming voice filled the house.

"So, you are the interlopers." The voice was deep and rich. There was no malice in its tone. If anything, the speaker seemed to regard the troupe as mere annoyances. "I do not welcome you here; as such, I will feed you to those who work to protect me and my property."

"Judge," George said aloud to the rest of the group. He recognized the man's voice. "Judge Marcus, give it up and return Amanda to me now!" George commanded. "Stop all this, and no one gets hurt!"

From within the house, a laugh bellowed. "Ah yes, Amanda Thatch, your lovely cow," Judge said.

George bristled at the mention of his wife's name. "You listen to me, Judge; this has nothing to do with her. Let her go…if you need someone, then take me!" George yelled.

"I think I'll have you both, actually," Judge replied with great menace. George suddenly heard a shuffling noise from above and spied a form tumbling down the center of the stairwell. The form dropped abruptly in front of George with a snap.

It took a second to understand what he was seeing. His brain couldn't accept the person's identity swinging from a rope before him. Her dark hair, slightly tanned and freckled complexion, and hazel eyes. George's mind broke at the sight of the corpse dangled before him, and his world erupted in rage and sorrow when he realized he was looking at Amanda. Her bruised face, eyes fixed in terror, hands and feet bound together.

"Quickly, man cut her down!" George heard Vincent yell distantly. He reached out to Amanda's body, dropping his rifle in the process, and tried to lift her. Some part of him dared hope that maybe she was just unconscious. She was so cold and heavy; she was heavier now that she was limp. George pulled Amanda's limp body from the stairwell and onto the landing.

Sicily gently pushed George aside as Vincent pulled at the noose tied around her neck. Sicily felt for a pulse and listened for breath sounds. Robert pulled his Bowie knife and sawed away at Amanda's restraints. After a perceived eternity, Sicily looked up at George, her eyes wet with the tears of grief. George moaned, tears streaming down his face. He reached over to look at her, touch her skin; somehow, it didn't feel real.

He brushed aside the hair on Amanda's face, and George's eyes opened so wide that the others thought they might fall out. It wasn't Amanda. It was someone else entirely. Her face was pale, her eyes and lips sewn shut. She had dark hair like Amanda, but her features, eyes, and face were Asian. He had never met this person in his life. She wasn't in Amanda's clothes but in a uniform. A server, maybe. Her hands were severed and now ended in what looked like serving forks.

"What the actual fuck?" George exclaimed. Everyone looked at the same body with expressions of both shock and horror.

Suddenly, the body lying before them sat up and screamed, tearing the stitches that secured its mouth. The scream was purely primal fear and something mechanical. Clicks and whirls were heard in its torso and head as it screamed at George. George was too stunned to react before the body slammed its forehead into the bridge of his nose, sending George crashing backward and down the stairs.

Sicily was moving to a defensive position when the thing threw a reverse elbow, catching her in the throat and sending her sprawling down the stairs after George. Robert was nearly standing, and Vincent backed away when the creature threw itself to the floor and kicked its legs up and out. It spun on its shoulder, kicked Robert across the jaw, and knocked the Desert Eagle pistol from Vincent's grip as he raised it.

It finished its move by pushing off the floor with its bound hands and landing on its feet. The thing struck the edges of the forks against each other, creating sparks that fell to the floor and screamed its terrible scream at the party.

"Guys! We got company!" Phineas yelled.

Through his tears, George saw another woman dressed in the same uniform scaling down the wall behind him like a spider. The hands and feet were replaced with a knife and fork. The eyes were similarly sewn, but the mouth opened and closed as if trying to work its jaw for the first time. Another climbed down the stairs from the third floor, reminding George of a scene from *The Exorcist*.

At the end of the foyer hall, two more similar creatures spider-walked around the corner, clinging to the walls and ceiling as they did so. Each of them adhered to the same dress code and was equally mutilated. The thing between Vincent and Robert turned and gracefully flipped backward several times to stand with the other wall-crawling corpse spiders.

"I present to you a project my son, Thaddeus, and I worked on together." Judge Marcus' voice echoed throughout the house. "He so loved his dolls, that boy. I thought it was high time I put them to use."

"You sick fuck, I swear to God I…!" George roared.

"Oh, yes. Did you like my little trick, Officer Thatch? I just wanted to give you a preview of what I plan to do to your wife," Judge taunted.

With a roar, George snatched his pistol from its holster and fired on the corpse spiders on the walls and landing above. He fired and moved until he was able to grab his rifle. After George emptied the pistol into the nearest construct, he holstered the pistol. He raised his rifle in a fluid motion. George saw another pair of abominations crawling over the banister behind Robert and Vincent and leaped to the adjacent wall. They had the high ground, and George knew he had to attack fast and hard before they could overwhelm them.

The creature on the wall took a swarm of bullets to its thorax and left hip, causing it to fall to the floor below. The second corpse-spider crawling across the landing toward George took a single hit to the right shoulder before it scrambled and leaped up and across the adjacent wall behind him. George aimed and continued his assault to interrupt the monster's attempt to flank him.

Sicily coughed and gagged from the blow she took to her throat. She looked up, and through her haze of pain, she spotted one of the corpses running along the wall that framed the hallway leading to the sitting room leap to the floor and charge at her. Sicily fell backward in retreat and tripped on her shotgun.

The world slowed down momentarily as she reached out to stop the creature from leaping on her and impaling her with its forked hands. She could see the creature's yellow teeth, leathery skin, and glint coming off the blades that now sought her throat.

Sicily's hands felt the pistols Vincent had loaned her blink into existence within her hands. Without another thought, she pulled each trigger as quickly as possible. Each of the bullets tore through the torso of the creature, but it still charged.

Sicily fought against her instinct to dodge and instead shoved one of the pistols at the face of the golem, now screaming that terrible scream at her. The barrel filled its mouth, muffling that dreadful noise. She pulled the trigger and watched as the corpse's head exploded, splattering blood, gears, and brain matter on the ceiling above.

Sicily was panting when time returned to normal, and she found herself lying on her back, pinned to the floor by the corpse spider. Its head was completely blown away. When Sicily looked down, she was surprised to find both of its hands had missed spearing her by mere centimeters. She kneed and kicked the thing off her just as a pair of spider-like creatures in the stairwell moved to attack Vincent and Robert. She put the pistols in their holsters and grabbed the shotgun, blasting her way into the fray.

Vincent ducked just in time to avoid the corpse-spider as it chopped at him with an overhead slash. It buried the tip of its blade deep into the banister railing. It pulled to follow up with a backhand slash but found its knife hand had thrust too deeply. Vincent moved quickly and kicked the nearest leg at the knee. The knee cracked from the blow, and the thing buckled under the force of the strike.

With a crazed roar, Vincent grabbed the corpse by the back of its head and slammed its face against the banister repeatedly. Suddenly, after the third slam of the thing's head into the thick wood, Vincent was thrown off balance when the scalp of the corpse pulled free of its head. Vincent looked at his hand in horror and dropped the sheet of flesh and long, dark hair of his opponent. The head of the corpse, now lacking the flesh to cover the crown of her skull, turned to regard Vincent.

The monster screamed at Vincent, then its left hand chopped wildly at the entrapped arm to free itself from the wood snare. With several blows to its own elbow, the golem cut itself loose. The thing's face was smashed in at the bridge of its nose, and blood and a clear fluid leaked from its nostrils. It issued a wet growl and stalked toward Vincent.

In response, Vincent reached for the tool holstered on his back and pulled forth the massive chainsaw. With a quick pull on the cord, the chainsaw roared to life; blue smoke poured from the engine and filled the hallway. The crooked teeth that ran along the chain raced along their path, eager to catch a meal. The creature seemed unfazed by this display and charged ahead to attack.

While Vincent was not the fighter Mata or Phineas was, he overcame the corpse's thrust with his lunge. He ducked under the stabbing blade hand and thrust the chainsaw forward. The blade devoured the belly of the creature eagerly. With its hungry teeth, it pulled itself deeper into the chest cavity, seeking the one thing it wanted most—its victim's heart. Vincent couldn't fight it if he tried and pressed on with the cursed saw.

The jagged chains ripped through tender flesh and meat, shredded the internal organs, and chopped at the bone. The tip pushed through the creature's back and chewed its way up, up, up, all the way through and out the top of the skull. The two sides of the thoracic cavity fell away, and the corpse-spider fell to the floor.

Vincent stood before the mutilated body of twisted flesh and bone. He was covered from the knees up in blood, organs, and tissue. Inside his head, he heard and felt someone cry out. His vision was suddenly filled with the deaths of his two families, crushed by the force of the hurricane waters and the collapse of their houses .

This was the price of using this weapon. You paid with your memories and relived the pain you had caused another. He felt the hot breath of the demon that visited him in that hospital bed. Vincent accepted the pain. It was his penance, after all.

A corpse-spider targeted Robert and crawled on the wall toward him. When a shotgun blast tore into the thing's back, Robert had just gotten his rifle up. The corpse-spider turned and hissed at Sicily. Robert used this chance and began unloading on the creature. Bullet after bullet tore through the construct, predominantly its head. The golem fell to the floor, twitching as blood poured from multiple wounds.

Robert stood up and faced Sicily, panting. He gave her a quick wink and a smile. She was a beautiful sight indeed. Wild and fierce. He loved this woman and had for a long time. If they survived, he vowed to love her fiercely for the rest of his days.

He was about to walk over, and… Robert wasn't sure after that. Tease her? Kiss her? Anything if it meant being close to her. Just as he stepped toward Sicily, he caught her looking over his shoulder in alarm. He turned to see George charging up the stairs to fight off two 'corpse spiders' at once. One monster was wounded and did not move as gracefully, but the other had gained high ground in their battle and was about to pounce on him from above.

The creature leaped from its position on the wall just above George. The hands and feet were replaced with three-pronged serving forks. All of them were angled to strike George's head and neck. George moved to fire at the beasts, but the weapon answered the trigger's pull with a *"click."* He moved to try and block as much damage as he could with his rifle.

The corpse was suddenly stopped inches short of reaching its prey by Phineas's spike. It struck the creature's thorax and slammed it against the wall from which it pounced. The tip was followed by throwing knives, striking the head and chest. It screamed a recorded woman's scream.

The creature attempted to pull away from the wall, but suddenly the spike twisted deeper into its body. From behind the corpse-spider, drywall and dust fell as the tip sank deeper into the creature and the wall behind. Within a couple of seconds, the corpse-spider was secured to the wall. Another of Mata's throwing daggers hit the creature between the eyes with a loud *THUNK!*

The creature quit its screaming and went still, its head slumped forward. With a snap of his fingers, Phineas summoned the golden spike. It twitched within the corpse and then ripped itself free and flew back into Phineas's palm. The automaton fell from the wall and rolled down the stairs.

George's second opponent was injured but was still eager to get to the nearest person and maul them with its blades. It shambled toward George and was swiftly met with a hail of gunfire from Sicily and Robert, who concentrated their fire on the animated corpse, tearing it apart with assault rifles and shotgun blasts. George looked back at them both and nodded in appreciation. They returned the nod and immediately got to work reloading their weapons.

Sicily and Robert both turned to regard Vincent, who had mutilated his opponent with a chainsaw. They were shocked when they looked upon the gory scene before them. Vincent was covered in blood and viscera. They looked at the grisly picture and noticed that Vincent was trying to spot clean bits of entrails off his jacket. Both officers burst into a laugh at the man's effort to try and get a stain out of his sports jacket.

"What?" Vincent noticed their laughter. "I can get it out, really."

This inspired another round of laughter, now by the others in attendance. Vincent saw Phineas approaching him with a look of amusement and condolences. Vincent looked down at the suit and sighed.

"I just had it tailored and cleaned, too," Vincent said as he threw his coat over the banister railing.

The team returned to the foyer when Phineas and Sicily noticed the arrival of three people at the end of the hall, just in front of the table in the sitting room. They looked like groundskeepers or laborers. Sicily halted the others and raised her weapon.

"Get on the ground now!" she commanded.

The three men didn't flinch at her words. They just stood there and smiled. Phineas and Mata took a defensive stance, preparing the best they could for whatever may come next. Sicily saw both reaching for something in their pouches. Glass spheres? Each had a mixed grey powder in them. It looked like ash to her.

"All right, motherfuckers, this is your last warning! Get the fuck down on your stomachs!" Sicily shouted. She repeated the instructions again, this time in Spanish. The three men blinked simultaneously and tilted their heads to the right. It reminded Sicily of dogs and how they do the same to hear better. The three men held up their hands suddenly.

Sicily blinked. "I wasn't expecting that to work," she said.

Mata put her hand out to block Sicily from moving forward. Her usual look of joy and curiosity was replaced with focus. Sicily looked back at the trio at the end of the hall as they came together in a huddle. She watched as they put their heads together, and all came down to a kneeling position. Suddenly, they all began to shudder and quiver. The motion grew faster and more violent with each passing second.

Everyone watched as the three men started to come undone. The clothes and flesh on his back tore open. The bones cracked, and shards burst through the flesh. The other two convulsed and tore at themselves.

Sicily looked on in horror as the three men's skin knitted together, and they began to become one. The men became one writhing mass of brown and purple flesh covered in bony protrusions and angry boils. Within the blob, Sicily felt eyes on her, felt their stares, looking at her hungrily. She could see images of what the creature had in store for her as the monster projected its thoughts and feelings. Sicily's stomach churned, and she felt nauseous from the intrusion and nearly vomited when one of the many mouths flicked its warty tongue at her.

Phineas walked up next to her and placed his hand on her forehead. She heard him speak a few strange words in a language she'd never heard before. The visions and intrusive thoughts faded until Sicily felt in control again.

"As long as you are close to me, you are protected from this thing's psychic attacks," Phineas said with a smile. He quickly turned to the team. They needed a plan to stop the Marcus' and deal with this new threat.

"George, you and Robert, take Vincent with you and get Judge Marcus. The three of us will deal with this shitbag," Phineas shouted.

"Hey, why can't I stay here?" Vincent complained.

"You have more experience with this stuff, and they'll need your saw, I'm sure," Phineas said.

Vincent sighed audibly and looked at George and Robert, who were already starting up the stairs. With a huff and a growl, Vincent chased after them. As soon as he did so, the mass sprouted long, writhing appendages and moved quickly toward the party. Sicily gave a shout and fired the 12-gauge shotgun at the creature. Pieces of flesh blew off, bones splintered, and pustules burst with the assault. If there was any real damage done, the monstrosity didn't show it.

"Run!" Phineas yelled at George's team and his own. The corridor was cramped, and there was no way to flank this beast in the present circumstances. If that is, this beast could be flanked. Eyes that opened and shut moved above the mass of flesh and bone. Mouths burst open, bearing fangs or shark-like teeth; others were gaping holes with tongues seeking the next meal.

Mata grabbed Sicily by the arm and led her to the stairwell, headed downstairs, and back to the lobby. Sicily fired one more shot, bursting an eyeball and splashing the humor across the adjacent wall. The creature squealed at this, and a tongue groped the now-empty socket. As Mata and Sicily made their way down the stairs, Phineas reached into his coat and pulled forth a pair of orbs filled with powder and surrounding a small vial. At the top of the globe was a crude button.

Phineas pressed the button, and the fragile tube inside the globe burst and began mixing with the powdery contents inside. Phineas quickly threw the grenade as he felt the contents begin to react violently to the mixture. He then vaulted over the banister railing just as the glass orbs smashed against the massive creature. One of the orbs gave a bright flash, causing the monster to scream when many of its eyes were blinded. The second grenade exploded into pure white flame.

Phineas could smell the burnt flesh and hear the noise of fat boiling as he landed on the stairs right in front of Mata and Sicily. The trio had just reached the lobby floor when the shambling mass rolled down the stairs after them. The heavy oak table from the sitting room narrowly missed them and smashed into the doorway, blocking their escape. They turned to face their enemy to find flames still licking at its flesh.

The blob was undeniably over ten feet in diameter, and a giant maw filled with rows of teeth formed in its center. The creature let loose a roar that shook the walls of the building. Sicily and Mata shielded themselves from the noise and lines of spittle that flew from the creature's orifice. The monster's breath reeked of decay and feces so much that they covered their mouths and noses to stop from gagging.

"The dining room!" Phineas yelled.

Sicily pumped the shotgun and pulled the trigger as Mata ran toward Phineas. Empty. Sicily growled in frustration and threw down the weapon. She drew her pistols and sent a swarm of bullets toward the creature while she moved into the next room to meet the others.

Mata and Phineas had already made their way to the far wall and looked to be heading toward an exit at the room's far end. Sicily speed-loaded bullets into the pistols as she ran after them. Above them, lighting flashed, sending colors from the stained-glass windows splashing onto the walls.

Mata and Phineas were barely halfway across the room when the fireplace adjacent to them exploded, shooting bricks, mortar, and ash everywhere. Both of them were pelleted and battered by the debris and the ash choked them. The shambling mass roared and moved into the room. The abomination had increased and was now nearly large enough to fill half the massive dining room.

As the creature reached out with its tentacles, an explosion went off just behind it. The beast squealed from the pain of the light and sound of a flashbang grenade. A family of bullets pelted at it from the side as Sicily emptied her rounds into the beast. With preternatural speed, she then reloaded and fired again. The monster roared in frustration and slapped at her with a massive tentacle.

Sicily dodged the attack and jumped on the table. She ran to join Mata and Phineas when another tentacle slapped her right flank hard. The blow sent her flying and spinning through the stain-colored glass window.

"Sicily!" Phineas screamed. He turned, faced the monster, looked at the kitchen door, and then Mata. Mata had recovered from the choking ash cloud and was now raising her arms in a fighting stance. Phineas looked back at the kitchen and then tapped Mata on the shoulder. She looked at him as he pointed toward the kitchen with his nose. As another pair of tentacles loomed at them, both began running just in time.

George could hear the explosions and gunfire intermingling with the roars and squeals of some creature below his position. Part of him desperately wanted to join the fight, but this was overridden by the knowledge that Amanda was with Judge Marcus. He needed to save his wife and kill Judge, in no particular order. He just wanted to save her and get as far away from Haven Shire as possible.

As George and his team reached the top of the stairs to the third floor, each man had to take a moment to comprehend what he saw. At first, it appeared as though they were looking at tree trunks growing within the structure and leading up through the roof. George got closer and remembered the veiny roots he saw that terrible day at the factory. These were the same, only much more prominent. Each one grew through the flooring straight as arrows up to the ceiling.

George inspected each root and nearly yelped as he encountered faces inside the giant columns. They were of the townspeople, everyone who was thought to have moved away or had gone missing. Each face tacked onto the "missing persons" board flashed into his vision. As he inspected the thick, pulsating roots that rose or fell from the ceiling, he found faces that were once for him nothing more than poor copier machine recreations.

The room was a dome-like structure, and at the far end of the room was a set of large wooden French doors. The door was carved intricately with depictions of tentacled creatures in the throes of battle or procreation.

George scanned the roots and saw that the tubers were absorbing the captives. He looked up to the ceiling and saw smaller tendrils sprouting out from the larger ones that moved like a web of vines overhead. Within some of those vines were other victims;

some were in burlap sacks, while others were bound by their hands and feet.

Robert called George from what felt like a great distance. The room was enormous, but George struggled not to get lost in his memories. Memories of the Mickey Corners shooting, the death of that little girl, those people in the masks. Those eyes, that impossible smile. He had been walking in Robert's direction but wasn't looking where he was going; his eyes were turned inward and to the past. George bumped into Robert, startling both men.

"What's up, Robert?" asked George.

Robert looked up and guided George to what was pressed against one of the roots. It was Amanda. She was tied to one of the more extensive roots with twine and leather. Her face was swollen in several places, and she had a laceration on her cheek. George hurriedly checked for vitals. She was alive but unconscious. George scanned for added injuries and found a puncture wound to her right shoulder. George growled at the sight of his wife in her injured state. With grim determination and tears swelling in his eyes, he tore at the roots that clung to her skin and clothing.

Robert and Vincent assisted George and carefully pulled Amanda away from the wall. Some roots had already burrowed their way into her clothes and the flesh on her back. The injuries caused by this alien root system were minor, as were the injuries to her face, but the puncture wound on her shoulder could be severe if not treated soon. George could see angry lines forming around the punctured skin, and the tissue around the injury was swelling.

"We need to get her outta here, boss," Robert said.

"Yeah, but how?" Vincent countered. "We can't return the way we came with that monster downstairs."

"Maybe we can help them, fight our way through, and get her to a hospital," Robert replied.

"Gimme a sec, guys," George said. His head spun with scenarios. "Vincent, check that door there, would ya?"

Vincent looked at George and finally nodded. He slung the chainsaw over his shoulder and ran across the room.

"Holts, listen up. No matter what happens here, you gotta get Amanda out here. Far away from Haven Shire," George said. Robert looked up and then down to Amanda.

"Yeah, you got it, man," Robert said. "Only if you swear you're coming with us."

"Let's agree that each of us must do our best to survive this," George said. "Yo! Vincent! What 'cha got?"

George and Robert looked up and saw the large French doors were open, but Vincent was gone. They looked at each other, and neither of them had heard anything. There was nothing but darkness in the room beyond the doors. A cold, dank breeze flowed from within that void.

"Vincent?" George called out.

They waited for a moment for a reply but got nothing. George's senses flared to life, warning him that something deadly was near. He looked at Robert and then to Amanda.

"Quick, let's move her out of sight. If things get bad, well worse, then we're all getting the fuck out of here," George instructed.

"And come back with the army?" Robert replied with a wry smile. George nodded in approval after he dragged Amanda to a corner where a viny pillar met the wall.

They both stepped out and pulled their weapons, moving quickly to get to the door. As they approached, they both looked into the room for any sign of Vincent or danger. The interior of the room was obscured in shadows. Small candles were lit near what appeared to be an altar but provided little illumination.

They each took the same positions as they would before a breach. George signaled that they would move on a three-count. One. Two. Vincent flew through the open door on the three count and skidded across the floor. Robert moved to check on him while George covered them. George could see a massive shape in the darkness, something writhing and groping around it.

The shadowy image coalesced into the shape of a tall, broad-shouldered man. The man stepped forward, closer to the room of roots, until his cold grey eyes could be seen. From that darkened doorway, a deep voice rumbled.

"You gentlemen are all trespassing on holy ground and on my private property." Judge Marcus stepped closer into the room. He held his scepter; in the other, he held a wicked dagger. "I will have to escort you out, I suppose."

-CHAPTER 34-
FIGHTING ON TWO FRONTS

Sicily felt cold. She lay in icy, wet darkness, and part of her wanted to stay there. In this place, there were no monsters, no pain, no sorrow. She didn't have to think about her mother and how she was tortured and strung up like game after a hunt. Her mother. Her poor mother happened to meet some loser who ran off the first chance he got when he found out she was pregnant. Her mother had to work two, sometimes three jobs, just to keep food on the table and clothes on her back. Her poor mother.

"No! No! Fuck all that!" Something was waking in Sicily. Her mother was not just somebody to pity. She was strong! She worked her ass off to make sure Sicily didn't have to want for anything! She did all this all by herself. She died fighting. Sicily saw that from the bloody fingernails and busted knuckles. She needed to get back up and get the motherfuckers who hurt her. They all needed to pay with screams and blood. *"Wake up. Wake up!"*

Sicily's eyes shot open, and she winced from the headache and dizziness. She looked around to get her bearings. It had started raining; she was in the grass and mud. She moved slowly to her hands, and pieces of painted glass fell off her back and from her hair. Sicily let out a groan as she moved to stand and found almost everything hurt. Unsure if it was stiffness from the chill or the impact, Sicily moved slowly at first.

Everything on her body hurt, especially her right ribs and her head. Her left arm was bleeding. Sicily checked the injury and found a shard of glass had left a rather sizeable laceration on her forearm. Sicily nearly jumped to her feet when she heard an animal roar and scream behind her.

Sicily just remembered how she got where she was. That giant beast with the tentacles. She pulled the two revolvers Vincent gave her. No amount of magic luck would make these pistols powerful enough to take down that creature. She needed more firepower. Then Sicily's eyes and smile beamed when she realized how close she was to the van. She remembered how these monsters screamed when put to the flame. She found her firepower.

Phineas and Mata dove, leaped, and dodged the slaps and grabs of the tentacled beast. If one of the arms got too close, it was disappointed as it found either nothing was there or a slap of Phineas' mighty cane or a chop of Mata's kama. The nimble pair tried to run for the kitchen, but the creature could maneuver between the couple and their escape. They could run out the way they came, but it would continue to hunt them. The situation was untenable, Phineas realized. This creature was single-minded in its purpose, and Phineas and Mata's stamina was not everlasting.

Phineas recalled the hallway behind the stairwell. He thought it wasn't a large corridor; maybe they could lead it in and use the cramped hall to their advantage. Phineas ducked under another strike and jumped onto the table. The creature roared in frustration and moved to strike again until a globe from Mata's pouch smashed against the beast and exploded in bright pyrotechnics. The creature screamed and swatted at the air wildly. Mata followed her attack with an X-shaped slash into the flesh of the bulbous fiend. Phineas was worried they would tire before doing enough damage to the creature to even slow it down.

Quickly, Phineas chanted a small curse while clutching an emerald ring in his right hand. He had used this particular curse on someone who was stalking a friend. The spell turned Phineas' own body into a voodoo doll. Any touch, injury, or sensation he felt would also transfer to his target.

This was also an effective way to communicate with Mata when things got chaotic, or she needed to focus on her opponent. First, he tapped himself on his left shoulder. Mata glanced at her shoulder momentarily and then looked up at Phineas. He nodded back to the hole from which the monster came.

"You go! I'll cover you!" she signed. Phineas was glad he was proficient in this gestural communication. He dove off the table just as a tentacle splintered the half on which he stood. Phineas rolled and came up on his legs. He looked over at Mata as she began hacking furiously at the monster. The hole was directly behind her, Phineas saw, and he started running for it.

As he ran, Phineas reached into his pouch, grabbed three more globes, and threw them at the monster. Two of them were filled with vials that, when the orb shattered, the fluid would mix with the powder and create a powerful acid. The third orb exploded with a pyrotechnic effect similar to Mata's. The monster squealed and screamed from the acidic cocktail and blinding lights.

When Phineas arrived at Mata's side, he roughly grabbed his left ear and pulled it in the direction he was going. To Mata, this was like someone had held her by the ear and pulled her along. She silently let out a yelp and stumbled backward through the hole her opponent made. When she was through and had caught up with Phineas, she looked at him and slapped herself across the face. Hard. It had not the intended effect of sending pain to Phineas, and she only hurt herself in the process.

Mata looked at him both in confusion and anger. *"What the fuck? Why don't you feel it?"* Mata signed at Phineas.

"I altered the curse so that I wouldn't receive your sensations and..." Phineas began to reply, but before he could finish the sentence, he was cut off by a hard slap across his face. Phineas blinked at the pain, as did Mata.

"Also, don't you ever use magic on me without my permission!" Mata signed angrily.

Before Phineas could apologize, a powerful tentacle grabbed him around his ankle and pulled so hard that he fell onto the tile floor, smacking his head. Mata felt the pain of the head injury and the strength of the tentacle through their cursed bond and swore she would slap Phineas again for putting it on her.

Quickly, Mata grabbed hold of the banister and Phineas' forearm and pulled tight. Phineas tried to shake the sting of the fall away and reached into his pouch. Empty. Phineas cursed as he must have lost some of his homemade bombs in the scuffle.

Mata dared not to let go, knowing the moment she did, Phineas would most likely be dead. Phineas tried to bring a spell or curse to mind, but he needed to concentrate on using them. It was an arduous task at this moment as he soon discovered the tentacle around his leg was a tongue. The powerful appendage tried to draw Phineas into a tooth-filled maw, drooling with anticipation.

Suddenly, from within the dining room, a flash of light and heat began to pour out of the space just behind the monster. It screamed as flames rolled over it from behind. The smell of burning flesh filled the room as a line of napalm erupted again over the monster's back. If it had a back, that is. The pain was significant enough that the fiend let go of Phineas and tried to retreat from the fire that even now boiled the fat and peeled its skin.

Mata wished she could scream for joy as she cradled a dazed Phineas. Sicily erupted from the kitchen with the flamethrower she had used on the Grey Farmstead. She could see the woman was screaming like a banshee as she bore down on the monster.

The creature tried to retreat but must have had a more challenging time constricting itself than when it grew. The flames were devouring the thing, the fat hissed and crackled from the heat, the flesh peeled and fell to the floor, eyes popped and sizzled. The heat and odor of this vile creature made Mata gag, and she was forced to cover her face.

Phineas began to come to his senses thanks to the stench of burning flesh and animal screams. He looked over at a green Mata, who looked like she would vomit any second. Phineas sat up and swooned slightly from pain and dizziness.

"Don't you dare throw up on me? I love this coat," Phineas signed after taking a moment to recover. She first looked at him with pure venom and then a teasing smile. She pushed him off her and stood to gather in case the fight hadn't ended. Phineas retrieved his last two glass orbs and placed them in his pouch. Mata came over and touched him on his shoulder.

Phineas looked up and saw Sicily walking over to the pair. The creature burned brightly behind her, and the conflagration backlit the tall, beautiful indigenous woman as she strode over to the couple with the flamethrower nozzle resting on her shoulder. It occurred to Phineas that Sicily was an exotic beauty. It is a rare sight to see a woman of her strength and beauty outside of Mata.

Phineas suddenly felt a tap on his shoulder and caught the eyes of an angry Mata. *"You pig! You think she's hot, don't you?"* her fingers moved in a flurry.

"What? No! Why would you even suggest such a thing?" Phineas replied, a little more than scared right now.

"Because you still have your fucking curse on me, you dumbass!" Mata replied, pointing at her crotch. *"I can feel your boner!"*

Phineas' face turned bright red at this, and he immediately began reversing the curse. It was a simple matter. After he was sure the curse was reversed, he fully expected an assault. Instead, Mata rolled her eyes and walked away, shaking her head.

"Well, fuck," Phineas told himself.

"What the hell was that about?" Sicily said breathlessly after she watched the exchange. Phineas, so caught up with his drama, almost forgot Sicily was standing next to him. He immediately blushed again.

"No, it's nothing. We should keep going," Phineas said awkwardly, walking off after Mata.

"Hey, Sicily! Great job slaying that ugly beast!" Sicily said to herself mockingly. "Wow, Sicily, you're our hero! Thanks so much!" she continued. "Yeah, well, you're very welcome, you ungrateful fucks!" She finally yelled after the duo.

Phineas, Mata, and Sicily quickly moved down the hall. As they did so, they checked the doors, most leading to storage rooms, a reading room, or a broom closet. A large metal and mortar spiral staircase was at the end of the hall. The stairwell was supported in its center by a large pole and secured to the mortar walls. This area was older than the rest of the house. Phineas could see and smell something ancient about this place. It smelled like a grave.

The stairs were narrow and had to be taken single file. Sicily walked somewhat clumsily due to the flamethrower on her back. The damn thing was heavy and cumbersome, but she would not be putting a weapon down if she knew it killed these monstrosities. In many places, the mortar that secured the stairs to the wall crumbled, and as the trio descended, the stairs shook, and pebbles fell. Sicily couldn't help but notice Phineas and Mata were not their usual playful selves. Phineas especially seemed to be pouting about something.

When they reached the base of the stairs, they found they were in an underground cavern. Lights were hung along the wall to illuminate the way, and the path was curated into a cobblestone walkway. The walls were nondescript except for strange vines that oozed luminescent sap. The fluid smelled of infection and decay, making the party cover their faces to hide from the odor.

Phineas and Mata began to walk when suddenly Phineas felt a tug on his arm. He turned to see Sicily looking at him. She looked concerned about something. Phineas slowed, and even though he knew Mata was focused on the task, he was also aware of how sensitive her sense of touch was and that she could *feel* him speaking. He didn't want to make her madder at him.

"Hey, what's up with you two?" Sicily asked. "You two are always so close and get along so well. What happened?"

"Nothing, a misunderstanding, really. I screwed up," Phineas stumbled.

Sicily gave him that look that said, "Go on," and then waited. She used this technique when she knew someone wanted to talk but was afraid. Phineas sighed and recounted what had happened during their battle with the creature in the dining room. After he was done, he looked up at Sicily and expected something. He wasn't sure yet what, though. Disgust. Anger. Embarrassment.

She seemed to mull the story over again and then laughed heartily. So much so that Phineas worried someone would be alerted. He futilely tried to quiet her. She lowered her voice but chuckled and chortled, with the occasional snort. Mata had turned at this point, visibly irritated by the lack of urgency in their movement.

"Seriously, you thought this guy even had a chance with me?" Sicily said so that Mata could read her lips. Phineas feigned hurt by this statement. "Don't worry, sweetie, he's all yours." Sicily chuckled again. Mata looked over at Phineas, who was beet red in the face.

"Guys, look here, you two are adorable, but I need both of you in the game and fighting with each other. Not against," Sicily said with her hand on Mata's shoulder.

Phineas quickly signed an apology. Mata looked nearly as embarrassed as Phineas and issued an apology as well. Sicily thought the whole discussion was strange, especially when they were about to face some unknown evil.

They were two adults, but something about them both seemed as though they were arrested in a place and time in their maturity. They were both nearly in their thirties but still behaved like teenage sweethearts. Part of her envied that, she admitted. She also appreciated this drivel, which distracted her a little from her grief and anger. She needed that break.

"Now, back to work," Sicily said quietly as she watched the two walk down the pathway next to each other. Occasionally, Mata would elbow Phineas and say something in sign language, which drew a laugh or signed reply. Maybe she and Robert could play like this after this was all over.

-CHAPTER 35-
SUFFERING IS CURRENCY

As Phineas, Mata, and Sicily made their way through the underground caverns, they came upon a bowl-shaped room. The floor was smooth, with carved steps leading to the center. Large tree-sized roots descended from a domed ceiling and draped themselves to the floor. The roots oozed the same pungent glowing sap. Up and down the tree were bodies in various states of desiccation.

Between the roots were offshoots that branched out and wrapped themselves around nearby descendants. The image of a congregation holding hands in a prayer circle came to mind to Phineas. The room was massive, but deep within the grove of repulsive roots and their pools of sickening slime was a strange glow. The light was warm and alive, like candlelight.

They made their way down a flight of stairs. Along the edges, sigils were carved in ancient text. Phineas wanted to examine them further but then felt something change in the atmosphere. The pressure changed, and the air grew thicker somehow. There was a distinct smell of ozone in the air.

Phineas could feel dread hang in the air, like feeling a storm coming, but this storm was not just about to bring rain and thunder; it brought something hateful and malicious. It inspired anxiety and chilled his bowels. Sicily and Mata were sweating, and Phineas shared their gooseflesh.

"We've got to hurry," Phineas stated. Mata and Sicily looked at Phineas. At that moment, he realized he needed to show confidence and bravery in the face of this thing. He smiled at them both.

"Let's see what the boogeyman looks like before we kick him in the dick!" Phineas said with a grin.

Mata looked at Phineas and smiled. Then she ran up and gave him a firm kiss that made him tip a bit forward due to her height. She then turned and looked at Sicily, ran up to her, and kissed her on the cheek. Mata pulled out her sickle and chain, skipping almost merrily into the unknown. Sicily looked back at Phineas with some confusion and amusement. He just smiled and shrugged. He jogged after the short but powerful woman.

Sicily looked after the two as they ran into the unknown. After a moment, she shook her head and chuckled to herself. "Fuck, you two are weird!" she said aloud.

Sicily, Mata, and Phineas moved through the thickets of thick, slimy roots and into a vast, misty landscape. Sicily looked over to Phineas, hoping she hadn't completely lost her mind. He and Mata looked at the unusual scene, slack-jawed in amazement. The look didn't exactly inspire confidence in Sicily.

"This is powerful magic at work," Phineas said with what sounded like reverence. "Someone has created a pocket dimension of some sort."

"What does that mean?" Sicily said, having no idea what that meant for them.

"Someone created a spell that either pulled us into another, self-made dimension or…" Phineas explained.

"Or?" Sicily asked, somewhat terrified now that such a thing was possible.

"Or someone took space on the physical plane and expanded a section of that space to form this separate environment," Phineas continued. "Either way, we must be cautious. Whoever did this may have set up defenses of some sort."

The dimensions of the space before the trio were hard to determine. A thick fog lay over the landscape: smooth rocks with rows of knee-high green grass. Set in seemingly random locations about the field were what appeared to be statues. Each statue looked to be in prayer and draped with green vines. The vines sprouted tiny white buds. As they continued toward the glow in the center of this environment, the grass became sparser and gave way to stone and sand. Black sand.

Mata looked closer at the statues and then turned back to Phineas in alarm. She began signing frantically. Phineas rushed over to her and looked over the figures as well. Sicily walked over with the flamethrower, staying on guard for an attack.

"What's up?" Sicily asked.

"Do you recognize these statues?" Phineas nodded with his head.

"Not much of an art collector," Sicily replied, keeping most of her attention to the fog and what may lie beyond.

"No, I mean, does the statue remind you of someone you know?" Phineas asked with greater urgency.

Sicily looked closer at the statue. In a small town, everyone knew everyone, at least by face, and if they didn't know more, they make up the rest. In this case, Sicily recognized the female statue as representing the home health nurse who cared for her mother. Shirley was her name, Sicily remembered, and she had gone missing a month ago. She quickly moved over to another statue. It was a skinny young man in his mid-twenties with a cleft lip. Samuel Clark. He worked for the church as the secretary.

"These are townspeople," Sicily stated after looking over a couple other statues for confirmation. "Most of these folks had moved away supposedly or gone missing."

Upon closer inspection, each statue was a calcified husk of a human, their faces not of a pious worshiper but trapped in a painful scream. Their arms and ankles were wrapped and thus restrained by the vines. In some cases, the closer the trio got to the warm glow in the center of the space, the more the figures showed signs of degradation or destruction. Faces were caved in to reveal the person was no more than a hollow husk. Some of the victims were nothing but scattered pieces of white porcelain chips, as if they were a dinner plate knocked from the counter.

Sicily knew many of the victims and had even been friends with a few. Even Mata was not immune to this loss of life. Phineas noted tears welling up when she came across a statue the size of a small child and toddler bound together by the vines. Phineas thought of George at this moment; he wished their shared trauma had not separated them for so long. Pangs of guilt shot through him for not reaching out to him and his family sooner. He needed to make amends somehow, but first, he wanted to kill whoever caused this death and suffering.

When they made it past the calcified remains of the missing townspeople, they came upon a small structure. From the ceiling overhead, the roots twisted and intertwined, the length of which extended until it met the roof of the building. The viny roots poured over the building and its simple brick-and-mortar construction. The weight of the alien plants would crush any standard structure, but this building appeared to be bolstered by it.

As they approached the building, the details and design became clearer. It appeared to Phineas as a small Byzantine chapel. The bricks were black and grey and seemed as though they had a sheen that reflected the luminescence of the sap that oozed from the root structures. The trim around the door and the windows was gold with strange etchings and symbols. Phineas could recognize some of them as wards of protection from viewing and prevented access from unauthorized visitors.

"I'll need a minute to get past this security," Phineas sat cross-legged in front of the entrance. "Cover me, would ya?"

"Why don't I just take out the hinges?" Sicily asked as she took a step toward the door. Suddenly, Mata grabbed her by the arm, stopping her cold. Sicily turned to look at her in surprise. She found Mata shaking her head emphatically.

"Whoever set these curses on this place did so to cause great suffering to any who should enter in any unsophisticated manner," Phineas said with closed eyes. He began murmuring something unintelligible while drawing symbols in the air with his left hand. With the cane in his right hand, he made circular motions. Sicily conceded and turned away, feeling somewhat embarrassed by her rash behavior.

Part of Sicily still rebelled against what she had seen with her very eyes. She wanted to go back just a few days ago when she was dealing with sexism in the workplace, flirting with Robert, and going home to her very alive and overbearing mother.

Then there was the pragmatic, sensible bitch in her who told her that pretending this wasn't real would not bring Mom back. It wouldn't make the machismo of the police culture any more bearable. Maybe, just maybe though, she could get through this shitty day, and she and Robert could get that drink together.

Sicily was brought crashing back to the insane reality of her situation when Mata slapped her on the back. She turned, thinking the girl was fucking with her, to find Mata on guard. Sicily looked out into the graveyard of statues and listened. She looked at Mata, who pointed into the darkness between nearby victims.

Sicily saw it. Saw something, that is. A shuffling in the darkness, just outside the glow of the chapel light. Sicily pulled out her flashlight, aimed it at a space where she heard some movement, and then lit the dark with the torch.

At that moment, Sicily had wished she never knew what lived in the shadows. She was always terrified of the things that skittered in the darkness, her closet, under the bed. Sicily's mind recalled every nightmare that hid in her childhood.

Now that her torch lit up the things that lived there, she wished she could just forget it and return to blissful ignorance. The light bathed what at first looked like a spider the size of a border collie with a single red orb for an eye. Below the eye were mandibles and rows of jagged, sharp teeth coated with spittle and venom. The legs were long and skinny; every crepitus step echoed on the stones.

The most horrifying feature was revealed when Sicily shone her light on these creatures; they raised their abdomens in a defensive display to showcase the faces of the victims now frozen in the hellish statuary surrounding the dark chapel. The faces screamed at the light, the final screams of those same victims from whom these monsters were born.

"Jesus Christ!" Sicily screamed. So rattled by the visages, she dropped her heavy flashlight, breaking it on the stones beneath her feet. Mata immediately pulled a flare from her belt, popped it to life, and threw it between nearby statues. A pair of spiders screamed childlike and scurried into nearby shadows. Mata repeated this again and again until the area surrounding them was painted in the red light of the flares.

Sicily fought hard to think of an action that would help, some way to fight, but all she saw were those horrible faces. All she could hear were those screams. The men, women, and even the cries of innocent children emanated from hungry spiders' abdomens. Their glistening fangs and mandibles promised that same pain. The same place next to them in a nest of Hell.

-CHAPTER 36-
UNACCEPTABLE LOSSES

"Drop the weapons and get on your knees now!" George commanded. "Holts, talk to me!"

"I'm fine. I'm fine. The bitch just sucker punched me, was all," Vincent replied. Robert helped Vincent to his feet and then aimed his rifle at Judge.

"Last chance, Marcus! Down! Now!" Robert yelled.

Before anyone could act, Vincent leveled his .50 caliber pistol and fired a shot straight for the man's chest. The gun blast sent Judge Marcus skidding across the floor and back into the dark. George and Robert flinched at the pistol's report and the man's actions. Both looked at him wide-eyed.

"What? Oh, come on, the man is trying to murder the whole planet." Vincent said unapologetically.

All three men looked into the space for motion. Vincent pulled a magnesium flare from his belt of pouches, lit it, and threw it into the room. It looked like a chapel, more satanic than the typical Christian variety. It had two dozen pews, an altar, and a glowing pit covered by a metal grate before that altar. Whatever was in the hole reeked of infection and death. Lying on the floor in front of the crater was Judge Marcus. The three men approached him with their weapons drawn.

When they reached the body, they all donned the same look of confusion when they realized the man lying before them wasn't a man. Whatever it was had flesh and hair and wore the same clothes, but it lacked eyes, a nose, or a mouth.

"What the hell?" George whispered. He nudged the body with his boot, but they got no response. Suddenly, the body began to swell, starting from its torso. The trio backed away as the figure inflated, much like a balloon. The clothes it wore tore and fell away, jewelry snapped and fell from wrists and neck. The skin stretched to the point it became nearly translucent. "Everyone, grab some cover!" George shouted after he finally shook away his disbelief.

Just as the body exploded, the trio ducked behind pews and pillars of root and stone. Red powder flew in all directions, the cloud so thick that no one could see more than a meter in front of them. The stench of rot and corruption that followed made each man gag and vomit. Through tear-filled eyes, George tried to locate his men. He wanted to call, but when he opened his mouth, he immediately began to cough.

Vincent groped around and finally found the wall of this twisted church. As a young man, long before he accepted his true calling as a merchant, he was a volunteer firefighter. Odd, he thought to himself now, that after all these years, the one thing he would remember of his training was the ability to find his way out of a room. Not the "handcuff" knot, how to perform proper CPR, or even how to make a decent pot of chili. For whatever reason, this one thing stuck after all these years. Vincent hugged the walls and stayed low, hoping that the cloud of gas was lighter than air.

Robert coughed, gagged, and tried to make his way to the exit when he suddenly felt a rush of air. Before he could understand it, a large object flew through the red cloud and smacked him square in the chest. The impact sent him flipping head over heels over the pew behind him. Luckily, his vest absorbed most of the damage, but he still had to answer to several bumps and bruises later.

Robert rolled to his left and began low crawling on the floor. There was a sudden crash of wood above him, and the two pews he crawled beneath rocked. Robert looked up to see another bench launched at him and crashed at the spot where he had once been. He quickened the pace of his crawl just as another pew slammed. Robert realized his attacker was as blind as they were.

George's vision was starting to clear, and his stomach had run out of things to retch. He could see more as the room slowly vented the smoke and smell. He saw pews from the rear of the room hoisted and thrown with ease. He couldn't quite make it out, but it looked like a large man was simply picking each bench up and throwing them like a javelin.

George stayed low and moved in a crouched position toward the nearest wall. The move didn't take long, as he had cleared his head enough to visualize a mental map of the room. This was a skill George emphasized to his trainees: get the layout and know what direction you are facing at all times.

He moved with the wall in the opposite direction as they came, knowing it would take him back to the entrance. He trained his gun on the pew-wielding attacker and aimed when he was parallel with the figure in the smoke. George was so focused on the attacker that he hadn't noticed a cylindrical concrete pillar. He bounced into it but recovered quickly and rolled behind it. George rolled again, this time to glance around the side of the pillar and take aim.

George realized then that it was quiet. No more sounds of wood crashing, or blurry images in the smoke. The haze had cleared enough that George could see Vincent across the room. The man was crouched low with his desert eagle clutched in his hands.

Vincent was indeed a sight with his blood-spattered dress shirt and pants, now all covered in vomit. The haze lifted just enough that George could see that Vincent wasn't alone. Standing behind him, Judge Marcus stood, dagger in one hand and scepter in the other.

"Vincent!" George yelled, trying to warn the man. Vincent started to look behind him when Judge plunged his dagger into the man's left flank. The force of the strike seemed to nearly bend Vincent in half as Judge lifted him into the air and, with the scepter he held in his opposite hand, smashed the man to the floor.

Judge spat at the injured man and then kicked him with enough force to send him flying to the room's entryway nearly fifteen feet away. Vincent slapped against the wall next to the doorframe and slid to the floor, leaving behind a blood spatter.

George roared and opened fire on Judge. Bullets struck the man's knife hand, upper arm, and shoulder, causing Judge to lose his grip on the blade. George fired another burst, but the man fell to the floor, and the bullets chipped at the stone wall behind him. George scanned the spot where the man fell, looking for any sight of him. Suddenly, from within, George felt his nerves come alive and his skin prickle on his back.

Behind me! George thought and spun to his left, bringing his rifle up to block the attack.

The blow struck the rifle with enough force to wrench it from George's hands. The improvised shield helped reduce the hit but could not absorb the full impact of the blow as George took a hit from the scepter Judge carried. The octopoid carving smacked George across his ear and jaw, sending him sprawling to the floor. His ear rang from the blow, and he was sure he nearly fractured his jaw. George desperately held onto his senses, rolled over, and pulled his sidearm simultaneously.

Judge was gone.

Slowly, not that he had a choice, George stood up to find Judge calmly walking out of the room. George glanced to his right to see Robert crouched low as well. They both moved to Vincent, who now lay in a sizeable bloody pool.

George and Robert moved Vincent into a seated position against the chapel wall. The man groaned from the motion. Vincent looked so pale to George; he was sweating profusely as well. He was in shock. He was dying.

"That bad, huh?" Vincent said weakly. "I was afraid I wouldn't be able to get these stains out of the suit," he finished with a smile.

George looked at Robert and nodded for him to cover them. Robert moved quickly, but George noticed the younger man already had tears in his eyes. George admitted disliking Vincent, but he was helping them stop this insanity and save his wife. That alone was enough for George to feel his loss.

"What can I do?" George asked. There was no sense in denying what was happening now. "What should I tell Finn and Mata?"

"Tell those two they can keep the gym. Tell them I said thanks for giving me more time on this shithole planet…" Vincent coughed up blood. "One more… one more thing."

"Yeah, anything," George said.

"Tell those two creeps I love them. Tell them…" Vincent choked up, and tears welled up in his eyes. "Oh God, I don't want to go to Hell. God, please…"

"Come on, man, you don't know you're going to hell," George said, trying to sound soothing. "A fine, upstanding guy like you? Surely they have a place for you in… well, whatever happens after you die."

A shadow passed before Vincent's eyes as he remembered what awaited him. "Yeah, sure," he said distantly. "Do one more thing for me? Ya…you…hurt him…hurt him bad…now go away…need rest…"

"You got it," George said, choking back tears. Vincent weakly waved him away, and as George was about to stand up, he felt the dying man's grip on his right forearm.

George suddenly felt the weight of the Desert Eagle in his hand. He looked up and saw that Vincent was crying. Vincent didn't have any more words, only regret. George saw it in his eyes and wished he could comfort this man more than anything.

George patted Vincent firmly on the shoulder, picked up his sidearm in one hand and the pistol in the other. Robert picked up the chainsaw and slung it over his shoulder. They moved to hunt down Judge Marcus among the thick roots. George vowed that the man would pay for what he had done. His suffering will be the currency.

George and Robert dove out of the church's entryway, and each ducked behind a thick root. George heard Robert groan in disgust as he slapped against some putrid sap that oozed from his cover. George quickly peered around his shelter and saw Judge Marcus nonchalantly walking toward where they came in. Then it hit him. Amanda. She was still unconscious and defenseless, and he was walking in her direction. Maybe even toward her on purpose.

"Shit!" George hissed.

Robert looked up and immediately realized the danger. Before George could stop him, Robert took off after Judge. He raised his rifle and fired. The bullets each struck center mass, but Judge ignored them. Each shell fell impotently to the floor. George couldn't stop him now and only hoped that if Judge were distracted, he could flank him. Suddenly, George felt his alert system buzzing in his head and skin at his feet. He looked down and saw the floor beneath him was smooth and black, like obsidian.

George felt his left arm vibrate before he had a second to question it. He turned just in time as part of the floor erupted next to him into a deadly spear of obsidian. The jagged black rock barely clipped his vest, drawing an incision in the fabric from his lower abdomen to his left shoulder. The vest deflected the hit, but George saw that had he not moved when he had, he would have been impaled through the heart.

The move to dodge the black blade left George unbalanced, and he tripped and spun to the floor. He skidded to a halt behind a thick, slimy root. Immediately, he rolled and got to his feet. He wasn't sure how these attacks worked but knew that if he stayed still for too long, he was as good as dead. He peered around the root and caught sight of Judge, who no longer retreated but stood perfectly still with his arms at his sides. His posture invited their attack. At his feet, George saw Robert's bullets. George considered how good any of their weapons would be.

"Fuck you, you sonofabitch!" Robert yelled as he reloaded and began moving toward Judge, firing fully automatic. George used the moment to move closer but watched as bullet after bullet seemed to hit the air before Judge and fall to the ground. Suddenly, George felt a vibration from his left but somehow knew he wasn't the target. The realization came too late as he tried to warn Robert, who was now almost in a full run at Judge.

Robert didn't seem to understand what had just happened. Robert fell to the floor after tripping on something. Whatever it was, it snagged his right leg, just above his knee. The misstep sent him sprawling to the floor and sent Robert's rifle skidding away. He watched it slide across the floor a good five feet from him. *When did the floor turn into black glass?* he thought.

Robert heard George screaming in the distance and knew he would be in trouble if he didn't get up. He pushed up and tried to stand on his right leg. There was an explosion of pain, and he felt himself slip and fall back to the floor.

Robert tried to move again but felt a coldness creep over him. He looked down, and the next scream he heard was his own. Robert saw the black obsidian spear jutting from the floor, covered in blood. He saw the lower half of his leg just past it. Then he saw the pulsing gushes of blood coming from the stump of his right leg.

George saw Robert lying there, holding the remains of his leg, struggling with this impossible choice. The pull of his own needs versus the needs of those around him was so great that his psyche was paralyzed in its trichotomy. He wanted to save his wife, the dying man before him, and kill the man who took so much pleasure in this suffering.

George rushed blindly toward Robert. He let his instincts take over rather than weigh the options. He got to his fellow officer, whose cries were so childlike that it made George weep.

Robert was already pale and diaphoretic. George's grief felt heavy enough to weigh him down and drag him to the floor. Seeing this young officer, a man with so much potential, dying from blood loss before him. George knew he could somehow stop this tragedy if he was fast enough.

"Robert, hold on. I got you, man," George screamed through his tears.

"Ge… George… my leg…" Robert whimpered. "Get my leg…we can save it… we just need…"

Before George could react, he felt every nerve come alive in his abdomen and chest. Not for him, he knew. George cried as he tried to pull Robert free in time, only to watch as several obsidian blades erupted from the floor and lifted Robert's body up before him. Robert didn't have time to scream or cry as the spears punctured him from several angles, piercing his lungs, abdomen, and shoulders.

"No!" George roared as he saw the young man lifted before him, his scream cut short when something heavy crashed into his right side. Judge slammed into George with a thrust of his elbow and forearm. The wind was instantly blasted from George, and he flew through the air and was caught by the thick trunk of a nearby root.

George coughed and then gasped for air as he tried to recover from the attack. He looked up from his prone position on the obsidian floor to see Judge standing beside a hefted Robert Holts, held aloft by Judge's magical black spears. George rolled and moved to a standing position when suddenly, his warning system tickled his back. He spun with his guns coming up before him and backed away just in time to miss another magical strike from the floor behind him. George felt another warning and dodged to the right and again to the left. Each time, he narrowly stepped out of the attack's reach.

He aimed his pistols and fired at a slightly amused Judge Marcus. Before any bullets could reach him, Judge suddenly sank into the floor. George took a deep breath and moved toward Robert. He could see that the man was still breathing, but barely.

George then looked over where Amanda was lying on the floor. He needed to get her out of this place; he couldn't fight Marcus and protect her simultaneously.

Judge's laughter echoed throughout the chamber as if in response to his internal suffering. George moved in Amanda's direction with a roar that was as much grief as rage. He blinked the tears from his eyes and tried to steady his breathing as he advanced.

Just as he took another step, George was warned that danger was at his feet. He couldn't tell which direction the attack would be coming from. It felt like the whole floor around him vibrated. Suddenly, blades came at him from various angles; some of the attacks were wild and far from hitting him, while others had to dance or shift to avoid a skewering.

George stepped back to evade a blade only to have another pierce his boot, sending waves of white-hot pain up his leg. Just as he extracted his foot from the trap, Judge Marcus flew up through the floor next to him and brought his octopoid rod across his cheek. Stars exploded across George's vision, and the next thing he knew, he was lying on the floor several feet away from the wizard.

"Please, God, if you're there, please help me kill this sonofabitch," George pleaded between gasps. He saw Judge Marcus looking down on him with his usual dispassionate stare. George gritted his teeth as he prepared for the next attack.

Vincent had only one sale pitch left in him. He had only one thing of value to give, and time was of the essence. Vincent reached up to the jewel around his neck with his remaining strength. This bauble was given to him by Phineas to hide his soul from the demon who still hungered for him. The creature wasn't killed by Mata and Phineas the night they met. It was only slowed long enough for them to find a way to hide his soul from the infernal beast. Now that the talisman had been pulled away, the hellish denizen could finally locate him.

"Find me quickly, you cunt," Vincent said as he spattered blood from his lips. "I know you're hungry for this." Vincent grasped the medallion firmly in his hand. With a ragged breath, he yanked the necklace hard enough to snap the thin chain. He held the jewelry up to look at it in his shaky hand. After a silent prayer, Vincent threw the bauble as far from himself as possible.

Vincent did not have to wait long; he had always suspected the demon was close, always hungry for this chance. The shadows near him grew in depth and size, the ceremonial candles suddenly lost their flames, and the temperature dropped dramatically. Vincent's breath steamed in the cold atmosphere. The smell of rotting flesh and feces filled the air. It was almost here. Vincent reached deep within and fought to stay conscious, praying he would see the demon before passing out due to the blood loss.

"You summoned me, human? Tired of the chase?" the demon said in a nerve-grating and singsong manner. "Has the meat been prepared?"

"Not exactly, you disgusting bitch," Vincent spat back weakly. This response seemed to amuse the demon, for it gave a chuckle at this. "You eat the souls of greedy men, right?"

"My favorite," the demon replied in its broken English. "Their regret tastes yummy." A line of drool fell past jagged teeth and beyond the demon's lower lip. The spittle hit the church floor and sizzled.

"How about I make you a better offer?" Vincent said. A bloody smile stretched across his face.

A broad and wicked smile broke across the demon's face as well. It lifted its hand as if to cup its ear to hear what Vincent had to say. The demon chuckled in anticipation of the man's begging. The smile faded as Vincent presented the last and best sales pitch he had ever given.

George rolled just as Judge swung his heavy scepter down, not away from Judge but toward him. The overhead swing of the club missed George and left Judge Marcus overextended and unbalanced. Judge tipped forward at the waist, trying not to fall over. George looked up and delivered a swift punch to the man's crotch. George's effort was rewarded by a heavy grunt from his attacker, and he began staggering away, holding his groin.

"Yeah, that's right, fucker!" George laughed and shouted. "You may be magic, but no man is immune to a good dick punch."

George ignored the searing pain in his left foot and charged at Judge. Judge turned to face his attacker just in time to catch a flying knee to the bridge of his nose. Judge's nose breaking was the most beautiful sound George had heard in a long while. Judge fell onto his back, and blood poured from his nose. George looked around for his pistols and found the axe that Vincent gave him instead.

George smiled as he bent low to pick up the axe. He immediately felt the hunger for the cursed object he held. It wanted to bite into flesh, dig into the tissue, and taste blood. George didn't even bother to resist denying the weapon. He turned to look for Judge and to drive the blade into the man's skull. Except Judge was no longer there. George's eyes went wide, and he cursed his arrogance. He turned this way and that, looking for the man.

"Where the fuck did you go?" George roared. "Let's end this now, Marcus!"

In response, George felt his alarms ringing from behind him. He spun, swinging the axe at the same time. In the air, almost in slow motion, George saw the unconscious form of Amanda flying at him. The axe rejoiced at any target, and it took not just a mental scream but a physical one as well to shut out the hunger the axe imparted on him to commit murder. He stopped mid-swing and dropped the axe to free his hands to catch Amanda's limp body.

The moment the axe hit the floor, the image of Amanda's flying body turned to mist. In its place was Judge Marcus in a mid-air leap toward George. His scepter was held straight for a charge, and the head slammed into George's chest. His vest blew apart as Judge released the magic contained within the strike. Black bolts of magic hungrily ate at George's skin, and he screamed as his muscles spasmed and twitched as if lightning had struck him. George fell to the floor, clutching his still-smoking chest and face.

"You are so very right, Officer Thatch," Judge said, standing over him. "Let's be done with this."

Judge stood up to deliver another bolt of deadly magic. George watched helplessly as vile bolts of magic cracked and streaked across the scepter's twisted head. Judge raised the club over his head and swung to strike.

Then he stopped as something thudded into him from behind. His look of absolute victory turned into one of confusion. Judge's face twisted with pain and fury. George peered around the man and understood why. Robert's knife, another gift from Vincent, was lodged in Judge Marcus' lower back, just left of his spine. Behind him, Amanda knelt, her eyes filled with venom and her teeth gritted in pain.

"You cow!" Judge screamed, his voice cracking with rage. He slapped her across her bruised face, sending her to the floor. "I will now kill you very slowly in front of Officer Thatch. He will beg me to end your life!"

Judge Marcus moved to make good on his promise of pain when he was again stopped. He stared in horror and disbelief at something just behind Amanda. Amanda looked to George, whose blackened face was slack, and his eyes were wide. She noted that he started crying, and a puddle of urine began to form.

Like a prey animal, Amanda slowly looked behind her to find a ten-foot-tall feminine figure hunched over her. Its leathery brown and yellow skin was stretched tight over its massive bony frame; its fingers and toes ended in black fingernails that were chipped and thick. From the top of its sternum to the tip of its pubis was an open wound. In that wound was a spool of razor wire, constantly turning and playing a twisted song of pain and torture. The same cables erupted from the thing's shoulders, down several points of the demon's arms, and back up again. The face was mostly covered by long, oily black hair. What was evident was the gaping maw filled with shark-like teeth. The demon licked its lips with a thick black tongue.

"We feed now!" the beast cackled in its nerve-wracking, high-pitched voice. The demon rushed forth to feast.

-CHAPTER 37-
CLAWING THE WAY OUT

Sicily felt the eyes of the unseen creatures in the dark crags of the underground cavern. Her skin shuddered as something projected images of the hungry mouths lusting for her flesh into her mind. She felt and pictured the scenes of those she knew from town, bound and helpless, as they were feasted upon and filled with the venom of these creatures.

Sicily wanted to kill them and make them pay, but what if those who died at the fangs of these beasts never left? What if they still felt pain? What if she died this way? What about those children? What if? What if? What if?

Then, there she was. Serena. Sicily's mother. Not the woman struck down by a stroke or a lifetime of regrets. The most authentic version of her. She was there beside her now. Sicily felt her firm, warm hand on her shoulder.

"Sis, you need to get through this for me. I can't say how proud of the woman you are. Not now," Serena said. "I wish I could have been as strong as you."

"I'm scared, mama," Sicily said. "I can't do this alone. I don't think I'm good enough …"

"You were always good enough," Serena said sternly, "I'm sorry if you ever needed someone else to tell you that. Now, I need you to kill this evil. Kill it and save the others."

Mata spun her sickle and chain, striking out at what little she could see in the dark. She impaled one of the spider-like things in the pitch; it shrieked a death rattle interrupted by the monsters pouncing on its dying body. Mata was fortunate to be unable to hear those jaws tear into their fallen comrade.

Despite the creeping doom she felt, Mata couldn't stop acting. Sicily seemed frozen, turned stone by her horror, leaving no one to protect Phineas. If she failed, he failed, then they all failed.

Then hope returned as a line of hungry flame reaching out to touch all that was evil and impure. Hope lit the shadows, chasing away nightmares. Hope comes from those who refuse to quit. It came as a raging Sicily with a flamethrower.

The spider-things screamed as they were brought to light and engulfed in Sicily's rage. Mata felt her skin percolate with the excitement of witnessing a warrior-made flesh when she gazed upon Sicily. How proud her ancestors must be, Mata thought. How proud her mother would be right now.

The line of flame licked the gravestone statues and arachnid horrors, dragging them all into fiery light and consuming them. The monsters screamed and writhed in the throes of searing white death. None, however, screamed so loudly, sang so beautifully, as Sicily with her flamethrower.

Mata rushed over to Phineas, who was already standing, and checked to see if they were ready to finish this battle. A smile crept across her face when she saw he was happy. Mata signed to him, inquiring about the outcome of his ritual.

"I see Sicily fighting. I was worried for one single second. She's pretty terrifying when she wants to be," Phineas signed with his fingers.

Mata looked at him curiously and nodded affirmatively. That's when she realized he wasn't trying to break any curse or unlock any ward. Phineas was summoning the strength Sicily needed to fight these abominations. She needed to feel the love and safety only her mother could give. Phineas pulled her spirit here to fight by her in the darkest moments. Mata looked in awe of Sicily in all her furious glory.

Phineas opened the door to the small chapel and was instantly taken aback. Inside the chapel was another pocket dimension. The room's interior was round, not rectangular as the exterior suggested. The room was more prominent as well. Floors were paved with smooth stones, the walls were all bare, and there were no windows.

Opposite the entryway stood a mirrored surface. Phineas knew the mirror was not designed for reflection but as a portal. Here, his powers of perception returned, and he could see beyond the gateway and through the Veil. Through the opaque surface, Phineas heard the screams, roars, and hissing of the denizens awaiting entry to this reality.

The dimension beyond was a place of chaos and violence. The landscape constantly changed as it roiled and bubbled. Mountains burst with explosions, throwing black soil and ash into the air. Creatures flew over the land only to be pierced by lifeless tree branches or grabbed by carnivorous plants. The sky was a deep purple, with stars swirling above one moment and violent storm clouds blooming the next.

Mata tapped an entranced Phineas on the shoulder and pointed to the figures in the center of the room. An elegant woman was wearing a purple and black robe. Standing next to her was a large middle-aged man. He was slightly overweight but well-muscled. He wore a simple brown suit that was ill-fitting for his frame. Phineas could see his arms barely fit in through the sleeves. The woman stood, her arms out to the side and her head slightly bowed as if silently praying.

"You are the lady of the house, I presume?" Phineas said with a sly grin. He looked over to Mata, who was eyeing the large man. Her expression reminded Phineas of a cat stalking its prey. "I assume you, sir, are here to..." Phineas let the question hang.

"I'm her brother, you fuckwit, and I'm here to make sure no one interrupts the ritual," Herman Montrose said. The large man scowled at the trespassers and tightened his fists around a thick baton. The club's end crackled with electricity with the push of a button.

"Would you care to do the honors, my dear?" Phineas asked and signed to Mata. Mata smiled wickedly, her eyes never leaving her target. The large man laughed heartily at the notion of fighting Mata.

"Are you fucking kidding me?" Herman laughed. "As soon as I'm done spanking your little bitch, I'm going to f—"

Herman didn't get to finish his sentence. Phineas had enhanced Mata's strength and speed by tapping into magical ley lines across her body. Phineas had similar enhancements, but Mata was born with natural gifts that made her the better fighter.

Once activated, the enchantments lasted only so long, and as a result, they needed to be used strategically. George and his officers witnessed the ritual at his home. To them, it appeared only as an application of body paint and smoke. Those without magical insight or talent couldn't see her muscles charged and empowered by magic.

Such was the case for Herman; as imposing as he was, he was just a man. Formidable, strong, and dangerous, but ignorant of how someone barely five feet tall could move so fast.

Herman grunted as he raised his arm to block, just in time to catch Mata's knee to his forearm. His eyes went wide from the power of the strike, one that nearly broke his arm. He took a few steps back and shook the tingling sting of the hit from his hand. He grinned at Mata as he understood now why Phineas allowed her to challenge him.

The large man lunged at Mata and swung the baton from his right to the left, hoping his reach would catch the woman across her temple. Mata quickly ducked the swing and sprung into a double backward somersault. When she landed, she immediately assumed a boxing stance.

"Well, ain't you nimble," Herman grinned. "I'm really going to enjoy playing with you after I kick your and your boyfriend's ass." Herman punctuated this threat with a lick of his lips.

Herman strode forward, covering the distance quickly and swinging the baton in a chopping motion. Mata dodged the attack nimbly and then countered with jabs to the man's flanks, neck, and chest. The metal spikes bit into Herman's flesh and drew blood, but if he was hurt, it didn't show. Mata sprung back just as the man tried to catch her with a left hook. Herman's mirth faded as he swung again with a backhand assault and missed again. Mata's smile taunted him with each of his missed attacks.

Phineas focused on the woman as she began singing a prayer to those who lived beyond the Veil. He didn't understand her language but knew that the prayer was an offering as she summoned the spirits that still dwelled in the land that Haven Shire was built upon. He saw motes of light as they were pulled from the obsidian pool she stood upon and watched as they were absorbed by the monstrous gate.

Each light represented a soul that empowered her spell to thin the Veil further. Soon, the Veil would be gone, and the evil beyond would spill onto this plane. Phineas slightly shuddered as he remembered the death and devastation he witnessed in his prophetic dream.

-CHAPTER 38-
PAY THE TOLL

Amanda scrambled as quickly as she could away from the demon. The stench of the beast alone made her nauseous, but the mere presence of the Hellspawn sent her mind spiraling into panic. Amanda didn't see the twisted, putrid vines, the impaled body of Robert Holts, or the man who had kidnapped and tortured her. She saw George bloody and bruised and now sitting in his urine, paralyzed by the truth. There is a hell and demons in that unfathomable place of suffering.

"George, baby, come on," Amanda stammered, caressing George's face and wiping his tears. "Babe, we have to get the fuck out of here."

Amanda turned, expecting the demon to be there, ready to deliver untold agonies. To her surprise, the beast wasn't moving. It stood before Judge Marcus, who was now more composed and preparing to face this otherworldly creature. The demon just smiled and drooled as it watched Judge prepare his defenses.

"Ah, yes, mage, prepare yourself, give hope to self," the demon hissed. "It makes your suffering tastier."

Judge called on the energy from beyond the Veil and pointed at the demon. Thick black tentacles rose from beneath the beast and wrapped themselves around the demon. The Judge began chanting a spell in the ancient language of the outer gods. Those eldritch limbs coiling around the devil began crackling with black bolts as they squeezed the infernal being. Nothing could be seen of the demon caressed by the limbs.

Somewhere within the tangled mass came a high-pitched tone. Judge's face screwed up in confusion and discomfort, so terrible was the sound of wires drawn across each other. Suddenly, a blur of motion erupted from beneath the tangles of the tentacles. The eldritch limbs ceased their movements briefly and then began to shudder and twitch. Piece by piece, the tentacles fell away, landing on the floor with a sick splat and then dissolving into pools of ooze. The demon rose above the bubbling piles of gore, lifted by the razor wires that twisted and turned within its heart cavity.

"More, wizard, show me more," the demon taunted. "I hope you don't need all your fingers, though; I am so hungry, I can't wait."

The demon produced a finger and slowly began to chew on it. Amanda vomited at the sound of the cracking bone and the slurping noises the demon made as it sucked the flesh off the digit. Beyond her own vomiting, she heard Judge scream painfully and looked to see him clutching his hand. A hand now shy an index finger.

Amanda quickly turned and looked into George's befuddled eyes. "I'm sorry, sweetie," Amanda said right before she slapped him across his face. "Get the fuck up!"

Pain. The stinging pain across George's face snapped his attention away from the demon to look at his new assailant, Amanda. George blinked and then threw himself into her, embracing her tightly. Then he saw Judge casting bolts of entropic energy and stabbing at the beast with those obsidian blades. The demon accepted hits from the magic or blocked some of the attacks with its arms.

"What the fuck is that?" George knew the answer as soon as he asked. Something internally recognized this creature fighting Judge Marcus. The blood, his flesh, everything down to his DNA knew that this was the enemy of humanity. "A fucking demon? How?"

Amanda looked helplessly at George. "We gotta go, honey," she said.

"Yeah, just have to get Robert; he's hurt, but maybe …" George began until he looked at Amanda. He looked at Robert and found him still impaled on those insidious blades. Tears started rolling down George's face. "Oh, God, Amanda, not him."

"I'm sorry, George," Amanda said, holding his face, tears swelling in her eyes, too. "He was such a good young man, but now we must get back to our girls. We have to tell people what happened here."

George nodded and let Amanda help him to his feet. Behind a column of slimy roots, an explosion of fire and light nearly knocked George and Amanda to the floor. George looked up to see the demon on fire. The monster laughed with glee in a screeching voice. Judge was just over ten feet away, blood oozing from a cut on his brow. George gained some pleasure at seeing the man fearful and breathing heavily.

George never thought he would cheer for a demon to win, and yet here he was. Amanda pulled his right arm, and he saw her looking up at him, pleading. He nodded and began limping away from the battle. Each step brought a wince and hiss from him as his adrenaline wore off and his injuries became more apparent. From behind George, he heard a roar of rage come from Judge Marcus.

"Yeah, fuck you, Marcus. I hope you die screaming," George whispered like it was a prayer. The demon laughed and screeched with joy, almost as if it heard him. As he and Amanda made it to the stairs, George found the duffle bag Vincent had been carrying. He smiled to himself when he remembered the explosive contents within.

Judge Marcus called upon curse after curse that would slow the infernal beast before him. He never trucked with the damned or those that lived in the lower planes. The risk was rarely worth summoning one of their kind. It was difficult enough to keep the masters beyond the Veil, and the outer reaches of that plane, pleased and gain access to their power. They were chaotic beings but not like the infernal ones. Denizens of Hell followed any and every impulse that brought suffering, even if it meant causing themselves harm.

Judge dodged as a line of razor wire sang past him, nearly cutting off his right arm. The attack slashed through one of the thick roots that continued to funnel the energy from the souls below. The root fell and immediately disintegrated and turned into ash. Judge's face belied to the demon how important the roots and all those trapped within were.

"Important to you? They are plant flesh, nothing more," the demon hissed. "They are in my way. I clear them now."

"No!" Judge Marcus roared. He ducked and threw himself to the floor just as the demon threw open the gash in its chest. The room became a squeal of metal on metal, and flashes of sparks flew as the nightmare became a tornado of razor wire.

The whips reached out the entirety of the room, slashing against the stone walls. The demon began spinning, dancing over

Judge, as it whipped its internal workings all about itself. Judge looked up just in time to see the officer's corpse he had impaled minced into chunks of flesh and bone.

Just as quickly as it started, the dervish ended. Judge looked around the room in horror as his work and efforts began to fall apart. The roots of the alien plant from beyond the Veil started falling from the walls, ceilings, or wherever they were suspended. The victims he had collected over the decades past were all destroyed. Those who had not been killed by the parasitic plant lay bleeding and dying with expressions of horror and confusion. Some crawled from their fleshy prisons, dragging their entrails or trying to find loved ones.

Judge's attention was brought again to the present by the cackle and orgasmic moaning of the demon. It squealed in delight as it held a victim, once trapped in the alien roots, high and laughed as the woman screamed. Judge surmised she would soon die; her missing limbs and spilling entrails told him that much. He needed this moment to escape and garner support from those beyond the Veil.

Quickly, Judge rose to his feet and began running for the stairwell. He was near the top of the stairs when suddenly he heard the sound of screaming metal. As he leaped for the landing, the Judge felt something slap his left calf. Then his leg exploded in searing hot pain as he felt the razor wire bite into his flesh and grab hold of him. Judge's leg was jerked so violently he didn't ready himself for the fall. He fell flat, his stomach and face slamming onto the stairs. His already broken nose smashed against the corner of a stair, sending a pyrotechnic display of pain to Judge's eyes and brain.

Judge felt his world spinning and growing dark, but he was not allowed the mercy of unconsciousness. The demon's whips coiled within itself once again, dragging Judge across the floor. Judge felt ice-cold fear worming up his spine, his bowels twisted, and his groin had retreated somewhere within his abdomen.

Judge looked about for salvation and found hope in the form of a wicked chainsaw. He recognized it as the one the young cop had. He was dragged closer to it, but it was over six feet away to his left.

Pushing past the pain in his leg, Judge rolled off his belly toward the weapon. As he rolled, he heard the terrible scream of razor wire coming for him. By his third roll, he was close enough to grab the tool. Judge's hand gripped the saw as several more razor whips wrapped around his other leg, abdomen, and torso. Judge screamed as he felt the whip bite into his flesh. He gritted his teeth and pulled the cord, bringing the saw to life. The moment the saw roared, Judge felt his body dragged so fast that he was at the demon's feet in the blink of an eye.

The razor whips work on his flesh as they retract themselves, gliding their edges across his body. Judge screamed as the razors sliced through his skin, muscles, and tendons. He peered up at his attacker, who crouched over him now, laying its palms on the floor and legs straddling him.

"Filthy human, what is chainsaw going to do? You believe you can escape?" Drool flowed from the demon's maw, and a drop landed on Judge Marcus' forehead.

Judge's breaths were coming quick, and he felt weakness beginning to set in. He looked down, and from within the demon, living tendrils of razors reached out and caressed his body. Almost gently, they slipped around him, wrapping him in an embrace. Judge felt them lift him up. He realized then that he was being pulled into the demon's body.

With a sudden burst of fear-induced adrenaline, Judge swung the chainsaw at the demon, cutting a few razor whips. The demon screamed in rage and stood straight on its legs again, lifting Judge. The wizard still felt pulled into the thoracic cavity of the devil, which was full of spinning razors. Judge felt his now useless legs caught by the spinning spool of razor wire and blades. His tendons were severed in several places, making his legs too weak to pull away from the slicing action of those awful blades. He screamed as he felt his tissue and muscle cut to ribbons.

Judge inverted his grip on the chainsaw and stabbed it in the demon's chest cavity. To Judge's surprise, the demon screamed in pain as sparks and metal were ejected from the wound. His mask of elation that he hurt the monster changed to utter despair as it began to moan with pleasure.

"Oh, yes, I feel you so deep," the demon cackled lewdly. "Come, I need to feel you closer. Give me a kiss." The monster sneered as it grabbed Judge, its blades tightening around Judge's torso and placing a hand on the back of his head. The perverse touch was as gentle as a lover's.

The razor wires sawed into Judge, digging deeper into his muscles and bone. Judge's scream was cut short as he became transfixed in the horror before him. The demon's mouth opened, and rows of shark-like teeth were in its maw, wet with anticipation. Beyond the teeth, its black tongue reached for his face. His mouth.

Razor wire sprang from the demon's throat and wrapped around Judge's head. Each one worked across his face, eyes, and skull like the whip that had nearly finished cutting through the man's waist.

Judge thrust the chainsaw deeper into the demon's chest by sheer force of will. Blood from both combatants spilled across the floor and sprayed on the ceiling as the chainsaw worked its way through the demon's back, and Judge Marcus was sawed, then folded in half. With a loud snap of his spine, the monster began pushing his body deep inside itself, forcing the chainsaw up through its own body.

Just as Judge Marcus's life had come to its end, he heard something fall hard behind him and slide to the demon's feet. Weakly, the mage turned his head and saw the duffle bag tip over onto its side, spilling its contents. Several sticks of dynamite, a grenade, and a brick of plastic explosives lay exposed beneath him. A red timer slowly counted down.

Judge screamed not because he was afraid of the inevitable explosion but because the little time left on the clock would not end his life before this infernal monster did. He would be dragged to Hell to be consumed and tortured for eternity.

The maddening scene of horror and gore suddenly came to an explosive end. The demon folded into itself when it finished delivering to its bowels what was left of Judge Marcus. There was a wet sucking sound from within the beast and then a violent rush of air as the demon imploded. The room then exploded in flames, the force of which shook the whole structure of the Forgotten Church down to the caverns below.

# # # #

Maria felt the explosion and the loss of her husband. She could not grieve the man, however. After all, he was responsible for the deaths of her beloved sons. He constantly belittled her talents and thought of her as nothing more than a conduit for the energies of the Veil. That, and a receptacle for his useless seed. He hadn't brought her any joy for so long that the man's demise only inspired her to sing to the gods with joy. They filled her with more of their blessings and empowered her to finish the ritual and defeat her enemies.

She sang louder as she felt the Veil's energy stream become more concentrated. It filled her mind, body, and soul all at once. She moaned in agony and ecstasy as she took in more of the Veil gods' blessings and power. Maria was concerned she would either lose her mind or physically explode as she felt those ancient beings pour their essence into every corner of her being. She began to moan with pleasure as their touch began to flow from her and fill the room. She looked at her body and watched as she became the stuff of shadows, corruption, and madness.

Maria bellowed a song of victory as she accepted becoming a thing of the Veil. Immortal, forever immune to sickness or age. She felt her body tremble with pleasure and the ache of her muscles and flesh growing. Her skin became as hard as obsidian and just as black. She was more now, not just a human woman. Someone to be abused or treated as lesser. A goddess of nightmares, she told herself.

Maria became oblivious to her brother's battle with that fierce woman, somehow blessed by those of the first tribes. She no longer cared for the shadow of death that stalked her, now approaching her with those eyes and that cane. She only wanted to set Formoria loose on the world and rejoice in its suffering.

-CHAPTER 39-
THE FERRYMAN WILL NOT BE DENIED

Phineas watched as Maria Marcus, the priestess of the Formoria, became infused with the Veil's power. The inky blackness of corruption crawled across her flesh and became her mantle. Her human features were washed away as she became one with the obsidian disc in the center of the room.

She slowly turned to face Phineas, and as she did, her joints sounded like glass ground between two stones. Phineas grimaced at the creature she had become. Her face had once been beautiful, but she now appeared like a candle melted by an open flame. Her features melted together to resemble a statue of Mother Mary wearing a Veil and her mouth fixed in an open scream. Or a laugh.

"What have you done to yourself, Maria Marcus?" Phineas said, feeling a twinge of pity for the woman. It was a fleeting emotion as he considered what he was about to do. Maria did not answer in the traditional sense. Maria laughed at him for his weakness.

Maria had no idea what the cost of her newfound power was. She had been driven mad, clearly. She had evolved into something more significant than a human. Oblivious that she was damned for eternity as an undead thing, to walk without rest as an abomination.

Phineas whispered in the language of Gehenna, the land of the dead. He constructed a shield to protect his body and soul. At the same time, Phineas built a protective barrier around his mind. Finally, he spoke the word of power that would activate those enchantments on his flesh and bones, just as he had for Mata. He felt the power of those enchantments send their energies into himself. Ley lines across his body became places for magic to flow, just as his veins transported blood and oxygen.

Phineas moved toward the undead creature that was once Maria. Just as he was about to reach the obsidian circle of flooring, he saw it was no longer made of that volcanic glass. Too late to stop himself, Phineas' foot plunged into shadow, and he went along with it. Phineas twisted in midair as he fell, and he turned to grab the edge of the floor before the drop. The shadow stuff was icy cold, and Phineas could feel his body already losing strength against its grip. Phineas' grip slipped completely when a pair of jagged claws grabbed his shoulders and pulled him into the dark.

Mata struck a series of blows to Herman's torso, sending him stumbling backward, when she saw Phineas pulled into a black pool. She instinctively ran for him, abandoning her fight with Herman. Mata dove and slid to the pool's edge, missing Phineas' hand. She peered into the inky dark of the pool and screamed silently, once again, cursing her inability to speak.

All Mata could see in that pitch black were the motes of lights representing all the souls who could not escape the hills surrounding Haven Shire. She prayed that Phineas was not included among them. Mata stood up to jump in and try her best to save Phineas. It was the very least she could do for the only person she loved.

Just as she was about to make the leap, Mata was struck from behind. The impact was followed by an electric discharge that caused her muscles to jerk and seize uncontrollably. The pain forced her to fall flat to the floor. Mata breathed through it and tried to focus on what had hit her. She looked up to see Herman holding his baton, the end of which was outfitted with a taser.

Herman smiled down at her with his wide, bloody grin. Mata tried to roll and escape, but her body was incapable of listening to her mental commands. Herman reached down with his massive hands, grabbed Mata by her braid, and lifted her off the ground. Mata hissed against the pain of the pull on her scalp. Herman's face was a mask of mocking laughter.

Herman swiftly thrust his forehead forward and smashed it against the bridge of Mata's nose and forehead. Her vision exploded into a fireworks display, and the pain stole her senses. She couldn't smell anything except her blood, couldn't see through her tears, and could taste nothing but her bloody spit. Anxiety swelled within her as she realized she was effectively senseless; she could not know the world around her except the pain. Mata tried to breathe and focus again, trying to see past this hurt.

All Mata felt was a blast of Herman's fist to her abdomen. The other hand still held her braided ponytail, and he used it to slam her face to the floor. Mata felt the world blur and dim, and her brain screamed to give into unconsciousness to escape this pain. Mata struggled to resist the call to slip into the merciful nothingness. She had to convince her body to cooperate and fight against the electricity-induced spasms.

Mata's spasms from the electric discharge of the taser only lasted a few seconds. Still, Herman efficiently used that time to inflict pain on her. Herman landed another solid kick to her ribs, blasting the air from her lungs and sending her skidding across the floor. She felt her right eye swelling, her nose broken, and several ribs fractured. Now, he prepared to use his baton on her again.

As Herman brought the baton down to smash her across the face, Mata rolled and clumsily stood to face him. She reached into the runes drawn across her arms and legs and asked the energies imbued within those ley lines to give her strength and speed. The magic was forthcoming, but Mata knew she had little time left before the enchantments wore off or her muscles would tear under the strain.

Herman came in with a backhand swing of the baton. Mata bent over backward, and the slash of the metal club flew right above her nose. She felt the distinct buzz of electricity arcing between the two prongs at the head of the club. Before Herman could recover and come in for another attack, she stood straight and delivered a powerful right roundhouse kick to the man's ankle. The kick hurt the man but didn't cripple him, but that wasn't Mata's intent. The kick forced his leading right foot to be knocked out from under him, driving him off balance. Mata followed the low kick with a leaping knee to the large man's face.

Herman's head snapped back sharply from the force of the strike. Mata did not waste a moment and followed the stumbling man, charging in with her cestus. She punched and slashed at the large man's legs and groin. The spikes on her forearms pierced, sliced, and crunched against flesh and bone.

Herman roared in pain and reached out for her with his left hand. Mata ducked the attempt to grapple and dipped in close. Slipping under the extended arm, she pulled a throwing dagger from the back of her corset. Setting the blade between her two middle fingers, Mata began pumping her fist in a series of quick stabs to Herman's flanks and ribs.

Jolts of electricity rocketed through Mata again, just as she pulled away from the close encounter, leaving her blade wedged between the fourth and fifth rib. Mata tried to clear herself of the attack, but her right leg made a wet popping noise in the center of her hamstring. Mata couldn't scream aloud, but an audible gasp escaped her as she fell. This was all Herman needed to encourage his next attack.

Adding insult to her pain, Herman's thrust of his taser baton stabbed her where her neck met her shoulder. Mata's neck cramped and spasmed, causing her head to bend awkwardly. She fell hard on her back, twitching and silently crying out in pain.

Herman moved to follow her, but then his brain finally registered the pain and damage in his legs, groin, and flank. Every move he made, even breathing, sent pain throughout his body. He fell forward on his hands and knees, his weapon sliding away. Herman stayed in that position for a few ragged breaths before moving to a sitting position.

Herman was hurting and having a hard time breathing. He felt the stabbing pain in his ribcage and reached for the throwing dagger between his ribs. He pulled the blade free with a quick jerk, wincing in pain from the extraction.

"You fucking bitch ... you whore ..." Herman said, taking deep gulps of air. "You fucking stabbed me!"

Herman stood up and looked down at the prone Mata, crying and clutching her right leg. He limped over to her and reversed the grip on the blade, which seemed tiny in his hands. He dropped to his knees beside her and grabbed a fist full of her braided hair. Mata stared at him with such hate and rage, refusing to let her final moments be of her crying at the hands of this man. He looked back and smiled wickedly. He lifted his meaty right fist, gripped the dagger tightly, and brought the weapon down.

Phineas looked around in the cold pitch he now floated in. All around him, he saw the souls of those who had died over the centuries, floating lazily in the darkness like jellyfish. He sensed their confusion. They had a purpose; to keep this land, make it fertile and prosperous, and maintain a garden of the first ones. Phineas heard their cries for help; once they had one moment, they swam together with their families in a river of eternal life and love;

now, they floated separate and alone in a cold dark. Phineas took a deep breath and tried to calm himself. He needed to find a way out and guide those lost souls home.

Phineas felt another presence in the dark. No. Multiple beings watched him now. Phineas peered into that blackness and found several eyes on him. Tentacles swayed in rhythm with the flow of souls, and teeth snapped at those that came too close. In the forefront of those chaotic shadows was the shadowy and elegant silhouette of Maria Marcus.

Maria glowed a pale blue aura that barely lit her features in the darkness. She was naked now, thin, and gaunt. Her curves and feminine features had eroded away, and she was left with a skeleton clothed in tight-fitting, stony flesh. Her mouth was agape in an eternal scream, and deep within her melted and shrouded face, her eyes bore into his mind.

Phineas tried to call out to her, possibly trying to move through the void, but he found his voice stolen somehow. Phineas resisted the urge to panic; he needed to stay calm and logical and focus on his next move. Just as he began to formulate a plan, he heard the light, playful laugh of Maria Marcus pierce the darkness behind him. Phineas turned to find Maria behind him, her face mere inches from his own.

"Just what can you do against us now, boy?" Maria teased mockingly. "What power could you bring to bear against Cthulhu? Against Yog-sothoth? The Formoria?"

Maria punctuated her statement with a blast of pale light that hit Phineas, burning through his defenses and sending him flying farther into the darkness. He fell on a cold, gritty surface, and as he cleared his eyes, he saw that he was no longer in some void. He turned his palm over and saw his hands covered in black sand. The sound of water filled his ears, and Phineas turned around to find himself looking at the ocean.

"What the fuck?" Phineas yelled in shock. He looked up and down the beach, and it seemed like the black sands went on forever. There were no signs of civilization that Phineas could see. He began to climb the beach to approach a hill for a better vantage of the landscape. Just as he made his way to the base of a dune, Phineas felt the curious sensation of the wind pulling on him, and the skies overhead became overcast in thick, angry clouds. He turned and immediately fell backward from the sight. A mile-high tidal wave rushed toward him from the sea, and with it was carried the weight of inevitability. Behind the tsunami, Phineas could make out a disastrous tempest.

Bolts of eldritch lightning streaked across the sky and raced inland. Then Phineas made out what had caused the rising wave as a slash of lightning backlit the wall of water. Phineas saw that beyond those waters, a titan hundreds of meters tall at the shore, with massive bat-like wings and an octopoid head. Hundreds of tentacles wriggled around the monster's body from its face, waist, and back.

Phineas felt so small in the face of this being as he felt it intruding his mind with maddening thoughts of despair and self-destruction. Phineas felt he could do nothing but hope Mata made it out of the church in time. The monster roared loudly, filling Phineas with a panic that made him wilt.

Yet, in the background of his fear and feelings of insignificance, Phineas felt as though this was all wrong. There was a lie here, and if he could somehow push past this assault on his mind, he could defeat it. Phineas fell to his knees and planted his cane as deeply into the sand as possible. If he was wrong and this was truly happening, then he would at least have a story to tell in the hereafter.

The inescapable wave crashed over the beach, and Phineas felt the waters smash into him and carry him inland. He held his breath and prayed to whoever listened that he would not be impaled on something or have an object crash into him. Phineas held his breath, but the weight of the cold waters squeezed him and twisted him and inevitably took a few mouthfuls of water. His body was racked with pain and cold, and he was about to lose consciousness when he felt himself slide across a hard, smooth surface. When he finally stopped moving and the water suddenly receded, he opened his eyes and looked around.

Phineas was surrounded by buildings in some war-torn city. He scanned the area, looking for a familiar landmark, and realized he had been tossed into downtown Kansas City. He saw the hotels and convention centers were on fire or severely damaged. Papers and debris blew in the wind, and Phineas caught the scent of burning flesh in the air.

Screams soon erupted as a mass of people shambled down the street. They moved as one rolling mass, all screaming and tripping over each other. As they drew nearer, Phineas understood the reason for their confused and clumsy motions. Nearly a hundred people were tied together with barbed wires, rope, and chains, and each of them had their eyes clawed out.

Phineas saw large shambling forms chasing them, whipping them with spiked tentacles, raking their flesh with wicked claws, and biting at the panicked masses. No two Formoria looked the same, and none held their shape long as they moved across the street surface on legs, slimy bellies, or using their shapeless masses to grab nearby objects and pull themselves forward. Phineas realized that the monsters were herding the crowd toward something. But what?

Then he heard a deafening roar. At first, Phineas thought it came from a siren, a warning of a threat until he heard animals howling and screeching within that chaos. So large was the sound that it seemed as if it came from everywhere. Phineas ran away from the mob and their keepers to get distance and develop some sort of defense. When he turned the corner at the end of the street, he nearly tripped at the sight of the massive creature before him.

It was as tall as Cthulhu. Phineas couldn't bring himself to stare at it for too long. The sight of the monster sent his mind reeling as it couldn't fully comprehend what exactly he was looking at. One moment, he would see a clawed arm, only to blink and have the limb obscured by a mass of eyes, then again to see them fold into its own bulk and produce a giant maw filled with countless teeth.

To Phineas, it resembled an angry, morphing blob, a tumor that sought a defined shape and then rejected it violently. It roared again, and as it did so, it projected images into the minds of any who heard its call. Images of human suffering flashed before Phineas. The monster tapped into Phineas' imagination and forced him to construct methods of torture for himself and all those he cared about. Now Phineas understood why the herd of screaming humans had no eyes. They must have clawed them out themselves.

Phineas erected his psychic walls, gripped his cane, and looked for a way to safety. Before he could even determine the direction to escape, Phineas felt a powerful hand grip the nape of his neck and throw him to the ground. He turned to look at his attacker, and there was the obsidian form of Maria. Before he could move to defend himself, he felt the world blur around him, and he was back in Haven Shire.

Phineas lay dizzy from the teleportation on the same spot his dreams foretold. He tried to catch his breath, but the motes of ash choked him. The smell of the burning flesh nauseated him. Maria swept her arm out toward the town, his hometown. All the buildings were nothing but blackened skeletons. Burned bodies of those frozen by Maria's spell lay on the ground, their faces preserved in agony.

Beyond the town, Phineas saw the landscape was now bare, the life of the land drained and barren. The sky and its horizon were choked by smoke from multiple fires. The gentle mists of the Shire were replaced by a fog of smoke and the scent of the dead. It looked like a nuclear winter as ash floated and danced in the breeze. Then, it occurred to Phineas that this was what had killed everyone. Everyone except the Formoria and their gods.

"Praise be, what a sight to behold," Maria cackled beside Phineas. She pointed to the horizon, and there in the distance, and still impossibly massive, walked the Old Gods. In the sky above them floated Cthulhu, who dispatched flying tentacled creatures to the surface. "The Gods are good, yes?"

"Fuck you, bitch!" Phineas roared. He gripped his cane and swung at the corrupted witch. Before he made contact, however, he was once again frozen by the horror of what he saw before him. Behind Maria was a field of pikes, black and twisted, that led all the way to the Forgotten Church. In the forefront were all those he knew and cared for.

George and Amanda were skewered by the same pike, and their faces and bodies were frozen in an embrace of suffering. Vincent was impaled through his rectum, and the spear erupted from his mouth and several feet beyond. Robert and Sicily were similarly gored but dismembered, their genitals torn away.

Then he saw Mata and Phineas began to moan sorrowfully at the sight of this beautiful woman being brought so low and broken like this. She was nude so that her wounds were visible to all. Judging from her injuries, Mata had been horribly violated and then disemboweled, her entrails still steaming in the cold. Tears streamed down Phineas' face as he walked to where she was crucified.

He reached up to touch her with his left hand when he realized he was still holding onto his cane. Despite being thrown around by a tidal wave, teleported to various locations, and even attacked by Maria, he never let it go. Then, it occurred to him as to why.

"None of this is real," Phineas chuckled and wiped away his tears. He suddenly remembered stabbing his cane into the beach when he saw the vision of Cthulhu. His cane was his most potent magical item for many reasons, including its ability to anchor its wielder in reality. Once the spell was enacted, he had a focal point to help him discern truth from illusion.

"Oh, but it will be," Maria said, amused. "Your meager powers of perception and use of cursed artifacts won't help you against a spell used by those beyond the veil."

Donning his evil grin and mentally preparing for an assault, Phineas gripped his cane tightly as he stabbed its point into the ground before him. A pale green light erupted from the dark, lacquered wood, wiping away the illusion around him. Once again, he was in the void filled with the souls of Haven Shire. They floated about like fireflies and were occasionally pulled into what appeared to be a bright gash of light in the distance.

"The Veil," Phineas surmised. "You are using these poor souls to feed the insidious tree. The tree weakens the Veil, separating this plane from the Formoria and their gods. You also use the souls to create a pathway for the Formoria."

"You are cleverer than most men, but none of this will stop the Formoria from entering and devouring your world," Maria said. "You are too weak and frail to stop me!"

Maria launched her obsidian self at Phineas, swinging hard with a right-handed sweep of her clawed hand. Phineas countered with a block with his cane. He could see her hands crackling with the dark energy of the Veil. Phineas spun away just as Maria released the power as a bolt, narrowly missing his head.

"You are right, Maria. I'm not strong enough," Phineas said. "Not by myself, anyway."

Sicily took great pleasure in the dying screams of the nightmare's arachnids as she threw a line of flames at anything that moved. There were enough of the monsters burning that she could easily see the field of nightmarish monuments and the hanging roots beyond. It occurred to her then that those roots were falling and turning into ash. Some disintegrated where they stood.

"They did it!" Sicily said to herself and praying to whomever was out there listening, to protect George, Robert, and even the old douchebag, Vincent. Sicily blasted another spider with a gout of flame. The momentary flash of light illuminated three things for Sicily at that moment.

Firstly, the pocket dimension, as Phineas called it, was shrinking. Sicily considered it was due to the destruction of the alien plant. Secondly, there were more spiders than she thought, and as the space around them compressed, the spiders were now more visible and pressed together. Finally, she was running out of fuel.

Sicily quickly reached for a flash-bang grenade hooked to her vest. She pitched the grenade as far as possible, landing the explosive within the congealing mass of arachnids, blowing many of them apart and stunning others. She followed the explosion with another grenade, a concussion grenade this time. She watched spiders writhe in pain from the bright lights and deafening noise. She threw a line of flames at those creatures, too stunned to run away.

Sicily repeated this until she was out of grenades. For a moment, Sicily thought she had made a dent in the elusive creatures' numbers. She pulled a road flare from a cargo pocket in her pants, lit it, and threw it as far as possible.

To her horror, Sicily now realized why the little bastards didn't rush her. They had the numbers. The clever monsters knew that Sicily would run out of fuel sooner or later, so they sent out small numbers to draw her fire and force her to use the fuel in the flamethrower. She was out of grenades, and soon all she would have were the two pistols Vincent loaned her and her 9 mm police-issued sidearm. Sicily would have to retreat into the chapel where Phineas and Mata went, barricade the door, and pray they didn't follow. Or take a stand and hope those two would somehow end this nightmare.

Phineas called on his greatest gift, to commune with the dead and summon spirits. Using his cane as a conduit, he reached out to every soul trapped within the void and beyond. Phineas felt their rage and pain and shared their sentiments. He promised them all revenge, a way to be set free from the prison that was Haven Shire. Not a single soul had been given a choice if they wanted to spend eternity in the land. That was a curse laid down by the first tribes of humanity.

Phineas gave them focus for their ire in Maria Marcus. The curse on the land was unfair, but what she had done was a total violation. She violated the order of nature, murdered the townspeople, stole their souls, corrupted their community, and now she intended to spill her brand of vile evil out into the world. Phineas shared his rage with them and promised to destroy Maria Marcus together.

Phineas called upon the souls of the dead and collected their energy and rage into white-hot lances of light. Maria screamed and threw a bolt of corrupt, entropic energy at the necromancer. Phineas summoned a shield of light from the same power gifted to him by his new allies. The baleful bolt struck the shield and slid around Phineas. He responded with a magic attack of his own by pointing the head of his cane at the Veil priestess.

Four white lances launched forward at Maria. Phineas saw she started to use her spells, the first to become insubstantial as shadow. Phineas called out to the first lance.

"Don't let her escape! Hold her!" he cried out both physically and psychically.

The lead lance exploded just before hitting Maria, and white light washed over her body. The light spread over her like dust, making her glow and lighting her monstrous features. The spell coalesced the light into a shell of spiritual energy tightening around Maria, binding her form and holding her in place.

The second beam lanced through Maria's upper leg. The stony flesh cracked and threatened to fall apart. Maria howled in pain as she thrashed back and forth, trying to shake her spiritual shackles. Another shaft of light pierced through Maria's other leg. The final attack struck the witch, stabbing through and out her back between the scapula and spine.

"Give up the souls, close the Veil, and leave this place, Maria!" Phineas commanded. "This will be your only chance to concede."

"You think this will bind me? You think this will break me?" Maria screamed back at him. "You are nothing to me or the Old Gods beyond the Veil! I will crush you and eat your soul!"

"I was hoping you would say that" Phineas said with a wicked grin, and he began chanting an ancient spell, calling forth spiritual energies for a powerful ritual.

Maria summoned her own energies from beyond the Veil, fighting against her restraints and working to free herself. The light that held her faded as the energy from those souls began to run out. She threw her arms wide with a primal scream, both human and inhuman. Maria laughed, thinking herself free and soon victorious.

She looked up and found Phineas floating above her. She heard him speaking ancient words of power she had never heard before. Maria could still discern that this spell was mighty indeed, and she needed to stop him quickly.

Maria began to cast a curse of her own, a powerful bolt of entropic energy. Her chanting was interrupted however, as she heard a great crashing and roaring sound approaching. A terrible chill ran through Maria's body, and the cold hand of dread gripped her by the throat.

Mata wanted to resist, roll, and fight, but her body was either reeling from that last shock from the taser or trying not to pass out from a severe muscle tear on her leg. She knew one thing; she would not let this man see her give up. She looked up as he raised the knife she left stuck between his ribs and could do nothing. Then Mata blinked, not out of fear or pain, but because an unexpected splattering of blood onto her face.

Herman stopped his attempt to plunge the knife into Mata's face. The left side of his neck exploded, and blood spurted out. He looked more confused than in pain. He turned to see his attacker, and so did Mata. There, at the entryway into the chapel, stood Sicily. In each hand, she held the revolvers that Vincent had loaned her. Her long black hair was soaked with sweat, as were her clothes, and she was no longer wearing the flamethrower.

Mata wondered briefly where the flamethrower was. Her question was suddenly answered in a brilliant display outside. A globe of fire erupted on the other side of the chapel doors, and Mata heard the screams of several of the arachnid creatures they had seen on the way in.

Herman saw Sicily and growled. He turned at Mata in a rage, determined to finish her before he died. His attack was interrupted by explosions of gunfire, followed by holes blown through his head, neck, and chest. There was a few seconds of quiet, and then the sound of Herman's fall echoed off the chapel walls. The knife he held fell out of his hand, and Mata watched Herman die, his now vacant gaze fixed on her. She stared hard at him until his eyes dimmed, and he was unresponsive and breathless.

Sicily ran over to Mata, who could see her look of concern. She knew full well the beating she took. Mata, however, was only concerned with Phineas. Mata gripped Sicily by the front of her vest and slapped her chest. Sicily looked at her with confusion. With tears of frustration rolling down her face, Mata pointed at herself and then to the last place she had seen Phineas. The very center of the room. The obsidian plate on the floor before the twenty-foot-tall mirror.

Sicily looked at where she pointed and nodded. Mata sighed and wept again as she helped her to her feet and assisted her to that spot. At the very edge of the ebony circle, Mata peered into the polished, black, volcanic glass, and her one good eye went wide. Sicily looked at it as well but couldn't see what had caught Mata's attention. She could only see her reflection.

Phineas called upon the power bestowed upon him in his journey into the afterlife. In his brief journey into the land of Gehenna, he met his mentor. The man, if he was that anymore, bore the title of Charon. The Ferryman. He tended to the spirits who were not promised any planes of existence after death, transporting them to the city of Enoch.

The city for lost souls was deep in the lands of Gehenna, and to get to the city, a soul had to be ferried across the river Styx. If any being tried to swim across, dead or not, the river's waters would devour it, thus erasing it from all existence. If a soul attempted to find a crossing, they would be lost to the cold-iron desert to feed the stygian beasts that roamed there.

Phineas learned many things from Charon during his stay in Gehenna. This was the exchange- To learn the ways of spirit magic, necromancy, and given knowledge of cursed items and weapons that could be used to assist him.

After Phineas' death, he would assume the position as the next Charon, transporting lost souls through Gehenna to the city of Enoch or planes beyond. It was as much a prison as it was a position of power since he would be trapped in that limbo until another successor was chosen.

Power? Knowledge? Control? Phineas had none of these as a child. So, it was an easy choice for the boy who had not yet lived. That was before Mata. Before Vincent. Even before Lizzie, the biggest, most beautiful, and best dog he had ever known. Now he would do anything to avoid a fate of eternal separation from those he loved. All he had to do was never die. How hard was that?

Phineas used the skills he was taught and brought to bear all the fury of those souls who had been robbed of their afterlife by the Marcus family. He used their energy and his own wrath to tear open a portal that would divert part of the river Styx through this pocket dimension. In front of Phineas, a ball of green fire flared into life. The flame began to fly in a circle, and with each rotation, it quickened.

Within seconds, the ball of flame was no more; it had transformed into a ring of fire. Within the center of that ring, Phineas no long stood; only a door opened beneath the river Styx. The portal was as tall and as wide as Phineas. Once the portal was completed, the cold waters rushed through that doorway and came crashing upon Maria.

Maria tried to bring her spells and curses to bear, but the waters summoned by Phineas caught those magics and washed them away. The force of the current was so strong that Maria could only scream wildly as the waves rolled over her and pushed her toward the tear within the Veil.

Already, the Formoria had seen the tear as an opportunity to escape their prison. They came to the gash, making a mad dash for freedom, only to be caught by those unforgiving waves. Their screams echoed through the void as the flood crushed them beneath its weight. Those caught within those waters withered into nothingness, erased from every existence.

"Take a bath, you fucks," Phineas said with an evil smirk.

From the rushing waters of the Styx, the melting form of Maria burst forth. The entropic rapids dissolved her obsidian shell, leaving the remains of her soul, weak and defenseless. Phineas flew through the void and grabbed her essence. She struggled weakly against his hold, trying to escape to the Formorian plane.

"Oh no, dear, not you," Phineas said as he raised the pale blue soul, "I have something special in mind for you,"

Phineas gripped her spirit by the back of her head and turned her to face the Veil. Maria writhed and clawed at his hands as she watched the Formoria rushing through into our plane, only to be destroyed by the river Styx.

"Look upon your all-powerful army, your almighty gods, as they are washed away. The Ferryman cannot be denied," Phineas whispered into her ear. "Where are your gods now bitch?"

Phineas drew a sigil on the back of Maria's soul using his index finger. He whispered old Sanskrit words, the oldest curses, into that rune. He pulled the soul of Maria close so she could hear every syllable he had to say.

"You shall not meet your gods. You will spend your eternity separated from your power," Phineas hissed as he etched his curse upon her soul, "You will exist as these poor souls have for all these centuries. Tied forever to the land powerless."

From within his coat, Phineas pulled the double-headed spike. He whispered a word of power into its tip. The weapon levitated from his palm, spinning and beginning to glow with an inner fire. Phineas raised his hand as though he held the artifact in his palm and then commanded the cursed item to strike.

The cursed spike slammed into the sigil drawn on Maria's back and drilled into her soul. The priestess screamed in agony as the tip worked its way into her incorporeal form. Maria clawed at her spiritual self, trying to dig into her soul and tear out the offensive metal that burned her and tormented her. Phineas released the ghost of Maria, confident she wasn't going anywhere now. The missile pulled her into itself, her soul imploding into the golden artifact.

After Maria had been consumed by the weapon, it launched out of the void. Maria's spectral wailing could be heard as it rocketed out of the church. Somewhere within the hills of Haven

Shire, the spike buried itself like a coffin nail. Maria's voice was silenced by the rocks and soil of the Shire.

Phineas was about to close the gate that gave the river of the dead a place to flow when suddenly an explosion came from behind him. Four pairs of giant clawed hands gripped the sides of the small gateway Maria had created. They began to pull at the gate, trying to widen it.

Phineas began calling to the souls of Haven Shire. He had to close the gate from here; otherwise, the Formoria and their gods would enter our plane. The souls heeded the call to arms and gave Phineas their strength. He couldn't kill the likes of Azeroth or Cthulhu; the best he could do was prevent their entrance.

Phineas commanded the souls to weave themselves like a spider's web and knit the rift shut, the same way a doctor would sew up a patient after surgery. The ancient beings beyond began to pull at those brilliant chords, snapping those threads under its power.

Phineas's heart faltered as the wormlike head of Yog-Sothoth appeared, peering through the entryway. Tentacles came forth and began to probe the tear in the Veil. The gate that Phineas used to call the Stygian tide faded, and the waters no longer prevented entry into our world.

Behind the bulbous obscenity, Phineas saw the army of the Old Ones. The shambling masses of teeth and eyes poured over each other toward the portal. Phineas reeled from the fear and disgust welling up within him as their howls of victory filled his ears.

Phineas worked to stifle his panic. His body and mind wanted to retreat from this place. Where would he go, though? If he failed here, there would be no place to hide. This corruption and madness would consume the Earth and every living thing. He took a steadying breath and tried to formulate a plan.

Another limb attempted to push itself through the weakened portion of the Veil. The souls worked furiously to close the gateway Maria had created. The gods of insanity and chaos would tear them apart if Phineas didn't act fast.

Phineas realized he would most likely die in the fight to stop the abominable advance. If it meant saving those he loved, the rest of the world be damned, then so be it. Phineas began sculpting souls into spears. He launched each spear into the torn edges of the Veil.

Phineas began pouring his life energy into shaping each spear into bridges and supports that would bolster the repairs to ruptured space. Beads of sweat rose across his skin, and his breathing became more labored from the effort of holding back the ancient god and its army.

Suddenly, a colossal tentacle pushed through part of the Veil that hadn't been fully repaired. Phineas roared in frustration as it probed around, trying to find a purchase to pull itself through. Some beings from beyond the Veil also attempted to squeeze in. Phineas dispatched them with arrows of light, empowered by the few souls he could summon quickly. This would only slow the inevitable, though. They were going to break through.

Phineas didn't have the power, much less the stamina, to fight this deity. Phineas focused the remaining souls and his life essence into a massive blade. It wasn't enough, and Phineas knew it. Tears and sweat ran down Phineas' face as he continued to empower the magical blade regardless.

Phineas thought of Mata then and desperately wished he could tell her he loved her. And George. He had just found his brother and had also considered a future with him in it. Phineas wept as he continued to forge the weapon. The soul blade he forged grew brighter, and blue flames licked its edges.

Suddenly, a gentle hand fell onto his. Phineas looked up and almost fell over. There, holding his hand, was the brilliant specter of his mother. Phineas fought to not shield his eyes from her brilliance. In an instant, he was a child again, wanting nothing more than her warmth and love.

"Mother?" Phineas said, feeling tears welling up in his eyes. "I'm so sorry. I wanted to help you, tell you that I could see the spirits like you and that you were right all along."

Judith Thatch reached out and embraced him. Phineas felt her warmth and love in that embrace. He felt a spectral kiss planted on his cheek, and her hands caressed his face. Phineas looked up to see his mother staring at him tenderly.

"I'm so sorry I wasn't there for you and your brother," Judith said. "I watched you both grow over these years; I never left your sides."

The intimacy of the moment was broken by a horrific roar. Phineas looked to the limb now thrusting its way into our plane. He looked down at the glowing soul blade in his hand and then back to his mother. Phineas gave Judith a grim smile and gave a resolved nod.

"I wish I could say I'll be seeing you soon, but I am committed somewhere else in the hereafter," Phineas said with a wry smile. "I will always love you, mom."

"I love you, too. I love you both, forever and always," Judith said.

Phineas choked up at this and then took a deep breath. Before he had his chance to attack, the spirit of Judith Thatch ripped the blade from his hands. Phineas tried to resist but was so weak now that Judith's strength surprised him. Gently, yet firmly, Judith shoved Phineas away from her and turned to the monstrous extremity, trying to claw its way into our reality.

Phineas screamed as she charged the creature, empowering the sword with her love and spiritual strength. That blade burned brightly, honed by her desire to protect her children, her greatest blessings. Phineas floated helplessly in that void, watching her flying at the evil god-like monstrosity like a fairytale knight charging a dragon.

The sword plunged all the way to the hilt into the thrashing tentacle. Judith released all the energy in the blade with a mighty scream. The result was an explosion of light and spiritual fire that blew the tentacle to pieces. Phineas was thrown by the force of the blast and felt himself falling, heels overhead, into the void.

As Phineas flew away, he heard the maddening scream of pain erupt from the evil and corrupt god. He watched as the flames became a wall that cauterized and sealed the tear. The wound made by the Marcus family was cleansed by fire, and that power forced the Formoria, and their gods, to retreat back into their dimension.

No longer able to resist the pull into unconsciousness, Phineas let the void take him and fell into the darkness.

# # # #

Mata and Sicily saw a great ball of light in the darkness of the obsidian disk. Both wondered about its origin but then realized the light was growing rapidly. Standing by the edge, they began to feel the floor beneath them shake. Not taking any chances, Sicily scooped up Mata and began retreating for the door that would take them out of the chapel. They had not gotten far when the light erupted from that void, the force throwing them both to the floor.

White light washed over them; both women covered their faces to shield their eyes from the blinding eruption. That brilliance filled the room and then swept out of the chapel. The remaining monsters outside the chapel screamed and turned into ash as the light burned them all out of existence. Their collective howls of pain and horror were so loud that Sicily had to cover her ears.

Both women stood up slowly and found themselves in the complete darkness of the chapel. All the candles had been winked out in the explosion and the only other light source was the strange, mirrored surface adjacent to the entryway. The near two-story mirror and the obsidian disk on the chapel floor were shattered and whatever power they had seemed lost.

Sicily was suddenly startled when Mata began pounding the ground with her cestus-covered fists and breathing heavily. Tears streamed down her face, and her mouth was open wide in a terrible but silent scream. At first, Sicily didn't understand, but then it occurred to her that she hadn't seen Phineas. Was he trapped in the rumble of that volcanic glass? She walked over to Mata, who was now sobbing uncontrollably.

"Mata, look at me. What happened just now? Where's Phineas?" Sicily asked as she grabbed Mata's shoulders and got her attention. The question brought another bout of sobbing. All Mata could do was point at the once smooth black disc. Sicily ran to it and looked for clues about what had happened. All she could see was the shattered remains of volcanic glass. "Where was Phineas?"

-CHAPTER 40-
ON THE SHORES OF STYX

"You don't belong here," said a voice from behind Phineas.

Phineas lay on the cold, silver sands next to the raging river Styx. Gehenna's lands were bathed in purples, greys, and oranges. It reminded him of dusk back in the land of the living. The land of the Quick as the tribes here called it.

Phineas sat up, scratching the sand from his hair and brow to look at the speaker. He knew this man, had known him for nearly a century in this place. His gravely Scottish brogue always seemed to carry a weight to it. Regret? Grief? Or maybe it was just knowledge earned through several millennia in human years.

"Pardon, Charon? I wasn't aware I had trespassed," Phineas replied to his mentor. He immediately got to his feet and looked to remove any evidence of himself that might desecrate this spot.

Charon, the ferryman of the river Styx and ruler of Gehenna, raised his hand to calm his pupil.

"Steady Phineas," Charon said sincerely. "I apologize for disrupting your morning meditation."

Phineas was flustered at this. Charon did not often apologize, and his manner of speaking was more informal than usual. It was rare that this being had referred to him as anything other than "servant" or "child." If Phineas was summoned by any other title than that, it was not for the best of reasons.

"How may I assist you, Lord Charon…" Young Phineas began with a bow, still nervous that he may have displeased his teacher.

"I have done you a great disservice, lad," Charon said, his eyes looking across the horizon.

Phineas was lost now. This man, if he could be called that, had been strict but otherwise shown him nothing but fairness and respect. He gave him a home in this alien place, taught him magic, and gave him his friendship. How could anything he had done been wrong?

"I should have not kept you in this place," Charon answered, seeing the quizzical look on his apprentice's face. "I should have sent you back straight away."

"Lord Charon, no offense but I didn't want to go back." Phineas replied honestly. "I took my own life. I made that choice. There was no way to return from that."

Charon's brow furrowed at this. The man's normally impassive face seemed pained now. This being radiated kindness and warmth to Phineas, but also regret. His Lord was going to help him finally understand his burden if he was just patient enough. Phineas held his tongue and waited for his teacher to speak.

"Before I had died, I had lived an incredibly long life. One filled with victory and loss, hope and despair. I had loved on more than one occasion and had been blessed with the grief of their loss," Charon began solemnly. "When I happened upon this very bank, I met my master and Lord Charon of that time," Charon continued. "He told me that he had wished to honor me with his title because I had lived so fully and with little regret in the end."

Phineas had known that the name Charon was actually a title and station but had not been able to ascertain how someone achieved this position. It had to be given to someone deemed worthy, then?

"I was given the choice," Charon explained. "I was asked if I could be the one to guide the souls of the dead to their hereafter, wherever that was. I had been offered this and allowed to accept it. Something I had intended to do for you."

Phineas's jaw dropped at this. Was he about to be offered the prestigious title of Lord Charon, the Ferryman of the river Styx? Charon looked up at the young man and suddenly began to laugh. This drew a somewhat pained expression from Phineas.

"No boy! I am not going to offer the job to you yet. You missed my point!" Charon said between chuckles. The man sobered and looked hard at his apprentice. "You have yet to live. You have known pain and suffering, the love and loss of his parents, but you have not truly allowed yourself to live."

Phineas absorbed this assessment of his existence. Part of him was hurt by his master's words, but he also conceded to the truth in them. Phineas died before his twentieth year. He had not achieved anything, known true love and companionship, and had never discovered his purpose. His life was lost to his grief and pain and desperation to be free of that.

"Be gentle with yourself, boy," Charon said, reading his expression and thoughts, "you are not here by choice. I kept you here."

"Master, what do you mean? It's not like I could have left," Phineas said incredulously.

"True, but I could have sent you back at any time," Charon said, his face now brimming with shame.

"What? Why would you? You know my suffering, my loss, and the shameful acts I committed to bury all that," Phineas said, tears threatening to escape his eyes.

"I made the choice to keep you here because I was a lonely old man without a friend on this plane," Charon said, grief now creased his face. "You saw the spirits around you, interacted with them, even touched them. Very few could do this, even here. Do you understand what that means?"

Phineas looked blankly at his mentor. He considered this for a moment. "That means that every person you have ferried to Enoch, or the Heavens, or the Abyss, never knew you existed?"

Charon nodded and finally said, "I have been alone all these years until you came along. Someone who could take my place as the Ferryman of lost souls. This is the way. Find a soul who could see me and learn from me, and then ferry me to the city of Enoch."

Charon took a deep breath and shook his head at the wrongness of an idea, the injustice of which was more than he could bear. "I couldn't complete the task and give this title because you have yet to live. Do you understand, boy?"

Phineas nodded and was about to protest but the Charon held up a hand. "I cannot accept you as my successor at this time. I demand that you return to the land of the Quick."

Phineas was about to object, but some curse bound his tongue. He looked at his teacher in confusion. Phineas began waving his hands back and forth as though the action could deny his mentor's wishes. He growled and cried until Lord Charon placed his hand on Phineas's shoulder. His face was not one of disappointment or rejection, but of pride. The sort of love someone held in reserve for their son.

"I demand you return to life, a second chance given to you, and be allowed to live a full life. A life filled with love and purpose,"

Charon said, with tears streaming down his face. "Go forth and with the knowledge I've given you, be who you were meant to be."

Before Phineas could object further, Charon punched the young man in the chest. The shock of the blow sent electricity throughout his body. Phineas felt his soul grabbed by some force beyond the Veil that separated the land of the living and the land of the dead. It pulled furiously and before Phineas could fight or object.

Phineas awoke this time in the pocket dimension Maria had built, battling the forces from beyond the Veil. He felt drained physically, spiritually, and emotionally. Phineas began to weep as he grieved the second loss of his mother. He was shaken from his lamentations by the sound of another person crying. The pain he heard and felt was much like his.

Phineas gasped when he understood it was Mata. He felt her calling for him, grieving for him and needing him now more than ever. Her pain touched his very soul and Phineas needed to do everything in his power to help her.

All around him Phineas felt the pocket dimension beginning to collapse. What was once a void, lacking form or structure, was soon to become his grave if he didn't leave. Mata was his way back home, his anchor to life, she was the safe harbor for him to return to.

Phineas turned the bulb on the head of the cane until he heard a sharp *"click."* The bulb split open, revealing a small green crystal. He whispered a spell he used to find treasures occasionally, and there was no more fabulous treasure to him than Mata. Suddenly, Phineas was pulled along with great haste through the darkness. Above him, he saw a tunnel of light.

-CHAPTER 41-
ON THE OUTSIDE

Outside the Forgotten Church, George and Amanda held each other and wept. The explosion that took Judge and the demon sent them tumbling down that last flight of stairs, landing them right in front of the decaying and disintegrating corpse of the monster that attacked Phineas, Mata, and Sicily. George told Amanda about Phineas' return.

George wanted to run back into the church and help him now, but Amanda was too injured and terrified to go back. Truth be told, so was he. His adrenaline had drained from his body, leaving George with pain and fatigue. George hurt everywhere and felt as weak and afraid as a newborn deer. The only thing they could do now was wait and hold each other.

Both yelped when there came an explosion, this time from below. George and Amanda questioned so much for those next moments. Had Phineas succeeded? Were their loved ones still alive? Was that the sound of the Ancient Ones or the Formoria invading and thus the end of the world?

After an eternity of breaths, a great flash of light escaped the building through every exit and window. This was followed by another tremor and several screams heard from within the mansion. George recognized the screams as those of the Formoria.

"Where are you, Finn?" George asked aloud. After a half hour, George had had enough and began getting every weapon he could from the van's cargo. Amanda told him that she would be going as well. George tried to protest but simply gave up when he looked into Amanda's determined glare.

"George Thatch, if you think you are going anywhere without me ever again, you have another thing coming," Amanda said, her voice between frustration and pleading. "Now, give me a gun!"

George conceded and handed her a pistol and a shotgun. He and Amanda hopped with a start when George heard Sicily's voice.

"You better do what the lady says there, George," she said.

George looked beyond the van and saw Sicily, Phineas, and in his arms, Mata. Amanda breathed an audible sigh of relief, and

George dropped everything and rushed to the trio. They exchanged hugs or something akin to it with their injuries. Phineas looked about the vehicle. Sicily did the same.

"Robert?" Sicily said, her eyes pleading.

"Vincent?" Phineas followed up.

George looked at them both and slowly shook his head. "I'm so sorry, guys. Both of them were murdered by Judge Marcus." Phineas' lips drew tight, and tears threatened to escape his eyes. He looked over to Mata and considered how he would break the news to her.

"What about Judge?" Sicily asked through gritted teeth and tears already streaming down her face. "What happened to his sick ass?"

"Last I saw, some sort of demon was working him over. The last I heard of it was his screaming before the explosives went off. I'm pretty certain he's dead now," George said. Sicily could no longer keep her grief at bay, and she fell into George, sobbing into his shoulder.

Phineas looked as though he was consulting some unseen person behind him. "I have it on good authority that Judge Marcus is in hell where he belongs."

Sicily and George looked at Phineas and just accepted it. Neither of them had the energy to be skeptical. Everyone piled into the van; Mata was laid on the bench, her leg braced. They left the Marcus estate and drove to the police station to pick up Lizzie. The dog greeted everyone joyfully, but even she noted the missing presence of Vincent and Robert. After stopping by the local doctor's office and pharmacy, where they obtained bandages and medicine for pain control, they drove around the town looking for survivors.

All except Mata and Amanda walked the streets for an hour, only to find that any affected by Maria's spell had died; most of the lifeless bodies appeared uninjured, but they couldn't exist without their souls. Then some were murdered by the Formoria; the sight was horrific, but it served as a reminder to Sicily of what had happened to her mother.

The party had lost the will to continue with their search. Each of them was too exhausted, too injured, or just too aggrieved to continue. Each started considering how to explain the situation when a low rumbling underground suddenly came. Initially, there was only a slight vibration beneath their feet. However, this vibration increased in intensity, and some of the mortar began to fall away from the old buildings downtown Haven Shire.

Phineas suddenly shouted for everyone to head to the van. It didn't take long for them to understand why as the hill leading up to the Marcus estate suddenly seemed to buckle. It appeared as though some great and invisible weight fell upon it. A moment later, the hill crumbled again. Rock, dirt, and trees tumbled toward town.

Everyone piled into the van; Sicily took the wheel. Before anyone could secure themselves or their belongings, Sicily slammed her foot down on the accelerator. Her human and canine cargo yelped from the force imposed on them. She drove furiously down Main Street, the only street in and out of town.

Phineas peered out the back door window and saw that the hill was sliding down and crashing into the town and sinking. Then the town itself was sinking. The streets behind them fell and became great pits as sinkholes opened up. The pavement spilled and buckled. Flames erupted from the ground as gas lines were ignited by arcing power lines and sparks. A sinkhole fell open, this one large enough to swallow a building. The path of destruction seemed to rampage after the van like some giant predator.

"Think maybe we should drive faster?" Phineas yelled.

Sicily snapped back, "Hey! This is your van, fucker! If you wanted to drive faster, Shaggy, you shouldn't have brought the mystery mobile!"

Suddenly the van lurched as a portion of the street jutted upward before sinking. Sicily shifted the target of her ire to the van now. George held onto Amanda tight as she cried into his shoulder. Lizzy shifted nervously in her pen and whined while Mata held the bench seat the best she could. Every bump and slam sent waves of pain through her body. Phineas rushed to her side and held her.

The van had hit another fresh crack in the road, causing it to bounce roughly and fishtail. Sicily hissed and cussed and was able to regain control. The chaos stopped when she drove past the "Welcome to Haven Shire" sign. They drove nearly a mile just to be sure. Haven Shire's sinking and the hills' landslide stopped at the city limits. Phineas had Sicily stop, and he and George got out to investigate the town.

"What just happened, Finn?" George finally asked.

Phineas looked out over the steaming maw of the fresh sinkhole. Fires and sparks occasionally lit the hole's interior, but its depths were obscured by thick clouds of smoke and dust.

"The roots had left those hills and this land a husk," Phineas explained. "When they were destroyed, nothing was supporting the surface."

"Well, fuck, there goes the evidence," George stated in dismay.

"Who would you tell? What would you have said?" Phineas asked. "Are you going to tell the authorities, whomever that may be, that a family of cultists was trying to summon horrors to come and murder the world? That there are other worlds out there, and they are teaming with hungry evil fuckers who want to wear your skin like a pair of footy pajamas? Or try to explain how this place sank because a giant otherworldly alien plant sucked it dry?"

"All right, I get it," George said, conceding to the logic. He was quiet for a moment and then finally asked. "What am I supposed to do with this?"

"Sinkholes happen ..." Phineas said with a shrug.

"Not that. This knowledge, my memories, all of it?" George said as he tapped his temple.

"Not sure, brother. For us, memories are a curse. They pain us, shape us, and we bear them the best we can. I embrace them now, and the curses I bear are as much a part of myself as Mata and Vin— " Phineas stopped suddenly, cursing his memory and fighting back tears. "You don't have to decide tonight, that's for damn sure," he said finally after collecting himself.

Phineas paused for a moment and finally took a chance. "You and your family are always welcome to call and lean on us if you need it." Phineas held his breath slightly as he waited for George's response.

George looked at him and seemed to consider this proposition. "Yeah, sure thing. I mean, thanks. Let's start by getting to a hospital first. I think I'm about to pass out from blood loss," George said, laughing dryly.

Together they limped back to the van, which sped away. Phineas watched the ruins of his childhood hometown fade from sight out of the back windows. So much of himself, his and

George's shared suffering, his broken father, and their mother's love. Phineas thought this wasn't the worst way to see it go if he had to let go and bury the past. He chuckled at that and watched as Haven Shire faded away. All the while, he wore his crooked smile.

-EPILOGUE-
RECONSTRUCTION

Never pick up hitchhikers. Simple enough rule and Gordon Jorgenson had always followed it. He traveled for work and rarely saw a hitchhiker anymore. This time, it felt different though. When he saw the girl, nude and covered in blood and walking along the side of the road, he *needed* to pick her up.

He swept the girl up off her feet, laid her gently in the backseat of his station wagon, and covered her under a blanket. The rest of the day's drive was a blur after that.

"JUST DRIVE," A watery voice spoke to him, directly into his mind. The sound of her voice was sweet and cool in his ears. He could feel her words coiling the base of his skull. ***"DON'T TURN AROUND."***

Gordon felt it was best to do as told. Not that he could turn or move anyway. Tendrils were burrowing through his skin, reaching into his muscles, gripping his spin, and churning in his guts. He couldn't feel the pain thankful be he was aware of the movement throughout his body. His body would jerk a little as it tried to resist the invasion.

"Where are we going?" Gordan asked as a tear fell from the corner of his eye and rolled down his face. He felt dulled somehow, yet still compelled to do as he was told, but whatever was happening to him was so very wrong.

"Away from this place," The girl spoke with her lips and mouth this time. "As far away as you can take me."

"What are you? Who…" Gordan started to say until he felt something pull sharply in his abdomen. He looked down to see the tendrils had made their way to his intestines. The snake-like appendages squirmed just beneath his flesh. Even though he felt no pain, he still felt strangely hollow, less of himself.

"DON'T CONCERN YOURSELF WITH WHO OR WHAT I AM," the voice spoke more forcefully into his mind.

"Are you going to kill me?" Gordon whimpered. The fear took hold of him just as those tentacles took hold of his innards.

"YES," the voice replied. Gordon felt some measure of glee coming from the thing in his backseat.

"Why are you doing this?" Gordon asked pleadingly. One of the tendrils broke out from within his abdomen. He looked down and saw that it looked a centipede with several segmented parts and tiny legs. The appendage ended with a tiny mouth filled with needle sharp teeth and a pair of pincers that flexed open and shut. The thing returned to its work and squirmed past Gordon's waistline and down his pants. It was followed by a few more of its kind and Gordon felt the things rummaging around, seeking a cavity or place to insert themselves once again.

Gordon couldn't watch anymore and looked up only to gasp as a ghostly-white face appeared before him. In his rearview mirror, a young Asian girl's face appeared. Her smile was sweet and playful but her teeth were short and sharp. The shark-like grin glistened with saliva. Gordon whimpered as he saw those eyes, wide and round, and completely black. The smile on the girl's face widened impossibly so.

"Oh sweet Gordon," the passenger cooed in his ear. "I have to. I can't drive."

A long purple tongue reached out and licked his neckline. Gordon was still frozen by whatever power this thing had on him. He managed a tremble as he sobbed.

"And we do need to eat along the way."

ACKNOWLEDGMENTS

Thanks to those who helped put together the bones of this book. If not for the efforts of Brian Hershey of Reader2Writer Press, Allyson McNitt my first editor and avid fan, and all those who were inspired to write as I had been inspired by others.

I could not have authored this book if not for my mother. Her stories and love for horror films only encouraged my obsession with the macabre.

Thanks to all the writers and filmmakers out there who gave me nightmares that inspired me in my writing and challenged me to scare others too.

ABOUT THE AUTHOR

Zachariah was raised on horror. From Friday Fright Night movies his love of the scary and macabre was born. Today he lives in the Kansas City area, a 12-year veteran of firefighting and EMS. He has seen the best and some of the worst human beings are capable of.

Zachariah also works with his community to increase awareness about mental wellness and strives to remove the stigma of mental illness. He hosts a peer group weekly and is part of the Johnson County Suicide Prevention Coalition.

It is the human condition that inspires his writing.

He is a proud father to two girls, husband, and dog lover.

Printed in the USA
CPSIA information can be obtained
at www.ICGtesting.com
CBHW031258050724
11009CB00007B/520

9 781088 166758